DOWN TO THE SURFACE

Gent's face looked eerie in the upwelling light. "You've crossed over," he said softly. "They won't forgive you now."

Urban was shaking. "Dammit, Lot, you know he's right. It's over. It's the monkey house now . . . or cold storage. For all of us. After tonight, they won't let us out in the life of this city."

Which might not be too long, Lot reflected. He looked at Gent, and saw in his eyes a quiet expectation. They had only one option left. "We're leaving the city tonight."

Urban blinked. "Lot?"

Triumph gleamed in Gent's eyes. Lot nodded, feeling detached, as if instinct alone was moving him through the patterns of a dance that had been written for him long ago. "We're going down the Well."

Bantam Books by Linda Nagata

THE BOHR MAKER
TECH-HEAVEN

Deception Well

Linda Nagata

BANTAM BOOKS
New York • Toronto • London • Sydney • Auckland

DECEPTION WELL

A Bantam Spectra Book / February 1997

SPECTRA and the portrayal of a boxed "s" are trademarks of
Bantam Books,
a division of Bantam Doubleday Dell
Publishing Group, Inc.

ISBN 0-553-57629-1

Published simultaneously in the United States and Canada.

Bantam Books are published by Bantam Books, a division of Bantam Doubleday Dell Publishing Group, Inc. Its trademark, consist-
ing of the words "Bantam Books" and the portrayal of a rooster, is
Registered in U.S. Patent and Trademark Office and in other coun-
tries. Marca Registrada. Bantam Books, 1540 Broadway, New
York, New York 10036.

PRINTED IN THE UNITED STATES OF AMERICA

OPM   10 9 8 7 6 5 4 3 2 1

for my dad
who gave me the habit of science fiction

Part
I

Part
I

Chapter
1

Lot wriggled toward the open vent, his slender, eight-
year-old body crushing a path through the brittle foam
of rotting insulation that coated the interior of the air
duct. A light breeze brought the dust forward, where it
lingered in a cloud that beguiled his headlamp, getting into his
eyes, his nose, his throat, and clinging to the moist, teardrop-
shaped surfaces of the sensory glands that shimmered on his
cheeks. He could feel a wet cough down in his lungs, itching,
burning to get out. His shoulders shook as he fought with it.
Captain Aceret had boosted him into the ventilation system
with instructions to proceed with full stealth. He couldn't let
himself be discovered. Jupiter's army was counting on him to
get through.

He dropped his face against his arm just as the cough
ripped out of his lungs.

And it wasn't just one small cough. For a few seconds it felt like he was going to hack his lungs right out. The
air duct shook. The organic fingers of his headlamp squeezed
tighter against his brow. Streams of dust swirled off in the
slow breeze. He imagined Silken troopers in the corridor below, listening to him, laughing at his distress. Tears started to
run out of his eyes and he didn't try to stop them.

Jupiter. He grasped at his father's name in half-
formed apology. *Jupiter, I want to come to you. I do.*

He felt his smallness then. He was nothing more than a tiny spark: flash, burn, die, in the black reaches of the void. It was the same for any of them. They were a border people. Half the troopers in Jupiter's army had lost their first families to the mechanized assaults of the old murderers. Some had wanted to run away to the Hallowed Vasties. It was said that no weapons of the Chenzeme could wreck the human civilizations there. But the Vasties were achingly far: from their former home in the star cluster known as the Committee, it was over eighty light-years to the nearest cordoned sun. Anyway, Jupiter said they didn't need the Vasties. He'd found sanctuary for them in the Well.

The coughing fit wound down. Lot listened for any untoward sound from the corridor below, but there was nothing. Maybe he'd gotten lucky . . . if *luck* was the proper word for it. Every step forward was a step closer to the deadly world of Deception Well. He tried not to think about that as he wriggled toward the vent. He believed in Jupiter Apolinario. Jupiter had survived the Well. He'd found in it the hidden world of the Communion, where self and other might be forever joined into a singular state of nirvana, alien/human/alien, blended in a living matrix that had existed for at least thirty million years, unsullied by the evil of the Chenzeme. Jupiter said they could be part of it too, if they trusted him, believed in him.

I do believe.

He swiped at the sticky droplets of his sensory tears, vainly trying to clear their clogged surfaces. He'd come into the city of Silk with Captain Aceret, as part of the advance mission. They'd arrived here aboard a shuttle under the pretense of friendship, never mentioning Jupiter's name as the great ship Nesseleth settled into a distant orbit beyond the fifty-five-thousand-mile limit of the space elevator that supported Silk. Captain Aceret had launched his commando raid to seize control of the elevator system, just as Nesseleth dropped her cargo slug containing the regular army: fourteen thousand troops, men, women and children, with Jupiter at their head. By the time the slug moored at the upper end of the elevator, Captain Aceret had secured lift control, and Jupiter's army began to descend.

That should have been the end of it. Jupiter Apolinario had no interest in the city of Silk. It was only an inconvenience that Silk had been built on the elevator column, two hundred miles above the seething green equatorial forests of the Well. The army had no choice but to pass through the city. They would have preferred to go peacefully, dropping straight down through Silk's unpopulated industrial core. But the Silkens wouldn't allow it. They were scared of the Communion. They never went down the Well, and they were determined to stop Jupiter's army from going down too. They'd cut the tracks where the elevator passed through the city, forcing the loaded cars to stop on the upper industrial levels, trapping the army in separate, sealed loading bays.

Captain Aceret couldn't help them. His tiny force was pinned down inside lift control by the frantic efforts of Silken security. Only Lot had been able to slip out undetected, escaping moments before air locks in the duct system closed, sealing off lift control. There was no going back. But that was okay. Lot knew the moves. Jupiter had kept him in commando training since he was five. He knew how to pack his sense of self away in cold storage, fear and doubt chilled down to a static background hum. He hauled himself forward.

His lungs burned, but soft little coughs helped to ease the pressure. The vent that he'd struggled toward came into view through the swirling dust. He whispered to his headlamp to switch off. Then he peered down through the grating.

The corridor below was dark. Motion sensors controlled the lights, so that meant it was probably empty. Better, the sticky drops of his sensory tears didn't detect any human presence. He lay still for a moment, concentrating on not getting scared. Then he ordered the headlamp back on. The beam pierced the dust, revealing a dead end to the air duct: a closed air lock just a few feet beyond the vent. It wouldn't be long before oxygen ran out on the other side.

Reaching to his waist pack, Lot took out the pocket torch Captain Aceret had given him. It made a soft hiss when he turned it on, then spat loudly as the white flame cut the seam that sealed the grating. An acrid smoke made Lot's eyes water and his lungs itch. Coughing softly, he moved the hot grate aside before it could self-repair.

He still didn't hear any sounds, or detect any human sense from the corridor. Captain Aceret said the Silkens had only a few security troops. If any one segment of Jupiter's army broke out, the Silkens would be quickly overwhelmed. He touched his headlamp. "Hark, release," he whispered to the Dull Intelligence that controlled the device. The organic fingers loosened their grip, and the lamp came away in his hand. He tucked it into a pocket, then grabbed the vent's hot rim with his gloved hands and dropped to the floor, landing with practiced quiet.

Lights flashed on, revealing white walls tinged brown with mildew or perhaps with age. The smart fibers in his camouflage suit instantly shifted in color and reflectivity to mimic the dirty white walls. The camo paint on his face shifted too.

He could see for maybe a hundred yards in both directions, before the corridor curved out of sight. A heavy door was set against the inside curve. Jupiter would be waiting just beyond it, trapped in a loading bay along with a small section of his army.

The Silkens had disabled the electronic system that controlled the pressure door, and there were no manual overrides on the interior. The army had tried using assault Makers to dissolve the door and the surrounding walls, but the molecular-scale machines had inexplicably failed. So it was up to Lot to open the bay door by hand.

Captain Aceret had thoroughly drilled him. First thing, find the control pad. It was set high in the wall, and Lot had to stretch to reach it. He slapped the reset button, then turned to the manual lever.

The door had been designed to protect against accidental decompression; it wasn't a security device. So long as the sensors registered equal pressure on both sides, it could be opened manually. In a minute, Jupiter would be free. The army would move out again, this time on foot, winding down through the spiral corridor of the city's industrial core, down and down to the lower elevator terminus, for the final descent to Deception Well.

Lot hesitated. He kept thinking of the Communion as a gigantic slime creature wrapped around the surface of the planet, disguising itself with a hide of forests or oceans or deserts, but really, under the skin, it ate anybody who came close. Soon, it would eat them. Jupiter had said so. And it would change them. Lot wasn't really clear on how. Sometimes, he wasn't sure he wanted to find out.

I do believe.

Seizing the large handle, he shoved it down with both hands, then slammed it to the side. The satisfying thunk of a heavy steel mechanism inside the door rewarded his efforts. He waited a moment, then pushed again. The door slid on smooth tracks back into the wall.

Yet the entrance remained blocked. Lot found himself staring up at a barrier of overlapping combat shields. The shields scintillated with a dark, distracting iridescence that was hard to focus on. Amid the slippery surface were hard knots: Lot started as he recognized the muzzles of grenade launchers protruding through sealed cuffs in the shields, and the glassy stare of video eyes.

"Wait!" he squeaked, and jumped back, pressing himself against the wall, so that his camouflage blended almost perfectly with the musty white.

"Corridor clear," a gruff voice announced. There was a sharp *crack!* and the finger-sized body of a scout remote shot down the corridor, its wings beginning to vibrate with an angry buzz as it rounded the curve and disappeared. Another took off in the opposite direction.

The combat shields opened as a unit, turning sideways like baffles on an air vent, admitting a humid burst of tension into the corridor. Then troops in gray armor darted out the channels, their faces grim behind the clear visors of their helmets. The first unit carried incendiary grenade launchers. The second wave was armed with slender missile launchers, their buzz-winged ammunition—like the scout remotes—guided by an onboard Dull Intelligence. Half turned up the corridor, half turned down. Two more waves armed with bead rifles followed, and finally, a tactical unit, their helmets opaque as they operated on the data supplied by the layered realities evolving on their internal screens.

Then the combat shields fell back on either side of the opening. A patch of light from the corridor spilled a few yards into the loading bay. Beyond that, the bay was dark and silent, though Lot could scent the readiness of hundreds of huddled troops in the cavernous space. He'd started to straighten up, thinking he should report to somebody, when Jupiter Apolinario strode forward into the light.

Lot caught his breath, staring up in awe at his father's tall, imposing figure. Like the advance troops, Jupiter wore gray body armor, but without the helmet. His long blond hair lay neatly across his shoulders, framing a stern though handsome face. High on his cheeks shimmered the silvery droplets of his own sensory tears. Only Jupiter and Lot had them; Lot wasn't sure why.

Jupiter seemed more youthful than most of his officers, though Lot knew that was only appearance. He watched as Jupiter's gaze searched the empty passage, lingering on the open ceiling vent. Captain Antigua and Captain Hu stepped up on either side of him. They conferred beneath the arch that divided the corridor from the loading bay.

"They've found us," Captain Hu reported. "Resistance downhill at less than three hundred yards."

The deep *whump!* of a grenade launcher slammed up the corridor, followed immediately by a flash of superheated air. There was a brief silence, swiftly broken by the harsh buzz of DI slugs peeling off after their targets.

Jupiter gazed in the direction of the firefight, as if he could see the action taking place around the bend. "Phase two," he ordered softly. He fell back to the side of the passage. Captain Hu did the same. Lot had to scramble to get out of their way.

"Squads two through twelve!" Captain Antigua barked. "You have your assigned targets. Get those other loading bays open and get our troops out *now*."

"And remember," Jupiter added, the tone of his voice seeming soft, though it rose in volume over that of Captain Antigua, soothing and reverberant at once. "The main body of the army is depending on you: the children, the wives who are with child, the noncombat members of our family who rely on your arms and your alertness for their own survival. Remember them. Believe in them. Believe in me."

That last word hung in the air for a moment, and then Captain Antigua stepped in again. "Go, go, go!" she shouted, and the troops hauled off like a river of stone, churning and raging as they deployed throughout the narrow passage.

Lot felt a hand caress his head. He looked up, to see Jupiter gazing down at him with an odd, squinting expression. "Switch off your camouflage, Lot, you're straining my eyes." His voice carried effortlessly over the thunder of the passing troops.

Lot felt his cheeks go hot beneath their cover of camouflage paint. He hurriedly knocked a wrist panel and the suit's camo function flicked off, leaving him clothed in dull gray. He snapped off his hood as the last of the assault troops rolled out of the loading bay. Captain Antigua moved out with them, heading downhill, toward the lower elevator terminus.

Jupiter crouched beside Lot and ruffled his tangled blond hair. Rare approval floated on the air between them. "You've given us victory," he said. "You are more than my only child. You are my right hand."

Lot stared at him, momentarily stunned, feeling his mouth open in a silly grin. Jupiter grinned back at him, and that made it even worse, leaving Lot crazy-happy like some of the women would get at convocation.

Jupiter touched his hair one more time. Then he straightened, and stepped across the corridor to confer with Captain Hu.

Lot coughed softly, trying to vent the mean, racking spasm he could feel building in his lungs. He felt warmed by a deep sense of pride. He'd opened the way for Jupiter. He'd let the army into the underbelly of Silk. He was Jupiter's right hand, and he was not going to give in to another spasm of coughing. That was not how a trooper conducted himself.

He coughed again, then swallowed hard several times. Across the corridor, he could hear Captain Hu relaying progress reports:

"Loading bays two through six have been opened. Approximately twenty percent of the army has entered the corridor system. . . ."

"And Nesseleth?" Jupiter asked.

Lot moved forward at the name of the great ship, the sculpted entity that had carried them across the void.

"The great ship is still coming down," Hu said grimly. Lot caught the scent of disagreement in those words. "She has approximately two hours left, Jupiter, before she burns."

Lot couldn't suppress a cry of dismay. "Nesseleth?" He scrambled forward, forgetting for the moment a trooper's proper reserve. "Did the Silkens hit her? Have they killed her?"

Jupiter frowned down at him, his angry mien impacting against Lot's sensory tears, and suddenly Lot felt stricken. He looked down, covering his mouth to stifle another cough. His eyes were watering. He could scent Jupiter's disapproval and he knew he should back away, stand quietly on the side, wait for orders. But the ship was going down. If Nesseleth died, they would have no way out. No way back.

Dread realization crept through his brain. "You've ordered her to crash, haven't you?" He backed away a step. *"You've killed her."*

Jupiter barely looked at him. "She was human once. She seeks her own salvation. To follow the army is her own wish."

"No, that's *not* why." Lot shook his head. "It's because she loves you. She's doing it because she loves you." Suddenly Lot felt jealous, fiercely jealous, because he wasn't sure *he* loved Jupiter that much, enough to lay down and die for him, no questions asked, and he wanted to be able to love that much, to believe. . . .

The cough that had been working at his lungs finally slipped out in that moment of stress. It started small, but after the first hack Lot lost all control over it. He turned away, throwing his hands over his face as his body shook with the convulsions. He felt as if he were choking, as if his lungs were melting, as if he couldn't get a breath. And all the time he was picturing Nesseleth and wondering if it would be worse to strangle, or to burn.

He was on his knees before it was over. In his hands he could see blood-colored mucus. He could feel the weight of Jupiter's gaze, and the sense of his anger all around.

Then Jupiter was there. He swept Lot up in his arms, holding him against his chest as if he weighed nothing. "What have they done to him?" he demanded of Captain Hu, and the fury in his voice made Lot shrink. "Have the Silkens used assault Makers against him?"

"We can't know that yet, Jupiter." Hu took two stomping steps toward the loading bay. "Medic!" he bellowed. "Dammit, where's that medic?"

"Get a tactical squad on this," Jupiter growled. "If the Silkens want to play germ warfare, then let them. We'll see how their museum Makers hold up against a modern arsenal."

Lot started to protest. The dust in the ancient air ducts had irritated his lungs. There had been no assault Makers. But another coughing spasm took him and he couldn't get the words out. Blood sputtered out between his lips, smearing across Jupiter's armored chest. Then strong arms were grasping him from behind, pulling him away.

Jupiter bent quickly, kissed him firmly on the head. "We'll be together again."

"No, wait!" Lot croaked, reaching for him. "I didn't mean it. Don't leave me." But Jupiter was already gone.

Chapter
2

L ot could not remember a time before the great ship.
He'd been born on the long outward passage from the
star cluster called the Committee. Nesseleth had been
his world. In her warrens he'd known a hazy, timeless sense of
permanence, as if his life there might go on forever with no
real change. The new world to which they were bound had
seemed as theoretical as death, a phantom specter lying far,
far over his personal horizon.

Then Lot had turned seven—over a year and a half
ago now—and Jupiter had taken him to his strategic chamber
aboard the great ship. There, he showed him a holographic
schematic of their destination.

Lot studied the star system. A faint white nebula
veiled the G-type primary, enwrapping it like the woven nests
some spiders spun around their eggs. The nebula looked nothing like the warm, dark spheres that enclosed the cordoned
suns of the Hallowed Vasties. "That star is Kheth?" Lot
asked, unsure what was expected of him. Jupiter nodded.

Under the veil, Lot could see only one planet. Its
image was exaggerated in scale, a lovely terrestrial world
wrapped in a meld of living green and blue. Within the
planet's orbit, the density of the nebula was very low. Puzzled,
Lot looked up at Jupiter. "Where are the other planets?" he
asked. "Where are the moons and the asteroids?"

Jupiter gazed thoughtfully at the display. "This is all that's left. If there were other planets, they're gone now, or dispersed into the stony nebula. The Chenzeme must have scourged this system."

Lot felt his heartbeat quicken. He knew all about the ancient war of the Chenzeme. It had been fought a long time before people even existed—a terrible alien conflict that had left no known survivors. The Chenzeme were gone. But their weapons still prowled the void, attacking great ships and frontier worlds at unpredictable intervals. Still, Lot had never heard of the Chenzeme actually tearing a planet to pieces. That would make them as powerful as the people of the Hallowed Vasties. . . .

An objection occurred to him. He looked cautiously to Jupiter, assaying his mood, searching for any hint of dark temper, but he uncovered only a quiet anticipation. "I don't understand," Lot said softly. "The Communion's here, and you said the Communion *ended* the war."

Jupiter smiled. His hand rested lightly on Lot's shoulder. "Peace wasn't made overnight." He pointed to the green-blue living world under its nebular veil, and the view zoomed in, sending the edge of the image rocketing off into the walls. "What was fashioned here required millennia to accomplish, and millions of years to refine."

Lot studied the planet, wondering what Jupiter wanted him to see. There was the gossamer thread of the space elevator, built by human settlers only a few hundred years before. He could make out the swelling of its anchoring mass some fifty-five thousand miles beyond the surface of the world. And low on the elevator, just above the main mass of the planetary atmosphere, a tiny bump that contained the city of Silk.

Except for the anchoring point of the elevator, the world itself revealed no evidence of technological life-forms, though the continents and seas were reputed to teem with living things—a biological mélange comprising many different genetic systems, including the coding structure of the insidious plagues left behind by the ancient regime.

Chenzeme plagues could be found on seemingly pristine planets, in the tails of comets, in the dust among stars. They were a constant hazard to great ships that mined almost all their raw materials from unknown sources. Jupiter had almost died when one such plague destroyed Nesseleth's original crew. That had been a long time ago, maybe over a hundred years. Jupiter had been the only survivor and it had been the Well that healed him.

Lot's gaze shifted, to a point some fifteen thousand miles beyond the swollen end of the elevator. There, circling the Well in an independent orbit, was a silver torus the size of a small moon. Lot pointed to it. "That ring is a weapon," he said. "Will the Silkens use it against us?"

Jupiter scowled, and Lot felt his heart quail. He looked down at his hands, while Jupiter's soft menace bedded itself in his sensory tears. "The Chenzeme war isn't over. We all carry the seeds of destruction within us. Boys grasp for weapons as soon as they have learned to make a fist. The war erupts again."

Lot felt a hot flush burning in his cheeks. It was true. The weapon had beguiled him. He knew it to be a swan burster, an artifact of the ancient war. *Swan* meant something like darkness. Swan was the direction in which the looming silhouettes of molecular clouds traced the inner edge of the Orion Arm. It was the direction from which the Chenzeme had come. Had it been functional, the ring would have had the capacity to destroy all the life-forms of the Well . . . and deep down Lot had wanted to see that happen, just for a moment, to see what such a thing might be like, how it might feel.

"What is the proper name of this world?" Jupiter asked, still with that edge in his voice.

Lot swallowed hard. He wanted so much to please Jupiter. In the great ship's records the world was called Deception Well. But Jupiter spoke of it as—

"*The Communion*," Lot whispered.

Jupiter nodded, though he did not seem pleased, as if he knew Lot always thought of it by its other name. "Within the Communion all life is sacred," he said, his voice soft, so Lot held his breath to catch every word. "No species is sacrificed to the greed of another. Within the Communion we will learn the ways of cooperation and peaceful coexistence, just as the Chenzeme were forced to learn. We will forget our yearning for weapons, and for power. We will become part of a greater whole that has endured despite the lingering evil of the ancient war for over thirty million years."

"We will be safe," Lot whispered.

Jupiter nodded. "We will be home."

* * *

He woke to a sense of dire fear. It seeped through his sensory tears and into his veins. It forced its way past the membranes of each one of his cells. He cried out softly, and felt a responding ache in his lungs.

Jupiter.

A hand touched his shoulder. "Shh, Lot. It's all right."

He turned his head at the familiar voice. "Alta?"

She sat beside him in the half-light. Alta was Captain Antigua's daughter, and already eleven years old. She was good at commando games. Sometimes she treated Lot like a baby, but she'd partnered with him once, and that time he'd lived.

Now she looked nervous. She kept glancing to the side. "You have to wake up quick, Lot. The medic doesn't know I took the sedative patch off. She'll be back soon."

Lot remembered the medic, but he didn't remember falling asleep. "I feel scared." His voice was a hoarse croak. He coughed softly to clear his aching throat.

"I feel scared too. Everybody's scared. The Silkens want to panic us. They've bombed the air with a psychoactive virus. It'll clear soon. We'll be all right." She glanced again to the side. She had black eyes and black, wispy hair that clung to her chin and her throat above her armor. Her skin was very pale.

"You look funny in armor," Lot said.

She frowned at him. "You look funny asleep, so *get up,* before the medic slaps another patch on your neck."

Her anxiety pried at him. Coughing softly, he pushed himself to a sitting position. They were in the cavernous loading bay, though it was almost empty now. Light spilling in from the corridor was augmented by a few headlamps on the floor. Nearby, five women sat cross-legged, infants cradled against the hard breastplates of their armor. One of them rocked gently, her eyes squeezed shut. Lot could hear his heart running fast. "Why are we still here? We're supposed to follow Jupiter."

Alta leaned close. Her lips moved beside his ear as she spoke in a barely audible whisper. "Not everyone's going to make it down." She sat back a little. "That's why you have to wake up. We have to go *now*. Only a few elevator cars are running below the city. The corridor is packed with people waiting for a turn. It can't last. We have to get to the lower terminus before it's too late. Don't be afraid. I've waited for you. We can do it together."

His sensory tears grappled with her scent. A sticky, pervasive fear seeped out of her, but that was undercut by a gleam of confidence, delightful in its unexpected presence. He fed on it, and felt his own mood lighten. "Where's the medic?"

"In the corridor. She'll try to stop us—"

A strange sound stirred in the far distance, a muffled roar blended of deep bass notes and high-pitched accents that set Lot's nerves on edge.

One of the huddled women muttered, "Oh, I hate that sound." Someone else hushed her. A baby fussed.

Alta surprised Lot with a quick hug. "Don't worry. That's nothing. Just the Silkens, trying to scare us."

Lot thought she might be wrong. "I want to look." He got to his feet and edged toward the door. Alta followed, her approval sliding coolly over his sensory tears.

In the corridor Lot saw more people—several hundred armored troopers sitting on the floor, their backpacks on. There wasn't room to walk between them. They were silent, but their anxiety spoke loudly in the absence of words. They stared vacantly: at the walls, at their hands. Lot knew they were listening. He listened too.

The distant roar grew louder, the keening overnotes more strident. Lot could almost believe he heard Jupiter's name in that wail. Alta nudged his elbow. "If we stay calm, we'll be all right."

"Something's wrong down there." He could taste it on the air, panic and terror like dark sparks flashing against his cheeks.

"It's not good," Alta admitted. "But Lot, *you* could get through. The troopers will let you pass, and I'll take care of you. We can get there together—"

A startled voice interrupted her. "Lot, what are you doing awake?"

He looked up, recognizing the medic who'd taken him away from Jupiter. Sweat glistened on her cheeks. He could smell her quiet terror. Still, she tried for a reassuring smile. "Come back inside. You're not well. You should be sleeping. You need to give your medical Makers time to heal you."

"I don't like to sleep."

"He can't dream," Alta said. Lot could tell she didn't like the medic.

The medic didn't seem too fond of her, either. "We all have our duties, Alta Antigua, and mine is to keep the two of you safe. Come inside. We'll be following Jupiter before too long."

Alta caught Lot's hand. He looked in her eyes, and knew she wanted to run. But there was no room to run in the packed corridor, and the sense drifting up from below was only growing worse.

"Let's go inside, Alta. Just for now."

Her anger cut sharply across his senses. He felt suddenly self-conscious. The troopers were watching them. He could feel their tension climbing, a cloud of flammable emotions building over their heads. He didn't want it to ignite. "*Please*, Alta."

Accusation lay in her eyes. But she went with him back into the loading bay, where the medic gave them both a drink and a ration packet before taking up a protective position at the door.

Lot ate standing up, listening to the murmur from the corridor. The wailing had faded, but the fear was thicker than ever. Lot could feel it tripping through his heart. He tried hard to ignore it. "I saw your mama," he told Alta. "She went down ahead of Jupiter."

"I know. If I were nine years older, I could have been in the advance troops too."

Lot remembered the flash of the incendiary grenade and felt glad that she was only eleven. But he didn't say it out loud.

He thought about his own mother. She was a captain too, and had her own troops to look out for. "They'll wait for us in the Well."

"Hey." Alta's mood suddenly brightened. She stuffed the last of her ration packet into her mouth, then caught Lot's hand. "Come with me. I want to show you something."

She wouldn't say what it was, but her gaiety was infectious, so he ran with her across the loading bay's open floor, toward a faint glow of white light. As they drew closer, he could see that the light was seeping up from a crescent-shaped pit. It lit the surface of a massive, curving wall on the pit's opposite side. A narrow channel ran in a vertical path up the wall's face.

Lot edged closer. A transparent shield surrounded the pit, sealing it off from floor to ceiling. He stood with his hands against the shield, looking down. Alta stood behind him, grinning.

The curved wall descended deep into the pit. Several levels below, a bright light shone against it. Lot could see a scoring, a warping of the wall's surface there, as if it had been partially melted. Below the damaged section the wall was dark. But he could see it again farther down—much farther down—where it plunged into a glowing green crescent. Except it wasn't a wall anymore. Distance had resolved it into an infinite silver cylinder.

"The elevator column!"

"You're right, Lot. They'll be waiting for us. They'll be waiting down there."

He stared into the pit, knowing he was looking at a two-hundred-mile drop into Deception Well.

Into the Communion, he corrected himself, feeling a nervous tingling on the back of his neck, as if Jupiter might overhear him.

Movement caught his eye. Far below, something was sliding along the elevator column: a tiny black capsule. It burst out of shadow and into Kheth's brilliant light as it sped down the shaft. "Alta, look!" he shouted. "There! An elevator car." In seconds, it was lost to distance. But even before it disappeared, Lot had sighted another capsule, this one moving upward, toward the city. It vanished into shadow just as Alta craned her neck to look.

"It's gone now, but I saw them. I saw two cars." He sucked in a sharp breath. The army was leaving Silk. And Deception Well was waiting for them, looming like a trap, just beneath the floor.

Believe in me, Jupiter seemed to whisper.

I do.

Alta's mood played slick and steely against his recurring doubts. "We have to get on one of those cars," she said.

"I know." Yet fear resonated in his blood. It flooded the air. A thousand variations of a common emotion. Holding Alta's hand again, he tracked the scent back to the door. The medic crouched in the entrance. She was staring down the hall, past the huddled troopers, her mouth open as she sucked in little gasps of air. Alta squeezed Lot's hand. "I want to go *now*."

In that moment, the keening took hold again, starting in ragged bursts, like the terrorized cries of individual voices, then rapidly gathering force. In only a few seconds it was fully orchestrated, and far louder this time than it had been before. This time, Lot was sure he heard Jupiter's name in the ghastly chorus. This time, there was no denying that the macabre roar was a melody of human screams.

The startled troopers mounted to their feet. An anonymous woman's voice rose over the anxious murmur. "Jupiter's down there!"

"You're right," a man said. "They're calling to him. I can hear his name."

"They're calling him back," someone else cried. "He's leaving without us. He's leaving us behind!"

The medic stepped into the corridor. Alta pushed after her, dragging Lot along. "No, wait." Lot tried to pull free of her grip. The air in the corridor was thick with an emotional energy poised to ignite. He didn't want to get caught in it. This wasn't what Jupiter had planned. "Alta, let me go!"

As if sparked by his voice, the troopers surged forward. Lot felt pressure from behind. He found himself stumbling down the sloping corridor, people shoving forward all around him. Alta held on to his hand while he struggled to keep his feet. The pace picked up. The troopers were running now, pushing to get around the bend and down, down the long corridor to the lower elevator terminus. Lot was forced to run too. Bodies pressed upon him from all sides. He felt himself lifted off his feet. He tried to scream, but there was no air in his lungs. Alta's grip slipped. Instantly, she was swept away. Knees and elbows bumped against him. Then the floor was under his feet again, and he was struggling to stop, to go back. Someone hit him in the shoulder. He spun, slamming up against a wall. He clung to it while troopers brushed past him, the static-roar of their voices mixing maddeningly with the raw scent of their terror.

"Jupiter!" he screamed. "I'm not going with you! I'm not. I'm not." He spun around, preparing to defend himself against anyone who would force him to go on. But the corridor was empty.

* * *

It took a long time to work up the courage to follow. Lot sat hunched against the wall, listening to the distant screams, afraid for Alta but too frightened to go look for her. Listening for her to come back. The lights went out, and he was left sitting in darkness.

Hours passed. The screams had long faded to silence when he found himself walking. He moved slowly, the beam of his headlamp picking out the abandoned armor, the backpacks, the bead rifles left lying on the floor. The corridor descended in a slow spiral. Bay doors stood sealed at intervals on the inside wall, their manual levers buried beneath white, scaly growths, unusable. Tunnels branched away on the opposite side. Lot peered up each one, moving his head slowly back and forth as he sought a human presence, but the only sense he got was stale. The tunnels seemed well placed to take people up to the city. Debris littered their floors, and he guessed that a lot of troopers had gone out that way. So he wasn't the only one who'd been scared. But Alta wouldn't have turned aside, he was sure of that. So he pressed on, determined to find her.

After several minutes he came across a cluster of three bodies. Two of the troopers were facedown, but the other—a young woman—lay on her back, her dry eyes gazing at the ceiling. After that he found bodies every few feet: mostly infants and children, but young women too, and even a few men.

None of them was Alta.

He reached the lower terminus without realizing it. The corridor came to an abrupt end at a set of bay doors that stood half-open, their runners blocked by fallen bodies. Loathsome vapors drenched the air.

It was then that the corridor lights came back on, spilling out across a loading bay crammed with corpses pressed up against one another so that most of them were still standing, their vacant, horrified eyes staring into emptiness. Across the charnel room, bodies were piled up against the transparent shield that walled off the elevator shaft, so that the sea of corpses seemed to rise on that side. There was no elevator car in the pit.

Lot told himself that Alta was not here and that Jupiter had escaped, and that Mama had gone with him, and they were waiting for him now, down below.

Believe in me.

Suddenly his amplified hearing caught the approaching buzz of a small remote unit. He jumped. Hard training moved his exhausted hands. He flicked on his suit's camo function and grabbed his headlamp, dropping it into a pocket. Then he pulled up his hood and pressed himself against the wall just as the little remote unit buzzed around the long curve of the corridor. No bigger than the end of his thumb, the round, golden remote darted past him on beelike wings, to enter the loading bay, where it flashed back and forth across the ghastly territory. Three other remote bees quickly followed it, and shortly after, Lot could hear the soft tramp of footfalls.

A patrol of Silken troopers jogged around the curve of the corridor. There were five of them, three with bead rifles, the others holding devices Lot could not identify. He studied them surreptitiously, his eyes mostly closed so they would not give him away. The Silken troops wore beige armor, the design similar to the armor of Jupiter's troops. Lot could see their faces beyond their helmets' transparent visors, so apparently their tactics were overlaid on hard reality. They wore tense expressions, not quite looking at the bodies on the floor. Several civilians followed behind them, all dressed in soft coveralls.

The Silken troopers came to an abrupt halt when they caught sight of the loading bay. It must have looked worse in reality than through the images generated by the buzzing bees. Lot pressed himself against the wall, trying not to breathe. One of the troopers stepped forward. She was a big-boned woman, massive in her armor. Her gaze swept the sea of corpses, and in her aura lay a hollow structure of disappointment and disbelief. "By the Unknown God, what have we done?"

Her language was foreign. Lot understood it, though it sounded different from the version he'd learned, almost cruel, each syllable hard and coarse in a stranger's mouth.

Most of the civilians lingered well down the hall, but one man and a woman had come forward too, threading through the knot of stunned troopers. The woman was slim and lightly built, reminding Lot of his mother in the way she carried herself. She almost brushed against him as she stepped up beside the armored trooper. One of the remote bees swept in from the bay, to hover a few feet off her shoulder. Soft anger filled her voice: "I'll tell you what we've done, Clemantine. We've destroyed Jupiter." She turned to the man who had come forward with her. "And didn't we agree that would be *right*?"

"So," Clemantine said. "We did a damn good job."

The man frowned. He was an imposing figure: tall and strongly built like the trooper, with dark skin and sharply intelligent eyes. His black hair was fixed in a thick mass of tiny braids, one of which had been used to loosely tie the others behind his neck. He brought a strange, cool-metal taste to Lot's sensory tears. "You know it wasn't meant to go this way. We didn't guess Jupiter had so many people." He said this regretfully, as if he might have done things differently had he known. Lot wondered. He couldn't find any taste of shame.

"We should have guessed," Clemantine said. "Dammit, Kona, we should have seen it coming."

Kona. Lot silently repeated the name. *Kona.* The dark man to whom it belonged glared at the carnage.

"At least get more crews down here," the civilian woman said as she watched the remote bees continue to hunt among the bodies. Her long black hair was loosely bound, hanging in filamentous curves against her cheeks. Earrings glistened in the shadows behind her finely sculpted jaw. She didn't look like a frontline trooper, and Lot wondered why she was here. "We need to sort this carnage through. These people can be restored."

Clemantine lifted off her helmet. "Yulyssa, we don't have more crews. Security's fully occupied with the refugees, so all dead and critically wounded are to be routed to cold storage."

"For how long?"

Kona answered that: "Yulyssa, we just don't know."

Lot blinked, trying to make sense of this. He'd heard of cold storage. In his fixed memory he carried a map of Nesseleth that showed vast banks of cold-storage units at her core. He'd never been to that part of the ship, but he knew the facilities were supposed to be used for emergency shelter, not medical repair.

Now another trooper moved forward. He looked confused; the point of his bead rifle dipped toward the floor. "I can't believe it's come to this," he muttered. "I just can't believe it." He pushed his visor up, looking from Clemantine to Kona, and then to Yulyssa. "Were they all insane? What kind of stupid sots would follow a madman like that anyway?"

"Maybe a stupid sot like you," Yulyssa said gently as she put her hand on his arm. "If you'd ever met Jupiter, you'd understand."

"Uh-uh." The trooper shook his head, his expression adamant. "This whole thing's crazy."

Yulyssa sighed. "David, have you ever been in love?"

He frowned. "Well, sure."

"No. I mean *really* in love. You'd-die-for-her in love?"

David looked suddenly wary. "That's kind of dramatic, isn't it?"

"Passionate. Yes. Irrationally passionate. That's how Jupiter could make you feel. The scariest part was, you'd *like* it."

"Not me."

"Even you," she insisted. "Deep down, we all want to give into that kind of crazy faith. To be part of something bigger than ourselves; something that'll outlast us. It's a need inside us all."

But the trooper wasn't buying it. "Huh. You can get that from a patch. I'm using a patch right now so I don't puke my guts out."

Yulyssa's lip trembled slightly as she admitted, "So am I."

"It's all chemistry," Kona growled.

Yulyssa glanced at the remote bee that still hovered near her. "And does that matter?"

"Yes it matters!" Kona's deep voice seemed to expand to fill the corridor. "Jupiter was beguiling people, and he must have been using psychoactive viruses to do it."

Clemantine said, "I think it's more complicated than that."

Yulyssa nodded agreement. She turned again to David. "You're very young. You don't remember Jupiter from before, and the people who do—" She looked significantly at Kona. "—don't like to talk about it. But you should know that he once lived in Silk without city authority being aware of him. He persuaded hundreds of citizens to keep his presence secret, despite the possibility that he carried a Chenzeme plague. He assembled a society around himself the way you might assemble your morning wardrobe. I'm talking about *our* people, David. The very same people you'll pass on the walks today. Maybe even your mother or father. *And not one of them betrayed his presence to city authority.*"

"Charismatic personalities." Kona spat on the floor. "Human history would have been a lot less bloody without them."

"Put the blame where it belongs, Kona," Clemantine said. "*We* did this. Not Jupiter."

"We did what was needed."

"I hope so," Yulyssa said. "By the Unknown God, I—"

She had reached out to rest a hand against the wall. Lot tried to dodge her inadvertent touch, but he was tired and slow. Her fingertips brushed across his hood. She gasped and snatched her hand back. "There's someone here!" She darted away, giving the trooper David room to work. He snapped his visor down, at the same time swinging his bead rifle in Lot's general direction. Clemantine moved in quickly to back him up.

Lot cringed. He glimpsed the light of changing tactics displays flashing across David's visor. Then David's rifle zeroed in on Lot's skull. He felt his head on fire at that point, as if the bead had already hit and even now it was chewing a path through his metallicized bone.

But David didn't fire. Instead, with a grunt of surprise, he let the rifle's muzzle swing down until it pointed at the floor again. "It's a kid," he announced.

Lot flinched at the harsh Silken accent.

"Hey, it's okay," David said. He crouched, bringing himself to Lot's level, ducking his head to get a look at Lot's downcast eyes. "You startled us, that's all. Want to shut off that camo? It's all over now."

Lot wanted it to be over. But he was so scared he couldn't make his hand move.

"C'mon, kid," David urged, as the remote bee hovered overhead. "You're hungry, aren't you?"

He was hungry. He remembered the ration pack he'd shared with Alta, and wondered again where she was. Not here. Please, not here. "I want to find my friend Alta."

"We'll help you find her. But turn off the camo."

Breathing in some of the trooper's calm, Lot moved a slow hand to his wrist and flicked off the camo function. He slipped off his hood. That was easier. He felt almost light, as if he might float away if he could just relax a little. . . .

"Shut off the camera bees," Kona said. There was a hollow note in his voice. "Now."

A chill touched Lot's spine. He looked from David to Kona to Yulyssa. "It's done," she said, as the buzzing ceased abruptly in both the hall and the loading bay. The remote bee at her shoulder dropped to the floor with a sharp *crack*.

Lot felt Kona's anger build to a frightening explosion. "It doesn't end!" he shouted, his fist impacting against the wall.

"If we're lucky," Yulyssa said softly, "that's true."

The rest of the troopers had come forward now. They exchanged puzzled glances. "What's the matter?" David asked as he backed away from Lot, getting some cautious distance between them.

Yulyssa didn't answer. Instead, she knelt in front of Lot, studying him with soft eyes that were full of concern. "What's your name?"

Clemantine stepped up close beside her. "He's dangerous, Yulyssa. Come away."

"Clemantine, this is a child. He's not Jupiter."

"Not yet," Clemantine said. "David!"

"Ma'am?" The young trooper stepped forward smartly.

"Get him out of here."

"And keep him away from the rest of the refugees," Kona added. "Well away."

"Yes, sir." The trooper looked uncertainly at Lot, then forced a nervous smile. "Hey, kid. C'mon with me. We'll get you something to eat."

Lot hesitated. It didn't feel right to simply give up; but neither did he want to put up any resistance. Maybe David sensed that. He laid a cautious hand on Lot's shoulder, guiding him away from the wall. "C'mon. You know it'll never get any worse than this."

Chapter
3

Lot lost track of things after that. He was tired, and when
he noticed David carrying him, he only shifted a little,
hiding his face against the young trooper's armored
chest before dropping off again. When he woke up the next
time, it was in Captain Antigua's lap. She was speaking to
someone in the hard-edged Silken language, something about
compensation and retraining. Her voice sounded strangely
empty, almost machinelike.

He gazed up at her, staring at the fatigue lines that
netted her serious face while her commanding voice echoed in
his memory *Go, go, go!* as she ordered the first wave of troops
out of the loading bay while Jupiter looked on. He jerked
hard. Captain Antigua had gone down the corridor just ahead
of Jupiter. Why wasn't she in the Well?

Her cold explanation broke off in midsentence. She
looked down at him, and he could see the anger in her eyes, a
deep-down fury. The scent of it started his heart racing.
Reaching up, he clutched at the padded neckline of her gray
armor. "Where's Jupiter?" he asked, in the graceful, lilting
language that had been the common tongue of their polyglot
crew. "What happened to him? Why did you come back?"

A soft breath hissed out between her teeth. "Those
are the same questions Alta asked when we pulled her out of
the tunnels. And I'll give you the same answer. Jupiter's

dead." She spoke in the Silken's language, and she seemed to take a mean pleasure in saying the words. "The elevators wouldn't run. Jupiter died in the crush at the lower terminus, and half the army with him. You saw it. *Everybody* down there died."

Lot stared at her in open shock. His fingers closed even tighter over the edge of her armor. "That's not true," he whispered. He had looked into the elevator pit. He'd watched the black capsule descend below the city until it disappeared with distance. "You know that's not true!" He wrenched his hand free of her armor, then spun out of her lap, fully awake now.

Suddenly, he was conscious of other people around him. He turned slowly, to see Kona seated on a crescent-shaped sofa, surrounded by strangers. *Silkens.* They sat on the sofa or stood behind it with hips half-cocked on the sofa back, watching him curiously. They seemed subtly foreign, like a familiar object viewed through a slightly diffracting lens, so that the difference was elusive, but real: chins carried higher than natural, eyes that stared too long, and their scent . . . not unpleasant, but *unsettling*. . . .

Behind them, a long wall glimmered deep glassy black. Lot could see a vague image in it, just beneath the surface, a woman, her lips moving in speech while dark figures shuffled slowly behind her, tired troopers, hunched in defeat. A projection wall? Tuned to minimal brightness. Despite the tenebrous quality of the image, he recognized the woman as Yulyssa, the one who'd come down the corridor with Kona. He could hear her voice faintly: "*City authority estimates casualties will run into the thousands. . . .*"

He looked away. More glass bounded the other side of the room, this time a great, curving panel filled with points of amber and white light. An older boy leaned against it, his dark eyes coolly curious.

"*Lot.*"

Dread settled around his shoulders as he turned to Captain Antigua. She glared at him from a seat on a sofa that faced the Silkens. "Sit down," she ordered him, in *their* language, using the same cold, machinelike voice with which she'd pronounced Jupiter's death.

He shook his head, backing a step away. "You don't understand. Jupiter's alive. I saw an elevator car going down. Alta was with me, and she—"

"You saw no such thing!" Captain Antigua barked. "And neither did Alta. I've talked to her, and she saw nothing. Jupiter is dead. It's over. And if you start any rumors to the contrary that get the surviving members of the army stirred up, I will personally see you delivered into cold storage. Do you understand that, Lot?"

She was lying. But the anger in her aura warned him not to argue. Not now.

"Do you understand?" she repeated.

He nodded slowly, wishing he could disappear.

"Then sit down and shut up."

Cautiously, he settled to the floor. It had a soft white carpet. As his legs folded under him, he sensed a hint of anger from the boy at the window. Lot glanced at him, and the boy extended a slight nod toward the adults, while a brief expression of contempt flashed across his face. *Pointless,* the boy seemed to say. Arguing with them was pointless.

Lot wondered.

Kona observed this exchange. He'd changed out of his coverall, into a soft felt vest and loose slacks. His sharp eyes lingered on Lot, as cool as twin scientific instruments designed to assay the quality of human intent. Lot eyed him warily, wondering if he had ordered the psychoactive virus to be released.

On the muted projection wall Yulyssa's faint image was gone, replaced by a dark field, featureless but for a poorly resolved image glowing dully red. The red deepened into the outline of a great ship, its extended cooling fins arranged in a pattern both distinct and familiar. "*Nesseleth,*" Lot whispered.

Kona followed his gaze curiously, then scowled. "Why is Yulyssa playing that again? Haven't we seen it enough?"

Nobody answered.

Lot's fingers dug into the carpet as Nesseleth's image dwindled in size. He saw the lowest fin flare to white, then vanish. He thought he saw the side fins crumple too, but he couldn't be sure. She'd become only a faint red blur on the dark wall, and suddenly that was gone too as incandescent white sheathed her entire hull in a brief flash that lasted less than a second, before she vanished completely.

"It was a mistake," Captain Antigua said, in that

awful, hollow voice. "We would leave, but our ship is gone. We must find another way."

"There is no other way." Kona leaned forward, his braids shifting slightly, a slow tide. "Unlike you, Captain Antigua, we did not come to Silk by choice. We were abandoned here, left to die. But we didn't die. And we won't let you die either. You and your people."

Lot hunched against the poisonous scent of Captain Antigua's fury. "These people are not my people, Kona Lukamosch. They are from many worlds. They were brought together by Jupiter, and without him, they are nothing at all."

Lot flinched. That wasn't true. They were one people. Jupiter had made them into one. He wanted to shout it, but he couldn't form the foreign words through his stunned surprise.

Kona Lukamosch didn't seem pleased with her answer either. "They are your people now, Captain. You are the only surviving officer. You are the closest thing to a leader they have left."

Lot felt his heart catch. *The only surviving officer?*

"They won't listen to me," Captain Antigua insisted.

Mama had been an officer. Lot felt a flurry of emptiness swirl around him, as if the darkness in the muted projection wall had slipped out to flood the room.

"You will make them listen, Captain Antigua. That is your assignment. That is the price of your freedom. If you ever want to be more than a ward of this government, then you will make them listen."

A little choking sound escaped Lot's throat. Jupiter was gone and Mama was dead and Captain Antigua despised their people. He could see that now. What he'd taken for fury was really hate, and maybe she'd already betrayed the army and maybe that's why Mama was dead. She didn't deserve to receive the faith of Jupiter's army. She didn't deserve it, the lying, lying, dirty coward.

He rose quickly to his knees. "You don't need her!" he said in his own birth language. Kona looked at him in mild irritation, while Lot searched for the right words in the language the Silkens used. "You don't need her," he repeated. "Let me do it. Let me talk to the army. They'll listen to me. They will." His accent was bad. The words came out with soft edges, but Kona understood him.

"That may be true, young man. But if it is, it's more a

problem than an asset." He turned to Captain Antigua. "Exactly what is he, Captain? A clone of Jupiter? Or a full psychological incarnation?"

Captain Antigua's lip curled in what could only be contempt. "He's neither. Lot's just progeny, that's all. Jupiter tried years to get him, but he's natural, I'm sure of it. Check his genotype if you like. You'll see he's no Jupiter."

"I'll do that. In the meantime, would you regard him as dangerous?"

Captain Antigua snorted. "He's a dog. Jupiter's favorite pet. Run and jump when the master calls." She looked at Lot, and contempt seemed to flow off her shoulders and down over him in an invisible molecular flood. He breathed her anger inside him, where it resonated, and became his own. *Jupiter's dog.* He glared at her, outraged by simple unfairness, unkindness, undeserved hatred.

And to his surprise a sudden, nervous sweat broke out across her cheeks. Her eyes widened and she flinched back in her seat. Her gaze cut to Kona. "Get him away from me."

Kona pursed his lips thoughtfully. "He's your charge."

"No." She was breathing hard now, and trying even harder not to show it. "I'll do what I can with the rest of Jupiter's people, but I won't take responsibility for him. I won't."

On Kona's lips there appeared a hint of a cold, cold smile. "That's acceptable, Captain Antigua. You may go to your people now. They've been quartered in factory spaces, but housing is being prepared for them. You'll explain their obligations and the civic requirements of citizenship." He nodded, seemingly satisfied. "With reason and patience we may yet find a new level of normalcy in this city."

Captain Antigua stood. Lot started to follow, but a cutting glance from the captain stopped him. A door opened in the dark projection wall, and she left along a garden path lit by amber lights, an escort of Silken security before and behind her. The door closed. Lot settled back on the floor, feeling the weight of Kona's gaze upon him. He kept his own gaze fixed on the carpet. "Let me go with her," he whispered.

"She doesn't want you. Why is that?"

He didn't know. His hands started to shake. Deception Well flowed beneath his feet, mocking him with its nearness. "We didn't want anything from you," he croaked, his voice broken with the presence of unshed tears. "Why didn't you let us go?"

Kona didn't answer right away. Then: "We did you a favor. The Communion is a myth. Deception Well is nothing more—and nothing less—than a complex biological machine, with molecular defenses more capable and more adaptive than anything we can field. It harbors plagues that would kill us. It would have killed you."

"No." Lot shook his head in solid denial. "That's not true. It didn't kill Jupiter. Jupiter was there. He was dying of a real plague and the Communion healed him."

Kona spoke softly, but his words were firm. "Jupiter lied to you. He was never on the planet."

Lot felt as if his breath had been stolen away. He sat back, stunned. *Jupiter lied to you.*

The world seemed to shift around him, as if every molecule had turned at right angles to some unseen dimension to create an entirely new order of reality.

He watched his fingers work at the soft carpet. From his fixed memory came the image of his mother laying him on a white carpet after his bath when he was a baby, still learning to crawl. "Will you revive the dead?" he croaked. He looked up at Kona, trying hard to hold on to his tears.

But the bitter expression on Kona's face crushed even this last hope. "We don't have room for our own grandchildren." He stood up, suddenly impatient. He looked to one of the Silkens still lingering behind the sofa. "Alonna, get another security detail."

The Silken shifted slightly. "Where do you want to put him?" she asked, glancing questioningly at Lot.

"Where do you think?"

"The monkey house, then."

"And make sure he stays there. I don't care what the doctors say. I want him kept away from Jupiter's people until emotions have cooled. *Urban!*"

Lot jumped at the sharp bark of command. The boy by the window had moved up silently behind him.

"Stay away from him, Urban," Kona warned.

"Why, Dad? He's not going to bite. Are you, Lot?"

Lot studied him warily. Urban looked several years older, and he stood at least a head and shoulders over Lot. He had skin like mild brown tea and short black hair fixed in about a hundred braids that bobbed around his face as he

crouched in front of Lot. He was more than halfway to man-
hood, and there was a wildness on him that set Lot's heart
pumping. "You hungry?" Urban asked in his harsh accent.

Kona shifted, his irritation clouding the room. "He
can eat at the hospital."

"I'll get you some food," Urban said.

Kona swore softly, but he let it go. One of the other
Silkens was asking him something, and he let his attention
move off that way while Urban strode out of the room. Lot
pulled his knees up to his chest and bowed his head. He felt so
tired. When his forehead came to rest against his knees, he
didn't try to lift his head again, not even when Urban sat
down next to him. "Hey, you awake?" When Lot didn't respond, he leaned closer and whispered, "The real people will
deep-run through your head if you let them."

Lot felt a twitch of trepidation. He raised his head a
few inches and frowned at Urban.

"Here, eat something," Urban said, and shoved a
plate at his face.

There were two rolled crepes, thin skins like irides-
cent butterfly wings wrapped around a creamy green filling.
Steam spiraled from the open ends. "Come on," Urban said.
"You want it or not?"

The smells had already set Lot's stomach growling.
He started to reach for a crepe. But his hand was soiled,
sweat-sticky, coated with the residue of ugly emotions, tainted
by death. He rubbed his palm against his thigh. Jupiter had
always commanded him to cleanse his hands before taking
food, because grace was found in ritual and respect.

Jupiter was gone.

Hesitantly, Lot picked up a crepe. It felt silky
smooth. He took a tentative bite. Sweet green flavors exploded in his mouth, and then he ate ravenously. Urban
grinned at him. "Now, listen," he said, leaning close to Lot
and talking softly. Lot glanced curiously around the room,
wondering why Urban bothered to whisper. Amplified hearing had been a pretty common asset on Nesseleth. But nobody
seemed to be paying attention. "You don't want to stay long
at the monkey house. They like to switch you off in there, and
you'll never know what they've done to you while you're
under."

Lot reached for the other crepe. He didn't want to
admit to Urban that he didn't understand. So he said nothing.

"Give them enough time," Urban said, "and they'll deep-run through your mind. They'll turn you into a happy monkey."

"Have you been there?" Lot asked, forcing the foreign words around a mouthful of food, so it was luck Urban understood him at all.

"Not yet. But I know people who have. You like being happy?"

"Yeah."

Urban's expression skewed into contempt. "Then you'll like it there, monkey. You can float high enough to be happy all the time."

Lot stared at him. He could already feel the glucose from the food running through his arteries. It slammed into his cells, overwhelming systems stabilized at starvation levels, leaving him giddy, frenetic, shaking with a mean buzz. "I'm not a monkey!" he screamed. "I'm not a dog. Don't call me that."

"*Urban.*"

Lot looked around at the stern voice. Kona was eyeing them again, but Urban hardly glanced at him. "If you're that mad at me," he said in a low voice, "why don't you hit me with that evil eye, like you did the old lady?"

Lot sat back in sudden confusion. He sensed no real animosity in Urban, just a calculated curiosity. "What are you talking about?"

Urban shrugged. "Hey, it's okay. You can tell me about it later."

The door slipped open again. Lot twisted around, to see an armored Silken come in. Urban shifted closer to his side, his hand tight on Lot's shoulder. "Listen," he whispered. "If you want to get out of the monkey house fast, then tell them anything they want to know. Make it up if you have to. And be happy. As happy as you can."

Part
II

Chapter
4

A fist-sized transparent slug grazed a slow path across the apartment ceiling, rasping at faint shadows of mildew. The light spilling from the toilet hutch glinted against brass flecks embedded in its body. Its stomach was a black sack surrounded by fleshy gel.

The slug had been in nearly the same position when Lot had gone to sleep four hours ago. Watching it now, he wondered if it had grazed in a circle around the entire room, or if the Universe had simply winked, skipping over the hours, time gone (where?) and nothing changed. Wink, and the past has fallen four futile hours away. Wink again, and ten years have slipped by.

Lot raised a hand, to rub at his sensory tears. Coarse golden hair on the back of his arm caught the dim light. Veins stood out just beneath the skin. What would he say if Jupiter were to suddenly come in the door of his breather and ask, *What have you done with your time?*

Wink! Four hours and ten years gone. No need to answer the question though. Jupiter wasn't coming back.

He sighed and sat up, tossing back his long blond hair. During the night, the microscopic Makers on his skin had gathered up the dust and sweat of the previous day and pushed it away. His body was clean, though a rime of dirty oil soiled the bedding. Even that would be gone in a few minutes, broken down to simple molecules, mostly carbon dioxide and oxygen, with the rare elements suspended in more complex chemical structures that would be carted away in a sinuous, liquid nanodrizzle.

His gaze swept around the tiny confines of his breather. The sleeping pad commanded half the floor space. Another quarter went to his carnivorous-plant collection, sundews and pitcher plants and fly traps growing in clear glass pots on glass saucers that pressed circles into the brown carpet. A set of shelves over a narrow bar provided a stock of food, though he rarely ate at home.

A glint of gold motion drew his eye to a corner of the ceiling. He glanced up, to see Ord wedged in the angle like a four-legged spider. The little robot's supple golden body—like a square-shouldered bottle with a cap—could have fit neatly within the palm of Lot's hand. It clung to the ceiling with two long, tentacular arms, each tipped with an adherent disk. Its squat, scuttling legs helped it balance. "Lot's sleep period's inadequate," Ord announced, its soft voice pitched to soothe. It studied him with pale optical disks. "Anticipate chemical imbalance."

"Why are you always trying to get me back in the monkey house?"

"You're a good boy," Ord said. "I love you."

Ord was a limited cognitive intelligence primarily designed to fuss and worry. City authority had assigned the little robot to harass him after he'd gotten out of the monkey house that first time. It was supposed to function as his guardian, and in that capacity it made regular reports to Dr. Alloin that supposedly described Lot's social behavior. Lot had read a few of those reports. Apparently Ord had as much trouble as any parent in seeing the deficiencies in his kid.

"I'm okay, really. Anyway, it's quiet this early. Only a few peaceful ados around. You like that."

"Good Lot."

The Silken social division between ados and real people had been easy for Lot to grasp. It was a natural system. Adolescents—anyone under a hundred years old—were considered to be lacking in experience and therefore not too bright. They needed looking after; they couldn't vote. Real people were older, more responsible. They made good decisions. Life had been like that on Nesseleth too. There, Jupiter had been the real one, while everyone else played the dumb ado role.

In the toilet hutch, Lot pulled on gray generic slacks and cloth boots. Looking at his image, he finger-combed his blond hair. It was long: almost halfway down his back. The doctors at the monkey house didn't like it, because Jupiter had worn his hair that way. Lot wore it for the same reason, and also because it reminded the staff at the monkey house that they had failed to change him, though they'd tried and tried through almost three years, employing gross surgery and nanomechanical tools against his sensory tears. He'd been sense-blinded, at times for days, cocooned in a balmy, claustrophobic absence of right awareness—for his own good, always. They tried to strip Jupiter's influence out of him, down to a last, spiteful shot at rewriting the color and texture of his hair, but it had all failed. The defensive Makers he'd been born with had neutralized every modification. Still, it had hurt and it had scared him and he hadn't forgotten how that felt. Neither had he forgotten the shame of his secret hope that it would succeed, and the silent disappointment after, and the confusion: How could he want and not want the same thing?

He stared at his image. The cream coffee eyes staring back at him seemed guarded, anxious. The faintly gleaming beads of his sensory tears were only a surface manifestation of a more profound difference that lay tangled up inside his brain. Stirring in his fixed memory, an image of Dr. Alloin once again acknowledged defeat:

"We like to think we can do anything, but of course it isn't true." That had been less than a year after that day. Kona Lukamosch had come for her report, while Lot huddled in a corner chair, his knees pulled up to his chin, waiting for judgment to fall.

Dr. Alloin offered the facts as she saw them: "Lot's brain tissue is netted with a filamentous structure, similar in its gross design to a common communications atrium, yet with details that are . . . unique. Mechanical more than biological, though it doesn't respond to EM signals. Only chemical stimuli. And it's directly parasitic on the cells to which it's attached." She shook her head. "I've tried to dislodge it, but I can't."

Kona's scowl had been fierce. He'd made it clear when he walked into the room that he'd come for better news than this. "If he's a hazard—"

"I don't think he is."

"Then your recommendation?"

"We learn to live with him."

"That's all?"

"He's not a bad kid."

"So just turn him loose?"

"Why not? What could he do?"

"*Nothing*," Lot whispered to his image. He looked like Jupiter but he was not Jupiter, and most days that felt like a safe line to walk, though he was not always proud of it.

The apartment door slipped open. In the dead silence the unexpected click made him flinch. "Lot!" Urban called. "Are you ready?"

"Almost." He did not look at his image again as he pulled on a black shirt and stepped out of the toilet hutch.

Urban was crouched on the floor, tapping his finger across the sticky paddles of a sundew. Urban hadn't changed much in the ten years Lot had known him. Sure, he'd gotten taller, he'd put on muscle. He was twenty-three now; not a boy anymore. But his thick black hair was still bound into small braids that reached to just below his ears and bounced when he moved, and he was still an ado. He grinned up at Lot. "There's a camera bee buzzing outside your door."

"Did you bring it with you?"

Urban laughed. "I didn't have to, fury. The mediots know you're a factor in this election. Even if you don't."

"Maybe that's because you never stop telling them."

Urban had drafted two initiatives on ado and refugee rights, and was presently engaged in gathering enough support to force them onto the ballot of the next election. They'd been tailored to get Lot citizenship, and everybody knew it.

"I don't care if I ever vote in a Silken election," Lot said.

"That's hardly the point." And before Lot could argue, "Netta's saving a table for us. Let's go before I starve."

Ord followed them out of the breather, clinging to the wall with its tentacular limbs. The little robot might not show itself again all day, but it would be there, observing, ready to intercede if Lot showed signs of emotional intemperance. Dr. Alloin mistrusted his emotions.

The apartment door had hardly closed when Lot

heard the low drone of the camera bee. The device cruised down the shadowed hall, slowing as it passed him. Lot glared at it, wondering what mediot rode behind its bulbous eye. "Leave us alone," he growled.

"Be nice," Urban chided. "You're a public figure now."

But the bee didn't go away as it was supposed to when dismissed, and it was then Lot noticed the two green stripes encircling the body. "It's city security." And why were they harassing him? "Hey Clemantine," he said, stepping toward the hovering camera. "I haven't done anything. You know it, so *leave me alone.*"

"Easy fury," Urban said and Lot felt the cold sting of his concern. "We don't want trouble."

The way he said it, Lot knew something was up, but he also knew better than to ask. "Sooth, it's just a joke."

Curious and a little worried now, he followed Urban to the end of the hall. Open-air stairs led down to the street, but it was easier to vault the railing. The drop was only a few feet, and they landed with soft slaps on a street aglow with a dim white light. It was still early, and dawn light had not yet begun to compete with the faint, milky haze of Kheth's nebula that washed the night sky beyond the vault of the city's transparent canopy. Muted stars gleamed through the nebula's veil, some of them members of the Committee where Jupiter had gathered his army long before Lot was born.

Within the nebula's coarse dust, the Silkens had discovered tiny entities of artificial origin called butterfly gnomes, after their minute, winglike solar panels. The butterfly gnomes were capable of storing an electric charge, which they would use to blast apart chunks of nebular material that had accreted to an ounce or so in size. Lot had seen them in a display of preserved specimens in the city library. For gnomes they were uncommonly large, being just visible with unenhanced optics.

Many other varieties of gnomes were found within the Well itself. All of these were microscopic in size. Rare specimens had even been discovered within the city—though these were felt to be isolated populations left over from the years when there had been traffic with the planet. The city gnomes were elusive and fragile, tending to collapse under extremes of heat or cold, or upon contact with molecular-scale analytical tools, so that attempts to study the details of their structure and function had produced few results. Indeed, their populations seemed to be in decline as their own micronscaled ecosystem was gradually overwhelmed by Makers of human origin.

A sudden bright flare drew Lot's gaze as a chunk of nebular material—probably no larger than his fist—vanished under the invisible beam of one of the city's meteor-defense lasers. Even the butterfly gnomes could not attend to every pebbled mass.

"Lot."

He flinched, aware of her a moment before she spoke. *Clemantine.* He would have picked up her presence earlier if he'd been paying attention, and then he would have left from the other side of the apartment complex.

She stepped away from the dark, columnar form of a pillared banyan tree. He caught her amusement, but it was mixed with a touch of anger. "Did you want to talk to me?"

A flush of heat touched his cheeks. "Not really. No." Urban stood close behind him, shedding uneasiness into the air.

"Oh," Clemantine said. "I must have misunderstood."

Lot felt embroiled in helpless anger. Why had she come here? He'd done nothing wrong. He did everything he was supposed to do, and nothing he was not, and still they harassed him. "I'm innocent. Why don't you leave me alone?"

He saw her tense; anxiety rolled off her. "Do you want to do that?" she asked softly.

He averted his gaze, suddenly scared. He'd let himself get angry. Dr. Alloin wouldn't tolerate that. She claimed his influence seeped out around him. *Charismata:* that was the romantic term she'd coined for the elusive pheromonal agents she claimed Lot generated through the chemically sensitive "atrium" in his head. When he gave into anger his body produced a charismata that went straight to the fear center of most people's brains. Even Clemantine could feel it. But for now, his retreat seemed to have satisfied her. "You're a good boy, Lot," she said. "Don't start trouble."

She turned to Urban. The light from the street glinted on her face in broken triangles that split apart when she smiled. "Urban. I was surprised to see you in the refugee quarter tonight."

The words were not addressed to Lot, though perhaps they were meant for him. The camera bee swept close, capturing his surprise. City authority never allowed him within the walls of the refugee quarter. Sometimes, though, the refugees would be allowed out, carrying a pass to conduct business in the city. Lot had seen Alta that way. He'd tried to talk to her once, but Ord had tranked him. It had been Lot's fault, yet they'd punished Alta, confining her to the quarter for most of a year. Lot had been bounced back into the monkey house, where he'd feigned interest in Dr. Alloin's tired explanation of how his charismata would have a destabilizing effect on the refugees. As if anyone was stable.

"I go down there sometimes," Urban said. The chill that rolled off him did not have much in common with the casual shrug he showed Clemantine. "Some of the girls are pretty."

"Sooth. They are, aren't they? But you weren't with the girls tonight. Or is it this morning? Whichever. It was a strange sight to see you drinking coffee with Gent Romer, though I'm sure it's nice to make new friends. Let me guess what you and Gent have in common. Could it be . . . Lot?"

Lot felt a flush of heat, like the fever he'd once had when his mother had given him a new Maker to quicken his muscular response. He turned to Urban, fighting hard against a sense of betrayal. Gent Romer had been the youngest spouse in Jupiter's group marriage; of Lot's family he was the last living member. Gent had survived that day, though he'd spent a week in a body bag, recovering. He'd emerged into the vacuum of leadership left by Captain Antigua's defection, still preaching Jupiter's philosophy of Communion. City authority considered him a troublemaker; they'd waited years for an excuse to seal him in cold storage. Lot knew this, because Dr. Alloin had told him.

Urban leaned close. Lot could feel his dark confidence like a bead, chewing through his skull. "Take it easy. She's just trying to rattle you."

She'd done a fine job of it. Lot guessed that Gent had given his approval to the initiatives. But what else had he done for Urban?

A gutter doggie waddled into the silence, shuffling on its short legs, its closed carry pouches bulging beneath squishy-looking brown skin. It looked them over with baleful eyes, determined they were not on its list of objects to be cleaned, then walked on. Lot felt a sudden, squirming impatience to be gone. "Hey Urban, I'm hungry."

Urban said, "I'll buy you breakfast."

Clemantine smiled, letting them know she'd accomplished her purpose. "Have fun, boys. I expect we'll be seeing one another again soon."

Chapter 5

In the neighborhood of Ado Town the buildings were mostly low-rise, no more than three or four stories, ugly stacked apartments built less than a hundred years ago as a concession to the city's growing population of adolescents.

Lot and Urban trotted uphill, negotiating the winding streets. After a few minutes, Lot thought it was probably safe to ask questions, but Urban raised a hand, shaking his head. *Not yet.* Lot nodded, and fell into step behind him. It felt natural; he'd tagged at Urban's heels since he was nine. Then, Urban had been an awe-inspiring fourteen and already living like a crazy ado. He'd rescued Lot from the sanctimonious baby-sitter city authority had assigned him. He taught Lot the city, and the difference between ados like themselves, and the real people, those over a hundred, who were old enough to vote. *We outnumber them,* Urban said. *But they make every real choice in our lives.*

Most ados didn't care. But it was everything to Urban. He wanted his fair share of political power, and the fastest way to get it was to get the vote and vote an ado into office. He had his candidate already chosen: *People like you, fury. They're drawn to you, just like they were drawn to your old man.*

Lot denied it, but Urban only laughed.

*   *   *

They breakfasted at a small, open-air restaurant on the grand walk—the highest, narrowest level in the conical city, closely encircling the walled core that housed the elevator cable. Here, the transparent canopy arched barely a hundred feet overhead, held up by the pressure of air. The nebula glowed in a thin, milky wash across the night.

A sparse crowd decorated the grand walk, ghostly forms adrift beneath the sprawling branches of bougainvillea trees that leaned this way and that from the anchoring cubes of their planter boxes. Patience had replaced Lot's initial curiosity; he didn't try again to question Urban. There would be time to talk later, after they'd eaten and satisfied at least briefly the demands of enhanced physiologies that burned energy almost faster than it could be taken in.

Netta greeted them at the restaurant gate, in a dress that left the smooth curve of her shoulders exposed. She smiled gaily, so it startled Lot to feel an acute shard of unhappiness embedded in her aura. "Netta?" he asked, his brow furrowing in concern. "Are you okay?"

Surprise flashed in her eyes. "You always know."

"Don't let him hurt you."

She looked down at the gate, using both hands to push it against a clasp that held it open. "Real people want too much."

"They want it all," Urban agreed.

"I'll only see ado boys from now on."

Lot said, "You know you'll never be lonely."

Her smile caught the faint light and slowed it. She touched Lot's hand. "It feels good to be around you."

He felt good too. In the soft warmth of her fingers he could touch the simple pattern of days, dawn to dusk to dawn in Silk, a circular flow of food and sex and fellowship that seemed at once both ancient and timeless. So naturally did the Silkens inhabit their city that it startled him to remember they had not built it, that they were refugees, *just like us,* with no way out. The ancient people who'd made the elevator and hung the city of Silk upon it were long gone, taken by plague less than ten years after they'd reached the Well . . . over five hundred years ago now. For half that time the city had been empty, its automatic systems recycling air, water and nutrients for the sole benefit of rampant gardens and overgrown parks—until refugees from the Chenzeme-ruined

world of Heyertori had been force-landed at the end of the
elevator column.

"What are you thinking about?" Netta asked him as
they walked between the tables.

"The Old Silkens."

For some reason, that impressed her. "Oh. My mama
says that when she and her sisters were little, they could still
find bones under the thickets in Splendid Peace Park."

"Why would anyone crawl into the thickets to die?"
Urban asked.

Netta thought about it. "I don't know. I never found
any bones."

"You looked?" Lot flashed on an image of Netta
thrashing through the thickets in one of her filmy dresses,
digging down through five centuries of humus with her soft
clean hands . . . and grinned.

"What are you laughing about?" she demanded.

"Nothing."

"You don't believe me."

"Oh I do."

"Maybe they were making love."

Lot frowned, lost by this sudden twist. "Who?"

"Under the bushes. When they died."

"If they died," Lot said, wondering how the fate of
the Old Silkens fit into Jupiter's teachings. He had never mentioned them.

"Of course they died," Urban said. "Their bones
were all over the city."

But how could they have died? The Old Silkens had
moved freely between the city and the planet below. They
should have been sheltered by the Communion. Instead, the
Well had killed them.

Netta passed a hand in front of his eyes. "Hello,
hello. Are you still there?"

"Huh? Sorry."

Sudden humor sparkled in her aura. "I think I'd better feed you quick, before you drift away from us altogether."

She left them at a table by the railing, where the view was
best. Lot stood, looking out over the slope of the city. Silk
hung like a conical bead on the string of the elevator cable.

Only the outer slopes of the bead were inhabited; the interior was given to industrial space.

Below him, the braided, luminescent streets of Ado Town glowed like a capillary network, infusing the slope with light. Ado Town split the circle of better neighborhoods like a visible stress fracture, zigzagging all the way from the grand walk down to the encircling belt of Splendid Peace Park, some two thousand feet below. Beyond that, past the transparent canopy, he could see the dark curve of Deception Well.

Silk was a city of over six million people, yet it was only a tiny realm perched above a closed world. No one was allowed down the elevator; neither was there any point in going up—no ships waited at the end of the cable to carry people away. Silk was a trap, with both ends sealed. And still it seemed big enough to Lot.

He sat down, just as a group of boys came in. Urban waved them over. Netta brought coffee and they chatted about unimportant things and ate, until finally Urban checked his watch and said that it was time.

They left the restaurant just as dawn light began to wrap itself in a pearly crescent around the Well's eastern rim. Lot could feel Urban's anticipation rising as they negotiated the growing crowd on the grand walk. "You're up to something," he said. "And it's to do with Gent. What is it?"

Urban half-turned, glancing back over his shoulder. His stride slowed, but he didn't lose his distinctive gait: a half-liquid flow, as if momentum was constantly shuttling on a long path through all the muscles of his lean body. A discerning smile rode his lips. "I could tell you. But maybe you'd report us to city authority. You're such a good boy."

"*Fuck you.*"

Urban laughed and took off. Lot swore some more, then bolted in pursuit. It was an old game between them, and they ran down the grand walk in a silent charge for two hundred yards until Urban suddenly changed directions and vaulted an ornate, waist-high fence surrounding a restaurant that wouldn't open until well after dawn. Lot leaped after him, cutting madly through the maze of tables. He'd almost caught him when Urban ducked around a carefully disciplined hedge, disappearing into one of the restaurant's private alcoves.

Lot stopped, put on guard by some inner sense. Walking slowly now, he edged around the end of the sheltering hedge.

Urban sat cross-legged on a banquet table, his back to Lot. He looked out on the city, or perhaps to the planet beyond. There in the Well, the first pale arc of dawn light had already brightened, smearing across the atmosphere in a searing white band.

Lot walked around the table and sat down on it too. "What have you gotten Gent into?"

Urban leaned back on his elbow, to regard Lot with a teasing smile. "Trouble. You guessed it. But hey, he's not in it alone."

Like that mattered.

"You think you're sharing the risk? Authority will put him in cold storage. They *told* me. It's not like he's Silken. It's not like *his* daddy runs the city council."

"Hey fury. It's not like he's a coward either."

Lot winced at the sharp edge of unpleasant truth. On the rim of the planet mountains stood in silhouette against the dawn light, like tiny, rasping teeth.

"You've let them scare you," Urban insisted.

"It's not a game. You weren't there."

"Life goes on. Gent knows that. He's working for you now. Everything he does is for you—and you won't even talk to him."

"If I did they'd arrest him."

"He's willing to take the chance. So am I. Everything I do is for you, too. I wrote the initiatives for you."

"I know."

Urban's first initiative would turn ados into adults by lowering the age of majority from one hundred years to twenty. His second initiative would ease the psychological standards for citizenship, allowing Lot to qualify despite the entangling net of his moods.

A spear of sunlight lanced the city. Urban's gray shirt responded, flicking on in an iridescent rainbow of colors seen through a haze of smoke. "The real people are laughing at us, Lot. They know it's all for you, *yet you won't give us one word of support.*"

Lot hunched his shoulders. He didn't want to say it out loud, that he *was* scared—and not just of being bounced back into the monkey house.

Gold glinted at the base of the hedge. Lot watched with a sense of fatalism as Ord slipped into sight, scuttling across the alcove's floor.

Urban hadn't seen the robot yet. "There's a rally tonight," he said. "The ados want you to come."

Lot shook his head, as Ord disappeared under the table. "I *can't.*"

Urban's displeasure bittered the air. "Why? It's not illegal."

"That doesn't matter. City authority doesn't want me there. It'll be trouble."

Ord's golden tentacles slid onto the table's surface. Its body followed a moment later. Lot drew back. *Stay calm,* he urged himself. *Stay calm.*

Ord stood on its short legs, its optical disks fixed on Lot. "Lot's tired?" it asked with gentle concern. "Come home."

Urban stared at the thing, his distaste brushing Lot's sensory tears. "What if you don't speak?" he suggested. And for the first time, he sounded uncertain. "Just be there."

"Why? What good would that do?"

Urban's mouth was half-open, already forming an answer when abruptly, he stopped. "I don't know. Maybe nothing."

"Nothing," Lot echoed softly, enjoying the shape of the word in his mouth. *Nothing.*

"You'd like that, wouldn't you? You're scared of what you might be able to do."

Lot's heart rate spiked. "That's not it!" he lied. "I just don't want to go back in the monkey house."

Ord caught the change. Its tiny brow wrinkled in an imitation of concern as it reached out with a gold tentacle to softly tap-tap against the back of Lot's hand, trying to extract a chemical measure of his emotional state. Lot slapped the tentacle away.

"What *do* you want?" Urban asked. "Have you ever thought about that?"

Lot didn't answer. He stared at the emerging curve of Kheth's searing face, his pupils stopped down so far against the light that the cityscape around him vanished behind a shroud of relative darkness, thinking *I want to know what really happened.* The grasping fingers of Deception Well's northern continent raked at the expanding crescent of light.

Scudding lanes of clouds ran perpendicular to the fingers of land.

What was happening down there? City authority had to know more than they were saying. They patrolled the surface constantly, via semiorganic wardens. The wardens could explore in both macro and molecular scale. The data they collected went into the library, and now and then a scholar would announce a tentative theory that sought to describe the structure of the Well's elusive defensive gnomes: the "governors," in popular parlance. The Silkens credited the governors with brewing new Chenzeme plagues. In Silken mythology, the governors were the villainous source of the mysterious plague that had destroyed the people of Old Silk while cannibalizing their biological data for the Well's own growing library.

The Silkens denied the concept of Communion. But Lot had to wonder if the governors could be its agents, set the task of blending all life into the matrix of the Well. If so, then the Old Silkens were not really dead.

Nothing is lost in the Well. Though everything there was subject to brutal change, driven in a reeling dance of forced evolution. Molecular-scale data shuffled constantly between microscopic life-forms and sometimes even into macro-scale life. Inept results presumably died off quickly. Only the rare successes survived, but that was enough to feed the next cycle of the Well's engines of diversity.

How it all worked, and why, remained a mystery. It seemed likely the term "governors" itself was misleading. Rather than being subject to a single type of gnome, it was far more likely the Well worked on a biomechanical system containing hundreds, thousands, or even millions of distinctly different components.

So maybe city authority really didn't understand the Well. Maybe no one did—except Jupiter?

City authority insisted Jupiter had never reached the planet, and if the wardens had found evidence to the contrary, it hadn't been reported to the library.

Lot wanted to look for himself. He'd requested permission to link with a warden, but that was denied. Only a select few were allowed access—a safety measure, it was said, based on the untested theory that the wardens' activity might disrupt the volatile biosphere. But to Lot the policy only suggested the presence of something in the Well the Silkens preferred to hide.

He felt Urban edge up close beside him. "It's only two hundred miles to Deception Well if you jump. Are you going to jump? Suicide sacrifice for your crazy cult leader?"

"Shut up!"

The retort was out before he could stop it. But he didn't let it go farther. He stared at Kheth's fiery disk, trying to deny his anger, trying to deny that he felt anything.

But Urban wouldn't let up. Urban was different from everyone else Lot had ever met. The *charismata*—if they were real—never affected him at all. "You're a slave, fury. Jupiter's got his fingers threaded through your brain. Is he your mastermind? You his toy?"

The touch of Ord's probing tentacle was more than Lot could stand. He reached out in a blind strike, and slapped the robot off the table. Then he wrenched his gaze away from Kheth, to the comparative darkness around him.

At first he could see nothing. Then his pupils dilated. A more subtle light slid across his vision. Urban crouched beside him. "Everybody knows Jupiter's dead. Why don't *you* believe it?"

"Because I saw the elevator car descend!" No matter what city authority said, Lot *knew* Jupiter had reached the planet. And he had to believe Jupiter was still alive, because if that wasn't true, then everything Jupiter had ever said about the Communion was wrong. And if Jupiter had been wrong about the Communion, then he'd led seven thousand people to their deaths for nothing, and he'd been a madman, just like the Silkens said. And his madness was inside Lot, tangled in his brain, waiting only for the proper set of circumstances to emerge.

Ord was back. It swung up on the table, hissing, *"Good Lot, good Lot,"* its raised tentacles glistening with some transdermal mood-stabilizing cocktail.

Urban saw it, and snarled. His hand shot out in a snake strike too fast to follow. Fingers set like stiff prongs, he skewered Ord, sending tendrils of gold gelatinous ooze flowing across his wrist. He brought up his other hand to secure his grip, as the tendrils began to retract back into Ord's main body mass. "Fury, you have such a gift. But you have to learn to control it. Use your aura, your charismata—whatever you want to call it. Use it when you need it, and you'll be as good as your old man."

Ord kicked and squirmed, struggling to slide off Urban's fingers. "I don't want to be like him! He left us behind to die."

A sheen of sweat stood out on Urban's forehead as he struggled with Ord. But he watched Lot closely, like a soccer coach, evaluating his star player. "You can hate him, fury, and still use what he gave you. He had a gift. You have it too."

Lot shook his head, confused at this sudden shift of direction. "I don't hate him."

Ord's little body had expelled Urban's impaling fingers. But Urban still had the robot squeezed tight in his doubled fists. Ord looked half-melted by the effort to reach Lot, by the need to rock him back onto the calm plane city authority had decreed he should occupy. Lot wanted it too. "Let Ord go." He could feel himself slipping down a dark emotional spiral. Ord's cocktail could pull him back up. Happy monkey. "*Let it go.*"

Urban glared at him. Lot knew that he hated Ord. Hated the way the little robot always fussed over Lot, calming him, damping his moods. "You *want* city authority to control you. You like it that way." He shifted his grip, and with a snarl, he flung the robot over the railing. Ord's golden body sailed in a long arc, dropping like a gleaming firework until it disappeared into a cluster of houses far down the slope.

"*Shit, Urban!* Do you *want* Clemantine knocking on my door?"

"It's only a matter of time anyway. Some people get to change who they are. Not you. The monkey house docs couldn't do anything with you. So now it's my turn."

Lot felt the rasping bite of Urban's dark confidence chewing down through his bones and he knew it was crazy. *Crazy.* They were *all* crazy and maybe it was inevitable. They were frontier people. Their ancestors had consistently fled the stable cultures of the Hallowed Vasties. Selection had worked on them from generation to generation. Those not restless enough, not deviant enough had been left behind. Only the crazy would dare to push into the Chenzeme Intersection—and here they were, trapped in Silk, a single election somehow critical to their lives.

"Do you want to be a dumb ado for another eighty-two years?" Urban demanded. "Do you?"

Craziness undulated in the air. "There are worse things."

"Not for me." Urban's hand closed over the lip of the table. "I'm going down to cold storage with Gent Romer. We're going to find out if Jupiter's really there. You can come, if you like."

Lot felt as if his breath had been pulled from his lungs by a sudden change of pressure. Cold storage was in the city's industrial core, and access was strictly controlled. "Into the tunnels?" The proposition pleased and horrified him at once. To return to the industrial corridors . . . His nostrils flared, haunted by a ghost aura of death. He didn't ever want to go back there. But to prove that city authority had lied, that Jupiter was not there with the dead . . .

"Yeah," Urban said. "Maybe if we find your old man's body, you can stop waiting for him. Maybe you can start living your own life."

Lot did not understand this animosity. "He *is* my life." Jupiter blazed in his memory like a sun holding his spirit in close orbit. In Urban's mind that made him a slave. But was it any better to be like Urban . . . and believe in nothing at all? Could a man's soul be as empty as the void and still be the soul of a man? But, Lot realized, the void wasn't empty. It was prowled by the war weapons of the Chenzeme.

His gaze rose, to the brilliant white column towering above the peak of the city, the great wall of the elevator cable hard and bright in the full light of Kheth. "We won't find Jupiter in cold storage." He stood up, defiance coursing through him. "You don't believe that now. But you'll come to believe it."

Urban laughed. His eyes were unfocused, dark windows where vague shapes moved, shadowy dreams of power. "Either way, I want you to come to the rally tonight. You'll do that for me if I take you into cold storage. You'll do it for Gent."

Lot felt his enthusiasm descend to a cooler plane. "You mean if we aren't arrested for trespassing."

"That won't happen." He glanced over his shoulder, winking at a faint sheen high up on the green wall of the surrounding hedge—a slick, round reflection, no bigger than the cross section of a girl's arm—all that was visible of a security camera mounted there. "We're not alone, you know. Clemantine's off-duty now. This shift is on our side."

"*You've got security behind you?*"

"I'm not going to answer that, fury. Not until you're sure you really want to know."

Chapter
6

They waited until the street below was empty. Then they dropped over the railing and trotted east. Here, town houses clustered against each other under veils of climbing ivy, clematis, and thick-trunked wisteria. The vegetation split the morning sun's horizontal rays into sprays of gold that glinted against address plaques and puddled water, so that a hundred times Lot thought he saw Ord returning.

But each time he was mistaken, and they were still alone when they reached the first of the narrow green bridges that arched across Vibrant Harmony as the stream boiled down the stepped slope of the eastern city. Urban raced over the narrow span. Lot followed silently, a step behind. From there they bounded down the winding path that paralleled the stream, skirting the patios of opulent homes squeezed close upon the water.

Lot's knees ached and his lungs were burning by the time they reached the broad pond at the bottom of the city's long slope. He pulled up, to stand with his hands on his hips, head thrown back, drinking in lungfuls of sweetly humid air. In the pond, orange and white koi saw him and swam over, their heavy tails splashing loudly as they harassed each other, seeking the best begging position. Here, the stream path joined a white-paved street that ran beneath the arched entrance of the walled refugee quarter.

"Come on, fury," Urban urged, his breathing already beginning to slow. "We have to meet Gent."

Lot gazed anxiously into the quarter.

Jupiter's people had settled here, moving into a cluster of ornate pyramids separated by lines of street trees. The pyramids loomed over the neighborhood's enclosing wall. They were fifteen stories high, with balconies around each floor, and progressively fewer apartments on the higher levels. They'd been unpopular with the Silkens because they were at the base of the city, across from Splendid Peace Park, and the view wasn't so good.

Lot had never tried to enter the refugee quarter before.

Such a good boy.

He grimaced. Ado defiance began to work at him, and finally, he trotted after Urban.

It started when they were only a few steps into the quarter. Some kids kicking a ball through the white street stopped their game abruptly when they saw him. The ball bounced away into a bed of ferns while the kids huddled together, their whispered debate easily audible: *"It's him. It's him."*

"Jupiter?"

"No, stupid, that's Lot."

"Shut up, you dumb ados! Remember what Gent said?"

Farther down the street, two women stood chatting beside a doorway. Recognition sparked in their eyes. "It's him." One stepped forward, but the other laid a gentle hand on her arm as if to hold her back. They exchanged a quick look.

Lot felt his pulse rise. His sensory tears tingled subtly, and suddenly he felt *linked* to these women, bound to them by a tenuous connection that glinted faintly silver in his awareness. His will flowed outward upon molecular links. Their will flowed back to him.

His pace slowed. A few dozen steps away, an open-air restaurant filled the alley between the broad bases of two pyramids. It was packed, and many of the patrons had already noticed him. They stood at their seats, jabbering excitedly. His name leaped out from all the meaningless noise, *Lot, Lot,*

Lot . . . the same way Jupiter's name had threaded the chaos of panicked human screams down in the tunnels.

Lot felt his perceptions begin to slip. Over a period of seconds the light around him brightened, blurring the structures and vegetation into an increscent silver glow while the people themselves became fluid, melting into humanistic icons, their individuality seeping swiftly away. He stopped in the middle of the street, blinking hard. *What was he seeing?* His natural vision ran from the visual down through the infrared range. He could see heat as well as light. But this vision did not fit anywhere in the electromagnetic spectrum.

A different interpretation, then?

Chemical sight. He was seeing *faith* . . . like a silver wash spilled on the world, dissolving it, homogenizing it, melding it into a skin that enwrapped him, an invulnerable silver armor. He owned these people. He could command them; he could wear their will like a flawless silver hide. . . .

The tide shifted. Against his throat he felt the cold press of a hand. His own hand shot up, to close hard around a wrist.

"Look at me, Lot." The voice fell like a shadow across the silver glow. "Listen to your heart. It's flowing like a river. Try to slow it down. Slow it down."

He could hear his heart. It rumbled like the rake of air across a ship's skin as it dipped into atmosphere, dumping velocity. Fear darkened his vision, and his grip tightened on the wrist. "That's right, Lot. Listen to me. Try to see me."

"Gent?" His voice was an ugly croak in the fading light.

"Sooth. It's me. You're okay now, aren't you? Sure."

Lot's hand ached. He looked down, to find himself still clasping Gent's wrist in a grip so tight the veins stood out, red on white against his knuckles. He let go and Gent quickly lowered his arm, to rub at a band of four parallel purple bruises.

Lot felt drained. He glanced around: at the street, at the pyramidal buildings rising past the trees, at the breakfast crowd in the restaurant, now returned to their seats though Lot could feel them still, vibrating just beneath his vision. His gaze shifted again. Urban stood behind Gent, his arms crossed belligerently over his chest while tangled skeins of jealousy and anger ran off him. Finally, he looked at Gent.

In Lot's personal mythology, Gent didn't stand out

as a big man—an impression derived, perhaps, from the quiet way he'd always moved on the periphery of Lot's life. So it surprised him that he had to look up to meet Gent's gaze. When Gent reached out to squeeze his arm, Lot felt the strength in his hand, and knew that Gent could have broken the grip Lot had held on his wrist, if he'd chosen to. "You shouldn't have stayed away," Gent said, his voice softly chiding. "We've tried to respect your wishes on it, but it hasn't been good for you."

Lot felt a bit of color return to his cheeks. "It wasn't my choice."

Gent's face was all sharp angles and narrow planes, as if some slow inner heat had melted all the softness out of him. His hair was a mix of blond and black threads woven into eight braids that were waxed and formed into perfect rings pinned just beneath his ears. Lot touched his shoulder. He wore a thin gray shirt, and through it Lot could feel the warmth of his skin, and the rough vibration of blood stumbling through the capillaries. He could wear Gent if he wanted to. He knew it. He drew in a sharp, startled breath and turned half away, shaking with the temptation.

Was this how Jupiter had felt?

He closed his eyes, forced himself to breathe long and slow, calming himself, the way the monkey-house docs had taught him . . . trying not to hear the distant chorus of screams reverberating through the tunnels. The taste of bile was suddenly in his mouth. *"Why are we here?"* he croaked. He turned around, his gaze seeking Urban. "Why did you bring me here?"

Urban's face was stony, his resentment a foul simmer in the air. "Everybody wants something." He jerked his chin at Gent. "He wants you. He brought you here, fury. Not me. That was his price. Best if you know that."

Cautiously, Lot raised his gaze, to look into Gent's eyes again. Steady eyes, that looked back at him with quiet affection. Lot could feel the subtle field of his faith. "You're not like the Silkens."

"Let's go inside," Gent said. "We only have a little time."

What am I doing here? Kheth's rays fell hot against his face. The air was very still. He could feel himself at a threshold. A soft voice whispered that it wasn't too late. He could turn around. He could walk out of the refugee quarter, take the transit to Skyline, where he worked every morning tending estate gardens that belonged to families of the very real. As easily as that he could be back inside the boundaries of his routine, and city authority would show its approval by leaving him alone, leaving him the hell alone.

Maybe he'd been alone too long. Good monkey.

Ado defiance nibbled at him. Gent had been part of his family once. Together they were the last surviving members of Jupiter's household. Maybe Lot wanted some of that relationship back.

"Okay," he said, trying not to see Gent's faint silver aura. "It's good."

"It will be," Gent said. He held his arm out, inviting Lot to accompany him.

They crossed the street, then went through heavy plastic doors cast in a stylized solar design. Urban caught his eye. "You okay, fury?"

"Yeah, I guess so."

Urban looked doubtful. "You looked . . . half-gone. Vacant. I've never seen that before."

Lot didn't know how to answer him. He looked to Gent. "Did you know it would be like that?"

"There was a chance."

"So what was it? What happened out there?"

Gent gave him an odd look. "You know."

"I don't."

For just a moment Gent looked impatient. "You're the gate to the Communion, Lot. The focusing lens through which we'll all pass. You gather the essence of your people. Through you, they become one."

Lot shook his head. "I don't understand."

Urban said, "That's because it's shit."

Gent glanced at him, and shrugged—a gesture that chilled Lot. If doubts translated to defensiveness, then Gent had no doubts at all. Lot rubbed nervously at his sensory tears. "I never felt this way with Silkens."

"That'll come," Gent assured him. "Given time, you can touch anyone. The difference is, we're ready to give ourselves to you, while the Silkens, I think, still resist." He looked to Urban, and gave him a broad wink.

"*Shit.*"

Lot gave it up for the moment, and looked around. They'd come into a small lobby. The carpets and walls were a wash of light yellow, a bright contrast to his own disquiet. An elevator opened on one side. Beside it, a wide sweep of stairs went *down*. Lot looked at the stairs in surprise. He'd never seen a building with access below ground. Silk was a surface city, and only utility engineers were permitted in the inner levels. Urban's mood shifted as he took some pleasure from Lot's surprise. "You'll like this," he said. "It's cute."

They trotted down the stairs, the impact of their footfalls absorbed by the carpet. The stair bent back on itself and descended another flight. Lot caught her presence while he was still on the landing. "Alta!"

He bounded after her trace. At the bottom of the stairs stood a second set of double doors cast in the sun symbol they'd seen above. Her presence teased him. "Alta?"

One of the doors swung open. Alta looked out past it, seeming a little surprised to see him. "Lot. Hello. I didn't think you'd come."

She'd had ten years to finish growing. Lot had watched her at the task, following her at a distance whenever he chanced to see her about in the city. She'd become an ado girl of extremes: black hair, black eyes, pale skin. No shading and no bright colors to distract from her elemental nature.

Lot had missed her sorely and he had always imagined she felt the same way, so he'd been ready to grab her, hug her, maybe hold her hands and dance—but those intentions evaporated as he ran up against the slick surface of her aura.

I didn't think you'd come.

With painful abruptness—like running into a wall— he understood that Alta had not been missing him, though she smiled at him now in a friendly way. "You look like Jupiter. Almost exactly like him."

"Sooth. It gives the monkey house fits." That earned him a short laugh. But he couldn't enjoy it. He was remembering how he'd abandoned her when panic had ignited in the tunnels. "I looked for you that day."

"We all did our best." She pushed the door open wider. "Come. Time's short. You should hurry."

He followed her into the dimly lit chamber. Immediately he felt a difference in the atmosphere, a soft, moist warmth, as if the air had been freshly made in the cells of tropical plants. It reminded him of the air aboard Nesseleth.

He smiled. It reminded him of the air in his own breather; it felt good to know he wasn't the only one who remembered.

The room appeared small, though it was hard to be sure because the light was sculpted, and deceptive. The walls were hidden behind opaque interference patterns manifesting in shifting silver curtains that destabilized any attempt by the eyes to focus, so that the walls didn't seem fixed, but instead floated in the consciousness with the fluidity of dream images, moving slowly in, pulling away. Isolation and communion in a slow holographic dance.

Jupiter had been seeking isolation when he'd first chanced upon the Well. That had been over 120 years ago, when he'd left the Committee with his first crew of faithful, bent on finding a world of his own somewhere beyond the Chenzeme Intersection. A fossil plague ended those plans. The virus got into Nesseleth's systems, overwhelming her defensive Makers and sweeping through her crew. By the time she sought help at the Well, Jupiter was the only person left alive.

The Silkens had greeted him with cautious sympathy, offering their own index of defensive Makers, even as their asteroid defense system fixed on Nesseleth. A plague ship could not be allowed to dock.

Nesseleth had assumed a stately orbit in the trail of the swan burster. Adrift in his terminal fever, Jupiter had gazed on the ring, while listening to Silken stories of the Well and its curious amalgam of genetic systems. His mind engaged the puzzle while his body failed. How could traces of plague exist on the planet without destroying all life there? How had the swan burster been tamed? And what would happen if a new plague was brought to the planet surface? Might it be subdued too?

The Silkens believed the Well fatal to humans, but Jupiter was already dying. He persuaded Nesseleth to let him take a shuttle to the planet's surface. There he stayed for nearly a month, while a molecular war raged inside his body, and dreams of aliens, human-aliens, and nirvana filled his mind. He found his cure. But more than that, he uncovered the force that had finally abolished the warring civilizations of the ancient world.

Now Alta took Lot's hand, leading him deeper into the holographic maze. Lot felt himself descending. Just slightly. The angled floor soft beneath his feet. When he looked back, Urban and Gent could not be seen, only the silvery walls with tiny vertical flaws of black embedded in them, and he knew they were a miniature reflection of himself and Alta, repeated over and over and over.

Within the enclosing walls the flaw became beautiful.

Why not? That was Jupiter's philosophy: that every individual could be contained within the Communion, there to change, to transcend the limits of their separate lives without losing selfhood.

Jupiter had drawn an analogy to the structure of cells. Somewhere, he'd met a designer, and for him the encounter had been resonant with implication:

"She showed me a cell diagram, pointing out the various parts—the nucleus, the reticulum, the mitochondria. 'The mitochondria,' she said, 'appear to be descendants of bacterial life-forms which were captured by some ancestral cell. Drawn into the cellular body, they became an essential part of its metabolic system. And here they are still: protected, nourished, widespread, and still with their individual DNA. The cell couldn't live without them, and they couldn't live without the cell. Here then, are two life-forms which have become one.' Her words re-echoed in my mind, though at the time I didn't know why. Only later did I come to understand that we could make a similar synthesis with the Well. Each of us a small but valued organelle in that ancient vastness."

In the Communion they would yield themselves to the unknowable computations of a purposeful biological system armed with thirty million years of experience. The Communion had ended the ancient war. The Communion had absorbed Jupiter's plague and changed it, tamed it, without destroying it. The Communion would sublimate them in the same way—or so Jupiter had preached.

Believe in me.

Lot shuddered. Doubt filled him, and he wondered—briefly—if Jupiter really had been running on a plan. He'd convinced everyone it was so, he'd seemed to always be pushing for its outcome. But what if he'd just been acting? Delivering up the faith because that's what people wanted, what they lived for, truth be damned, truth's too ugly, give us some illusions and we'll die for you.

"I've seen enough," he said softly. "I don't want to be here."

Alta's disappointment carried the weight of stones.

"It's not a thing to be afraid of, Lot. It's just a place for reflection."

"You've been scared too," he said. "You left the tunnel that day."

"They took me out. My mama found me."

Captain Antigua. Alta remained a refugee, but her mama had gotten Silken citizenship. Captain Antigua was the only refugee who had. "Your mama lied about Jupiter."

"I know and I'm sorry." Her graceful fingers touched her breast just above her heart. "I know he's still with us. I feel him every day."

The weird light in the room had cast a sheen of silver on her hair and skin. It was color he could breathe, pulling part of her inside himself. "I don't remember it like this."

"You're older now."

"Was it like this with Jupiter?"

He caught from her a tiny trace of surprise, and . . . something like fear, understated. "You know it was," she said quickly. "Now go. You have to be done before the shift change."

Alta turned, and was swiftly enfolded by the walls, lost to view. He heard her speaking with Gent at the door, though he couldn't make out the words. A wall receded, and Urban appeared close beside him, shaking his head. "That Alta is one crazy ado." He looked at Lot again, closely, this time. "Oh, fury. She got you, didn't she?"

"No."

"She's crazy, Lot. Don't fall for her."

Lot moved his head slowly back and forth, letting his sensory tears harvest traces of her from the air. "Why are we down here anyway?"

"So they can mess with your mind. Besides, there's an access tunnel, down at the lowest point of the floor."

So they followed the slope down, while the black reflective darts in the walls became things with inherent volition, mating, blossoming into complex patterns composed of darkness as much as light. The symbology struck Lot as obvious and oppressive and he was relieved when, in a few steps, they'd found the hatch, and Urban unlatched it.

"When did you come here before?" Lot asked.

"Last night. But I haven't been below."

"How do you know Alta?"

"I don't *know* her, fury. She was with Gent last night. She's not my girl, so don't snarl at me."

"I didn't mean it like that."

"Just forget it." Urban lifted the hatch, exposing a dark pit. Lot could make out a ladder descending into it.

"Go on," Gent said, from close behind them. "It's a maintenance tunnel. The lights will come on."

"Sooth." Lot remembered the tunnels. Sweat slicked his hands. Fear pressed like a spike against his belly, holding him back.

He wasn't in the mood for that. Not anymore.

He crouched on the hatch rim, taking a moment to gather his courage.

She was with Gent last night.

He jumped, plunging past Urban, feet first through the hatch, preferring to impale himself on his fear than to let it control him again.

The lights flashed on. He caught the hatch rim to slow his fall, then dropped to the ground, hitting solid, his knees bending to absorb the shock. His chest grabbed for air in a loud wheeze while his irises strained to clamp down against the brilliant light. *I hate this.* He could feel his face wet with sweat, but his heart rate had already begun to slow. He looked around.

A tangle of pipes ran along the floor and walls. He saw that it hadn't been too smart to drop blind through the hole. He could have hit a pipe and pitched himself good. Dumb ado then. Urban dropped silently beside him. He would be resenting Lot's rush to be first. But he knew how Lot felt about tunnels. He didn't say anything.

Gent climbed carefully down the access ladder, burdened by a loaded backpack. How well did he know Alta? Lot wondered. She wasn't a kid anymore. Aboard Nesseleth she would have been married. He rubbed at his sensory tears, wanting more of her. Gent's hand clasped his shoulder. "Are you okay?"

"Sure. How's security down here?"

"Everywhere. Just like above."

Urban took a long, slow look up and down the corridor. "But Gent's fixed it so nobody's watching this shift. Have you caught on to that yet, fury?"

"Not quite yet. Guess I'm slow."

Gent's eyes twinkled in amusement. "Jupiter still has friends in this city. Don't forget he once lived in Silk."

"Sooth," Lot said. "But that was over a hundred twenty years ago." How could anybody remain constant for so long? He didn't understand real people, and he wondered sometimes if they were real at all, or only dumb programs running over and over and over.

Urban nudged him in the ribs. "You could ask Gent for names. It'd be good to know who's on your side."

He looked at Gent. He seemed to expect it; maybe he'd been offering. But Lot only shrugged. "I'm not asking. Not now." He felt a faint blush across his cheeks. He could ask for names, and Gent would tell him. He could ask about Alta too. But he wasn't sure he wanted to know.

Gent shrugged. From his backpack, he produced three thick beige vests. He hefted one and passed it to Lot. It was heavy, but supple. Lot noticed the nub ends of two small plastic tubes poking out from either side of the collar. "Put it on," Gent said. He patted the fabric. "It's a rebreather rig, with supplementary oxygen squeezed in the cells. We'll need it farther inside. You remember how it was, Lot? Captain Aceret had to pump up the pressure in the industrial corridors before anyone could disembark."

Lot looked at him, trying to see through the remark. "I didn't know that, Gent. I was asleep most of the time we were in the control room."

Gent considered that briefly. It couldn't sit well in his personal mythology. But he just shrugged. "Anyway, the pressure's kept low in the core. It's a conservation measure that doubles for security. We'll need the oxygen."

Lot slipped the vest on. It pulled snug around his shirt, sealing down the front. Gent gave him a transparent oxygen mask and showed him how to link it to the vest's tubing. The unit would function as soon as he put the mask on. For now though, he let it dangle at his chest.

The corridor ran level. They followed it for two hundred yards, moving quickly but carefully over the crisscrossing pipes. Nanotech drizzles ran sideways along the wall: tiny portage streams a few meters long, made up of a procession of Makers carrying some recovered element to a collection point.

Lot smelled the sour rot of a gutter doggie as they passed the opening of a narrow crawlway.

Finally, Gent stopped before a locked hatch. It was oval, only about a meter high. "When were you here before?" Lot asked as Gent punched in a security code.

"You don't know?" He looked hurt. "We received permission last year to hold a memorial service in cold storage. Twenty of us, plus an escort. Authority wouldn't let you come. I asked. I thought you'd hear about it, though."

"No."

The hatch opened onto a small lock. Gent ducked in first. Lot followed. Urban squeezed in behind and closed the door. They took a moment to fix their oxygen masks over nose and mouth; then Gent bled the pressure and opened the opposite hatch. The air on the other side was very cold; the tunnels, too familiar. Lot stepped outside. His lungs hurt. His teeth hurt. His vest started to heat up.

Gent left the hatch open. The corridor curved in a familiar slow spiral, rising to the left, descending to the right. They jogged upward for almost twenty minutes. Finally, Gent stopped beside another hatch. He punched a code into the pad, then cracked the seal. No pressure differential this time. They climbed through. "These locks are new," Lot said, his voice muffled by the mask. "Since that day."

"Yeah. Bad element in town, you know?"

Lot grinned, and that helped. He felt better. "I remember that day, when it was all over—Captain Antigua warned me I'd wind up in cold storage if I stepped out of line. Guess she was right."

Gent chuckled. "We've got Placid Antigua's soul stashed on ice too, against the day she's ready to reclaim it."

A short passage took them to another hatch. Gent coded it, then swung it open. "This is it," he said. "Cold storage."

Chapter 7

Lot peered through the last hatch. The chamber on the other side was low, only about eight feet to the ceiling. It appeared to be toroidal in shape, wrapped around an immense central pillar, and where walls and ceiling met, the corners were deeply rounded. It seemed to be completely empty.

He stepped through, feeling a gust of disappointment. Gent stepped up close beside him. "Storage is beneath the floor," he said, pointing beyond the narrow apron of decking on which they stood. "See?"

Lot nodded. The floor was a polar grid of black panels laid down on a gray frame. Lot stepped onto the first panel. It lit up with a red display of amino-acid codes running in parallel lines, appearing at one side of the panel, vanishing at the other. Gent said, "Each panel codes for one of us."

Lot frowned at the frantic display. "Is this the only identification?"

Behind his transparent oxygen mask, Gent looked apologetic. "In the city library each individual's biological map is linked to a four-digit identification number, but we can't access that. The best we can do is look for a familial match with your own genetic pattern."

"How?"

He slipped off his backpack and reached into it. Out

came a waferlike instrument, some four by six inches, mounted on a short handle. Embedded in its black surface was a sculpture of a scarlet anthurium, its heart-shaped red bract freshly opened around a thick, erect white spike. Just above the flower, a miniature pair of finely sculpted androgynous lips—recessed, so they didn't protrude from the surface—smiled slyly. Lot took one look at the thing and burst out laughing. "A mate finder?" he croaked. "Come on, Gent!"

Even Urban lost his sour look. He grinned at Lot, quoting commercial scripture: " 'Hunlo's Mate Finder: Whether you're seeking millennial marriage, a one-night affair, or anything in between, we can help you find the perfect . . .' " His grin faded, as his voice trailed off in surprise.

" 'We can help you find the perfect genetic match,' " Lot finished for him. He turned to Gent, suddenly anxious. "Will it work?"

Gent held the device in two hands. "Why not? It has an optical scan that can access the data in the panels. We'll just tell it to look for familial similarities." He pointed to the smiling lips. "Put your finger here. Let it take a cell sample."

Lot had seen ados play this game in the drunken hours after midnight. He pressed his finger against the lips. They mouthed his fingertip and moaned suggestively, touching him with a hint of warmth and moisture, though there was no tongue. When he took his finger away, the lips moved, and a low, androgynous voice cooed, *"You're in me now. Would you like to define a personality file? Or are you a bioexclusivist?"*

Gent touched the vox tab. "Bioexclusivist. Look for a mate with at least fifty percent genetic similarities."

"Ah." The mate finder seemed intrigued. *"There's no place like home."*

"Did you have any other relatives?" Urban asked.

Lot smiled faintly. "Dozens." He glanced at Gent. Group marriage had been the custom aboard Nesseleth. Gent had lived in Jupiter's household as a full adult partner, one of seven spouses in the family warren. "But not by blood."

Gent handed the mate finder to Urban. "Jupiter's genetic system was . . . not compatible with most women. None of the children in his household were his by nature." He drew another mate finder from his pack, and held it out for

Lot to touch. "Jupiter wanted a child. So in the abyss he took another wife."

"You're in me now."

He shoved the mate finder into Lot's hands and went on with his story. "She was very young. She'd been born on the voyage out, and there were some that said she'd been especially made for him." Gent said this as he pulled a third mate finder out of his pack. He didn't look at Lot, just held the instrument out. Numbly, Lot touched the lips. He'd never heard any of this before. Gent glanced at Urban. "Maybe it was true, because she didn't conceive off of us, and we'd had children with our other wives. But after a few anxious years she got Jupiter his child."

"You're in me now."

Lot yanked his hand back.

"Bioexclusivist?"

He started when Gent squeezed his shoulder. "You should know these things."

"But you're saying I'm no part of my mother after all. She was a vessel."

"I have not said that! Jupiter called you a natural child and it was never my place to question him. Neither is it your place. He loved her. We all did."

And they were all gone now, every member of Jupiter's household, except Lot and Gent.

Urban touched Lot's arm. "Come on. Nobody's natural anyway. You can work out the family history later. Let's see what we can find, okay?"

Lot nodded, trying not to hear the accusing voices in his head. His memories of his mother were clear and detailed. She had *not* been an empty vessel. She'd been fiery and proud. He remembered the solid strength in her lithe arms, her hard belly. He could remember how it had felt to nurse at her breast, and hear her heart beat, cradled on the bed between her and Jupiter, long before he could walk.

"Lot."

He started at Urban's insistent voice, then nodded shortly. Remembering the mate finder in his hands, he looked down, forcing himself to examine it. Turning it over, he found a scanning window in its base. A similar port existed in each one of the floor panels. Holding the mate finder at waist height, Lot swept it over a panel window. Optical data cascaded in invisible streams between the two instruments. The mate finder sighed in a careworn way and whispered, *"No match."*

"Don't be looking for scandal where it doesn't exist," Gent said. He swept another mate finder over an adjacent panel.

"No match."

Lot nodded and stepped forward to the next square.

"No match."

Urban worked on his other side. They moved around the circumference of the grid, and by the time they'd completed one circuit, the sighs of the mate finders had grown increasingly despondent. "Patience," Gent urged. "We're not trying to find Jupiter. We're trying to prove he's not here, and that means we have to check all seven thousand one hundred and ninety-six panels."

"Is that the count they gave you?" Lot asked, as they stepped forward in a slow line from panel to panel.

"No match. No match. No match."

Behind his mask, Gent's face was grim. "That's what they said. Add that to the known survivors here in Silk, and we've got nine hundred seven unaccounted for."

Lot looked at him sharply.

He shook his head. "It's doubtful more than a handful went with Jupiter. Most of those unaccounted for were lost when the Silkens attacked the upper tracks with the meteor-defense lasers. An entire car was dislodged, you know. It fell into the atmosphere."

Lot hadn't known that.

"No match."

He told Gent, "I requested access to the planetary wardens once. Authority denied it, of course."

"It doesn't matter."

They completed the second circuit in silence. They'd been at the task two and a half hours, and Lot could feel tension building inside him. There were only a few hundred more panels to go. If they could get past those with no matches, then they would know Jupiter had made it out of the city. They could prove city authority had lied.

Urban had been working the inside track, so that he'd completed his circuit well ahead of Lot. He'd gone on to start his third pass and was almost out of sight around the curve of the chamber when he called back to Lot in a low voice, full of trepidation. "Hey fury. There's a match here."

Lot felt the skin on the back of his neck tighten. His heart began to boom. *"No!"* he whispered. He started to bolt toward Urban, when Gent's voice barked out a command: "Hold on!"

Lot looked back at him. "Don't assume the worst. Now mark that square before you move. We're not done with this survey yet."

Lot looked around quickly, trying to decide the best way to mark his position. Finally, he laid the mate finder down on the streaming lines of code illuminating the panel. Then he took off after Urban.

Urban's mate finder was still happily cooing about the genetic similarity when Lot stepped up to his side. Urban looked up from the panel display. "Sorry fury, it's a false alarm. This one's female."

"It's Helena, then," Gent said, coming up on the other side. He craned his neck to see the panel display. There was a slight catch in his voice as he added, "It has to be her." She'd been Gent's wife as much as Jupiter's.

"Your mother?" Urban asked.

Lot nodded.

"Shit. Let's move on."

Gent flinched at the profanity. Lot shook his head. "No. I want to see her."

Urban drew back, an expression of distaste on his face. "Why? You can't bring her back, fury."

"Sure. No shit. I know the rules here. But I want to know for sure it's her."

"I do too," Gent said.

"We don't have time!"

"Get out of the way!" He turned to Gent. "How do we open this thing?"

Gent touched a series of pressure pads on the panel display. "Stand back," he warned. With a smooth, electronic whir the panel lifted on a hinge, revealing a hollow beneath. Lot gazed into perfect darkness. A musty odor rose up, worming its way past the seal of his mask. A light snapped on just below floor level. Another electronic whir, and a metal frame rose smoothly out of the hole. The light was fixed to the frame's top. It shone down on an inflated silver body bag.

"The corpse will be vitrified," Gent said. "It will appear glassy and artificial. And it could be badly damaged. We don't know how she died."

Lot nodded, drawing in a long breath to steady himself. Urban stepped up close to his side. Gent reached up to the top of the bag. With his gloved hands he slipped the bag off its hook and flipped the seal. A gush of musty air raced out and the bag collapsed to the floor in a crumpled silver heap, revealing . . . *nothing*. Lot stared, trying to make sense of the scene that presented itself to his stunned eyes.

"There's no body!" Urban burst out, each word sharp-edged with an incredulous anger.

Gent bent down to probe the empty bag, as if he expected Helena to suddenly materialize there. Lot watched him, his throat dry as he sucked in harsh gasps of air. *"They've lost her!"*

Gent shook his head. "No. This storage cell has a full biological map. She *was* here."

"They found out who she was, then. They destroyed her."

"But the record is still here! Look, neural maps!" He waved his hand at a knitted three-dimensional display of intersecting lines on the lower side of the cell's raised panel. "The record is still here. They haven't destroyed her. Only the body—"

Possibilities and suspicions boiled into existence. Lot couldn't put them into words. Not yet. He leaped past Gent, dropping to his knees on another panel.

"Lot!" Gent caught his shoulder. "What are you doing?"

Lot puzzled over the display, then punched in a slow sequence to open the cell. Urban watched him closely. "You think it was just her, fury?"

Lot didn't answer, though he could feel Gent's grip tighten even through the padded vest. He sat back as the panel opened, as the inflated silver bag rose in its frame. Urban reached up to undo the bag. Again, the gust of air. The bag collapsed. Empty.

Lot stared at it for several seconds before turning to Gent. "Did you actually see any bodies when you were down here last year?"

Gent let go of his shoulder. He took a step back, his eyes wide. "Yes, sir. We did. We looked at several on the periphery, to check the storage conditions."

Urban turned and walked deliberately to the outer edge of the chamber. He bent down, worked at the display on a panel, then stepped back as the aluminum frame rose. He opened the bag to find it empty.

Lot rose to his feet. "Come," he said, crooking his fingers at Gent. He trotted back to the entrance. "Do you remember which ones you examined?"

"We did it randomly, sir. We started with this one, I believe. Yes. That's it."

"Open it."

Gent did. It was empty.

By this time, Urban had cracked six more at random points around the circular chamber. All empty. He stepped up beside Lot. "The bodies were here last year. Now they're gone. Why?"

"Authority found something. They heard from him."

"Get off it. It doesn't take ten years to make your presence known. He's dead."

"Then why? Why now?"

"Maybe it's you, fury. Maybe they're scared of you."

Lot snorted. Urban was always working on him. Urban valued that cult-leader persona. It could play so well in his hands.

Gent spoke up hesitantly. "We're not done, Lot."

Lot frowned at him. "You want to finish? The cells are empty."

"The data's still in the panels. We have to know if Jupiter was ever here."

"He's right," Urban said. "Come on. It won't take twenty minutes."

A camera bee cruised slowly past, its wings buzzing hard to maintain its elevation in the thin air. It circled once around Urban's head. *"Shit,"* Lot whispered.

Without warning, Urban lunged at the thumbnail-size device. With a sweep of his hand he tried to knock it out of the air, but it gracefully evaded the blow, whispering past the tips of his fingers to settle in front of Lot, hovering on a golden blur of wings.

Lot glared at its bulbous eye, as smooth and curved as a drop of water.

"Who's on it?" Gent whispered (as if the bee couldn't detect a whisper).

Lot scowled. "Authority. Who else?" Despite Gent's promises, they were logged in, and he and Gent were going to the monkey house, maybe to cold storage—there was room enough.

But Urban had moved up softly to his side. *"Shut up, Lot,"* he said softly. *"Just shut up."*

The camera bee backed off, then turned and sped away, quickly disappearing down the curve of cold storage. Lot glared after it. They would have only minutes, at most, before security officers arrived. "Let's finish it!"

He sprang away, racing across the black panels to the point where they'd left the mate finders. Red display lights exploded under his pounding feet. He could hear the thunder of Urban and Gent following several paces behind him. Then the camera bee was at his shoulder, its wings buzzing hard like nasty toddlers' tongues, full of contempt. It hovered beside him, staying even as he half-turned and dropped to the ground. Smoothly sliding past the mate finder, he grabbed the device and came up on his knees on the next panel *No match.*

And the next panel *No match.*

And the next *No match.*

Grimly delighted with the continuing negative results, sadistic delight in the sad sighing of the mate finder's artificial voice, in the equally sad laments of Urban's and Gent's mate finders bemoaning their dismal luck.

A sudden, soft, rapid percussion sounded from the direction of the lock. Lot stepped forward to the next panel. The reverberant clacking grew louder. Gold flashed on the edge of his vision, and a moment later he heard the close, cold rattle of Ord's scuttling limbs. "Don't touch me," he warned the little robot. "Stay away."

Ord stepped in front of him, its tentacles raised in an inverted V. That was Ord's shot at a pleading gesture, but the sentiment wasn't reflected in its pale eye disks. "Come home, Lot," it wheedled. "Rest. Counseling."

Lot stepped grimly over it, activating the panel that it occupied *No match.*

"Please Lot."

No match.

"Come home."

No match.

"Good Lot. Good boy. City authority doesn't need to know."

"They already know. Get out of my way." He could hear Urban coming up behind him. They only had a handful of panels to go. They had to finish. At the least, they had to know.

Ord scrabbled back in front of him, its tentacles dancing around his ankles, not quite daring to touch. "Authority doesn't know, Lot. Good Lot. It's not too late."

They rounded the curve. Lot had expected to see security forces at the lock, but there was no one. He stepped onto the last panel in his circuit. *No match.*

Only then did he notice the camera bee resting motionless on the floor in front of him. It lacked the green stripes that would mark it as a device belonging to city security. Instead it carried the emblem of a news service. An eerie feeling swept over him. Carefully, he stepped around the bee, then glanced back. Urban was just finishing his circuit. Gent had ten or twelve panels to go. And security still hadn't arrived.

Abruptly, the camera bee lifted into the air. It hovered between Lot and Urban, its water-bead eye reflecting the dark, curving walls. *"How much do you know?"* it demanded, in a tiny, tinny, feminine voice. *"Do you know why cold storage is empty? No. I can see not. That shock on your faces. Shao? Stop recording. We have enough video to do the story. Now I want to know why."*

Lot and Urban exchanged a glance. "It's Yulyssa," Lot said, recognizing the lilt of her voice even through the camera bee's lousy audio. Yulyssa had taken an interest in him from that first day in the tunnel. Not a professional interest. Though she was a mediot, she'd never done a story on him. But in those first years she'd spent time with him, taking him on fun excursions to a soccer game or a concert, or to the surf pool in Spoken Verities, or for a wild ride in the VR crash chamber, which he hadn't liked, or—most often—to lunch at tiny restaurants known only to the very real. She'd helped him with his accent and made sure he learned Silken table manners. He'd liked those times, but as he'd gotten older he'd seen her less, until finally she stopped coming around.

But apparently she hadn't forgotten him. "We came looking for Jupiter," he told her resentfully.

"You didn't find him."

Lot glanced questioningly at Gent; caught the slight, negative shake of his head as he switched off his mate finder. "No. City authority lied. He's not here. He never was here—"

"Dumb ados will believe anything," Urban interrupted. "But you're one of them. You knew better, didn't you?"

The camera bee dipped slightly. Was that an answer? Lot stepped forward, a fist clenched in frustration. "I saw the elevator car descend," he insisted.

Yulyssa said, *"I saw it too."*

Doubt had eaten at Lot so many years, this simple confirmation left him stunned. "You knew? But you never said anything. . . ."

The camera bee dipped again. *"It seemed right at the time. So many people had already died."*

"At the time . . . ?" Urban mused, a look of fine ado cynicism on his face.

"You weren't there, Urban," Yulyssa said. *"You didn't see it."*

Lot felt his guts twist. "So what did they do to everybody?" His hand swept out across the panels.

"That I don't know. I don't know why cold storage is empty."

"I do," Lot said. "It's because Jupiter's alive."

Yulyssa demurred. *"That wouldn't be my first guess—"*

But Gent interrupted her. "It's time to go. We only have a few minutes before—"

Urban cut him off with a sharp look. He turned to the camera bee, his eyes dark with a feral excitement only half-concealed. "Do your story," he told Yulyssa. "We're not afraid of that, though of course it'll lead to our arrest. But if you've got any sense of justice, you'll hold off releasing it until the rally tonight." He grinned. "After that, it won't matter who knows."

He crooked two fingers at Lot. "Come on. Let's go." Lot hesitated, looking back at the camera bee. Yulyssa had seen the elevator descend and yet she'd never said anything. What else did she know?

Gent touched his elbow. "Come on. Urban's right. We don't have any choice now."

Chapter
8

I n Lot's carnivorous-plant collection there were several sundews started from seeds that Netta had given him. The sundews were tiny. If Lot made a circle of his thumb and forefinger, each plant could fit within it. They had no stems, only thin petioles growing from a central bud, each petiole supporting a sticky paddle at its end.

One of the seedling sundews had caught a small fly. Lot leaned closer, remote implications suddenly resonant in his mind. He had to wonder: Of what use were the tiny insects to the well-being of this city? They were pests. They dove into fruit salads and sweet wines and flew too close to people's faces and died on countertops in untidy heaps. But they were here, having successfully tagged along with their human cousins through the waves of migration that had expanded the Hallowed Vasties, venturing uninvited all the way into the Chenzeme Intersection.

He watched the tiny antennae of the trapped fly wriggle helplessly, while its legs sank deeper into the sticky goo that coated the paddle of the sundew. The paddle itself was no larger than the white crescent at the base of Lot's thumbnail. It sprouted minute, dew-studded rays in a breathtaking, delicate architecture. Some of these bowed over the body of the fly, sealing it deeper in sticky juices. Sweet juices, irresistibly attractive to the little insect. Now the fly's body would slowly dissolve, becoming part of the sundew's tissue.

Lot wondered if the fly would have followed the sundew's sweet scent if it could have comprehended the danger ahead of time. And he decided that it probably would have. Consciousness did not negate instinct. It only provided a post for self-observation.

The disembodied voice of the apartment's majordomo interrupted these thoughts: "A call for you, Master Lot Apolinario. Madam Yulyssa Desearange. Will you receive it?"

He realized he'd been half-expecting to hear from her. "Hold on." He got up and dug around in his cabinets until he found the headset for his rarely used phone. "Okay."

He slipped on the visor and Yulyssa's image appeared overlaid against the background of his room. She still looked much the same as she had that day in the tunnel, when she'd come down with Kona to view the dead. "I wish you had stayed home," she said.

"Are you holding the story?"

"For now. I want to talk to you."

"I have questions too."

"Do you know where my cameraman Shao lives, in Vibrant Harmony?"

"No."

"I'll send a bee for you then. Twenty minutes?"

"Five's okay."

The fly still kicked and struggled on the sundew's glistening paddle. Lot was aware of it, in the corner of his vision.

Lot never learned if Shao was home. The bee led him through an open gate to a garden patio behind the house, where Yulyssa was transferring two steaming plates from a service 'bot to the table. He presumed Ord had followed him, though it had kept scrupulously out of sight.

"Lunch by Savuti's," Yulyssa announced. "Hope that's all right."

"We ate there once."

"You seemed to like it." She poured a pale wine into long-stemmed glasses. Her aura felt dry as afternoon air, marbled through with baked scents of pleasure and anxiety and vaguer things he could not quite name.

She took a seat. He sat down too, his fingers curling immediately around the stem of a wineglass while he asked the question he had never before been allowed to ask. "What happened to Jupiter after the elevator car left the city?"

"I don't know." She answered so smoothly she might have been practicing. . . .

"What do you mean you don't know?" he burst out. "You're part of authority."

"I'm not. I'm independent."

He moved his head slowly back and forth, encountering something like truth on the air. Yulyssa was very real. In her news reports she often seemed to know more about city business than the junior council members. Yet she hadn't known cold storage was empty.

He felt naive because he wanted to believe her. "Who *would* know what happened to Jupiter?" he asked, feeling gullible and penitent at once.

"Nobody knows." Her hand rose in a gesture meant to slow his natural protest. "There's been no sign of him in the Well. I do know that. I've accessed the planetary wardens and looked myself."

"Somebody knows," Lot insisted. "Someone's seen him. It's why they emptied cold storage. They're afraid he'll revive the army."

Yulyssa picked up her glass, a half-smile on her face. "Try the wine, Lot. Shao found the recipe on a deep run in the city library."

Lot was surprised to rediscover the glass in his hand. The wine tasted of honesty. Yulyssa gave him time to savor it, before indulging her own curiosity. "Did Jupiter ever talk to you about the Hallowed Vasties?"

A sourceless tension ran through him. He studied her warily, the fumes from the wine addling his sensory tears.

"What's wrong?" she asked.

"I don't know." Still, he could feel a memory on the edge of recall.

"You know something." She was very curious, leaning forward, her dark eyes hungry.

"I'm not sure. Maybe." Did he *want* to satisfy her? He wasn't sure. He picked up chopsticks, nipping at the marinated dumplings on his plate. Her curiosity mobbed him, though it was cut by a heavy share of anxiety.

"Lot?"

He put the dumpling in his mouth and chewed, but he didn't taste it. "There's nothing to tell. All I've got is a feeling." A feeling of dread. But he knew he could pull more out of fixed memory if he tried.

His fixed memories were an eclectic collection. Jupiter had given him some: spare facts and essential data that could not be allowed to degrade in organic memory. Others had crept in when he'd been an infant and still others had been burned in by trauma. But most were of his own choosing: brief scenes and moments of no intrinsic importance, but that had appealed to him once, so that he'd taken a second to fix the image, seizing it with the same fleeting sense of conquest he might have felt stooping to retrieve a shiny sequin that had fallen from a girl's dress, or plucking an unusual seedpod from the garden—childhood treasures that gave him a powerful connection to a past that sometimes seemed little more than myth. He didn't often think about the past, but when he did he could unlock scenes that would play themselves out in his head like a virtual skit.

"The Hallowed Vasties," Yulyssa urged.

"Yeah." Her curiosity had worked its way inside him, to become his own. "Yeah, I do remember something."

He remembered waking abruptly deep in ship's night, brought instantly to full consciousness by a wiry sense of foreboding. He'd been maybe five, six at the most. Sliding out of bed, his heart had hammered with the harmonic stirrings of his own answering fear. Around him, the soft breathing of other children blended in a pneumatic chorus, their dreams filling the darkness with madly jumbled sense.

He stepped cautiously out of the creche, his commando training letting him move across the planking of the garden deck without a sound. Torches burned low over the vegetation, casting quivering shadows that seemed to grab and scrape at the night. He moved his head slowly back and forth, letting Nesseleth's humid air run over his sensory tears, its message of dread etching stark lines of shadow across his mind.

He glanced back. Other doorways opened onto the deck. He half-expected his mother or some other member of the marriage to emerge from one of the dark arches and testily order him back to sleep. But all he heard was the soft fussing of a baby.

So he stepped down onto the path, his fingers trembling and a cold-messy sense chewing at his gut. Through the garden and out the arched gate into the warrens. Dim footlights came on. He passed the gates of neighboring compounds, though he didn't peer within at the gardens, the private courtyards. From unseen fountains the trickle of water reached him. Night blossoms pumped their heavy perfumes onto the air. This was his world, and in his mind it had taken on a sense of permanence despite Jupiter's admonitions that Nesseleth was only one step in a journey to transcendence that had begun long before Lot's birth. Tonight, for the first time, he felt the evanescence of their lives.

Down four levels on a spiraling stair, his weight growing in oppressive increments as he descended. A round foyer at its bottom, on its opposite side an ornate black and red lacquer moon gate that opened on to Jupiter's strategic chamber.

Lot edged across the foyer floor. A dim illumination spilled out from the room. When he peered past the round gate he could see that the light came from an astronomical projection. At the room's center, embedded in a field of white and reddish stars, a dull red sphere glowed faintly—a cordon of the Hallowed Vasties. It appeared to be a solid object, but really it was a swarm of orbiting habitats so dense they hid the light of the central star . . . or they should have. This cordon looked shattered, as if some recent blow had opened in it a network of wire-thin cracks through which a blazing white light glowed.

Jupiter sat in an armchair to one side of the projection pit. He watched Lot with eyes sunken into shadows. The dread that had pulled Lot from his sleep had now grown into a tidal pressure, and Jupiter was its source.

Lot cowered at the door until Jupiter crooked a finger. Then Lot sprinted across the dark space, scrambling into Jupiter's lap. *"What is it?"* he whispered, as if there was something sacred in the night's silence. *"What's gone wrong?"*

"There, look, you can see it," Jupiter said, nodding at the projection of the shattered red sphere.

Lot stared at it, thinking that perhaps the blazing lines of light had widened. "Is it a cordon?"

"It was."

"But it's broken."

"Yes." Jupiter's arms tightened around him.

Lot frowned at the projection. Now he was sure the lines had grown wider, and more intricate too. Very softly: "What does it have to do with us?"

He felt a brief burst of surprise from Jupiter. Then a sigh ran past his lips, and with it his foreboding began to change, strengthening to a wry determination. "What would I do without your counsel, Lot? Of course you're right. It has nothing to do with us. Not anymore."

Lot turned away from Yulyssa, disturbed by the memory and by a sense of complicity, for Jupiter had warned him never to speak of what he'd seen that night. But now Yulyssa was expecting an answer. He took a long draft of the wine, as if to numb himself for the task. "Jupiter said the Hallowed Vasties had nothing to do with us."

"Umm. I wish I could believe that."

He picked up a slight, disturbing tendril in her sense. "You're scared."

"Sooth. Just a little. It seems we have a new star in our sky. Or should I say, an old star listed in the astronomical catalogs has been observed from Silk for the first time."

Lot frowned at her, not understanding.

"We don't have good astronomical facilities, and living within the nebula we don't have good viewing. But we do have several dedicated hobbyists."

"So?"

"So have you ever heard of Ryo?"

He felt a sudden tightness across his chest. *Ryo.* "Yeah. It was one of the cordoned suns of the Hallowed Vasties."

"Was . . . ?" She seemed to hold the word in her mouth like wine, tasting its implications. "Yes, you're right. It disappeared under its Dyson swarm almost sixteen hundred years ago. But it's visible again. I saw it last night. Our astronomers noticed it only a week ago, though they say it could have been visible for months, or even years before that." He could feel her probing gaze. "You're not surprised, are you?"

Two tiny flies with glassy wings rested on the rim of his plate. "I've seen grand schemes fail before."

"I guess you have." She poured more wine. He could feel something dark and menacing under her calm demeanor, but none of that came through in her voice: "Ryo isn't the only one, you know. Quin-ken and Bengali are also out in the open again."

One of the flies began walking toward the cooling dumplings. He shooed them both away. "Why are you telling me?"

"Just to see what comes of it. Placid Antigua claims that Nesseleth wasn't made in the Committee."

"Sooth. Nesseleth came out of the Hallowed Vasties."

"How do you know that?"

Lot drank more wine and considered. "Nesseleth told me. Only it wasn't the Vasties then. The star was called Talent, and there were still planets. When she was a little girl, she lived by an ocean, and we'd go swimming every morning when the tide was low—"

He stopped himself, startled at the intensity of the recollection. He'd known Nesseleth through a personal interface, a little blond-haired girl, always just his age. He'd spent far more time with her than with any of his brothers or sisters. They'd played in her memories, and sometimes it was hard to distinguish what was his own past, and what was hers.

"I don't know what happened after that, or who made her into a great ship, or why. It didn't seem to matter then."

Yulyssa filled his glass again. "Did Jupiter come out of the Hallowed Vasties?"

Lot couldn't stop a soft chuckle. "I don't think even Jupiter was *that* old."

"Why?"

He blinked, unsure how to answer. "I don't know. Don't people get . . . strange? After a while?"

"You mean real people?"

He wondered how old Yulyssa was. She'd come from Heyertori, so she had to be over three hundred years. Except for a couple of officers like Captain Antigua and Captain Hu, the crew aboard Nesseleth had been relatively young, still ados by the standards of Silk. Comprehensible. By contrast the real people he'd met in this city felt . . . well yeah— *strange*. Half the time he couldn't tell where their feelings were coming from, or why. Their reactions were so weighted by experiences invisible to him, he could never hope to understand the process behind their moods.

"Just like you said," he conceded. "Strange like real people. Only worse. I mean, to reach the edge of the Hallowed Vasties it'd take . . ." He groped for a reasonable figure.

"Maybe five hundred years?" Yulyssa suggested.

"Yeah. Maybe."

"I'm quite a bit older than that."

Lot felt something rise in his throat. He swallowed hard against it, then gulped more wine.

"You didn't know."

"I heard it's possible."

She smiled in sympathy. "Most people become sessile long before they reach my age. Maybe that's how the cordons start. Maybe I would have gone sessile too, but it's different here in the Chenzeme Intersection; stability's more elusive."

"Sure." He felt obliged to agree with her. How could anyone who'd been alive so long be wrong?

"Don't look so scared, Lot." Her amusement warmed the air between them. "I'm not Jupiter. It's not like I ever learned the secret of life."

"*Shit.*" He knew she meant it as gentle ribbing, but it irritated him just the same.

"Now you're angry."

"I'm not."

"You are, and I don't like the way you're making me feel."

He sighed. The charismata again. His influence seeped out around him, whether he meant it to or not. "Sorry." He rubbed at his sensory tears, feeling suddenly dizzy. "I think I'm drunk."

"Eat some food before it's cold."

So he did. There was more wine. By the time they were done he was feeling warm. He gazed unself-consciously at Yulyssa, her finely sculpted face mottled by sinuous patches of greater and lesser darkness where the branches of a shading tree cast shadows. "You knew him, didn't you?" Lot asked.

Her smile felt like soft fingers against his skin. "You never asked that before."

The diamond studs of her earrings sparkled within the black strands of her hair. They cast a silver tint over her brown skin. He blinked, but the silver wash didn't go away.

Uneasiness stirred in her. "Don't look at me like that."

But he couldn't look away. "Did you love him?"

"No. He scared me. I don't like being intimidated."

"I'm scaring you now."

"You're not like him."

He thought of Alta and the slick surface of her aura, hard and smooth and not given to damage or change. "Sooth. I know."

"Don't be sorry over it. You've got your own life."

"And you?"

"Sometimes . . ." He thought he felt the gentle brush of her desire, but it was fleeting, lost too soon to a bemused smile. "I'm old enough to know better."

Dumb ado.

He stood up. Ord was skulking on the path and the sunlight seemed too bright. "I should go now."

Did she hesitate? It didn't last. Now she was nodding, giving approval to his decision. "Be careful, Lot. There is a difference between you and Jupiter, but that's not clear to everyone."

Chapter
9

He waited out the afternoon in his breather, watching the slug move slowly across the ceiling. He'd promised Urban he'd get some sleep before the rally, but it was hard. He kept thinking how city authority had lied to him. For ten years, everyone from Placid Antigua to Dr. Alloin to Kona Lukamosch himself had claimed Jupiter to be just another corpse in cold storage. They'd quashed his denials, repeating the lie over and over again until he'd begun to doubt his own senses, his own sanity, his own beliefs. Until he'd begun to doubt Jupiter.

Resentment simmered in his chest. *Happy monkey.*

Even Yulyssa had abetted the lie by keeping her own truth hidden.

He started to think about finding something to eat. Though Yulyssa had fed him well—with both food and information—it was never enough. Like most people, he lived life on the torch of a metabolism souped up so high hunger was almost a constant thing.

With a sigh, he got up, pulled some packaged paste out of the cabinets, and tore off the seal. The presence of oxygen set it to heating. He sniffed suspiciously at the aroma, wondering if Dr. Alloin had known the truth, that Jupiter *had* escaped the city. Eventually he decided she probably had not. Even Captain Antigua, in all likelihood, had only parroted what her Silken masters told her. Yulyssa had known. And Kona Lukamosch . . . ? Kona was the grand old man of Silk, the chair of the city council, the personification of city authority. He had to have known the truth about Jupiter, yet he'd lied to Lot from that very first day.

Through the long afternoon Lot stewed over the injustice of it. His outrage seeped into the close air of his breather, circling back to clog his sensory tears in a feedback reaction that steadily amplified his mood. Ord got nervous. It scuttled in agitated circles, its tentacles soft against his neck as it sought a clear measure of his emotional state. *"Good Lot. Calm Lot."*

"Leave me alone."

The hour marched on to early evening. He was supposed to meet Urban in half an hour, at a little restaurant just a block away. But a new resolve came over him. Kona knew what had happened to Jupiter. Now it was up to Lot to confront him, to demand an explanation. After ten years of baseless lies, Kona owed him at least that much.

The nebula was faint tonight, its glow washed out by the bolder light of the Well's artificial moon. The swan burster soared high in the west, a ring shape glowing almost incandescent with its own light. Seventy thousand miles up, and eighteen hundred miles in diameter, the burster tumbled around an imaginary axis, undergoing a fifty-four-minute conversion from a circle, to an oval, to a one, to an oval, to a circle. The interior of the ring was velvety black, a region of twisted space-time that would crush any object unlucky enough to fall into it. Even light could navigate the interior in a straight line only through a small aperture of normal space at the burster's center, so that if the ring's own light was masked, it was possible to see there a blurred circle of stars.

It occurred to Lot to wonder how many of the nebula's butterfly gnomes died inside the crushing geometry of the swan burster every hour. Did they know the danger? Did they ever try to nibble at the neutral mass on the outside of the ring? Or were their erosive activities limited to more familiar nebular material?

As he left Ado Town, the swan burster turned face-on to become a perfect circle. As its luminous surface increased, its light brightened: a silvery glow that fell across streets full with the usual evening crowds. Lot slid silently through them, individual faces registering as little more than heat signatures in his mind, objects to be avoided. No one called his name, though he could hear whispering in his wake.

He crossed the bridges of Vibrant Harmony, passed through Serenity Gardens, and finally reached the partitioned edifice known collectively as Old Guard Heights. The foundation of the Heights was a massive complex built against a U-shaped cove that cut into the slope of the city, forming a twenty-one-story windowed cliff that surrounded the tournament soccer fields at Splendid Peace Park. Above twenty-one stories, the Heights became five segmented "towers" that lay back against the slope like broken fingers, each phalange an estate separated from the next by walls and narrow gardens.

It was the best address in the city.

Lot dropped two levels, then followed a narrow, luminescent street under a canopy of flowering jacaranda. Blossoms were strewn on the ground, glowing like purple glass against the lighted paving. He reached the third address, then followed a narrow brick path to the door, past a stand of fruiting banana trees on one side and a sweep of waist-high ornamental grasses on the other.

At the door the house majordomo greeted him in a sprightly male voice. "Hello, hello. Such a surprise to see you, Master Lot Apolinario. And our most humble apologies are offered, for your gracious visit cannot be immediately entertained—"

"Is he home?" Lot demanded, cutting off the DI's social niceties.

The door pulled open, and he got his answer visually. Kona Lukamosch stood against a rectangle of yellow light, staring out at Lot with a faintly amused expression, his fine black braids loose down his back, and a glass of amber beer in his hand. Surprise predominated in his aura, but beneath it Lot could sense an emotional turbulence that included solid doses of wariness, annoyance, and a kind of low-level, cautionary fear.

He looked Lot up and down, and then he stepped back from the door and beckoned with his glass for Lot to enter. Ord took that moment to scuttle out of the stand of feathery grasses, slipping through the door ahead of Lot. Kona eyed the robot sardonically. "Do you think you'll need it?" he asked, cocking one eyebrow.

Lot felt a cold emotional cloak pull down around him. Ord existed at this man's insistence. "I don't need it."

"Not at the moment, anyway."

It felt odd walking into the apartment. He hadn't been here since that day, when Urban had fed him crepes, and the lies had first begun. The living room was·as vast as he remembered, with its island cluster of sofas, its white carpet, its view out over the soccer fields and the adjacent slope. The projection walls were tuned to an image of silvery mechanical parts moving against each other in silent, slow-motion copulation, several thousand variations on it around the room's two open walls. Lot walked slowly past them, examining the details of shape; trying to discern function. Kona watched him curiously, as if expecting some reaction. "Does it mean anything to you?" he asked.

Lot turned curiously. "Should it?"

"It's a neural structure of the Chenzeme."

Startled, Lot stepped closer to the projection, striving to see some meaning in the patterns. "Where did you get it?"

"It's an old project that's been stumbling along for a number of years . . . but you didn't come here to talk about the Chenzeme."

Lot caught the sudden, cool shift in Kona's mood. He turned his head slightly, relishing the silent touch of Kona's anger against his sensory tears, liking the way it resonated with his own resentment.

Kona sipped at his beer. "I hear you've joined the political campaign," he said. "I thought I might attend Urban's rally tonight. Give you a chance to mesmerize me—"

Lot chuckled darkly.

"—after all, I'm a voting citizen."

"Privileged."

"An earned privilege."

Lot looked across the room at him. "I was down in cold storage today."

That drew a satisfactory grunt of surprise. Kona set his glass down on a white, cast-stone table. His focus seemed to shift inward, and Lot could almost sense the raging stream of data flow spilling into the atrial organ in his head as he sought information on Lot's claim. The artificial organ existed as filaments within Kona's brain. Through it, Kona could communicate with the city plexus or even entertain the electronic ghosts of other people. In Silk, only real people could have atriums; ados had to get by with phones, or face-to-face chatter. Not that it mattered to Lot. No one on Nesseleth had ever owned an atrium; Jupiter had mocked them as exotic curiosities . . . only in his more cynical moments did Lot wonder if that judgment had been made *after* Jupiter discovered that his complex physiology could not support one.

But these doubts he kept to himself, while he watched Kona with a careful eye.

It was a sudden flowering of indignation and alarm on Kona's face that led him to guess supporting evidence for the raid on cold storage had been found, possibly from security cameras in the tunnels, but more likely, Yulyssa had floated her story.

The walls seemed to vibrate with detailed, silver motion. He told Kona, "The cold-storage cells are empty. You would know the reason for that."

To his surprise, Kona only shrugged. "The data's there. It's all that counts."

"Jupiter never was there."

A cool half-smile appeared on Kona's face. "And is *that* what's brought you here tonight? The fate of one man outweighs the disappearance of thousands."

That made Lot flinch. It startled him, like an unexpected shadow falling across his face. But he refused to be distracted. "You know he descended in the elevator car. I saw it! He reached the planet, didn't he? And he's still alive. The wardens have seen him."

"No."

Lot hesitated. Kona had to be lying, but he couldn't *sense* any deception. "Why did you empty cold storage, then? You must have thought he was coming for them."

"Coming for the dead?" Kona sounded incredulous. "Do you think he cared that much? He hasn't come back for you, has he? And I think you'd be easier to grab than a corpse."

Lot's fist closed in frustration. "You know what happened to him!"

"I don't care what happened to him."

"But you emptied cold storage."

"I emptied cold storage, yes. I've also emptied every other form of storage in this city with the one exception of the biointegument existing on the city's surface. You enjoy walking through our city, Lot. Next time, look closely around you.

You'll be looking at the better part of our remaining organic resources."

Lot shook his head. "I don't understand."

Kona snorted. "Of course you don't understand. What need did your kind ever have for reasoning? A simple mind serves your purpose best. That's the charm of dull intelligences. They can be assigned a task, and relied upon to finish, because they don't have the intellectual capacity to question their own natures."

"The city—"

"It's starving to death! Can you understand *that*? No recycling system was ever perfect. Nitrogen and oxygen are volatile gases. We can't lock them up at every stage. There are losses, and losses and losses. And no source of replacement, once all the stored tissue has been consumed.

"And it's all been consumed. Every resource tank. Every mass in cold storage. *We're dying.* Can you understand that?"

Lot took one cool step back, swaying slightly, feeling as if a chemical understanding had just been poured upon his head, an anointing acid that flowed down through his brain and over his face, stripping the film off his eyes, boosting the laden structure of his mind, so that for a flashing moment he could see the Universe as it was and as it would be. "That's why then," he whispered. "That's why he left me here." Time was a tapestry, and the pattern of the weave had been coded long ago. The realization came to him with the force of a calling, a clear conception of his own purpose that he'd never felt before. His wondering gaze turned to Kona. "You've seen it already, haven't you? You know you'll have no choice but to follow him down the elevator."

But Kona denied that truth. "There are always choices."

The mural's silvery machine parts vibrated in unsettling rhythm against Lot's consciousness. He found himself pacing a slow half-circle. "What choices?" he asked. "To die? To become code? Data stored in the hatch of a cold-storage cell?"

Kona shook his head and picked up his drink again, his broad shoulders touched by a glaze of sweat. "To die here or to die on the planet—the cult mentality is enamored with death. It's almost as if the Chenzeme still work through you."

He cocked an expectant eyebrow. Lot could feel his anticipation, as if he were waiting for *confirmation* of this slander.

Suddenly, Lot felt frightened for no discernible reason. "It's just that you don't understand the Communion," he blurted. "It isn't death."

"Tell that to the Old Silkens." Kona stepped up to the window. Beyond the city's sloped horizon, the swan burster had begun to squeeze down into a svelte oval. "For the moment I'd rather search for other options. The world is made of more than ones and zeros."

Lot frowned at the defunct alien weapon, a pretty moon above a pretty world. *Deadly moon, deadly world.* A functional ring could produce coherent bursts of gamma radiation of a magnitude that would boil off a planet's atmosphere and oceans, while sterilizing the rock beneath.

Lot felt his certainty begin to slip. He groped for a defense. "Deception Well—"

"Is a loathsome sewer."

"Jupiter—"

"Died of his own foolhardiness. Will you do the same?"

Lot glanced again at the slowly tumbling ring. Long, long before any human eyes had looked on the Universe, some unknown force had infected the ring, pithing its logic systems while leaving the physical structure untouched. He couldn't look at Kona without considering the analogy. "I won't die here," he warned softly. "I won't starve here while an entire world lies below us. We could live there. Jupiter did."

"You're an amazing instrument," Kona said, though his gaze lingered on the swan burster. "I can feel the pull of you, like an organic magnet. You caught Urban that first day, didn't you—?"

"No!" The force of his own denial startled him. "It's different with him."

Kona's expression hardened. "I couldn't feel you then. But you're getting stronger. That cult-leader package you inherited from Jupiter is kicking in."

"It's not like that."

Kona gave him an indulgent smile. "If you say that, you're lying to yourself. You can't help what you are, Lot. Any more than Jupiter could help it. It's amazing that such a complex genetic structure could survive sexual reproduction. But obviously, the package has its own protections. You were designed by a genius . . . or perhaps a madman. What else could you call someone who admired the Chenzeme enough to duplicate the neural patterns of their killing machines within the structure of a human mind? Within your mind, Lot. That's the nature of the neural organ that once so puzzled Dr. Alloin. Did you never guess?"

Lot took two quick steps back. *Crazy.* Kona had to be crazy to say such things.

Kona chuckled, amused at this reaction. "It's shocking, I know. But then, all kinds of obscenities have come out of the Hallowed Vasties."

"Jupiter came from the Committee."

"No. He wasn't made there."

Yulyssa had implied the same thing. They were trying to rattle him! But it didn't matter. Lot knew why he was here. "What happened to Jupiter?" he demanded. "You know."

Kona's smile broadened. "And still, you persist." He seemed oddly satisfied, as if his expectations had been fully realized.

Why? Lot didn't care anymore. Trying to understand the twisted needs of the very real was like trying to understand the motivations of the murderous Chenzeme. The task was beyond him, and he knew it. He faced Kona squarely. "The Well lies below, and we can reach it. No one needs to die."

"That's right, Lot." By the condescension in Kona's voice, he might have overheard Lot's intellectual surrender. "No one else needs to die. The seven thousand one hundred ninety-six murdered by Jupiter were quite enough. And no one else *will* die, despite Jupiter. Despite you."

When Lot heard these words, he knew he'd been defeated. Kona would never tell him anything. He should leave now.

But an idea had begun to take shape in his mind. He remembered Yulyssa through a haze of heat and wine: *I don't like the way you're making me feel.* And Urban: *You have a gift, fury. Learn to use it, and you could be as good as your old man.*

Use it.

At the insistence of the monkey-house docs he'd always tried to suppress the moods that brought out the charismata. But what would happen if he played along instead?

Use it. Jupiter had bent people to his will all the time,

strong-willed people like Captain Antigua, and Captain Aceret.

Kona was vulnerable too. Hadn't he said so?

Lot looked inside himself. It wasn't hard to find a bud of anger. He sank into it; let it flare up and surround him. His eyes narrowed in concentration. His stance shifted, shoulders turned perpendicular to his hips as he stepped forward, all the muscles of his body pulling taut—

Suddenly, his sensory tears could taste the cloud of his own mood and it was grim: a spine-penetrating anger mixed with the cold threat of abandonment, of bitter loneliness while he demanded yet again, *"What happened to him?"*

Kona's jaw dropped in open shock. The glass fell from his hand, an amber arc of beer streaming from it as it bounced on the white carpet. Lot almost lost the moment then, through sheer surprise. But he held on to it with an effort. He could do this! He stepped forward, ready to press his advantage, when Ord dropped on his shoulders, its tentacles tangling in his hair, its little voice whispering frantically, *"Good Lot. I love you, Lot,"* a murmur that didn't quite cover the sound of escaping gas.

Lot closed his nose and mouth and eyes, but it didn't matter. The custom trank slid into his system through his sensory tears, and his focus shattered. A cool current of air moved through the room, sweeping away the eroded bits of his will, and Kona laughed at him. "You're not quite your old man, are you?" Then he looked past Lot and said, in a stern tone, "It's about time you arrived."

Lot turned unsteadily, to see Clemantine in her security uniform coming through the open apartment door, closely followed by two other officers. "Hi ya, Lot," she called cheerfully, as she crossed the room to meet him. She had her trank gun holstered at her waist. "The report is, you've been having a real bad day."

"Hi, Clemantine." His tongue felt thick, and his voice came out husky. He struggled to focus on her face, but his gaze kept drifting down to the stylized C/S on her uniform breast.

"You like that?" she asked, stepping up beside him, a motherly grin of amusement on her face.

He felt himself flush. *"It's the trank!"* The effect had peaked, but the biochemical work of clearing it from his brain had left him dizzy.

"I know, son."

She started to reach for him, but he didn't want her to touch him. He took a stumbling step back. Ord, half-hidden under his hair, placed a moist tentacle against his throat.

He felt an awful calm invade him. The temperature of everything in the room, including himself, seemed to plummet. Motion became cool deliberation. Anxiety froze out. He could think clearly and see clearly and function at a level that felt very, very cool. He smiled. Looking past Clemantine, he surveyed the two other officers. Jiro, and—he failed to hide his burst of surprise—David. David from the tunnels. The same officer who'd carried him out of the corridors that day. David was an ado, only a few years older than Urban, and Lot knew they sometimes ran together. David was all right. Jiro, though . . .

Lot had met him in the monkey house. Technically, Jiro was an ado too, but he was only a couple of years away from being real, so it wasn't the same.

Jiro had his hand on his trank gun. He grinned at Lot, as if this was the funniest sight he'd seen all year, while David looked nervous. The gold wire of security headsets gleamed in their hair. Clemantine didn't need any supplementary communications device; real people always used atriums.

"You'll go with them quietly, I know," Kona said. "You've always been good that way. Admirably well mannered and conscionable—despite your background."

"Sure," Clemantine said, and this time she got a motherly arm around Lot's shoulders. He caught the clean scent of her sweat and her easy confidence. "It just gets a little rough sometimes, doesn't it, son?"

Lot glanced briefly at David, and caught a minute nod. "Sure," he said. "As you say." David was looking away now, but a nervous half-smile had appeared on his face. Suddenly, Lot felt an urge to be helpful. "Yeah, Clemantine, you know, I think it's time to go."

Chapter
10

Outside, the swan burster had completed its half-cycle,
folding into a thin line. The silvery light it cast over the
city had declined in luminosity with the decreased surface area, making the streets seem to glow a brighter white.
No one else was in sight, though Lot could hear voices and
laughter carried in from some distant quarter, maybe even the
amphitheater in Splendid Peace where the election rally must
be getting under way.

"Do you want to take a transit car?" Clemantine
asked, her arm still around his shoulder, control disguised as
affection.

Lot could hear the sharp intake of David's breath. "I
don't like the transit," he said quickly. "You know that."

She chuckled. "Well, people change. I thought
maybe, since you'd been down to cold storage, you might
have lost your aversion to tunnels." He didn't answer, though
he could feel the pressure of her gaze. "Why'd you go down
there, Lot?"

"To look for Jupiter, that's all."

"Did you find him?" David asked softly.

Clemantine gave him a harsh look. "Hush, son.
There's no need to ask when we already know."

She'd led them down through the Broken Fingers, to
the broad promenade that topped the Height's vertical apart-

ment complex. A chest-high granite rail loomed ghostly in the silvered light. It formed a vast, U-shaped barrier, half-hidden beyond the spreading branches of regularly spaced shade trees. The tournament soccer fields would be nestled in the curve of Old Guard Heights, twenty-one stories below. But this far back from the railing Lot couldn't see them; the granite columns seemed to be holding back an abyss populated only by a thin scattering of stars.

In the distance, Lot could hear a trampling vibration, a cacophony of excited voices. He tensed. Urban wanted him at the election rally tonight. How badly? Yesterday he would have said "not badly enough to interfere with city authority." But that was before they'd gone down to cold storage. With that act, Urban had crossed over to a new territory where the factors that limited his behavior still needed to be defined.

The distant crowd noise grew a little louder. Lot slowed, forcing Clemantine to slow with him; then he half-turned, to survey the slope. But he saw nothing.

"You're a good boy, Lot," Clemantine said, her strong arm tightening around him and a sudden puff of tension rising from her pores. "Everybody has bad days."

"Hey, I guess so." He moved quickly and without warning, shrugging out from under her embracing arm. "But I'm still going to the election rally tonight."

She smiled. "I don't think so, son." She reached for his arm in a friendly gesture, though irritation was rampant under that façade. He jerked away.

He could feel Jiro close behind him. David didn't move or say a word, but Lot could feel him getting frantic. The babble of voices hung like a mist in the air. In the still night, he couldn't get a fix on distance, or direction. Clemantine's expression hardened. "You're a good boy, Lot," she said again. "Why are you acting like this? Are you on something besides that trank?"

Ord was still tangled under his hair, so he took another step back, deliberately bumping into Jiro. The robot hissed at the mild impact and dropped silently to the ground. "I'm always on something, Clemantine." His eyes unfocused, as he tried to gauge the distance of the rowdy party. "We've all got pharmaceutical factories in our brains, always making drugs to roll us from one day to the next and the next and the next. I get so tired sometimes. Maybe I'll be a sculpted entity someday and be done with all this." Not human anymore.

That'd be all right. But he had to wonder if it was possible. Dr. Alloin couldn't do anything with him. "Maybe that's what the Well's all about," he said softly. "Deconstruction. Rehabilitation." The cluster of voices faded to silence. He raised his chin, listening, but no, the night had become ethereally quiet. A glance at David brought only a shrug of confusion.

Urban wasn't coming.

Lot turned away, to look out over the starry void, knowing he'd screwed up. He should have waited for the rally. He might have used that chance to disturb the fixed certainty of city authority just a little. But now he was bound for the monkey house . . . without the satisfaction of having done anything worthwhile.

He could feel a depression descending on him then, like a black mantle drifting down from the heavens, to furl around him, turning his blood to cold syrup.

"Stop it!" Clemantine hissed. "Don't play that game with me, Lot, or I'll see to it you never get out of the monkey house again."

He looked at her in surprise. The last of her humor had evaporated. Shadows pooled around her eyes. "You aren't going to tell me how to feel," she warned him. "We don't need another Jupiter around here."

"I'm not doing anything!" he protested. But he could see that wasn't true. Jiro was shaking, his trembling hand poised over his trank gun. David looked stricken; silver glinted on his features, more than could be accounted for by the ring light. He stepped forward tentatively; Lot felt the wispy touch of his faith. It brought with it a sense of power. Lot's mood rose on the faint edge of its tide. His mind opened again to possibility.

Clemantine must have seen the change. She lunged at him: a smooth shift from perfect stillness to absolute motion. But she didn't have the same enhancements as Lot, and her effort seemed comically slow. He jumped back out of her reach, just as her fingers brushed his sleeve. He collided with David. *"Be careful, Lot!"*

"Sure." But an ado recklessness had swept over him. He was not going to the monkey house. Not until that journey became inevitable, and worthwhile.

Jiro had his gun out. He pointed it at Lot's face, aiming for unprotected skin. David tried to slip between them, but Lot held him back. "Shoot," he told Jiro, and Jiro did, even as Clemantine screamed *"No!"*

The patch—as small and sticky as the paddle of a sundew—hit with a sharp slap against his cheek. Lot took a couple steps back, opening up the distance between himself and Jiro, while David stared at him, eyes wide with a kind of horrified fascination. Clemantine's gun was still in its holster, but she was looking openly pissed now, like she knew the assignment was screwed. Lot reached up and scraped the patch off his cheek, squinting into night vision so he could read the label.

"That's supposed to drop you within one point two seconds," Jiro said. His voice didn't sound too steady.

Lot smiled. He staggered back another step. His legs felt wobbly, but his heart was pumping hard, systems on full call-out, energy coursing through his body like a scouring current—feeling better already—his smile spread into a smeary grin. "Standard tranks never work the way they're supposed to on me," he told Jiro. "Because I'm not human." It was a raw boast, inspired by ado cockiness, but once the words were out he remembered Kona's accusations about the Chenzeme neural patterns, and suddenly he had to wonder if it might be true.

"Take it easy, Lot," Clemantine said, trying to ease in on him again, talking softly as if he were some frightened VR dog. He hadn't done the VR in a long time. There was no emotional sense in the VR and it just never felt real for him. Tonight didn't feel real either. Sometime in the last minute reality had tripped and fallen flat on its face, leaving the world to stagger on without the defining structure of social laws, and every object around him—the people, the promenade, the balustrade, the stars and the slopes glittering with lights—seemed suddenly spongy, malleable, as if their definitions could be changed with a swift kick, a hard punch.

Jiro seemed to feel it too. On his smooth face an expressive symphony played out—*variations on comical confusion.* He still held his trank gun, apparently unable to bring himself to holster it, but it was no longer pointed at Lot

—perhaps—

they couldn't control him, unless he allowed himself to be controlled?

David touched his shoulder in an intoxicating, silvered gesture. His astonished gaze met Lot's briefly, then shifted upslope. Lot's heart rate spiked. He swung around, to see a tide of darkness rolling down the illuminated streets of the Broken Fingers, a voiceless mob plunging down onto the promenade like an opaque gas of heavy molecular weight, rolling across the level surface, bouncing off the balustrade, sweeping around Lot and David and Jiro and Clemantine in an irresistible ado tide. Individual faces flashed in and out of focus. Shoulders bumped against him; fingers brushed him. He felt heated, accelerated by the contact. Bodies squeezed in between him and David and Jiro and Clemantine, inevitably separating them, blending them into the volatile matrix, leaving them no choice but to go along.

He wanted to go along.

He felt good.

He felt radiant.

He belonged nowhere else but here; he knew it.

It felt solid. So real.

Urban caught him on his shoulders and spun him around, both of them still stumbling in the rapid mob flow, and Urban was laughing out loud, his thick hair swaying in its confining braids while camera bees darted past his shoulders. "We *will* have our rally!" he shouted. "Now. Here. On the promenade."

Like David and Jiro, most of the ados had come wired for sound tonight. Even Urban wore the gold metal strand half-hidden in the spongy mass of his hair. He must have been the center of a multicast, because at his declaration the flow slowed as if it had hit an opposing current, and the direction of their progress shifted, turning gradually until the ados swirled in a broad eddy that had Lot and Urban at its slow-turning focus, and as Urban slid round a new face came into view, electric in her unexpected presence.

"*Alta!*" Lot shouted his surprise, feeling as if he were looking on a mirage. "How could you be here?"

Her smile unfolded in sly hooks. "We have friends!" She had to shout too, to be heard over the tumult around them. "More all the time! They gave me an open pass." She turned her hand palm up, revealing the dim blue glow of a data stamp. Lot touched it. His fingers were silver. They seemed to slide beneath her skin. Her smile faltered as silver oozed like blood to fill her upraised palm. She looked at him with astonished eyes. Her exclamation almost fell into incoherence: "*I can feel him! I can feel him inside you.*"

She snatched her hand back, rubbing at the blue stamp. But her palm was undamaged. "I didn't understand!"

Her cry was a protest. But her retreating fingers had traced a silver arc that still hung in the air between them. Silver glistened on her skin and in her hair. It burned on her fingertips, cool points of light like St. Elmo's fire that leaped outward as Lot watched, expanding in a rush to meet the surge of ados still spiraling down around them, haloing the anonymous bodies in an encompassing silver glow. *Chemical sight.* Lot was taken by awe as he watched the infection of faith spiral out across the crowd. They received it, and redoubled it, sending their devotion spinning back down on him like water accelerating down a funnel, superheated water, steaming, melting the faces around him in the same blur of devout Communion he'd felt only that morning in the refugee quarter, faith flowing over him, hardening around him in an invulnerable silver armor. These people belonged to him. He could cuckold their will. And this time, Gent wasn't here to pull him back.

Alta surprised him again with her sudden proximity. Her hands were on his shoulders. Her eyes glistened slyly only inches from his own. Her astonishment had all gone and she seemed to have found the night to her liking after all. She stretched up, her lips moving against his sensory tears. "*We all love you!*"

Then hands were grabbing at him. Her laughing face fell away to vanish into a silver sea as he felt himself lifted into the air. Shoulders like living earth supported his buttocks and thighs, boosting him into full view of the ado mob. The crowd roared at this sudden incarnation, and Urban leaped up beside him, screaming, "*Twist them!* Make them hear you."

A bright light flared from a droning festival lamp hovering over the crowd. Its beam fell square on Lot's face, addling his nocturnal vision. He couldn't see beyond it, but he didn't have to. If he had no optical facilities at all, he would still be able to perceive this congregation. He had them in his mind, a liquid-crystal composition of passion, curiosity, resentment, even outright anger. He could use it all. He knew he could use it.

"*Lot!*" His name, chanted across a chorus of adolescent howls. "*Lot! Lot! Ow-ooo . . .*"

He knocked the hair back out of his face then raised his hands, as if he could embrace every individual present.

Gradually, the shouts fell off beneath the breadth of this gesture. An eerie silence rolled away from him in a circular wave, broken only by the high buzz of the camera bees, the low drone of the light. He stared up into the blinding white beam, suddenly aware that a remote congregation must be participating too, hovering ghosts on the farside of a radio link, shades of influence, the real people, in their homes, in their offices. "Time is running out!" he roared at them. Swiftly, his early elation became something more stern that gushed out over the heads of the silent ados and buffeted the small bodies of the camera bees. "Nothing lasts forever.

"Certainly not the supply of oxygen, the supply of nitrogen, the supply of hydrogen this city needs to survive.

"Cold storage has been plundered! For the oxygen, the nitrogen, the hydrogen locked up in the physical mass of my people. Their bodies are gone. That's how close to the edge Silk has come."

Beneath him, shoulders shifted. He heard a grumbling of concern, of disbelief. He looked blindly out across the crowd, his exhausted retinas struggling to gather up a shadowed image. "Believe it!" he commanded. "The evidence is ready for anyone to dissect. By morning there won't be a question. The only issue then will be *What will we do?* And *Who will decide?*

"Who will decide?

"It won't be me. It won't be any of you here tonight. Ados! Fully half the population of this city—we can't vote. We have no voice in our own future.

"But the real people can change that.

"The election is in ten days. We need ten thousand signatures to put two initiatives on the ballot. One to lower the voting age to twenty. One to allow citizenship for our immigrant population. And after that, we can link on our collective future."

The DI in his retina finally tweaked his optical system, getting him a rough silvered image of gleaming faces. Their shock rolled in on him, immediately cooling his tirade. He became aware of his own heaving shoulders, of the sweat that poured off his face and the exhaustion in his muscles like a slow poison more potent than any trank.

Whispering broke out around him, sibilant arguments. The ado mob teetered on a pinnacle. He watched them, waiting to see which way they would fall.

It started by the balustrade, that ado howl again, and then the scattered hooting of a nascent ovation interspersed with deep bass screams of *L-o-t!* Ado boys feeling high, a natural contest to see who could be more wild. The hooting swept across the promenade, and an angry roar accompanied it as ados began to process what Lot had said, not really believing it, not yet, but asking themselves *What if it's true?* and *What would Silk be like if we could vote?*

There were so many of them; to have that kind of power! The Heights seemed to rumble, howl. Lot raised his hands again and shouted over the cacophony: "Ten thousand signatures! And I know where to start!"

He twisted around, sliding off the shoulders that supported him. The crowd loomed around him in silvery, anonymous volume. He pressed through, disturbing their array like a magnet in a field of iron filings. They clung to him. They fell in behind him as he moved swiftly through the streets. They *believed* in him. He'd caught them in Jupiter's cult tide and it felt good. He could give them what they needed, he could fill up all those chemical sockets in their brains that needed filling, that they couldn't feel whole or safe without having filled. He could draw out of each and every one of them a neurotransmitter mix that would keep the innate human fear of death at bay. He could give them the illusion of a future, and maybe that was all anybody needed: faith. Better than food and drink and sex and kids and love. Faith is love at its most intense and selfless. Society was built on faith.

Overhead, the swan burster had begun to expand into a feminine oval. Lot felt as if a goddess had opened her eye to look down on him. Yulyssa.

Yulyssa was well over five hundred years old, and she had known Jupiter.

The congregation was strung out behind him in a long running wave that filled the narrow streets between the Heights and Spoken Verities. Lot had brought them to the base of a tower. He gazed speculatively up at its face. "Yulyssa lives here?" he asked, and looked to his side, surprised to see Urban still there.

"I think so."

Lot stared at him. Alone among the crowd, Urban did not seem to be touched by the melting, silver wash of faith. *Why?* Lot felt suddenly uneasy. He wanted to patch up the deficiency, or eliminate it altogether . . . but not now. A sense of urgency had come over him. He looked again at the tower. "Yulyssa will sign the petition. Once we have her support, half the city will follow."

Urban laughed. "You're crazy, fury. No one's more real."

But somebody had already scampered around to the entrance, to check the doors. "We're locked out!"

"She's probably not home anyway," Urban said, his presence like a cold thermal cell in the heated night. "Let's move this thing into Ado Town, before someone gets hurt. Let the real people come to us."

Lot studied the building. It had a vertical face, at least twenty stories high. But each story had wide balconies, their rails glinting in the light of the ring. He could climb it. A hedge of oleander grew around the base, but Urban could boost him past that. "Come here," he said. He crushed a path through the tall bushes, twigs snapping and grabbing at his shirt.

On the other side he faced a concrete wall almost ten feet high. Urban moved up beside him. "You don't want to do this, fury."

"Boost me," Lot said.

A couple of other ado boys came up. They were ready to help. Urban really didn't have much choice. They picked him up, and when he stood on their shoulders he was able to reach the first railing.

Camera bees buzzed close as he seized two posts of the balustrade: rods cast in a design of stacked human faces, each carefully detailed in natural colors, their expressions ranging across the spectrum of human emotion—delirious, despondent, joyful, furious, bored—gazing out from every angle, reminding him unexpectedly that this city was made by strangers, and these faces—they were the faces of a dead people. Yet they seemed *alive* . . . so real he half-expected them to scream or bite or at least curse him soundly as his hand closed around their tiny features, but they seemed not to have the capacity for movement or for speech.

Chapter
11

He gripped the sculpted baluster, then pulled himself up, climbing to the top of the rail. There he balanced on the two-inch span while the ado mob packed into the narrow street below, roaring at his antics like some maddened piece of machinery.

He leaned back a little, to survey the distance to the next balustrade. He could reach it without jumping. So he took hold of the posts—just like the first, covered with tiny faces—and pulled himself up again, and to the next one after that, each with the same peopled railings, as if every individual in Old Silk had been represented on the face of this building. Camera bees swarmed behind him.

Now real people began to appear on some of the balconies. They talked to him. Some weren't happy. But most offered encouragement and advice. A few said they would sign the petition, but most just smiled when he asked. The camera bees picked up the dialogue, and with each nonanswer, the ado mob in the street below roared their disapproval.

Before long, Lot's shirt had become sweat-soaked, and his arms were trembling. Somewhere around the tenth floor, his vision dropped down to a dim representation of shadows. "Yulyssa!" he screamed. "Yulyssa, I'm calling you. Where are you?"

"Fifteenth floor," said a gentleman in a white beard, who leaned on his railing a couple of floors above, a beer in one hand and an expression of undisguised amusement on his face.

Lot hauled himself up until he was even with the man. "What floor is this?" he panted, breathing so hard he could hardly get the words out.

"Twelve, son. We don't have a thirteenth floor, so you've got two to go."

"Thanks." He stood swaying on the railing, ready to reach for the next level, when suddenly he became aware of another presence besides the helpful gentleman. He looked down between his supple black boots to see Ord climbing up the railing beneath him. A slow smile slid across his face. "What are you going to do?" he called to the little robot. "Trank me now?" And he leaped for the next railing, hanging in open space a moment before he caught the posts in both hands. "Go ahead!" he shouted. "I don't care. I'll just let go and fly." He hauled himself higher. Got his feet on the next terrace while Ord extended a long tentacle, using pliant, formfitting suction cups to lock on to the concrete flooring. "It'll be a bit of a mess," Lot observed as he scrambled up. "Bit of a mess in the street, but that's okay. Authority will just scrape it all up and tuck it into cold storage, plenty of room there. Or better yet, serve me up to the city for dinner—" Ord had started to pull itself up on its tentacle, but now it hesitated. "Yum," Lot said, balancing rather unsteadily. "Scrambled madman—" And the robot slowly lowered itself back down to the balcony below. The tentacle popped free. Lot grinned.

"Where are the flowers?"

His head snapped up as Yulyssa's distinctive voice floated down over him. He saw her leaning on her railing, smiling down from the floor above. "If you climb to a woman's balcony," she went on, "you're supposed to bring her flowers."

"Oh." He looked around quickly. On this floor, a wide, open-air terrace fronted the glass doors of an apartment. In an arbor over a cushioned bench there twined a vine of mandevillea, the pink flowers silvered in the ring light. He jumped onto the balcony, an action that brought an immediate yelp of surprise from Yulyssa.

"Lot! I was only teasing."

He neglected to pay attention. Striding quickly across the terrace, he knocked on the double glass doors. Hardly a second later one popped open, and a little girl stared at him. Only she wasn't a little girl, he realized on second glance. Despite her size, her apparent age, she was real—as real as Kona, Yulyssa, Clementine. He felt sure of it. There was something distinctive about the way real people carried themselves, and the way they interacted with the people around them. They seemed buoyed by a warm reserve, a measured calm that Lot could breathe in, but had never managed to adopt.

She told him, "I've been watching you."

He said, "I need some flowers."

"Oh, you can have that."

So he plucked a spray of mandevillea, though he knew it was a risk because the stuff leaked a white sap. And sure, two fat drops of the thick, sticky liquid soiled the terrace floor, gleaming like pearls in the ring light. He looked apologetically at the real child. "I'm sorry."

She shrugged, "It's okay," and tagged after him to the railing. He put the stem in his teeth, boosted himself onto the railing, stood there a moment taking the measure of space just over his head. Yulyssa was leaning over the railing, laughing hysterically. She was dressed in a close-fitting stretch wrap that hugged her body from breast to knee like a second skin; her five-hundred-year-old body. Her toes curled over the concrete floor. Her bare legs were thrust partly through the rail, and he was half-tempted to grab for them. But he caught the balusters instead, the mandevillea dripping white goo down his black shirt. Yulyssa laughed and laughed, like an ado girl who'd had too much to drink. Lot hadn't known real people could laugh like that. He felt himself begin to catch her mood.

He hauled out, and flipped over the railing. His boots hit the balcony. He grinned at her, his shoulders heaving while she giggled behind her hands. "I brought you flowers." He held the spray of blossoms out for her consideration. "Hope you don't mind."

She became suddenly quiet. Her ambivalence washed his sensory tears. She seemed on the verge of saying something when a camera bee buzzed past. She glanced at it, self-consciously straightening her shoulders. Then her gaze cut back to him. "I'll sign your petition."

From the street below the ado mob roared, screaming her name at the night. But the cheering sounded remote. It struck Lot then that Yulyssa might be acting. She was a mediot. Maybe she was just upping the ratings, playing to the crowd.

Or maybe not. He wasn't sure. And he was used to being sure about other people's feelings.

She caught his uncertainty with an immediacy that frightened him. Stepping forward, she put one hand on his and with the other she took the flowers, getting the sticky white juices on her own palm. All the humor had gone out of her. She looked somberly at the camera bee and said, "Go away, Shao."

That wouldn't do much for the ratings. The bee buzzed off. The public show was over.

She led him into her apartment. They sat together on the couch, very close, their shoulders touching. He could smell her sex, and it addled him. She felt very warm. She was quite a bit more than five centuries old. "You shouldn't have gone to see Kona," she told him.

"He says the city's dying."

"Umm. It seems that's true."

Lot tried to keep his temper in check. "You knew then? Another secret?"

She shrugged. "It wasn't a secret to anybody who cared to look. I looked today, after you showed me cold storage." Her lips turned in a smile of self-derision. "I've never been too quick."

"Yeah," he said bitterly. "Some people say I'm slow too." Slow poison? He wondered again why Kona had made his accusations about a Chenzeme influence. It was absurd! But it haunted him.

"Lot?"

He blinked. Yulyssa was gazing at him in gentle amusement. Suddenly he suspected she'd said his name more than once.

"What are you thinking about?" she asked.

"Something Kona said." He hesitated, unsure if he should tell her. He wanted to trust her. He caught nothing but warm interest in her aura. But the subject left him uneasy. "Kona said some things about the Chenzeme, that's all."

Her brows rose in amusement. "And why should that worry you? Kona's obsessed with the Chenzeme. For him, everything that goes wrong becomes a metaphor of the Chenzeme. They're the source of his profanity."

He gave her a guarded look. "It's more than that." How much did she already know? "He said there's been some sort of research project into Chenzeme neural patterns. He claimed . . ." A sudden flush touched his cheeks. "Well, he claimed they'd found some similarities with my neural patterns." He wanted to smile when he said it, make a joke out of it—*don't take this too seriously, okay?*—but Yulyssa's shocked expression quashed that intention.

He could almost feel the heat of thought behind her sweetly furrowed brow. "How could Kona know anything about Chenzeme neural patterns?"

Lot hunched his shoulders, feeling suddenly out of his depth. "From the library, I guess."

"No. There's nothing like that in the library. We don't even know who the Chenzeme were."

Lot's flush deepened. Sure. The Chenzeme were known only by their weapons. No one could say what they'd looked like, how they'd lived and thought, or why they'd left such a terrible legacy of destruction. In that vacuum of information it was easy to think of the killing machines as direct representations of the Chenzeme themselves. But in truth there was no reason to believe the logic systems of the surviving weapons reflected Chenzeme thought patterns in any way. It seemed more likely the weapons would operate on artificial protocols aimed at maximizing their dual functions of aggression and self-propagation. "Sorry," Lot said. "Kona referred to the weapons. Not the Chenzeme themselves."

"Umm. That won't work either. No one in our knowledge path has ever succeeded in examining a functional Chenzeme weapon."

She carefully left open the chance that somebody, somewhere, had done it. Not that it mattered. Knowledge moved slowly, if at all, across the gulfs of light-years. Radio signals might carry data in the Hallowed Vasties, but in the Chenzeme Intersection any radio signal strong enough for interstellar communication would draw the war weapons, so cross-fertilization between cultures was left to the occasional great ship. In the slow ecology of the void the spread of useful data was random and erratic. What was common knowledge in one culture might remain dark mystery in another as their knowledge paths diverged from a common root. Somewhere in the Chenzeme Intersection someone might have dissected a functional weapon of the old murderers, but that information had no way of reaching Silk.

Still, there was another possibility. "Would the weapon have to be functional?" Lot asked.

"You're thinking of the swan burster."

"Yeah." He remembered the thoughtful way Kona had gazed at it, while standing at his apartment window.

Yulyssa shook her head slowly. "We examined the ring when we first came here. The Old Silkens investigated it too. That's why they settled here, you know. They came explicitly to study it."

"And?"

She shrugged. "We know the swan burster warps the structure of space-time within its circle. It seems to draw its energy from the zero-point field, though we haven't begun to understand how . . . or why this particular specimen has become quiescent. The Old Silkens felt the decision-making structure within the ring had been corrupted so that it could not respond. That's still the best theory I've heard."

"Has any work been done lately?"

She shook her head. "Nothing's been reported."

"But city authority doesn't report everything."

Her eyes closed. "That's true. So true. *Oh, Kona!* I always thought we were on the same side." She shook her head and looked at Lot again. "What is he up to?"

"I don't know. But what he said—it's not true. It can't be true. Not if Jupiter came out of the Hallowed Vasties."

Her lips parted, and he caught from her a wisp of fear. "Did he? But you denied that."

"I just don't know! Okay?" She jumped at his outburst, and immediately he regretted it. "Yulyssa, I'm sorry."

"It's all right," she said, but her fear was real enough to sully the air between them.

He started to get up, but she laid a hand on his thigh. "Security's outside the door. They want me to open it."

He frowned at the closed door. How did she know? The house majordomo hadn't spoken. Then he remembered her atrium, and wondered if real people ever managed to be fully alone.

"I'll find out what I can," she told him.

"Yeah? Thanks." He appreciated her interest, but it

was hard to express that. His mood was closing in fast. In the quiet rooms of the monkey house, the doors never opened from the inside. Closing his eyes, he let his head tip back, feeling exhaustion press in around him. "What else do you know?" he asked softly.

The door swooshed open. Lot heard the step of a security officer on the threshold.

"I knew Jupiter those few months he lived in Silk. He survived a Chenzeme plague. He survived Silk and the void. Now, the commandant of wardens complains the Well is haunted. If it is, I think I can guess the identity of the ghost."

Haunted?

Through the blackness of his closed eyes, Lot felt the faceless officer reaching for him. He raised his forearm to block the touch. "No," he said. "No more tranks."

"Lot!" It was David's voice. "I can't do this. I'm not going to do this anymore."

Lot opened his eyes. David looked chagrined, and more than a little disgusted as he turned away. Lot sighed. David had gotten him free tonight. He'd risked his position to do it, and they'd never even been good friends.

Lot looked at Yulyssa, feeling cold and sticky and very, very tired. "I've got to go."

"I'm sorry." Her lips brushed his cheek.

David blocked the doorway. He'd popped off his comm wire and dropped it on the floor. Now he was stripping off his uniform shirt.

"David," Lot said. "It's okay. I'm ready to go."

"It's not okay." David slung the shirt hard against the floor, his anger like sharp needles in the air. "It's all wrong. I'm not going to bring you in when I know it's wrong."

"But this won't change anything," Lot said, puzzled. "They won't hurt me."

"It'll change me. It'll hurt me. Because it's *wrong*. I won't stand against you, Lot. Not ever again."

A faint silver aura still clung to David. It brought a chill to Lot's spin. "Thanks David." He edged past him, out the door. "Thanks for everything."

Believe in me.

Lot walked alone down the hallway, meeting a contingent of real officers at the elevator, so that they didn't even have to step off the car to take him into custody. Good Lot. Not that he was worried.

He looked back down the hallway as the elevator doors closed. David stood on one foot, stripping off his uniform pants. Yulyssa stepped into sight beside him, her gaze seeking Lot among the crowd of officers. "I'll have you out by morning," she promised him. Lot nodded. Somehow, he'd already known that.

Chapter
12

He rose slowly from the gray state of nonbeing he always experienced during sleep, into a dull awareness that he was interned in the monkey house, though he couldn't remember his arrival. He recalled riding in a transit car, the security officers talking to him, loud, jovial questions, their knuckles in his ribs as they tried to keep him awake. But exhaustion had dragged at him, blurring the cops' faces, stripping their words of sense.

Now he was in the monkey house. He didn't have to open his eyes to know that. One conscious sniff of the air, and his body dutifully notified him that the carbon-dioxide level was way too high—but that was just the monkey-house way of saying, *Be calm. Take it easy.* Dr. Alloin liked to employ the ethereal peace of oxygen deprivation. In her mind it was a safe trank. She preferred not to use anything stronger, never knowing for sure how his metabolism would react—even Ord's custom brews were mostly guesswork.

Of course the docs were always refining their guesses, watching him every minute he was in here. Hidden cameras in the walls. Molecular sniffers. Microscopic blood analyzers. Breath analyzers. Semen and shit too, for all he knew. It made his skin crawl.

He opened his eyes—

—to find himself lying on his side, on a sleeping pallet identical to the one in his breather. On the near wall there vibrated a frenetic mural of interlocking silver machine parts, like the one in Kona's apartment. Why had Dr. Alloin chosen that motif?

A tube led out from the wall and into his left hand. An IV needle had been slipped into a vein and taped down. They'd taken off his black shirt and his boots—probably analyzing his sweat—his skin felt clean, though the bedsheets still had a crust of crystallized oil on them.

He sat up, feeling heavy and slow. Carefully, he untaped the IV and slipped it out. Questions boiled in thick liquid circuits just beneath the surface of his mind, a potential hemorrhage kept in check by the deadening pressure bandage of CO_2.

He turned to glance at the door, half-hoping he was awake because they'd sent him a stimulant through the tube, and any moment now Yulyssa would walk through the door, having secured his release.

The door failed to open.

Turning away, he briefly considered giving in to the urge to lie down again on the pallet and simply wait. But even under the CO_2 lethargy, anxiety had begun to bubble up from somewhere deep in his mind, breaking the smooth surface of his emotions. Physically, he'd taken himself to the edge last night. He should have been sick, exhausted and starved. He would have been, if he'd slept only the balance of the night. But he felt okay. Which meant he'd slept hours past dawn; maybe even through the next day. What had happened in the city in that time?

With an effort, he pushed to his feet. This room was larger than his breather. Ornamental grasses with rust red tassels grew in wall-mounted pots near the door. The carpet was thick and white, with pillows scattered on the floor. The furnishings were simple. Besides the sleeping pallet, there was only a small table with a phone visor and two chairs. Looking at this last, he grimaced, wondering how many hours they planned to make him sit and chat with Dr. Alloin. Then he remembered where he was, and carefully, he forced all expression to fall from his face. For they would be watching him, and he didn't want to show them anything.

Responding to the needs of his body, he staggered to the far corner of the room, then pressed an icon on the wall. The toilet slid out of its chamber. He stared down into the smooth, peach-colored bowl. *Time to give them some piss to analyze.* When he was finished, the toilet retreated.

He tossed his hair back, out of his face. *Madman,* he thought, remembering his chemical vision: the electric aura of the crowd, the silver swirl of faces, the sense of control, of command, his body encased in an invulnerable silver armor. His heart beat faster, thinking about it. Immediately, he tried to suppress that reaction, knowing they would hear. But he couldn't deny the memory excited him. To feel such a quantity of energy at his back . . .

Quickly, he closed his eyes, breathing deeply to calm himself. The allure of power . . .

Why, he wondered, *does it feel so good?*

He remembered the swan burster, and the desire he'd felt that first time he'd seen it modeled in Jupiter's strategic chamber aboard Nesseleth, and Jupiter's rebuke:

We all carry the seeds of destruction within us. Boys grasp for weapons as soon as they have learned to make a fist.

An instinct as natural as breathing . . .

Jupiter had held fourteen thousand people in his fist.

There were over six and a half million people in the city of Silk. *Given the decline in oxygen, in hydrogen—how long before we notice our demise?* And what would be the first physical signs? He already knew. The first sign would be an increase of emotional pressure—and he could feed on that.

Uneasy now, he opened his eyes. The bed had folded itself into a couch with a blue floral print. A low table arose from the floor in front of it, bearing a plate of scenic cookies, each decorated with a different three-dimensional image. He picked one up. It showed a great ship moving in orbit over the slowly turning geography of the Well. At first he thought the ship was Nesseleth, but the lines were subtly different. Maybe it was Null Boundary, then, the ship that had brought Kona and Yulyssa and the rest of them from the ruins of Heyertori. He squinted, examining the planet's image more closely.

There was no elevator.

The familiar continent rolled past, barren of any anchored thread. Intrigued, he inspected the ship again. The Old Silkens had built the elevator. Maybe this was their ship. *Sypaon.* That was her name. Yulyssa had talked about her once. Sypaon had been a great engineer.

He put the cookie down and picked up another. It showed a tournament soccer game, the crowds vibrant with motion as the players scurried around the field. Another cookie displayed a garden bright with daylilies and iris nodding in a subtle breeze. He picked up the last one. Silvery machine parts vibrated in intricate motion across its face: the same motif as the wall mural, both here and in Kona's apartment. It was supposed to be a neural structure of the Chenzeme. It didn't mean anything to Lot.

He tossed the cookie back onto the plate, wondering if Dr. Alloin had arranged the snack as a kind of psychological test. He couldn't help but smile. Did she seek to gauge his sanity by the food he chose to eat? And what was sanity? Was it crazy to consider escape from a dying city?

Years ago, Dr. Alloin had sent him on a VR run of Silk—but not the Silk he knew. Urban's people had been force-landed here 252 years ago, dumped by the damaged Null Boundary at the end of the elevator column, knowing only that the constant radio queries they'd directed at Silk had gotten no response.

As Lot thought about it, a deep chill wrapped around his spine, like the first touch of cold storage. Kona and Yulyssa and a handful of others had gone first down the elevator column. In the VR run, Lot had gone with them: part of the exploration party, living remotes for the 5,000 incarnates (and the 212,000 in hatch storage) all crammed into the cargo slug at the elevator's end, every one of them waiting to learn if they had any future at all.

Closing his eyes, Lot could see again the skeletons that had inhabited Silk. City of Bones. That's what they'd called it. Human bones had littered the streets. On the balconies, knee-high weedy shrubs with dark green leaves and bloodred flowers sprouted from the detritus of decaying human bodies. In the park, skulls glistened like rounded mushrooms among overgrown meadow grasses. In a bedroom in Old Guard Heights he watched his own flesh-covered hand descend through a slow, reluctant arc (fully conscious of the skeleton biding inside it) to touch the smooth white skull of a child nestled in the center of a bed among parental ribs, enfolded like treasure within long, bony arms. The child had its baby teeth, and a second set of adult teeth embedded in the maxilla. Lot touched these, one by one, and more than the bones themselves those preemergent teeth testified to the potential that had once been.

The Old Silkens believed the Well had killed them. In

the city library, their sweat-soaked, emaciated images described how their medical Makers had been decimated and their lives stolen by a plague spawned in the Well's seething biomass. But no one really knew. The plague had died with its victims, leaving no evidence of its origin.

Had Jupiter died too?

In the City of Bones, maybe it was crazy to believe in even the surety of the next moment. But Jupiter had lived here, and he'd come away from this city preaching communion, not death. By that standard, the people of Old Silk could not be really dead, but just changed, become part of the Communion, their souls mixed up with the fragmented remnants of the ancient beings that had held this place to be their home. Lot remembered the feel of his finger sliding across the infant's double row of teeth. Many things could be hidden under the skin, in the bones. Jupiter had been down there, and he had lived.

The oxygen content of the room was rising. Lot felt more alert, and suspected Dr. Alloin might arrive soon. Restless now, he wandered to the table and picked up the phone visor. It seemed incredible that he would be allowed net access. And indeed, when he slipped the visor over his eyes no images appeared against the background of the room. It had been disconnected. He tossed it back onto the table, beginning to pace now, five short strides from one end of the room to the other. After three laps, he caught himself, took a deep breath of the rich air, then forced himself to sit down on the sofa. Minutes decayed at the leisurely pace of stable atoms. He had time to wonder if Urban had been arrested too, and the thought brought on a brief burst of panic: Urban had no defense against Dr. Alloin's therapies. Neither did Gent.

He jumped to his feet, paced the room again twice, his fingers trailing along one wall as he sought to discover the locations of the cameras. He wanted to look at Dr. Alloin, fix her with his best imitation of Jupiter's commanding eye. Finally, he stopped in the center of the room, arms stiff at his sides. "Dr. Alloin!" he called. "Listen to me. Listen: You won't touch Urban, or Gent. You won't change them. You know it's because of me." His words silver as a second skin. "Come see me. Come talk to me. You know it's me."

He shuddered, not so sure of that last anymore. Chenzeme neural patterns mixed with human emotions to produce bizarre results.

What am I?

He paced the room again. Tried the phone again. Sat down again. Another minute of his life decayed. And then another until two hours had burned away, and still no one came.

He got up and pounded on the door. "You want me out of sight?" he shouted. "You think I'm dangerous?" He whirled away, three strides to cross the room, hit the wall and turn. "I am dangerous." He muttered it, knowing the volume wouldn't matter. They could hear the very growl of his blood stumbling through his capillaries. "I *am* dangerous."

He raised his hand to strike the door again, but as he did so, the door popped open. Startled, he took two short steps back. Captain Antigua stood in the entrance.

She seemed softer, chubbier, maybe even shorter than the woman in armor he remembered from that day. Her coppery hair curled around the perimeter of a broad, open face. Her hand touched the doorframe, the fingers thick, friendly and hearty. He wondered how much of her changed appearance could be attributed to his own changing viewpoint. He'd been smaller that day, and more vulnerable. Still, he sensed the difference was real. Placid Antigua had force-fitted herself into a society that could not trust her. Given that, it wasn't really surprising that she would let her aspect evolve into something less threatening and more maternal. But who was she inside?

He couldn't begin to guess. She'd abandoned Jupiter to become a maker of useless trinkets and children's fads. She was a leaf fluttering in the wind, turning this way and that, one day loyal to Jupiter Apolinario, the next a stolid citizen of Silk. And the next?

He felt the hair rise on the back of his neck as he caught a sense of calm satisfaction from Placid Antigua. What could Captain Antigua have to be satisfied about? He widened the distance between them, retreating two more steps until he stood by the couch.

She watched in mild amusement, a friendly smile on her soft, matronly face. "That was an impressive debut you made the other night. You're better than Jupiter, I think, at least when your heart's in it." He saw a flash of green in her hand.

"Where's Dr. Alloin?" Lot asked nervously.

"Busy." Captain Antigua stepped fully into the

room. The door closed behind her. "You brought her a number of new patients." She looked around, her gaze taking in the mural, the furnishings, before settling again on Lot's face. Her anger surfaced. It hit him in a sudden pulse, rattling him badly. "You've heard from Jupiter, haven't you?"

Shock flicked across his face, a moment only before he had it under control, but she saw it.

She misinterpreted it. *"Devil!* How long have you known?" Like a chameleon's skin her face darkened from pale cream to the brown of singed paper. She raised her hand, showing him a glistening green lozenge about two inches long. Her index finger poised clawlike over the tiny spray head. Suddenly, the room seemed several times smaller. "The planetary wardens have seen the change. It's time, isn't it? He's coming back." She stepped forward, closing the gap between them. *"Answer me!"*

He was suddenly conscious of his heart, doing crazy things in his chest. Everybody was crazy. Where was monkey-house security? Where was Dr. Alloin?

"Answer me!" Placid Antigua screamed.

"I don't know." Lot kept his voice calm, quiet, but his gaze was fixed on the green capsule and the poised talon of her index finger, searching for any slight flexion of muscles.

She gave him a curious look. "Do you think I want to hurt you?"

"No." Maybe he answered too quickly.

"Lot, I didn't betray him."

He nodded, as calm as possible, doing everything he could not to provoke her. "None of us did."

"He sent me back up the tunnels to supervise the off-loading. But it was too late! The troops were already panicking. I couldn't bring order to that chaos. Lot, it wasn't my fault."

"Sooth." Had she been laboring under that guilt all these years?

"He left us behind," Placid insisted.

"I know."

She nodded, as if they'd suddenly become confidants. "I had a life before I knew him. He took that away from me." She pressed the cylinder against her chest. "He came to my house. I had a husband. I had children. But he got inside me. He took me away from them. And he won't let me go! I can still feel his presence, his *abiding* presence—that's what they call it in the refugee quarter—his abiding presence, alive inside me, always *accusing* me, *blaming* me, but it wasn't my fault—"

"I'm sorry," Lot whispered. "I'm sorry. Maybe Dr. Alloin could help you."

She looked at him with a half-smile. "I don't want help. I want to go back to the life I had before he poisoned me with this *need*. I want to see my other children again. I want to go home."

Lot swallowed hard, groping for an effective strategy. "I don't know how I can help you."

She smiled in a shy, distracted way. "That's okay. The wardens will take care of it. They'll dissolve any trace of him they find." She looked at the little capsule in her hand. "They're armed with a neat assault Maker."

"Captain Antigua . . ."

"You know it was always *his* fault." Her claw flexed.

Lot threw his hands over his face and dove past her across the room as the aerosol hissed from the spray head. He felt cold moisture on his forearms, his bare chest. His shoulder plowed into Placid, and then he hit the floor on his elbows. It hurt. He had time to wonder if he'd shattered bones, before his back slammed into the wall and he crumpled. He heard Placid screaming. Through dark spots of looming unconsciousness, he saw the capsule on the floor and he guessed that he'd knocked it out of her grasp when he'd jumped, but why didn't she pick it up again? He kicked at it, sending it skipping across the rug. His arms were burning. His chest too, and not in a mild, allegorical way. He screamed and reared back against the wall, eyes clenched shut and face screwed up, sure that someone must be holding a torch against his skin even if he couldn't see it. His medical Makers kicked in. Foam on a fire. Pain receptors blanked. His arms and chest went numb. Placid's screaming kept on and on. He forced his eyes open. A single glance told him she'd poisoned herself too. The aerosol must have spewed across her face when he'd bumped her. Her face was gone. Her eyes were empty sockets, her nose bone visible. Cheek bones. He could see the hearty roots of her teeth, blackened tissue pulling away around her skull, bubbling, dissolving.

Assault Makers. He hadn't even known the wardens had an arsenal. The Silkens: they could have used it that day. *But they hadn't.*

His arms were still half-folded over his face. Tentatively, he looked down at them, and almost choked when he saw twin slivers of white bone, running from elbow to wrist, glistening amid the pinched pink of exposed muscle. Corrupted tissue hung in a bubbling black globe from his right elbow. As he watched, it dripped off and rolled away from him. Another small mass of blackened tissue had already migrated across the carpeted floor. He didn't want to look at his chest.

Placid's screaming stopped abruptly. In the sudden silence he could hear his breathing and another sound. A soft frothing hiss: the sound of Placid's head and chest as they boiled with black corruption. A wave of nausea swept over him. He braced himself against the wall, glancing again at his own arms, but his exposed flesh was still pink. Wounds pitted his chest. He could see bits of ribs, a fingernail patch of sternum. But no degradation. The wounds were clean. The contaminated flesh had sloughed off and the wounds were clean.

Why?

Now the black corruption had spread across Placid's body. Lot could feel heat pumping off it. The fizz grew louder. He could almost make out words in it, but that was crazy.

Crazy, crazy.

Why was he still alive? That was crazy too. Maybe he wasn't human after all; maybe the bloody Chenzeme influence had protected him. He closed his eyes. "Get me out of here!" He still held his wounded arms mantislike in front of him. "Get me out!"

But the door wouldn't open with a hot agent loose in the room.

Airflow. The word came as a worried whisper from his subconscious. The ventilation system would seal in the presence of contaminants.

He listened to his panicked breathing, straining to feel even a hint of air movement against his sweaty face, but there was nothing. The collapsing black mound on the floor continued to fizz and bubble—destructive metabolic processes adding heat, stealing oxygen. Stealing from him. He couldn't stop the theft. But perhaps he could outlast it?

He envisioned stillness. He sought the stagnant order that lies on the edge of death, dropping into the ever-slowing rhythm of his breathing, his heartbeat, darkness like a cooling blanket while time seemed to accelerate around him. . . .

Chapter
13

He blinked hard against a layer of dust and oil that sought to seal his eyes shut, finally opening his eyes to discover only darkness. His shoulder ached. He lay on his side, on a cold, hard surface that slanted beneath him at an angle immediately familiar: he was in the spiraling tunnel of the city's core. He found confirmation of that conclusion in the stale panic and putrid decay that permeated the thin air.

He blinked on his IR function, and discovered vague mounds of radiance on the floor, glowing warmer than the surrounding air. A bobbing white light appeared below him, just rounding the curve of the corridor. Its clean rays stabbed his retinas, and he squeezed his eyes shut hard in instinctive reaction. The sound of footsteps reached him, and he struggled to sit up. His arms wouldn't function. He got his knees under him though. He was kneeling when he opened his eyes again. A clean white light bathed the floor around him, illuminating the mounded shapes, revealing them to be the bodies of armored troopers. A gasp caught in his throat. The troopers' medical Makers had failed to protect their flesh from corruption. Their bodies were decomposing, and the gases produced by that process had caused their heads and hands to swell grotesquely out of the confining shells of their armor. He ducked his head, only to discover that his own arms and hands had been reduced to a clatter of bare white bones crossed over his chest. Clean white.

"Aren't you coming?" Jupiter asked, his voice sharp-edged. Impatient.

Lot's gaze rose. Jupiter stood over him, dressed in gray body armor, his blond hair neatly arranged across his shoulders. He wore a headlamp like a crown, its light a soft radiance at the center of his brow. Looking at him, Lot felt a flush of dark emotion, as if a sordid mix of guilt and anger had been injected into a main arterial line. "It was you!" he screamed. "You made me stay behind."

He sat up, startled by the sound of his own voice. Sunlight filled the room, illuminating the white carpet and the soft floral pattern of the sofa on which he'd been sleeping. Through a window wall he could see the vegetated slopes of the Broken Fingers and beyond that, a green run of Splendid Peace Park before the prospect sank into the cloud-filled atmosphere of the Well.

Urban crouched in his field of view, his dark eyes anxious, his hand on Lot's knee. "Fury?"

"What was that?" Lot whispered. "I saw him."

Urban's eyes narrowed. "It was a dream."

Lot couldn't recall ever having a dream. "Do you dream?"

"Sometimes."

He looked down at his arms. They were crossed over his bare chest, wrapped in opaque cushions and supported in slings. Tubes ran out of the slings at his elbows. He followed their paths to two half-empty nutrient bags on a table behind the sofa.

He turned back to Urban, worry furrowing his brow. "Did they arrest you?"

Urban's face went waxy. "House arrest, that's all." In his Daddy's house. This was Kona's house.

"And Gent?" Lot asked.

Urban shifted position, to sit with Lot on the sofa. "I saw him arrested. But they won't tell me anything." Then he corrected himself. "They told me what happened to you. I'm sorry, Lot. I never . . ." He shook his head, dropping that unprofitable line, starting over: "It's been wild." There was a hint of pride in his voice as he explained: "Yesterday a few thousand ados blocked all the transit stations for an hour—to get attention, you know?—they wanted you released. That's why you're here now. Course, some real people are screaming for you to be confined to cold storage. But don't worry," he added quickly. "That's nothing. Authority won't go for it. The council's already under enough pressure. People are angry. They want the resource problem dealt with. They want the ados dealt with too. While the ados want *you*." He smiled in quiet triumph. And why not? Lot thought. It was his doing.

"Authority's been trying to keep things calm all around," Urban went on. "They've had the monkey house hosting formal reconciliations for the entire city—hey, maybe they haven't had time to mess up Gent—but you know this—" He nodded at the thick wraps on Lot's arms. "—this hasn't gone public yet. When it does, it's going to make things worse." Urban didn't sound entirely displeased at that prospect.

"How's Alta?" Lot asked.

"I don't know. Why?" Then his expression changed to something like distaste. "Yeah. That's right." Alta Antigua didn't have a mama anymore. "It wasn't your fault."

Lot shrugged. "Jupiter's still alive."

"He's not."

"Captain Antigua thought so. She said the planetary wardens have seen a change, and Jupiter's coming back. She sounded pretty sure."

"That's bullshit."

Lot didn't answer.

"You want some food?" Urban asked.

"No."

A few minutes later the door slipped open. Lot could scent Dr. Alloin's surprise even before she spoke. "Lot. Up already?" She circled the sofa and smiled down at him, her soft brown face as warm and reassuring as a patch of floaters: a façade that could not hide her tension. "You always beat my best tranks," she said as she picked up the nutrient bags and tucked one in each sling. "And a good thing, too. It was your odd physiology that saved you—I've never seen such a swift defensive reaction."

Lot felt the first ugly stirrings of anger. Dr. Alloin had left him in that room. She'd let Captain Antigua come in. She'd probably messed up Gent, too. He breathed softly, slowly, determined to stay calm. He kept his gaze fixed on the brilliant white carpet, his pupils stopped down hard against the sun's glare . . . until a shadow fell across his line of sight.

"Your temper tantrums are always so quiet, Lot. You really do have a lot of emotional control. More than Dr. Alloin gives you credit for."

Kona. Lot smiled in wistful satisfaction. Dr. Alloin only followed orders, after all. He started to stand. "Don't!" Dr. Alloin protested, while Urban laid a restraining hand on Lot's shoulder. "You haven't the strength."

Lot turned to Urban. "You should be helping me."

Guilt flashed across Urban's face. His lips came together in a tight line, but he nodded. He put his arm around Lot's back, got his hand under his armpit, and steadied him while he rose to his feet. Lot swayed a moment, startled at how weak he felt. Finally, he looked at Kona.

The strain of the past few days was evident in Kona's face. Taut muscles stretched in sharp relief beneath his skin. Worry lines furrowed his brow and his eyes seemed deeper set, somehow robbed of moisture. He seemed vulnerable, but that roused no sympathy in Lot. "You sent her," he accused. "You sent Captain Antigua."

Urban's supporting arm stiffened around him. "That's not true, fury. Daddy . . . ?"

Kona's gaze shifted to Urban. He nodded in reluctant admission. "It is true." He looked back at Lot. "I sent her to see you. Not for that purpose. She was to reason with you."

"You say that." His legs wavered. Urban's grip tightened.

"I couldn't know, Lot. There was no reason to suspect. She'd been emotionally stable for years."

"You've lied to me all those same years!"

Kona shook his head, and spread his hands helplessly. "It was necessary."

"It was wrong."

"You're sure?"

Lot glanced past him, out the window, to the emerald and aquamarine glow of the Well. Fragmented clouds drifted over the ocean in formless ranks.

"*Try* to understand how fragile our position is," Kona pleaded. "We don't know how the Well functions. We devise theories about the governors, but that doesn't mean we understand them. They slide off our analytical tools, and treat our Makers like raw material to be stripped and sorted. We are inferior here. To let anyone go down there would be murder. To give your people any reason to believe they should make the descent would be a gross irresponsibility."

Words. "He's alive, isn't he?" Lot asked. "The wardens have seen him."

From Dr. Alloin there came a small gasp of shock. But Kona denied it. "No. The wardens have not seen him."

Lot cocked his head, trying to strain truth out of a soup of anxiety. He had so little strength, that slight shift would have toppled him if Urban hadn't been holding on. "Someone else?" he asked.

"Some*thing*," Kona admitted with a nonchalant wave of one hand. "A weather phenomenon. It doesn't matter."

"I want to see it."

Kona gazed at him for several seconds. He might have been consulting with someone over his atrium. He might have been finding counsel in his own thoughts. Finally, he nodded. "Okay."

"Urban too."

"Now?" Kona asked.

"Tomorrow, fury," Urban said. "You need to rest."

"Tomorrow then," Kona agreed. "When you're ready, call me."

"And Gent?"

"Gent Romer was released this morning," Dr. Alloin said with a maternal smile.

Lot felt his hackles rise. *"Did you touch him?"*

She looked hurt. "We don't ruin people, Lot. We help them." She gazed at him a moment, than shook her head in resignation. "We didn't 'touch him.' "

"The council has agreed to support a general amnesty," Kona explained. "We will do what we can to achieve a reconciliation. I hope you'll consider the same."

He led them downstairs, to a private transit station beneath the house. Urban half-carried Lot down the steps. Kona offered to help, but Urban—perhaps sensing Lot's reluctance—shook his head. A car waited for them. Lot collapsed on the seat and let his head flop back, feeling his face glazed in sweat. He tried to raise an arm to wipe it away, but his arm didn't respond. Dr. Alloin leaned in the door, running down instructions on what he needed to do to take care of himself. Beyond the streamflow of her voice, he could hear Kona speaking softly to Urban: "*I want you to think about what I've said.*"

"Sure, Daddy."

"*Urban, we need you.*"

"*I've gotta go.*"

Dr. Alloin withdrew. Urban stuck his head in, then climbed past Lot and sat down. The door closed. "He's scared," Urban said. There was a mix of guilt and triumph behind his words.

Lot closed his eyes, feeling the car accelerate.

"What's happening in the Well, fury? Do you know?"

"No."

"Why do you think he's letting us look?"

" 'Cause it's not Jupiter."

"Sooth," Urban quickly agreed. "Still—"

"I think he owes me," Lot interrupted. He shrugged, and his wounded arms rose and fell in their slings. "This looks bad."

"He didn't plan that."

"Sometimes it doesn't matter." For several seconds silence filled the car. Lot felt the slight centrifugal tug generated by the slow curve of the track around the conical base of the city, turning away, always turning away from a straight line's path, moving in an infinite sequence of tangential motion. "I want to sleep for a few hours," Lot said. "But tonight we could go down to Splendid Peace."

He felt Urban tense beside him. "You're still in it, then?"

Lot shrugged. Wasn't he running on a program? Jupiter Junior in the chutes. He glanced tentatively at Urban. "Do you think . . . Captain Antigua could've been right?"

"About what?"

"About me."

"She tried to kill you."

"Yeah."

Twin beats of silence, then: "Shut up, fury. She was crazy." Lot didn't see that as a special distinction. Maybe Urban didn't either, because immediately, he got defensive. "There's nothing wrong with what you do. People need somebody to follow. They always have."

"People don't follow me because they want to, Urban. It's because they have to. What makes them feel that way?"

"It doesn't matter. Just get them to stop listening to city authority and we'll be okay."

A few seconds later the car stopped in Ado Town, at the Narcissus Street station. Urban boosted Lot out the door, then followed, never letting his supporting hand drop from Lot's shoulder.

They hesitated on the platform, looking around in surprise. It was the middle of the day, yet the station was empty. They crossed the tile, then climbed the stairs. Two security officers had been stationed at the top. They greeted Lot and Urban with cautious nods. Beyond them, Narcissus Street was utterly deserted. Urban greeted the scene with a low whistle of surprise. No one attended the shops. No lunch crowds chatted at the sidewalk cafés. Fancy filigree balconies rose six stories on either side, but no one lounged behind the grillwork.

"Get the message?" Urban said. "Don't start anything."

"I didn't start it."

"*Sooth.*"

They walked down empty Narcissus as far as Oasis, then followed the smaller street to Reini Lane, still without seeing anyone. Ord waited for them on the stairs to Lot's breather. It slipped a hesitant tentacle, to touch the back of Lot's hand. *"No good. No good."*

"Hey Ord."

They floundered up the stairs. Once inside, Urban plugged Lot into a new set of nutrient bags that had been delivered from the monkey house.

"I'm staying with you," he announced.

"You don't have to."

"Yeah? You can't even get your pants down to pee."

Lot felt a flush warm his cheeks.

"So I get to be your girlfriend for the day," Urban said. "What a privilege."

Lot laughed. But then he got to thinking again about Alta. He wanted to talk to her, to explain, but it was impossible to put a call through to the refugee quarter. Gent would take care of her, wouldn't he?

After a while Lot fell asleep to the sound of Urban's voice working the phone. He didn't wake until after dark. By then he could flex his arms a little, though his balance was still shaky. He reeled to the toilet hutch. Ord helped him with his clothes.

Urban had pulled a quiet crowd down to Splendid Peace Park. Lot sat on a soft sponge boulder in a grove of sterile sapote trees, his arms still cramped in slings across his chest. A few camera bees buzzed about curiously. Ord had slipped off into the vegetation.

They were far from the streets, and the night was very dark. The swan burster had set behind the Well, leaving only a few stars to prick the swath of Kheth's nebula. Urban had called for a flock of floating festival lights, but somebody in authority must have countermanded the request, because none had come. The ados didn't seem to mind. They'd gathered under the trees in dense throngs. Lot perceived them as glowing heat signatures, ghost trails of warm air blurring behind them as they moved.

David sat alert on the boulder beside him. He wore shorts and a sleeveless shirt, a glowing tattoo in the shape of a red dragon squirming on his arm, hair slicked back, pure ado, his ten-year stint as a security officer only a troubling memory. He'd come by Lot's breather early in the evening, to crouch ill-at-ease among the sundews, not saying much until Urban went out to get dinner. His ensuing confession had taken Lot by surprise:

"You've been part of me since that day. I didn't understand it then. You were just a little kid, and I couldn't see why the real ones were so scared of you. But after a while I started to feel your presence inside me. I got scared too, though I didn't say anything. I didn't want the monkey-house docs to know. I didn't want to be cured."

Now his face was a wash of silver; he was more susceptible to Lot's influence than any refugee. David hadn't known Jupiter; his loyalties were undiluted.

Lot watched him lazily, feeling the soft, enticing edge of a trance slip close. David noticed the attention, and turned, an aggressive edge to his mood. "If authority tries to break this up, we have to be ready."

"It'll be okay," Lot assured him.

David thought about it, then said, with a touch of sarcasm, "Yeah. We're only ados. We don't scare them."

Through the crowd a silver current: Gent, with a small contingent of faithful. Authority had felt obliged to ease back on their restrictions. Lot looked for Alta, but she wasn't with them. David eyed them warily. "They aren't supposed to be near you."

Lot's mood sharpened. "You still with authority?"

David stiffened. "Don't, Lot. I'm with you." He looked nervously at a passing camera bee. "Rule change?"

"Rule change," Lot agreed. "We make our own choices now."

"Sooth."

Gent approached, and gripped Lot's hand, nodding in greeting. He introduced his pack. Three men and two women, their faces gleaming silver in Lot's addled vision. He shook each one's hand, feeling his heart rate rise as the oils of their skin rubbed across his palm. He caught Gent's sleeve. "How's Alta?"

Gent shrugged. "The monkey house has her in light therapy. She'll be all right."

"I wanted to call her."

"In her heart, she's with you."

The soft, dark-party chatter of the ados had begun to chill. Silver tide rolled slowly, thinly across the gathering. Urban came threading through it, a spot of darkness, a light sink. Lot watched him, fascinated. *Different species?* Silver armor encased Lot's hand, but he couldn't use it to hold Urban, any more than he could hold a pocket of darkness.

Urban climbed on the rock, unaware of his distinction. "All ados," he said with disappointment.

David reprimanded him. "You know the real people are watching."

Urban glared at him. "Don't lose yourself, ado." He looked back at Lot. "Keep it soft, fury. Can you?"

Lot nodded. They didn't want to scare anybody. Not yet. He turned to David, drinking in his vulnerability, pulling it into himself . . . then sending it out again as a soft, silver blanket descending over the congregation. He felt his arms bound across his chest, but he didn't need them. He was a worm, with frictionless skin. He could burrow into the minds and hearts of everyone around him. David was his point of entry.

Lot lowered his chin, fixing David with a hard eye. "I am not worried," he said. And though his voice still had the nap of softly spoken words, it had hidden volume too, and carried through the shifting silver gathering like a slow electric charge. "I am not worried," he repeated as silence gradually fell around him. But he still spoke to David. David's eyes were wide, his cheeks hollow. The warmth had left his face. He might have been caught in the eye of the Unknown God. "There is no real division in this city," Lot told him. "We all want one thing—you, me, city authority—we want to speak for our own future."

David's lip trembled. "I'm with you, Lot."

The claim echoed through the silver tide wound between the dark trees. Lot scanned the glow. They lived, as did the trees around them and a few feet of oxygenated soil beneath their feet. A veneer of life above the static, honeycombed bulk of Silk. This was everything. There were no reserves left. "Our vitality is not diminished by the thin state of our existence. We are alive. We have a voice."

From under the trees a woman cried out: "But they would murder you!"

Lot smiled. "That helps, sometimes . . . when you want to be heard. . . ."

That night he slept with an IV plugged into the back of his hand. His medical Makers continued their reconstruction, and by morning enough muscle tissue had been replaced that he had partial use of his fingers. As he sat flexing them, a tiny motion drew his eye. The sundew closest to his bed had caught another fly. It wriggled on the plant's glistening yellow paddle.

Lot got Ord to heat a stew of beans and rice. He ate it, wondering how the flies got into the room. Did they wait by the door and slip through during the few seconds every day that it was open? Or did they come in through the ventilation system? He frowned, remembering his own slow passage through the air ducts that day. It wasn't an analogy he wished to pursue.

Urban came by and they set out together for the authority offices. A small group of mediots met them in Reini Lane. Yulyssa wasn't one of them. Lot stopped to talk while Urban stood quietly on the side. The questions were friendly. They complimented him on his media interest factor. Very high.

After that, it took half an hour to get down Narcissus. Ados wanted to chat. Some tagged along. Urban paced in circles, watching the shifting activity with wary eyes. "We'll have to take the transit from here," he said at last. "We'll never get there if we walk."

Chapter
14

Urban was in a queer, stiff mood. On the transit ride he kept glancing at Lot, as if he had something pressing to say but couldn't quite get it out. "You're scaring me," Lot said after a minute. "You know something?"

Urban shook his head, his gaze downcast. "Do you want to find him?"

Lot felt his heart lurch. "Sure." The word was off his tongue fast, say it quick before he could change his mind.

"I'm getting scared," Urban admitted.

So that was the strangeness Lot felt.

Urban said, "He was supposed to be gone. Long gone. Now we don't even know if we have a future."

The car stopped at the authority platform. It was an empty white cavern, with no direct access to the surface. Authority offices existed entirely underground . . . a controlling biochip secreted beneath the city's skin.

Lot got out first. His arms had started to hurt, and his neck ached from the weight of the slings. He flexed his fingers, staring across the platform to a pair of double doors, with RESTRICTED embossed over their surface.

A soft chime announced the pending arrival of another car. He turned curiously, just as the vehicle's bullet-shaped nose penetrated the gel curtain that confined a near vacuum to the tunnels. The car brushed to a stop with a soft whoosh. The door opened, and to Lot's pleasant surprise, Yulyssa stepped out. He felt a silly smile upon his face, and then a warm flush to back it up as he realized how much he'd missed her attention. She hadn't come to see him since he'd gotten out of the monkey house. . . .

Doubt touched him. Dozens of mediots had flocked around him, but not Yulyssa. That fact took on a new significance when, instead of joining them as he'd expected, she remained rooted by the track, watching him warily. Only after several seconds did she break the awkward silence. "I thought you'd be inside by now."

"We were slow getting here." His sensory tears tingled as he tried to untangle the skeins of her mood. He could sense no animosity, but that wariness . . . where had it come from? He took a step toward her. Immediately he felt her tension rise, and he pulled back in surprise. "What's wrong?"

Her gaze cut to Urban, then back again, to settle on his wounded arms. "I don't like what happened the other night."

"You mean the rally?"

She nodded.

"It got a little crazy," he admitted.

"But it's not going to happen like that again," Urban quickly assured her.

Her doubt filled the air. "I wish I could believe that."

Lot turned his head slowly from side to side, trying to puzzle out her mood. "But you were there. You were having fun."

"I was caught up in your tide! Just like the ados— except I don't like being manipulated."

Manipulated? He didn't remember it that way. Emotion had been shared in the communal tide. He'd given up as much as he'd taken. Now her retreat left him feeling vulnerable. He wanted to smooth over her doubts, and quickly. He took another step toward her. This time she actually backed away. He pulled up again, astounded at her resistance. She'd felt so close the night of the rally. So open and sympathetic. How could that change?

"I'm not going to sign your petition," she said. "I wanted to let you know that."

Urban touched his back. "Come on, fury. I told you she was too real."

"No." Lot couldn't look away from her. She'd promised her help. She couldn't just walk away from that.

"Stop it, Lot," Yulyssa warned softly.

He let out a sharp breath, breaking eye contact as her tension rose yet another notch. Ord stirred restlessly under his hair.

"Listen," she said. "I'm sorry. But there's just so much we don't know. If Jupiter came out of the Hallowed Vasties—"

Lot grimaced. "If he did come out of the Vasties, he fled it, like everyone else on the frontier. He was scared too. He knew the cordons were failing."

Urban stepped forward indignantly. "Who cares where Jupiter came from? The cordons are a million years away. The Vasties don't have anything to do with us."

"Sooth," Lot said. "It's what I've told her."

"But you're only guessing," Yulyssa insisted. "You don't know what you are, or where you come from. We need to be cautious. Placid Antigua's breakdown was a warning sign. We're under pressure—"

"Sooth," Urban sneered. "And we don't need real people making decisions for us."

"We don't need Jupiter's ghost in charge of our decision making either. I'm sorry, Lot, but if there is a Chenzeme influence—"

"Yulyssa!"

His protest came too late. Urban had caught the reference. "What do you mean 'a Chenzeme influence'?" he asked.

Lot turned away, reluctant to explain, fearing how Urban might react. "It's just a stupid theory."

"A theory about what?"

"About Lot," Yulyssa said, watching him with suddenly playful eyes. "He didn't tell you? I guess he's more independent than I thought."

Briefly, Lot met Urban's suspicious gaze. "We'll talk about it later." Then, before Urban could ask questions, he set off toward authority's double doors, telling himself it really didn't mean anything, that Kona had said it just to rattle him.

The opaque doors opened and Kona himself was there, his expression carefully blank as he glanced over the scattered trio. "I've asked Yulyssa to be the public witness," he said.

Urban stepped up beside Lot. "So you'll broadcast this?"

"After the fact."

They followed Kona into a large chamber that opened onto four long, diamond-shaped rooms. The offices weren't labeled, but Lot knew the divisions: city environment, city security, space systems, and planetary security. Work stations lined the office walls, each with a large video pond over it, at least five feet by five. Below each dark pond were consoles outfitted with grips and data-entry systems. There were only a couple of officers in each room. No video ponds were in use. "Where is everybody?" Lot asked.

Kona chuckled. "You're not impressed?"

"I thought it'd be busier."

He shrugged. "We conduct oversight from here. Not much else. Our officers work through remote links. And DIs subsidize the systems. Security's been decentralized since that day."

Lot nodded, remembering the now-demolished control room where Captain Aceret had won command of the elevators. It would not be so easy again to seize a city function. "But the environmental systems are controlled from here?"

"Only for the industrial core. The city is self-regulated, operating on a feedback mechanism involving a decentralized network of DIs. The Old Silkens seemed to have mistrusted the idea of a central authority."

"But resource supply is handled from here?"

"It can be."

They passed the first office and entered the second. Kona introduced them to the commandant of wardens, a grim-faced man in a security uniform who did not seem pleased at the idea of sharing his post with ados. He took delight in telling them that almost no "activity" had been observed in the past twelve hours. "Yes, yes. Unusually quiet. You could be disappointed."

Lot exchanged a glance with Urban. "And what is it we're not likely to see?" Urban asked.

"Let's wait," Kona said. "I'd like your unbiased opinion." He turned to the commandant. "The wardens are in place?"

"Four have been convened, as you requested."

"How many do you run?" Lot asked.

The commandant glanced at Kona, who nodded permission. "We try to maintain some seven thousand, on all landmasses and a sampling in the oceans. The number fluctuates. They're not long-lived."

"Why not?"

The commandant didn't try to hide his condescension. "It's the Well. Nothing lasts there."

Lot snorted softly. "Everything lasts there." The Well was a genetic museum and the governors were its curators. But he let it go. "Are the wardens armed? Captain Antigua said—"

"It's a precaution," the commandant interrupted, his Adam's apple bobbing nervously in his throat. "The spray has never been used."

Lot's smile was cold. "At least not in the Well?"

Kona said, "Our security's being reevaluated. But we can discuss that later. Let's get started, and see what we can find."

They followed the commandant to a side room outfitted with crash couches. The room was dimly lit, the air colder than in the outer chamber. Ord slipped off Lot's shoulder and disappeared under a couch.

Kona got them bracelets from a sidewall. He tossed a set to Urban, then helped Lot slip the bands over his wrists and ankles. The bracelets were about an inch wide, slick and soft and semitransparent. As each contacted his skin, it unfurled, dissociating into hair-thin tendrils that slipped up his arms, under his casts, and onto his bare shoulders in a branching pattern designed to sense every twitch of his external musculature. The bands on his ankles similarly mapped his legs beneath his slacks, so that his motion could be translated by a DI to the warden he would link with in the Well.

In the Well: the reality of it finally hit him. Until now his mind had treated this venture as an abstract potential. Now the Well loomed as the central element in his mental landscape. He felt irresistibly drawn to it, frightened and exhilarated at once. He would not be there physically, no. But it would seem as if he were. Almost.

Kona lay back on a couch, indicating that Lot and Urban should do the same. Lot turned to look for Yulyssa. She hung back, lurking just outside the darkened chamber. "You're not coming?" he asked.

"I'll be watching over your shoulder."

"Have you seen it before?"

"No."

He nodded, and settled into a couch, carefully guarding his balance against the dead weight of his arms. The air's chill seemed concentrated in the chair's fabric, and the bare skin on his back puckered in instinctive protest.

"Ready?" Kona asked.

From somewhere to his right Urban answered in the affirmative. Lot did the same. Before he had the word fully out, a shield slid down over his face, wrapping him in darkness, muffling the sounds from the room. The darkness lasted for a heartbeat; then Lot found himself blinking in the muted light of a cold cloud forest.

For a moment he felt unbalanced. The forest seemed to lift and spin around him, and he had to fight against a sensation that he was falling over backward. But after a few seconds, his mind accepted an artificial center of gravity, and his perspective stabilized.

He looked down to discover himself balanced atop an arch. Further inspection proved the arch to be part of a tangled system of tree trunks rising in short jags and loops so that the whole structure had the appearance of having been flash-frozen in the midst of an octopus-crawl across the slope.

The vegetation seemed startlingly tall, until he realized the warden he occupied was diminutive, perhaps only two feet high at most. He looked down at tiny, fragile gray-green hands. He tried flexing them, and after a few fumbling attempts, he got them to close. His body had become an undetailed blank of humanoid shape, gray-green like the hands, suggesting a sculpture that had never been quite finished.

A misty rain fell from the heavily clouded skies, beading every leaf in glistening crystal drops. Animal sounds came from the slope behind them: a high chirping, repeated in beats of three. And once, a low rustle of disturbed vegetation.

Motion drew his eye to the right. Another warden stood beside him on the branch. It was hard to make out against the mottled background of leaf and bark. Still, Lot could discern its vague, fragile physiognomy. It had Urban's face, cast in gray and green. His short braids looked as if algae were growing in every depression.

Lot couldn't suppress a grin.

Urban's pseudolips twisted in a crooked smile. There

was no mouth behind them. They skated on a solid marble surface. "I couldn't look half as goofy as you, fury."

"You say so."

But Kona's voice interrupted them. "We're not here to admire one another."

Lot turned. Kona stood on his other side, his stern face like a bas-relief sculpture in marbled algae-wood. Beyond him, a fourth warden had assumed the commandant's disapproving air. It looked out, away from the slope, and Lot followed its gaze to discover below them a bowl-shaped valley. From ground to sky, like a fault in his visual system, a broad, gray band neatly bisected the vista. "That's the elevator cable!"

He studied the prospect. An overlay in his optic field informed him that the elevator column was some 1.5 miles distant. It was anchored on a black platform that filled the circular valley floor, looming at least a hundred feet above the tops of the nearest trees. He could see the dark lines of the vertical tracks on the column's gray face. Three tracks were visible from his position, though all were partly obscured by tufts of vegetation that had begun to grow on the structure. Almost hidden by the dark bellies of rain clouds, a single elevator car hung some twelve hundred feet above the terminal building. Lot felt a chill on his spine, wondering if that could have been Jupiter's car. Softly: "What happened that day?"

Kona said, "We don't know."

Urban hissed his doubt, and immediately the commandant rose to the defense. "It's true!" he insisted. "No one was monitoring the wardens that day. We had other things on our minds."

"But the wardens are guided by DIs—"

"Yes, and their experiences are recorded, and uploaded to authority, yes. But not that day. Not from this area. We found no records in the archives. When we investigated this region, we found no wardens."

"They'd apparently been disassembled," Kona said. "It's not unusual. It happens."

"Not like that," the commandant countered. "When they vanish, it's always one at a time. But not that day. We maintain a force of at least ten wardens in the vicinity of the elevator column. That day, every one of them vanished, in a radius of some eighty miles."

The frustration, the anger in his voice: it startled Lot. He'd believed for so long that authority *knew*.

But apparently, no one knew.

Except Jupiter?

"There was damage to the column too," Kona added softly. "We found minor pitting and scarring over the lowest half-mile. That's where the plants took root."

"That's right," the commandant agreed. "It seems Jupiter stirred up the wrath of the governors against all things human-made: the wardens, the column, and his holy self."

Lot grimaced at the sarcasm. "You're just guessing," he accused. "You don't know."

The warden shrugged. "It's just a good thing the column held together, or we'd all be in cold storage now, adrift a million miles from nowhere."

Lot let his gaze wander as the commandant talked. A broken mist swirled slowly through the valley, chased by brief rain showers. The land smelled wet, and full of the healthy rot of microscopic life. He found it beautiful, and did not want to believe that sinister, molecular-scale guardians lay everywhere beneath it.

A sudden hiss from Urban made him jump. "Shift your optics to long-range, fury."

"Yes, yes, there," the commandant muttered, pointing into the valley, toward the base of the elevator column. "Look there. It's what you came to see."

To the north of the terminal building, where the mist tumbled around the ruins of the road that led out of the valley, Lot thought he could see something moving. In the mist, it seemed to be a gray, nebulous shape, human in outline, but not in detail. Like the shadow of a man, rather than the man himself. Shifting. Shimmering as it walked slowly down the road, like a warden suffering a failed camouflage function, except it was far too big to be a warden. Measured against the road, it seemed to be fully man-sized. He sighted another off to the right of the first.

Then the mist thickened. The men—or whatever they had been—were no longer visible. But several seconds later he saw them again. Now there were three. They were a good hundred yards from their previous position, near the trees that crowded the periphery of the roadway. The forest seemed to pour mist out across the open road. Soon, the images were obscured once more.

But in the brief time the apparitions had been visible, they had seemed to be gazing directly at Lot.

"We call them phantoms," Kona said, with a note of grim satisfaction in his voice. "You can see they're not human. It's a phenomenon only, that has nothing to do with Jupiter."

"But what is it?" Urban insisted. "What creates it?"

"No, no, we don't know that," the commandant said. "It's unknown—like the rest of this poisonous world."

"A phenomenon," Kona said again, as if by repetition he could force some standard of meaning on the word. "It registers faintly in the infrared, but it doesn't seem to have any solid physical structure. It may be a projection. It lasts for only a few minutes at most, and doesn't generate or respond to radio frequencies."

Urban moved up close beside Lot. "Do you know what it is, fury?" he asked. "Do you recognize them?"

Lot looked at him in sharp surprise. "No! I don't know." His own defensiveness startled him. "You think . . . this is what happened to them?" He shook his head. "No, it wasn't supposed to be like this. . . ." His voice trailed off. In truth, he didn't know anything. Jupiter had never really said what life would be like in the Well. He'd talked about the mitochondrial analog, two life-forms blending into one. He'd said there'd be harmony. An infinite union. Nirvana. Words as vague as the faces on the phantoms.

Lot stared at the drifting fog, willing it to move off so he could see the old roadway once more. Surely for every phenomenon there must be an explanation awaiting discovery. "Let's get closer."

With instructions from the commandant, he switched to observer status, allowing the warden's resident Dull Intelligence to assume motor function. Under the DI's guidance, the little warden slipped through the bedewed vegetation, as quick and quiet as any small jungle creature. It ducked around several large mounds of upthrust soil, and in less than six minutes he was on the old roadway—but the phantoms were gone.

Twenty minutes later Urban stood in the rain, shaking his head in frustration. "No scent trails. No footprints."

Lot tramped in a slow circle just off the roadway, watching the warden's tiny feet. They left almost no impression in the spongy mulch of leaves and rotting bark that carpeted the ground beneath the trees.

"If they're projections, then what's producing them?" Urban asked, of no one in particular.

The commandant shrugged.

Lot pressed his warden toes into the cold humus. "How long has this been going on?"

Kona answered—too quickly. "Not quite a year."

Lot gave him a sharp look, but could read nothing in the warden's marbled interpretation of his face. Still, he sensed some unspoken factor.

Urban asked, "Have you tried to identify the images as individuals? Do they match any data in city records?"

"No, no," the commandant said. "The resolution is too poor."

Urban crouched on the road bed, his gaze following its rise out of the valley. "This has to be something left from Old Silk. After all, the elevator column's still here. It's possible some other branch of their technology survived too."

"No." The commandant shook his head. "The wardens have been in this valley two hundred fifty years. If there was something here, they would have found it."

Later, they sat on the white carpet in Kona's apartment, sunlight falling around them while they drank beer and talked about the Well. Kona waved his hand, indicating the sprawling planet beyond the city's horizon. "This land . . . it's the most valuable thing in the system," he told them, "if only it could be made livable."

Lot stared at the golden bubbles rising in his beer. Though his fingers were steadily gaining strength, he didn't trust himself to hold the glass. So Urban had dropped a straw into it. Bubbles clung to the straw, huddling together on the column like refugees. No one alive today in Silk had ever intended to make this city their home. He shook off the thought, and forced himself to look at Kona. "Could you do that?" he asked. "Could you subdue the governors and make the Well livable?"

"Maybe. We need to move slowly. We need to look at all options. You understand?"

"I don't know." Though Kona seemed open, and ready to include them both in his deliberations, still Lot sensed something had been left unsaid.

"Try," Kona said. "We're facing difficult decisions. I

won't pretend I wanted you to be part of the decision-making process, but you are, and that means you have a responsibility to act in the best interest of the people—all the people. You could help hold us all together, Lot, or you could plunge this city into chaos."

Urban scowled. "Nobody wants that. All we're asking for is a vote, a voice. You could help us get it. Daddy?"

Kona stretched, cleansing his body with a long sigh. "I'll do what I can, Urban. All right? No promises. But I'll do what I can."

Chapter
15

"The official estimate is out today," the mediot said, his smile faint, his mood somber. "Authority predicts we have eight months, at current levels of use, before shortages become evident. Do you have any comment on that?"

"Eight months?" Lot echoed the mediot's question. It startled him to hear their remaining time summed in concrete measure. Eight months. He glanced at the faces of the watching ado pack. Camera bees buzzed over the blooming azalea bushes in Splendid Peace. Already, the ritual of the interview seemed old to him. He'd been through so many. Over the last nine days he'd become the nominal leader of a significant political party, though nearly all his supporters lacked voting rights. That would change with tomorrow's election. Urban's initiatives had easily gathered the signatures necessary to appear on the ballot. It was only a matter of time.

"Eight months will be enough," Lot said in a confident voice that called on people to sit up and listen, "if we work together. If we give an equal voice to all. If the distinction between ados and real people is forgotten. We'll find a consensus."

"You're confident the election tomorrow will give you the vote?"

Lot smiled. "Not me personally. I won't be twenty

for two more years." A ripple of laughter ran through the quiet ados. "But for many people in this city, yes. In the past, it's sometimes been forgotten that real people and ados are *not* different species. We're the same. The real people know that, and they'll remember it tomorrow when they vote."

Back in the refugee quarter, Lot stepped up to Alta's apartment door for the ninth time in as many days. Her majordomo acknowledged him. "Greetings, Master Lot Apolinario."

"Alta, may I see you?" he asked the door's blank face. "I would very much like to see you." He waited, but for the ninth time in as many days, she refused to answer him. She had not stirred from her apartment since learning of her mother's death. Lot had sent Urban to talk to her, but she wouldn't acknowledge him either. Gent had seen her, but he revealed no details of their conversations, saying only that she was grieving, but rational, give her time.

Lot could not bring himself to do it. Every afternoon he slipped loose from the ado packs and came alone to her door. He could not say exactly why. Part of it felt like love. She'd gotten inside him that day in the tunnel. He felt bonded to her and in consequence he desired to see her, care for her, share her grief and her joy. But love was an easy and nonexclusive emotion for him. He felt similar things for other girls in a shifting, adolescent version of Jupiter's own group marriage.

If it were only love he could step away. But his hurt was more complex than that. He'd felt the silvery touch of her faith the night of the rally. Her belief had ignited the crowd. The loss of that belief felt like a chink in the silver armor of his influence, a weakness that could grow like rot if he didn't patch it quickly. He leaned against her door for several minutes, considering. "Alta, please talk to me." The door remained stubbornly closed, the majordomo silent. Finally he sighed and straightened. "I'll come back tomorrow." But the election was tomorrow. Perhaps he wouldn't have time. "I'll try to come back tomorrow," he amended. He took a step away; but then he turned back. "I'm sorry for your mama, Alta. I never desired for Captain Antigua to come to any harm. It was an accident." He pressed his palm against her door, striving to see her, to sense her beyond the opaque barrier. "I wish that you would forgive me."

He waited several seconds, but the door remained stubbornly closed. He turned away again, feeling stupid. She'd probably switched off the majordomo's audio pickups as soon as he'd shown up, leaving him to talk to an insensate door. Great cult leader, oh yeah.

Gent waited in the street outside. Lot met him with a cursory nod, still distracted by his failure with Alta. "I have an appointment," Lot told him.

"Where?"

"Library."

"You've been spending many hours at that."

"Sooth." The election's persistent questions had awakened Lot to his own ignorance. He'd been profoundly shocked at the scope of it. "Authority says we only have eight months."

"More time than we need, I think."

Yulyssa's story about the phantoms had swept the city, creating a special stir in the refugee quarter. Gent would not account them yet as evidence of the Communion, but many in the quarter did.

They fell into step with one another, leaving the walled refugee quarter via the narrow lane that wound through the neighborhood of Nine Turnings. Here the small apartment buildings had rounded prows that seemed to push the lane into a sharp sine wave. Ancient tulip trees shaded the streets, their branches twining overhead, huge orange flowers catching the sunlight so that it seemed as if they walked under a winding river of fire.

Gent broke the silence. "Let me hear you say Jupiter's name."

"What?" Lot looked at him, abruptly conscious of the discordant tone of Gent's mood. "Why?"

"You haven't said his name in days."

Lot felt himself flush. "Gent—"

"Jupiter's name is not forbidden, and it's not profane." There was judgment in his voice.

Lot sought to defuse that. Softly: "That's not what this election's about."

"If you'll forgive me, sir, that's a polite lie."

"Gent!" Lot stopped in the street, a hot point of panic suddenly awake in his belly. If he couldn't hold Alta, if he couldn't even hold Gent, how could he expect to convince more than a handful of real people to vote for the initiatives?

Gent watched him closely. "Have you abandoned him?"

"No! You know that's not possible."

"But you doubt him."

Lot stiffened. "I have questions," he admitted.

Gent nodded somberly. He started walking again. Lot leaped after him. "I do believe in him! I intend to follow him someday."

Gent's eyebrows rose in mock surprise. "Do you?"

Lot stopped again. A camera bee buzzed into sight. It glinted metallic orange, reflecting the color of the flowers overhead. Lot watched it slow, seeking the best camera angle. "Go on!" he shouted at it. "Leave me alone."

The city's privacy laws required the mediot to obey. Gent watched the bee until it was out of sight. Then he spoke. "The Silkens like you, Lot. They say you have a pleasant aspect. But they don't trust you."

Lot could feel miserable truth descend around him. The campaign had been going well; he'd had some confidence. But now: "You think we're going to lose the election."

Gent shrugged. "If you do, it'll be because you're supporting a lie."

"*What lie?* Gent, all we're asking for is to vote."

"That's a surface issue. You're asking the Silkens to accept *you*—by denying Jupiter."

He winced. Miserable truth indeed. "*Sooth,*" he whispered, his arms stiff at his sides. "But what else can I do? They're afraid of him."

Gent shook his head. "You're the one who fears him. You'll never recover your faith by foraging through the library. Everything you need to know, you'll learn in the Well."

Lot considered that, then smiled. "You know, it's a bit easier to get to the library then to get to the Well . . . unless you've convinced the Silkens to allow us down?"

"You don't need permission. You could go there now."

Lot stepped back, stunned at this pronouncement. He sought some hint of deceit, but found none. Gent crossed his arms over his broad chest and nodded. "I could take you to the Well. I've been ready for a long time."

"But . . . *how*?"

"Silken security is naive, at best."

"I don't understand. If you have the means, why haven't you—"

Gent's patience snapped. "Our people are still here! You're still here."

Lot turned away, thinking, *I'm not ready for this.* The orange light around him seemed garish and hot. "I'm going to the library." He started again up the lane. "We'll talk about this later."

"Later. Sure, Lot. There's time."

The library was a place of ados. It had been inherited from Old Silk, whose people had used no atriums, living as detached from the city's information flow as modern youth. Constant access or accessibility had not been important to them—though neither had they cherished isolation. Their city had been designed with myriad social centers, the library being one of the most frequented.

It was a vast, half-round building that seemed to shore up the grand walk as it stepped down the city's slope in three neat levels. Lot crossed the first enclosed courtyard. Here the afternoon light was softened by the lush green leaves and pale blossoms of the white garden: roses, bougainvillea, jasmine, lilies, salvia, protea, and a host of others, all in milky monochrome. Flower scents mixed with the lusher smells of the cabana restaurants where ados clustered in knots of small talk. Lot slipped past them, out of the sunlight and into the calmly lit lobby. From the corner of his eye he saw the gold flash of Ord's small body, following him inside.

The lobby was crescent-shaped, at least a hundred yards from end to end, with a vaulted ceiling that soared some forty feet overhead. Aside from the glass entry, stacked shelves lined the walls, each supporting a swarm of hanging racks and boxes for storage of original works in degradable media. He crossed the ruby carpet, threading a path around clusters of couches and arm chairs, nearly all of them occupied. He slowed, his gaze scanning the patrons, all the while responding with unconscious grace to the soft greetings, the glances that ever marked his progress. Perhaps one in five of those present seemed real.

Why had they come here?

The library's resources could be accessed through their atriums from any point in the city. Had something else drawn them, then? A need for community . . .

Ord tapped his hand. Lot smiled at the little robot, then hefted it up so it could climb onto his shoulders. He presented himself at the librarian's station and was greeted by a guiding bee that hummed ahead of him, leading him through the tangled caverns beyond the lobby. Archival access booths hung at short though uneven intervals on the wending, intersecting maze of corridors, the whole laid out in the common chaotic fashion of Old Silk, as if that people had some deep fear of order, or predictability, of efficiency or the dictates of a central authority. Within seconds Lot knew he was hopelessly lost. But the bee plowed on, leading him finally to the black membranous door of a booth isolated at the end of a short cul-de-sac.

He pushed his way through the forgiving membrane. "Yulyssa?"

The room on the other side was dimly lit, the gray walls shimmering faintly, like stone in ring light, an impression that deepened and grew in detail until he felt himself to be in a walled garden, with vines crawling over the stonework and the dark bulk of a tree looming overhead, silhouetted against the backdrop of the nebula, while the glow of the swan burster filtered through its leaves. Yulyssa manifested then, as part of the holographic display. She sat cross-legged on a wooden bench, her antique diamond clips winking in her black hair.

Lot felt a sudden dark rush of disappointment. "I'd hoped you'd be real."

Her smile seemed apologetic, though he couldn't be sure. The projection failed to replicate the breath of her emotive mood—a minor flaw in the senses of most, but for Lot it felt like an amputation. "It's better this way," she said. "I can access library systems much faster."

"And besides, you don't want to be near me."

She sighed. "No, that is *not* true. But as we agreed once before, I'm old enough to know better."

Unhappily, he nudged a wooden armchair with his foot, and when it proved solid he sat down in it. Ord slid off his shoulders, dropping softly to the ground. He remembered his manners at last and said, "Thank you for coming."

"I hope I can help."

Crickets chirped in the rampant shrubbery. In the cool, nocturnal setting, intimacy should have been easy—would have been, if she were real. "I've been wondering," he asked hesitantly, "what happened a year ago? Kona said the phantoms first started appearing then. Why? Did anything significant occur, that might have inspired it? The librarian helped me search the archives, but I've found nothing in the public files."

She frowned. "Secure files aren't within my reach . . . but I can petition the council for you."

"I'd hoped you would."

Her diamond clips glittered with the slight movement of her head. "That's done. And next?"

"I've been thinking about Old Silk. Who were the people who built this city? Why did they die?"

"But that's well documented. Their own histories say they came to study the swan burster. . . ."

"There's history, all right. But little interpretation."

"Oh." She leaned back, her gaze seeking the thin light of the projected nebula. "You're after reason, not mechanism."

"Both, I guess."

"Their death is documented."

"Though not at all understood. We blame the governors and pretend that explains it." He could see uneasiness on her face, but it didn't move him. He felt isolated. Sealed away from the resonant influence of human presence, he felt as if his emotions were slowly settling over the base of his brain in nonreactive layers, leaving his cerebrum unencumbered, slick with a machinelike efficiency. "The Old Silkens lived freely on the planet for ten years, without incident. They must have felt themselves safe." He watched Yulyssa closely. "Now Kona wants to make the planet 'livable.' How? If he can't dominate the governors, how could he ever be sure we were safe?"

She nodded slowly. "You're fearing a new plague might arise, even after decades."

"No. I only wonder what method Kona would use to insure that couldn't happen."

She closed her eyes. "All right. The librarian is searching for suggestions."

"I've done that already."

Her dark eyes opened. "I can't access closed files."

And neither could any of Gent's nameless Silken friends. Lot frowned, struggling to put the right flavor on his words. "I thought you might know someone. . . ."

Her sharp gaze cut him off. "I won't violate council security for you, Lot."

He nodded and looked away, a flush warming his cheeks. His dignity seemed destined for repeated trampling this afternoon.

"Next?" Yulyssa's gaze did not soften.

Lot swallowed his misgivings, groping to express a line of thought that had puzzled him for days now. "The great ship that brought us here: her name was Nesseleth."

"Yes."

Childhood recollections encumbered him: the tight corridors, the close, sweet scent of a child's sweat, soft sounds of lovemaking in the night, and the voice of the stream in Jupiter's garden. Nesseleth had been his playmate, the projection of a pretty little girl, just his age. It had been her delight to show him secret places, and to share with him memories from her own youth on a world that was now gone, its mass broken and transformed into one of the swarming cordons of the Hallowed Vasties. "Nesseleth was human once."

"Sooth. That's the way of great ships."

"She died for him, you know. She didn't go down because of accident or sabotage. She did it to herself, at his request. So none of us could back out."

Yulyssa's face paled. She didn't answer.

Lot felt an inexplicable stirring of anger. "That was a very human thing to do, don't you think?"

"Lot—"

"Sorry," he said swiftly, and out of habit he averted his gaze, though of course the charismata couldn't affect her image. "Really, I'm thinking of Sypaon."

"The great ship of the Old Silkens?"

"Sooth. The librarian says she created this city, using her own body as the seed." Sypaon had become the city. She would have existed within it, as he existed within his own body . . . at least for a time. "She wouldn't have been susceptible to the plague that killed her people. So what became of her?"

Yulyssa sighed. In the cool glint of the ring light, her

expression seemed infinitely sad. "Her people . . . they must have been like children to her. It's cruel, to ask a mother to survive that."

Lot marveled at his cool reaction. He could not be drawn in by the synthetic pain of a projection. He told her, "Sypaon might not have been such a loving mother. She seems to have left the city at least a year before the plague hit. At least, there's no record of her in the library after that."

Yulyssa looked up in surprise. "No?" Her expression blanked, as she accessed her atrium.

Lot laid his central question across her questing silence: "Where could she have gone?"

"Perhaps another great ship came by—"

His brows rose at that speculative response. "And she joined with it? Two entities in one body?"

"I suppose it's not likely."

"No record of any visitors, anyway." His fingers tapped thoughtfully on the arm of his chair. "She made the city to run without consciousness." He looked up at Yulyssa. "That was why it was alive and still habitable when you came here."

Yulyssa nodded a slow yes, her gaze distant, remembering. "The parks and streets were overgrown. Everything so lush. The air was good."

"Could a great ship exist without consciousness?"

She frowned. "A great ship is active. It must navigate and forage, balance its environment, plan for lean times, and the appearance of Chenzeme weapons, negotiate with its human complement, and seek out others . . . like itself. . . . In short, the analog of a motile animal."

"And by contrast, this city is sessile."

"Yes," Yulyssa said. "Like a plant, anchored in one place, drawing energy from the sun, a constant source. And protected from the Chenzeme by the Well . . . ?"

Lot shrugged. "We do know the city's internal systems were designed to operate by feedback mechanisms, with no need for an overseer, no central control."

She nodded, cautiously following the thought. "And there was no need to forage for resources. Sypaon must have planned for the city to draw up all that it needed from its roots in the Well. . . . So, Sypaon *intended* to leave—that's what you're saying."

"I'm asking: Where did she go?"

Personas were often transferred from one substrate to another. Real people did that when they ghosted, gifting copies of themselves to dwell in the atrium of another. Yulyssa spoke to him now as an independent copy of her original persona, residing within the machinery of the archival booth. The great ship that had been Sypaon's body must have re-ceived her original persona in the same way. Sypaon had been a sculpted entity. Not a natural creature, but an electronic ghost that haunted the body of the great ship. He knew of no reason that would force her to remain in that body, if she had another place to go. . . .

"You think there's a structure on the planet," Yulyssa said.

Lot started. "No. I hadn't thought about that. There's no evidence for it?"

"No," Yulyssa admitted. "Still, we don't know the planet well."

"The commandant of wardens would disagree with you."

Yulyssa frowned. "You have another idea."

Lot nodded. "The Old Silkens came here to study the swan burster. Sypaon was supposed to be a great engineer, and very curious."

"The ring's not even a human artifact. She couldn't have found a proper substrate there. And besides, the ring's quiescent."

He cocked his head. "But what can we really con-clude from that?"

She glanced nervously at the milky sky. The swan burster was hidden behind the overarching tree, but its light spilled like lace across the garden. An anxious smile flitted across her face. "We can conclude it has not killed us . . . yet. Oh Lot, you can't seriously think—"

He snorted. "Sure, I'm slow."

"Oh, stop it."

He shrugged. "Sypaon built this city, intending to abandon it. She had to have some place in mind to go. And the records are clear as to why she came—she wanted to investigate the ring."

"That was over five hundred years ago."

"You've lived that long. What does time mean to a sculpted entity?"

She sighed uncertainly. "I don't know. Do you really think she's still there?"

He leaned back, his hands clasped behind his head. "You should ask Kona."

"I will."

He straightened. "I've been thinking about that day. Captain Aceret sent me to crawl through the air ducts. Our advance troops were trapped behind a sealed door. Their assault Makers wouldn't work against it."

He started at Yulyssa's sharp intake of breath. "They used assault Makers?"

He looked at her in dull surprise. Could such a prominent fact remain unknown? But then Captain Antigua had been the only surviving officer. She might have kept quiet, seeing no advantage in promoting an image of brutality. And the regular troopers had probably never known. "The point is, the assault Makers failed to function. Why?"

"City authority must have neutralized them—"

"I don't think so. Authority wasn't ready for us. They had access to assault Makers—sooth, the wardens are armed with them. But they didn't use that against us."

She seemed puzzled. "What are you saying?"

"I'm not sure. But *something* stopped our assault Makers. And long ago, something stopped the Chenzeme ring." He shook his head, trying to define his nascent suspicions. "We all know the Well has its own molecular defenses. The governors cause things to fail in the Well." He held her in his stare, willing her to see the same connection. "But things fail here too. And even as far out as the swan burster. I have to wonder if the enemy we're hiding from isn't living in our midst."

That drew from her a patient smile. "If that were so, Lot, don't you think we would have noticed?"

"I think we have."

Her smile faltered. "You mean the city gnomes. But they're harmless. They're almost extinct."

"For all we know, the city gnomes are governors too."

She shook her head. "If that were true, we'd all be dead."

"You don't know that. Jupiter survived the Well. And the Old Silkens lived with the governors for ten years—"

"Before they died."

"Yes. We need to know why they died."

The room slowly darkened, as the ring made its roll from zero to one. "You want to go down there, don't you?"

"We don't really have a choice. So I want to know what's there before we have to go."

That actually made her laugh. "Oh ho! That's something Jupiter never would have bothered with."

He felt mortified at that response. Like Gent, she *knew* how shallow his faith was. Could everyone see it in him? Still, he tried to defend himself. "I just want to be cautious, that's all. . . ."

"It's all right. If you're different from him . . ."

"I believe in him, Yulyssa. I do." And maybe if he said it enough, he could convince himself. "We belong to him."

"No, that isn't true, Lot. No one owns you."

"It doesn't really matter. Yulyssa, don't you see? The Well reached out across open space to take the swan burster. It reached up the column of the elevator to take the Old Silkens. It defeated our assault Makers only ten years ago, so we know it's still here, in the city. And Jupiter's part of it now. Don't think he's forgotten us. He'll take us if he can."

Chapter
16

He sat in the darkened room, several minutes after Yulyssa's ghost had departed. Ord hung motionless in a corner, like a giant spider perched within the reaching branches of the projected tree. Gradually, Lot's body began to accept the evidence of evening. He could feel his metabolism pick up—a half-nocturnal creature, always at his most active in the dark hours before midnight. In the cool air the only emotional scent was that of his own cold concentration. He breathed that in, amplifying his intellectual focus in a cascading feedback reaction.

He tried to move beyond the sticky web of questions that encumbered his mind. He sought to visualize himself one year into the future. Who would he be then? What would the city be like? Only a year. He could not make himself see the disaster predicted by all reasonable studies. In the long run, he had to believe there would be options. . . .

He stiffened, suddenly aware that the quality of light within the room had changed. A dark shadow had appeared, pouring from a hole in the garden wall. It flowed across the masonry, eclipsing the reflected, silvery glow of ring light. It flooded the sky, extinguishing the milky wash of the nebula. It swept around and between the complex shapes of shrubs and trees, erasing their forms like black ink poured over a painting, before it finally swept the patio stones at his feet, replacing substance with black emptiness. The chair disappeared beneath him, and for a disorienting moment he imagined himself falling. Quickly, he let his assumptions go. Dropped his expectations so that this new environment could freely write its own definition in his mind. In another moment the garden had vanished entirely and he felt himself floating in undimensioned darkness. Fantastic illusion. His body seemed to drift like a camera bee, a pinpoint observer in a nonexistent world. Ord had become a dim companion object visible only in the infrared.

Then a faint, three-dimensional silver patterning began to emerge from the darkness, as if the vanished ring light would reassert itself within the chinks and flaws of this unworld. At first Lot could see the silver presence only from the corner of his eye: a dimly glowing net. None of his enhancements could bring the image into better resolution. Only time could accomplish that. Gradually, the silvery pattern brightened until it was revealed as a working field of innumerable tiny, interlocking barbs, myriad tool shapes seizing and clutching at one another, at many others, tugging, twisting, reshaping and reordering a delicate silver mesh of tiny parts . . . like the mural in Kona's apartment and in the monkey house, except it didn't exist on only one surface, but instead surrounded him, embedding him within the depths of its structure.

The taste of the air changed. Humidity rolled across him, the moisture acting as a vehicle for a complex sensual array. Abruptly, he felt himself immersed in a stew of communicative emotional states, more complex, more detailed than he'd ever experienced before, like a crowd-buzz conversation of the senses, except that every inhabitant of the crowd spoke the same words, in the same order, only slightly out of sync with one another so that Lot's first impression was of chaos, but after that he swiftly began to discern a repeated and coherent sense of curiosity.

Speak to me.

He did not hear the words, yet he had them in his mind. "Who are you?" he asked, too startled to be afraid. ". . . Jupiter?"

The shivering machinework vibrated, flexed, pulled. It began to move past him in a slow, continuous stream, washing him with its substance until he felt coated with silver, a mineral being, the focused eye of a mob, briefly parting the current, only to have the silver stream close in again behind him.

The flavor changed: he sensed temptation. The current's speed increased. Velocity blurred the interlinking barbs into an undifferentiated flow. *Trust me.*

This was not Jupiter. It could not be. There was no real taste of him here, none of the tidal pressure of his compelling presence. And yet a vague sense of familiarity tugged at Lot. "Who are you?" he insisted. "Explain yourself. Now."

This brash demand solicited a wash of amusement. Lot felt it clearly. He had to smile in return. This game intrigued him. Who could have written this silent conversation? Who besides Jupiter? Evoked in the mood language of crowds. It was his own private language. In the city, he alone was conscious at this level.

He felt his silvered body extended far into the current. Details washed over him, and gradually, he grew aware of an unsettling strangeness layered within the human emotive pattern. An alien accent that he was shocked to find already within his memory. "Tell me who you are," he urged.

But the answer that reached him was only more amusement: *Guess.*

Okay. He did not think it could be Yulyssa. She didn't know him well enough to speak to him this way. Dr. Alloin, then? With her belittling pharmacy? He could not imagine Dr. Alloin playing frivolous games. He noticed Ord in the slow flow, its body disrupting the current like an insoluble stone.

"Ord?" he asked softly. "What do you think?"

The little robot seemed to come awake suddenly, snapping over in the current. "Psychoactive viruses line the chamber walls. They are producing olfactory elements."

"Slick."

"Bad," Ord countered. But it seemed oddly lethargic, and did not elaborate on this moral judgment.

Now the speed of the steam flow began to slow—no. Somehow his perspective had changed, and it was himself that swept like the point of a needle through the silver matrix so that his stomach clenched at his own perceived deceleration . . . now he moved only slowly against the flow. Once again he could perceive some of the frantic workings of the barbed network, and a presence. . . .

He caught her female scent a moment before he discerned her body. She surrounded him, carrying him through the current. He existed inside her . . . if she could be said to have an inside. Her body was not human, not silver-solid like his but like a woven net instead, or like beaded lace, each bead a mouth emitting a babble of scents, so that every part of her seemed to talk in chemical whispers: her feet, her calves, her thighs, hips, buttocks, belly, breasts, shoulders, back. Her face too.

He gazed at her face from behind her eyes, as if he were seeing a holographic surface from the wrong side. Her mouth seemed beaded of hundreds of tiny mouths; her eyes the same. Sketched lines of speaking mouths linked her features together, drawing a hollow suggestion of a woman, every part of her breathing incoherent histories that impacted his sensory tears, inspiring odd flashes of imagery in his mind: the swan burster aglow with a terrible white light that burns his retina; and himself, part of the ring, a mindless spark in a fascist rally, pulled to the will of all those other cells around him; and above him, blackened worlds; radio communications howling past him in languages that don't even inspire his curiosity, signals that abruptly cut out; in the void, a sexual merger as alien cells infest the familiar matrix, intoxicating in their diversity, he must sink inside of the other, watch his worldview shred as his assumptions fail the test of her experiences, he will become something new. . . .

"Sypaon?" he whispered.

Her mouth (linked chains of tiny mouths) smiled. Thousands of lips parted, to speak in brief synchrony: *The ring light coats you*—a burst of tiny voices—*you see it even when the ring is in eclipse.*

"Sometimes," he admitted, stretching slowly against a skin of silver armor so like the silver glow of the swan burster . . . the silver flow of Sypaon's current? He could feel a sense of discord from the matrix, and a swift soothing coo from Sypaon that closed off the discontent. "This flow," he said, "it's endless because we're moving in a circle, right? We circle the ring."

The cells are ever restless. They have their own opinions, and the aggressive ones must be soothed . . . though they all were made with a contempt for complacency. In a war, one must always change.

He shook his head, not understanding. Around him, Sypaon bestowed calm and patience and concord on the matrix, closing off dissent like a zipper forever sealing a rent in an otherwise harmonious fabric, around and around the ring we go. . . . How many circuits had she accomplished in five hundred years? She had an alien accent, and it reminded him of Jupiter.

Speak of it, Sypaon urged. *The Chenzeme influence. Where did you get it?*

Lot shuddered, gazing at his silvered hand while the current swept past them, a seemingly infinite river of dissent that Sypaon somehow knit into consensus.

We both perceive with the neural patterns of the Chenzeme, she insisted.

"No! I'm not like you."

But he lost the thought as her will flowed through him, soothing him, just as she soothed the cells embedded in the matrix . . . each one of them a node of dissent? of thought? consensus mind.

. . . we never want to change, she mused. *Who made you?*

He shook his head, wanting to back away but not knowing how.

Speak of it: Were you made to subvert the Chenzeme? Or have you been aimed at us?

"Neither!" His fist flared brilliant silver. "It's not like that. We came out of the Hallowed Vasties."

She closed around him again, calming him. *Aggressive cell,* she whispered. *Don't fire. Don't fire. I remember that time.*

He hesitated. What did she remember? "Sypaon . . . what happened to your people?"

Brief confusion spilled from her mouths. He could feel a flaw in her will, but it healed quickly. *So very young. You don't remember when I brought our people here. I've been away too long.*

Our people? Did she even know what had happened? Hesitantly, he asked, "When was it you left us?"

A twinge of guilt flowed from her mouths. *A few years, no? I've been distracted. Time is . . . hard to hold on to here. Oh, but it's not a reason to be sad. . . . Child? Why do you feel this way?*

If she didn't know, he wouldn't tell her.

She seemed apologetic. *The ring is my body now, and human thoughts are alien, very difficult to grasp.*

"What have you learned?"

That made her laugh, her multiple mouths all shaping different licentious expressions. *Evil. I've learned to destroy whole worlds, little child. I am one with the old murderers now. . . . Oh no, don't be sad for me. War is change. I am a weapon in the hands of my people. For the first time, I can protect you. All of you. I love my children. All of them.*

"I know you do, Sypaon."

Then convince them that it's right.

"What?"

But she was gone, the silver matrix washed out under a flood of blank daylight. The library's director stood looking in the open door, frowning at Lot as if he suspected the equipment had somehow been misused. "What's that smell?" he asked, wrinkling his nose.

Lot shook his head, squinting against the sudden glare.

"Well, anyway, they want you at city authority."

"Who?"

The director shrugged, examining the blank walls with a suspicious air. "Were you in here all night?" He sniffed distastefully. "This chamber will have to be cleaned. An hour of downtime, at least. Go on. Go on now. Or they'll be blaming me for not delivering the message."

Lot got slowly to his feet, every muscle wincing in pain. He felt suddenly famished, light-headed and none too stable on his feet. But he tried to hide that from the critical eye of the director. He was halfway through the door when the director scowled again. "Your personal attendant: you aren't going to leave it here, are you?"

Lot glanced back into the chamber. Ord still clung to a ceiling corner, motionless, and apparently unaware. "Ord," Lot said in soft concern. "I'm going."

A visible shudder ran through the robot's golden body. Then it dropped to the floor and scuttled toward Lot, muttering, *"Bad, bad, bad."*

Lot held out a hand to it, and Ord crawled quickly up his arm and under his hair. A soft tentacle patted at his cheek, and as he followed the director out of the tangled passages Ord whispered: *"Good Lot needs to eat; good Lot needs to sleep; what happened, Lot? No good."*

Chapter
17

He emerged from the dim interior of the library into air
that tasted cool and moist, scrubbed clean of emotion.
Kheth roved below the city's horizon, its honey rays
leaping up the prim slope to touch his face with a soft heat—
igniting unexpectedly a doubtful inner voice . . . for didn't
the library face the eastern sky?

Lot stopped short in stunned surprise as he realized
he'd stepped out into morning. But how could it be morning?
He'd entered the library in the afternoon. He could not have
been with Sypaon all night. "Ord," he called softly, trying to
ignore a sudden sense of dissociation. "What time is it?"

Camera bees swooped past as Ord consulted its internal clock. "No sleep. No good," Ord mumbled. "No record of night."

The courtyard outside the library was strangely deserted, the kiosks closed. But then he remembered: it was
Founding Day, the anniversary of the Silkens' arrival in the
city. They would be with their families.

"Messages," Ord said. "Lot is called to city authority."

"I heard."

"Lot must eat."

A good suggestion. He considered for a moment,
then headed for the grand walk. A handful of camera bees

followed, though he didn't see any people . . . not even when he mounted the broad stairs above the library and stepped out onto the walk itself. He gazed at the wide, empty expanse, wrestling with a sense of disbelief. Even on Founding Day, there should be people here. The camera bees recorded his reaction. He eyed them, suddenly wary.

"Lot is called to city authority," Ord reminded softly.

"What's happening?" Lot whispered.

Ord took an extra moment to answer: "A demonstration test has been scheduled. The event is accorded extremely high importance by media ratings."

"A demonstration?" A chill slipped down his spine. . . . *Convince them that it's right.* Suddenly, he thought he understood Sypaon's admonition. "They're going to activate the ring, aren't they? They're going to use it against the planet." That was the secret Kona had held to himself. How to make the Well safe? Sterilize it with the same type of Chenzeme weapon that had destroyed the Silkens' home world. It had a grim symmetry to it; a ruthless balance. But it caught in Lot's throat. "Jupiter's down there. And the Communion. . . ." Would the Silkens really sterilize the Well? Without ever understanding it. . . .

Hastily, he squinted past Kheth's glare, then turned, to examine the translucent blue arch of the city's canopy. But he couldn't see the ring. "How could Sypaon *do* it?" he shouted at Ord. "When her people might still be down there." *In some form.*

But then he realized: Sypaon couldn't know about the phantoms; she believed the *modern* Silkens were her people.

Panic slipped under his skin. The Well was a living entity, supple and adaptive and ever-vulnerable in its willingness to receive the other.

It must not be attacked.

The thought came to him with the force of revelation, firing him to action. At a flat-out run he took off for the nearest transit station, determined to do what he could to stop the assault.

He found a car waiting beside the platform. For him? Kona would know where he was.

Maybe Kona had sent Sypaon to beguile him.
Crazy.

The car door slid open.

"Lot wait!"

"Alta?" He turned, to see her rushing breathlessly into the transit station.

She ran to him, catching his arms, spinning around him to slow herself. "Where *were* you?" she demanded. There was impatience in her aura, and deep anger, and something else too . . . *shame?* "We've been looking for you all night. Urban and David and I. Gent too, but he was trapped in the quarter when the gates were closed. I was supposed to go back. They told me to go back, but I didn't. They wouldn't tell us where you were. Do you know what they're going to do?"

"Yeah. They'll try to fire the ring."

"The Well is our world, Lot. You have to make them stop."

The horizons of her face were frosted with a dim silver glow. He touched her cheek, getting some of the glitter on his own fingers.

She caught his hand, pressing it against her face, and suddenly he felt himself drawn down into a well of shame— her shame, though for a moment it was so intense he wasn't sure. She said, "I'm sorry for what Mama tried to do to you. Something happened to her that day. She wasn't the same. She blamed Jupiter. She didn't understand. But I do. I do. Can you forgive me?"

Lot blinked in astonishment. "For what?"

"For what she did—"

"It wasn't your fault."

"She was my mother."

"Lot," Ord interrupted, "is summoned to city authority immediately."

Alta nodded, the thread of a communications wire glinting in her hair. "They sealed off the refugee quarter because they're afraid of riot." Her shame—so intense only a moment before—was suddenly gone. Anger dominated now, spilling around him in hot ghost voices. She touched her throat mike. "Urban's on his way to the authority platform. He'll meet you there. Lot, I want to come too."

Lot drank in the elemental certainty of her aura, using it to harden his own determination.

She misread his hesitation. "You can trust me. More than anyone."

He moved his head slowly back and forth, exploring the slick, steely taste of her aura. "You were always good at commando games."

"I still am."

"You could be my bodyguard."

"You could need one." She smiled and took his hand, just as she had that day in the tunnel. "We'll make it all the way this time."

He nodded. She'd seen the old man inside him. It made a difference. Cool and slick and steely she remained, but he was on the inside now, not walled out anymore.

They ran together to the waiting car. She sat close beside him. He was acutely conscious of the curve of her cheek, the pale skin of her neck. Silver glinted everywhere, and he felt sure she understood what he was feeling. "Is Gent your lover?"

Her lips twitched in a brief smile. "Sometimes."

If she were married to Gent, she'd be married to Jupiter too. It seemed slickly efficient.

But then she surprised him with questions of her own. "And you? Is Yulyssa your lover?"

"No."

Her doubt clouded the air. "I watched you climb the railings. Why did you do it?"

"It felt right."

She didn't like it. "If you'd slipped, city authority would never have revived you."

"I didn't slip."

"You didn't get anything from her either."

He'd gotten information.

"Some people are born flawed, Lot. My mama was like that. She knew Jupiter. She loved him. But that love ate at her in a bad way. She saw it as something else. Yulyssa's the same way. She knew Jupiter. Yet she's not our friend. She'll try to hurt you."

Alta held his hand as she said this. She spoke to him as if he were eight years old. Lot felt the first stirrings of anger. "You don't know that."

"Gent says the same thing."

"Not to me." It was a cool, and smoothly efficient anger.

"He doesn't want to scare you."

"But you don't mind."

Alta hesitated, as the drifting charismata fell over her. "No, I don't want to scare you either."

That wasn't true. She would like the advantage it gave her.

Lot touched her throat gently, strangely unmoved by her budding misgivings. Beneath the silvered interface of his fingertips he felt the quickening pulse of her heart. "I'll always know it if you lie." Ord shifted uneasily under his hair. Alta's eyes grew so wide that they showed white all around the dark iris. Lot said, "Yulyssa is my friend. It doesn't matter if you like it. It doesn't matter if Gent likes it. You won't speak against her. You won't try to hurt her."

"I don't want to do that," Alta whispered. Her voice was hoarse, as if he were squeezing on her throat though he was not. "I only want to help you."

The scent of his charismata came back to him, cold and terrifying. "Then don't hide from me. Be there when I need you. Open your door to *me,* and not just to Gent—"

"*Stop it!*" She ducked away from him, her head snapping around so hard he might have hit her. "Stop it, Lot! Don't do this to me—" Her fingers scraped at the sealed door. Then she was pounding on it, demanding that the transit DI "Stop this car. Stop this car *now.*"

Lot watched this interesting display. He felt inexplicably detached, like a slickly efficient machine that could taste emotional issue without being changed by it. He'd never felt this way before.

Ord's small voice tried to recall him. "Good boy, good boy. Lot be good." Tentacles softly tapping.

Lot ignored it, feeling a flush of power in this strange and isolated state. *"Listen to me!"*

Alta froze, though she did not look at him.

Lot stroked her cheek with curled fingers while the car swiftly slowed. Her anger was wanton heat. He waited for it to dissipate, while the car came to a smooth stop and the door slipped open. Lot flexed his hand, watching the play of muscles that were still thin and weak from Captain Antigua's assault. Deep inside he felt a stirring of shame at what he was doing, but he pushed that feeling down. He would finish this. "Things are changing, Alta. I'm not a kid to be lectured to, or led around by the hand. You know how I feel. Don't use it against me. Understand?"

Her eyes squeezed shut, and she nodded.

"Fury?"

Urban leaned in the open car door, his gaze roving warily from Lot to Alta then back again. "Where have you been all night? Do you know what they're trying to do?"

"I know."

Alta slid out of the car. Lot followed. Alta touched his arm tentatively. When he ignored her, she withdrew her hand. It made a little fist at her side. Urban frowned at her. "Are you okay?"

"Sure." Her voice was soft, but steady.

Believe in me.

Lot looked away, refusing the shame that still wanted to come.

"Have they got full control of the ring?" he asked Urban.

"Yeah. They say so. It's only a test today, but eventually they want to use it against the planet."

Lot didn't like the ambivalence he sensed in Urban. "Do *you* want it?"

"Easy, fury. A lot of people don't like this thing." He glanced questioningly at Alta. "Where have you been all night, anyway? You look wired. This isn't going to play well in the media."

Lot figured he could handle the media. He started toward the authority doors. "What's the poll on this . . . 'test'?" he asked.

Urban kept pace with him. "No polls on election day. You know that."

"Sooth. But who wants it?"

"The very real."

The oldest citizens then; those who'd left the ruins of Heyertori. "You'd think once would be enough."

"They watched Heyertori die. Maybe they figure they're owed a world."

Alta caught up with them just as the doors slipped open. Her aura sang like a high, hard note. She wasn't calm, but she was working hard to get rid of the fear he'd put on her. That was efficient too.

An abundance of voices spilled out of the chambers. Lot caught anxiety, doubt, cold determination. He guessed at least a hundred people were present. The walls between the lobby and the space-systems chamber had been removed, creating a large room of an odd, sickle shape. A bit different from the last time he'd been here, but then, this was a great day.

"There's a sculpted entity in the ring," Lot told Urban, as they edged into the crowd. "That's how they worked out the control function." He scanned the room, looking for Kona. "It's Sypaon."

"Who's that?"

Lot scowled in irritation, while Alta answered for him: "Sypaon's the sculpted entity who made the city."

Lot caught sight of Kona deep within the diamond-shaped spur of what had been the space-systems chamber. "There's your daddy. Come on."

They worked their way forward. A holographic projection presided at the chamber's center, displaying a finely detailed image of the swan burster, glowing silver with its own light as it soared over the night-black limb of the planet. The space inside the ring looked like a black, satiny cloth, pulled tight and marred by shiny coruscations. At the very center Lot could make out a tiny circle like a window onto true night, with a handful of stars peeking through.

Kona stood on the far side of the projection, a circle of council members around him. He looked up at their approach, soft satisfaction lying deep in his eyes. Lot could not understand such desire.

He pushed forward, while around him the hum of excited voices gradually faded. Geometries shifted, and suddenly Lot found himself separated from Kona by an empty gulf, while the crowd pressed in on all sides. "You can't do it," Lot said.

The crowd muttered. But Kona—he responded in a tone of calm reasonableness: "It's only a test today."

"But it's wrong."

"Compared to what? We'll do what we need to do."

Kona's attention seemed only partly on him, and Lot wondered if he was really playing to the crowd, or perhaps engaged in some other, more significant conversation through his atrial link. Lot moved his head slowly back and forth, tracking Kona's sense, trying to guess his thoughts. An exercise in futility! It was impossible to understand the very real. "You can't bring Heyertori back by repeating the crime that destroyed her!"

Urban stepped up swiftly. "Easy, fury. It's only a test

today. There'll be a plebiscite before any action is taken. We'll have the vote by then."

Lot considered. Urban could be right. After the election tonight the ados would be able to vote their opinions, and they didn't carry the same scars as their elders.

Kona nodded, as if he approved of the rational progress of Lot's thoughts. "I told you before, there are always options. I wanted you here, to witness that. You're part of this city now. It's time you learned to make responsible decisions. Don't let yourself be pulled down by myth, or sentimentality. We'll do what needs to be done."

"You mean Sypaon will do it."

Kona gave him an appraising look, his head cocked curiously. "Did you enjoy her company?"

"Did you send her?"

"I didn't have to. She's fascinated by you. She sees herself in you, and no wonder. We could hardly talk to her before you came here. But when we copied your neural pattern onto a translation DI the language became suddenly clear."

Lot let the taunt slide past, refusing to be lured away from his own objections. "She's lost track of history."

"She thinks you're a hybrid, with the taint of the Chenzeme in you."

"She thinks we're her people!"

Kona shrugged. "Now we are."

"No. Her people are in the Well. Or some part of them anyway."

From a booth beside the display an officer announced: "Final systems check."

The room quieted. Lot turned to the projected image with some trepidation, remembering Sypaon in her endless journey around the ring, knitting each alien cell to her will. Kona might have read his mind.

"The swan burster's surface is composed of billions of cells," he explained, his voice misleadingly soft. "Each of those contains a selective neural architecture with well-defined values."

"Like 'Kill aliens,' " somebody muttered.

Kona nodded. "That's the essence. But Sypaon has modified those values. Before, a kill decision was reached by consensus. Now, she defines the target. Today it'll be the spectral image of a distant star."

"Then you've tried this before?" Urban asked.

"Not a full test, no." From Kona, Lot sensed a sudden uneasiness. "We ran a preliminary test nearly a year ago. The swan burster attained a state of high activity before the sequence was stopped."

"Why didn't you go all the way?"

"It was only a preliminary action. Most of the burster's cells are aggressive. When a fire/don't fire decision must be made, they generally opt for action. Sypaon understands these cells; she has them under secure control. But a small percentage of the cells are passive. Unfortunately, they tend to be large and massively interconnected. On that first attempt at a test firing, they overrode Sypaon's consensus, suppressing the aggressive cells. But she's learned how to neutralize them. There, you see that?" He pointed at the holographic display, indicating three minute red pinpricks evenly spaced about the ring. "We've removed three of the meteor defense lasers from the column, and shifted them to the farside. In just a few seconds, they'll fire on the swan burster."

"What?"

Kona's cheek twitched. Lot caught a puff of nervous unease. "When the aggressive cells detect the assault, they'll cut off the passive cells, and retaliate. It's part of the deep programming."

Someone growled, "Let us all pray to the Unknown God that the soulless bastards don't retaliate against *us*."

"Sypaon controls the aggressive cells," Kona insisted.

"And who controls Sypaon?"

The watch officer preempted any answer. "It's time," she announced. *"Now."* On the display, fine lines of white light lanced from the red pinpricks, impaling the silver glow of the ring. "Targeting successful. Ring geometry is deepening. Radiation levels are rising at a proportional rate. . . ."

"This is as far as we got last time," Kona muttered.

Lot watched the ring begin to blaze a brighter silver. Within seconds the blaze reached brilliance.

"The geometric gradient is climbing astronomically. Readings are approaching the historical values recorded on Heyertori. Climbing. Climbing. . . ."

The ring's image burned with a painfully bright light. The dark interior filled with a sheet of silver fire, marred only by a small circle of darkness lingering at its center. Stars were no longer visible through that aperture, their light overwhelmed by the burster's luminescence.

Then abruptly, the burster's light began to fade.

"It's failing," the watch officer announced. A murmur of discord ran through the assembly. "The burster's geometry is declining to quiescent levels. Radiation levels are collapsing. It's failed."

"It's failed." The comment soughed through the room like the passage of a ghostly chorus. Shock was the dominant expression on the gathered faces. Fear seeped onto the air. "It can't be."

Lot looked in amazement at the wide open, foolish faces goggling like ignorant children. "Why are you surprised?" he demanded of them. Startled faces turned toward him. Urban laid a restraining hand on his arm, but he ignored it. "The Well protects itself. Everything fails in the Well. That's what I've been hearing for ten years. From *your* mouths! And you knew the Well had caught the ring. Once, long ago. Did you think the passage of time had shortened its reach? Uh-uh. It has the swan burster, it has *us* within its reach and there's no difference, no difference at all if we live in the city or in the Well."

For several seconds after his outburst, no one spoke. Fear clouded the air, and suddenly Lot found himself leaning hard on a panicky memory of the packed corridor. He turned to leave, but the route to the door was blocked. People stopped him. Council members. Real people. They asked his opinion. Was a descent to the Well inevitable? Yes, he believed that. Were they already exposed to the governors, here in the city? The evidence for the Well's influence was clear.

Quiet expanded around him as he spoke. He found himself addressing the entire room. "*Try* to understand. Our situation is fragile. If we threaten the Well we'll be consumed, just like the Old Silkens. We must abandon the ring."

In that moment, he felt as if he held them in his hand. They would do as he said. They would descend to the Well. For what choice did they have?

Then, from the far side of the room someone muttered in angry syllables, "*He's a madman.*"

The words smashed against the budding confidence of the crowd. Lot felt his control crumble under a sudden surge of denial; a feverish flush of anger.

"*Fanatic*," someone close to him growled.

"*Jupiter's dog.*"

An ugly muttering arose on all sides: as if truth could be changed by name-calling. Their blindness sickened him. They could kill this city by sheer accident in their frantic struggle to deny truth. "Stop!" he pleaded with them. "Stop and ask yourselves why the Old Silkens died. Ask it and answer it, before you kill us all."

He left then, pushing his way through to the door, frantic to escape the room's seethe of negative emotions. In the sudden stillness of the station platform, Ord's background burr of begging, pleading, became the dominant sound. "Hush," Lot said, as a car swept throught the gray membrane that separated the vacuum of the tunnels from the pressurized station. Ord quieted: an unexpected obedience that confirmed for Lot just how much his situation had changed.

Chapter
18

In the transit car he felt sick, fever-flushed and trembling. What could do that to his system? The Well was in him. Maybe it would take him first, absorbing him just as some ancient cell had once absorbed an independent bacterium, forcing its evolution toward a subjugate cellular organelle: the mitochondrial analog. Was that process beginning in him now? He half-closed his eyes, his head lolling on the seat back. And what if it was? He smiled, suddenly sure that could not be a bad thing. He'd waited for this all his life. Inside, he still held a narrow core of fear, but for the most part he felt only relief when he considered that the waiting might finally be over.

Ord brushed his neck with soft tentacles. "Elevated body temperature. Lot needs to eat."

"Not hungry."

"Deprivation encourages unstable chemistry."

"Leave me alone."

"I love you."

The car stopped in Ado Town at the Narcissus Street station. Lot stepped out on the platform amid a swarm of camera bees, Ord clinging under his hair.

One of the bees told him, "City authority's attributing the swan burster's failure to minor technical problems. Do you agree with that assessment?"

He laughed. *Convince them that it's right,* Sypaon had enjoined him. She'd spent centuries cycling through the ring, learning a dead species' mad language. Of the living Well she knew nothing. He told the bee, "The Well defends itself. It always has. It adapts. It consumes. In its consumption, it forces the adaptation of others, including the Chenzeme." Jupiter had seen all of that, long ago.

Another bee, this with a feminine voice, then countered, "Yet the swan burster was not aimed at the Well. There was nothing to defend against."

"No?"

Ados on the steps moved aside for him, unwittingly interfering in the flight of the camera bees so that Lot stepped out alone onto the street. Already his fever seemed to be subsiding, but not the free clarity of his thoughts, the *acceptance* that had come upon him. If this was not yet the plague that would draw the population of the city down into the Well, still, he knew that time must be imminent. He turned back, to so inform the mediots hiding behind the glassy eyes of the camera bees, but to his surprise he saw that they had already withdrawn, buzzing away over the rooftops in a slow, glittering flock. Had Kona recalled them? So.

Silence filled the street. At the café tables, on the balconies, ados watched him with looks of expectation. The election was to take place today. Lot remembered that suddenly and wondered if it still mattered.

He might have stood there longer, considering things, but it occurred to him that indecisiveness didn't look so good. So he set off down Narcissus Street at a detached, determined pace. In the quiet of his breather he could think, and sort out what to do next.

But when he got there he didn't think at all, just threw himself down on the sleeping pad and lay at floor level staring at the sundews surrounding him in their glass pots. He heard Ord busying itself in the kitchenette, but he listened to his body, searching the pulse and wash of his metabolism for some sign of transformation. . . .

The door opened itself for Urban. He had Alta with him. She came in only far enough to avoid the closing door. Her cool gaze took in the room, and then she looked at Lot. "I underestimated you. I'm sorry."

"He forgives you," Urban said. Stepping long strides over the plants, he threw himself down next to Lot, his braids performing a jubilant dance against his cheeks as he grinned. "Fury, I'll give you points on the dramatic exit from authority, but the fact is, you left too soon."

Ord squeezed up between them and plopped a cup under Lot's nose. A pink paste filled it, shedding a vague, fishy odor. "Good Lot," Ord murmured. "Good boy. Eat now."

Lot wrinkled his nose. "Oh, that's foul." He shoved the cup far to the side. "Don't cook for me, okay Ord?"

Urban laughed, while Ord protested: "Lot's hungry."

"I like being hungry."

Ord patted tentacles against his arm. "Deprivation encourages unstable chemistry."

"Yeah, and you love me, I know."

Urban slapped the robot out of the way. "Will you quit playing with that thing and listen to me, fury? Authority picked up some radio gibberish after you left. They couldn't figure it out at first. It was more like a data stream than a language, and it was aimed at the ring."

"Chenzeme?" Lot asked tentatively.

"That's what everybody thought, at first. But it turned out to be Null Boundary."

"The great ship that brought the real ones here?"

"Brought 'em here and abandoned 'em. Yeah. The bastard actually came back . . . or at least he's cruising the system periphery. Whether he's got the mettle to actually come in-system—" Urban shrugged. "Anyway, he caught the telltales when the ring went hot, and went into a panic. Shot some decoy Chenzeme code at it to try to convince it to pass him by. He must have thought we were dust—again."

Lot nodded, recalling the history he'd absorbed during his years in Silk. Null Boundary had appeared like a scarred tramp in the thriving space above Heyertori only weeks before a swan burster swept that system. The ship had been an ominous sight with his dark hide split and pitted from some violent encounter, the wounds only half-healed. He carried no crew. For several days he'd prowled the outposts, trying to persuade some there to come aboard, but he got no takers and soon he vanished back into the void. The Chenzeme ring came soon after, moving undetected past the outposts until it stood in low orbit above doomed Heyertori. That it had followed the ship in from the periphery was an assumption never proved; nor could it be shown that Null

Boundary had somehow effected the mechanical failures at the system's outposts that had allowed the incursion. But the ship had survived where Heyertori had not, and when it ran again through the system a decade later a bitter faction of survivors had grudgingly contracted for passage out. . . . *Has a forced wedding between scarred lovers ever found success?*

Null Boundary wanted a replacement crew, but the Heyertorians spurned that intimacy, wanting only transportation out of hell. In hindsight, the falling-out could be seen as inevitable. From the start, the Heyertorians had refused to treat the ship as a permanent home. They kept most of their complement in cold sleep, and made no secret of their suspicions that Null Boundary had some hand in the destruction of their world. The emotional tensions must have been unbearable.

The break came eleven years into the voyage. Null Boundary claimed problems with his synthetics factories and announced that he could no longer support a human complement—though almost ninety-eight percent of the Heyertorians were in cold sleep and no draw on ship's resources. Declaring emergency breach, he abandoned them at Deception Well.

It was all ancient history to the ados. Urban shook his head, as if he couldn't quite believe his own news. "You should have seen the real ones, fury. They were about to shit on the floor. You know, I think they'd blow that ship out of the void if they could."

"Be straight. Soon as they cool, they'll be on their knees begging for passage out of this system."

"I don't think so. Not the way they were talking. Null Boundary's the same as the old murderers in their eyes. They'd rather deal with the Well than trust themselves to him again."

Alta shifted restlessly, her impatience like stinging cells. "You're thinking it's time?" Lot asked her.

"How much longer shall we wait? How many more signs do you need?"

He laughed at her. *Signs.* He'd never waited for signs, only evidence. No longer. "Soon," he told her. "It's playing out broadly." Jupiter had left him here to persuade the Silkens, to bring them around at this cusp of crisis.

"Sure, the election's tonight," Urban said, oblivious

of the taut demands stretching between Lot and Alta. "Tomorrow we're real."

The apartment majordomo inserted its masculine voice into the conversation. "A visitor for you, Master Lot Apolinario. Madam Yulyssa Desearange. Will you receive her?"

"Do it," Urban said, before Lot could decide. And the majordomo, recognizing his privilege, obeyed. Lot tasted ire from Alta. "Why don't you go home?" he suggested to her, as Yulyssa hesitated in the doorway.

That shocked her. Eyes too round, she started to object. "Lot—"

He only had to look at her. She nodded, though anger glinted in her eyes. "I'll wait for you."

But then he'd known that. He smiled in satisfaction as she slipped out past Yulyssa. The door whispered shut. Yulyssa seemed to listen for its closure, her lips turned down in disapproval. "You're learning," she observed. Beneath her casual demeanor he could sense a subtle field of fear. She still mistrusted him. Yet she'd come around. That pleased him too.

He let his tension flow away, rain sliding across the perfect curves of her face. Her skin seemed bloodless, but still beautiful. Her eyes though, looked tired and distracted. She glanced over his collection of carnivorous plants, then sniffed at the high humidity that kept dew beaded on the sticky paddles of the sundews. The slug crawled on the wall just beside the door, rasping at invisible patches of mildew. "Eccentricity's supposed to come with age."

Lot shrugged, baiting her with silence. Urban was into it, his amusement like silent laughter on the air.

Yulyssa waited a minute more, then sighed. "You had a lot of questions yesterday."

"Yeah." Yesterday, she had not been real.

She pressed her back defensively against the door, as if reconsidering the wisdom of this visit. "I just came here to tell you I may have found an answer. Authority tried to fire the burster last year."

"Kona said."

"I cross-checked the date with the commandant of wardens. It seems the first phantoms were recorded two and a half days after the test took place."

Urban hissed. Lot felt his own chest tighten. "Do you

think the two events are linked?" Did the phantoms know how dangerous the ring would be to use?

Yulyssa shrugged. "I don't know." A new resolve rolled from her. She stepped forward, placing her feet delicately between the glass pots, her brown legs as beautiful as anything Lot had ever seen. He scrambled up to a sitting position to make room for her on the pad. She slipped off her shoes, then sat down, casting a cool eye on Urban, who refused to yield his floor-level view of her thigh.

Lot felt pressure in her nearness. Her presence seemed to challenge him in a silent test of dominance. He didn't like it. He'd begun to think he'd gotten all the important systems in hand, but now his control was cracked again. He didn't let her see it. He held himself aloof, his gaze fixed on the bedsheets: a shimmering white sea of wrinkled waveforms, tangled inconsistencies. With the palm of his hand he brushed the sheet flat, feeling the demand of Yulyssa's gaze.

She said: "I find it hard to talk about Jupiter. What he believed . . . it disturbed me. It's not what I want to believe."

It seemed an odd thing to say. Yulyssa's desires could not define the world. The Universe had come preloaded with conditions and did not care a jot if those conditions pleased the human psyche or destroyed it.

"Nobody's talking about Jupiter in this election," Urban said.

Yulyssa ignored him, her gaze in a gravity lock on Lot's face. "I have avoided death for a very long time," she went on. "I have not always wanted to, but it felt like a duty. In a Universe that would destroy us, the most defining thing we can do is push on. Not for any real goal. There is no place of permanence, no golden existence, no finish line . . . not even in the Hallowed Vasties. Life can only exist on the edge of chaos, with all the turbulence that implies—or so I believed, until I met Jupiter." She ran a fingernail up and down the wall of a glass pot, studying the twisting pattern of the white roots, how they ducked and turned away from the glass, minimizing their interaction with the light.

"He caught me for a while. He had a presence that was hard to deny. It was paradoxical: a more profound sense of self I could not imagine in any man. Yet still he denied any value in independent existence, driven always by his 'mitochondrial analog,' this insistence that we should surrender ourselves to some symbiotic communal state."

"He only wanted us to live," Lot said. He glanced up at Yulyssa, then down again at the bedsheet, smoothing another wrinkle with his restless hand. Her doubt played against his sensory tears, but in a peculiar negative reaction he'd never experienced before. Instead of enhancing his own uncertainties, he felt them begin to crumble. *It could be okay,* to be part of something bigger. He knew it could. He'd felt the edge of it, every minute he'd been with Jupiter. "In the Well we'll become more than we are, safe from the Chenzeme . . . and from whatever is causing the Hallowed Vasties to fail."

"*So Jupiter said.* But myths have always been used to veil the finality of death."

Lot traced the curve of her cheek against the sheet, appreciating her doubt, but oddly unmoved by it. "The Communion is no myth."

"I don't know. Jupiter's '*surrender*' seemed too much like suicide to me. I pulled away from him. And then he was gone."

Lot smiled. "You think you left him? He could have held on to you. He let you go."

That angered her. "Why would he? He had no one. He left here alone."

"He left you at the Well." And finally, Lot saw that as a privilege.

"And why again? So I would survive? So I would live to be here with you? Talk to you about him? Make you angry enough that you'll follow him just to spite me?"

"You're the one who's angry," he pointed out.

"No one plans that well, Lot."

But Lot wasn't so sure. His fingers skated across the shimmering cloth, raising waves in their wake. "So you're free then. Are you going to leave on Null Boundary?"

That set her back. He caught a flash of overt fear from her, quickly suppressed. "Are *you*?" she asked softly.

On the white sheet he traced with his index finger a slow, inward-turning spiral, a descending orbit that ended in the Well. "I don't want to leave. I know that now. It's begun, and I'm not scared anymore."

Chapter
19

Lot spent most of the afternoon in the refugee quarter. Down in the cool bowels of Gent's church, the dancing reflections in the holographic walls mixed up his image in a manic imitation of sexuality, a Well-redoubled blending of self and self. Before his image shredded, Lot caught a glimpse of his face and was startled at his gaunt appearance. His cheeks seemed sharp and thin and bloodless, while his eyes were red, brooding from deep within their orbits.

Then Alta was with him, as if she had coalesced out of the shadows. She crouched beside him, her hands on his shoulders as she watched their distorted reflections writhe within a wall. "I understand you better now," she said.

"You've talked to Gent?"

"He didn't send me here." She leaned forward, and her lips brushed his sensory tears. "Your skin's so hot!" He turned his head and she kissed his mouth with a fierce determination. Apparently she had taken his admonitions to heart. He shut his eyes, as a pleasing sense of completeness closed around him. Her kisses continued, and it wasn't long before his exploring hands found her breasts beneath the restrictive architecture of her dress. She helped him get it off. She helped him with his shirt. Her fingers stroked his chest a minute; then she lay back, pulling him down with her. Her breasts swayed.

He caught one nipple gently in his teeth, drawing from her a sharp gasp.

Her fingers stroked his brows, his ears, his lips. They pushed into his mouth, dry foreign objects trespassing on his body. Next he could feel her touches at his hips as she tugged at his pants. He eased them off and then her fingers were wandering through his pubic hair, the soft inside of her arm brushing against the silken smooth skin of his erection. Her hand slipped down to caress his balls. He leaned forward, his hair falling upon her in twisting, gleaming, golden threads. Her skin puckered at its touch. Slipping his hand behind her head, he lowered himself against her. He felt the wiry brush of her pubic hair against his belly, the delicious, smooth kiss of her labia across the head of his member.

Their reflections had become an abstract mingling of his body and hers, repeated hundreds of times in the shifting holographic glow. Lot couldn't remember anymore why he'd been angry with her. She'd made him forget that. He could feel her smug satisfaction beneath the surface deference she wanted him to see . . . and something else. An influence that ran through *all* the refugees, and some of the real people too—he'd sensed it before, though he hadn't understood it: a subtle division of loyalties . . . a division that didn't exist in the ados of Silk.

He withdrew a little, suddenly wary, feeling a tenuous sense of danger.

"Lot?" Alta looked at him with questioning eyes.

Jupiter had been here before him. He'd left his mark on her. Lot felt the hair on the back of his neck rise in an ancient defensive response: territorialism across the millennia, across a span of ten years.

"Lot, what is it?" Alta's eyes widened as the threat of his defensive charismata brushed against her.

"I can feel him inside you."

To his surprise, that made her smile. Pleasure blossomed across her aura. "We all belong to him."

"No. I want you for my own."

She felt his jealousy. Oh yes. Her body became a hard shield around this trace of Jupiter. "Stop it, Lot," she warned softly, astounding him with her resistance. But then Jupiter would have armed her against sedition.

"We all belong to him," Alta repeated. "Even you."

She touched the sticky droplets of his sensory tears. "Lot? It's okay. He loves you still. He needs you."

Her soft chiding had its planned affect. He lowered his head, feeling a rush of shame. He sought her neck, her breasts: a show of desire to hide his jealousy. If he didn't look at it, maybe it would go away?

Her fingers slid through his long hair. His sensory tears rubbed against the treacly brew of her sympathy. "I love you too," she whispered. "We all love you."

"I know."

"And all things are shared in the Communion."

"Sooth."

She ran her hands over his buttocks, encouraging his penetration. *"Now, Lot."*

Her passion rode the exhalation of those words like a perfume, an aerosol intoxicant that brushed his sensory tears and sent his heart rate leaping. His metabolic processes accelerated too. Time seemed to burn faster, and his perceptions shifted in compensation. The shifting walls coalesced into a dull white haze, while Alta's body lay washed in silver. Lot felt himself sucked downward, sinking, past the barrier of her skin, past her muscles and the deafening swirl of her blood, until—for a moment—he seemed entirely inside her, their bodies crushed together by some irresistible gravity.

He heard himself cry out, but not in pain.

It seemed that some bit of time had been lost. Maybe only a second, maybe several. He found himself slack against her, a mean buzz in his head, his slick skin cooling in the shifting light while Alta's chest labored for breath beneath his weight. Ord squatted beside them, one gold tentacle pressed against Lot's neck, muttering some half-mechanical drivel: *"No good, no good. Not allowed."*

Lot slapped the tentacle away. "Leave u alone." He took his weight again, and kissed the cooling salt sweat of Alta's neck.

Then he rolled to the side, sprawling utterly slack against the soft floor. He watched her breasts slowly rise and fall, imagining what it might be like to be an oxygen molecule drawn forcefully into her lungs, exposed to gas-exchange over the alveoli, helpless freight rammed through the arteries, O_2 exchanged for CO_2 in the capillaries, depleted blood moving back to the lungs, subsystem of human life. Every molecule of air in Silk must have been breathed millions of times. From Alta's lungs, to his own, to the kids playing in the street outside, and from there around the city until everyone had shared the same breath.

And what then? How many times could one breath be made to go round and round?

Later, Gent took one look at him and asked—with an approving air—if he was fasting. Lot didn't know what that meant, so Gent explained, and Lot agreed that it was so. He hadn't eaten anything for over a day, but his metabolism wasn't slowed by the deprivation. If anything, his metabolic rate had picked up. His body was a furnace, swiftly burning off his mass, reducing his volume of flesh so that his innate pharmacopoeia of brain chemicals gradually became concentrated into a smaller and smaller volume. By evening he felt only lightly attached to his body, and everything around him carried a tint of silver.

As the day's light failed he walked outside with Alta, her hand cool against his own blazing palm. A celebration had been ongoing in the refugee quarter since the Silken curfew had been lifted in late morning. The burster had failed; the Well had been spared. The continuation of their journey down the elevator seemed inevitable now, for what choice would the Silkens have but to let them go—no, even to go with them? For no sane people would choose to starve.

Gent and David met them, and they sprawled together on a flow of lawn that ran between two of the pyramids, listening to a small orchestra dominated by the quickening rhythm of flutes and drums while the talk ran soft and eager around them: *How long would it be? How long, before the Silkens let them go?*

The city had swung into full darkness when Urban finally showed up, at the head of a pack of silver-tinged ados that must have numbered close to two hundred. Urban's grin faded when he crouched next to Lot and got a good look at him by the colored light of festival lamps drifting among the branches of the trees. "You don't look too good, fury."

Ord's tentacles emerged from beneath Lot's hair. "Nutritional deprivation leads to imbalanced body chemistry," it said, its little voice loaded with a full measure of worry.

"Which focuses the mind," Gent added.

"He looks like some crazy virtual prophet. Fury, the real people are already nervous. They aren't going to buy this shit."

Lot shrugged. Urban would always worry. It was his particular blindness that he couldn't feel the silver flow of the deeper world around him. "Trust me," Lot said. "The council's been exposed, the ring has failed, and there's only one way out of Silk."

"Yeah? Would that be the same way your old man got out? I heard that was a pretty scene."

Alta started to rise, her hands fixed in a combative stance. Lot laid a restraining hand on her arm. "It's okay."

"No it's not," Urban said. "You seem to be confused, so let me clarify. This election's about choice, not annihilation."

"I know that." Lot spoke calmly. It wasn't the time for conflict. He gave Urban a reassuring smile, letting the charismata of his confidence loose upon the air. But Urban seemed oblivious and the gesture fell flat, leaving Lot disconcerted and deeply troubled. What was Urban, anyway? "You'll have what you want," Lot promised, in an attempt to cover his unease. He got to his feet, his clothes slightly damp from contact with the grass. "Time to go down to Splendid Peace, you think?"

The people around him had seemed before to be paying no particular attention to him, but now, suddenly, a wave of quiet ran out from his position. Faces turned his way. "Yeah," Urban said. "I think it's time."

Splendid Peace Park ran in a belt around the foot of the conical city. It was only a few steps from the quarter to the park itself, but the main gathering tonight would be at the soccer fields below Old Guard Heights. They followed the park promenade past intervening neighborhoods, a mixed procession gathering behind them, refugees and ados falling into step, laughing, talking, buzzing like tiny, unconscious flies, swarming together out of instinct. . . .

Crowds thronged the greenway. The real people among them moved out of the way as Lot advanced, their eyes warily tracking the mob at his back. But his presence acted like an attractor on the ados, pulling them out, drawing them to him. He did not have to speak, or even raise his eyes. They came, their faces tinged in silver, lured by the energy of the mob.

Urban's mood lightened as he watched them gather. Soon he was grinning as if he had the election in hand, and Lot didn't doubt that it was so.

A white gazebo had been erected on the soccer fields. There were nine fields and the barriers between them had been removed. Already, the area was crammed nearly to capacity, mostly by ados, but with a heavy cut of real people too, under the drifting festival lights. Lot's arrival set off a pressure wave through the crowd, as the people behind him pushed onto the field. The air felt dizzying, almost overwhelming in its seethe of emotion.

At a distance, Lot saw three figures emerge from a glimmering fog in the gazebo. He blinked, briefly telescoping his gaze. The figure in the middle was Kona. The other two he recognized as longtime members of the council. David eased up on one side of him. "Clemantine's coming."

Lot glanced around, sighting the big-boned security officer making polite but determined way through the press. Urban muttered profanities under his breath, but Lot stayed easy as Clemantine gently elbowed aside the last ados standing in her way. She grinned at him. "Hey Lot, stepping up in the world, I see." Her words were friendly, but her animosity floated over him like a darkening fog. She squinted as she took a closer look at his face. "All prepared for the part?"

"You want something?" Urban asked with full ado surliness.

"Sure." Her grin widened. "Master Lot Apolinario, the council invites you to a brief question-and-answer session on the lawn." Her palm swept in a smooth arc, indicating the gazebo. "It seems the day's events have muddied some election issues, and the council would prefer to clarify points of debate before the vote is taken."

"Forget it," Urban said. "The issue is voting rights, and the choices are clear enough."

"No, it's okay," Lot said. "I'll talk to them."

"I said no, fury. They'll string you up."

"I *want* to talk to them. Urban, don't worry. It'll be all right."

* * *

He climbed the gazebo steps alone, feeling as if he were ascending temple stairs. Kona watched him. He sat with the two councilors in a semicircle, facing an empty chair. Meeting his gaze, Lot felt a brush of trepidation. Kona was in image, and Lot could get no real sense of his mood.

Did it matter?

Lot knew how Kona felt.

He gave the vacant chair a slight kick, determined that it was real, and sat down in it. Camera bees hummed softly all around.

"There seems to be some confusion about the election issues—" Kona began, but Lot interrupted him.

"It's voting rights," he said, echoing Urban's lead.

"It's more than that. We're concerned that any change in eligibility might dilute our electorate's capacity for judgment—"

"Because ados don't think?" Lot felt a dark mood dropping in around him, a contagious anger that swept both to and from the watching crowd. "How old are you anyway?"

A faint smile crimped Kona's face. "Three hundred sixty-three this month. I've lived your life several times over."

Not a day of it, Lot thought. But aloud he only said, "That's a long time . . . at least in human terms." He let his gaze rove across the surrounding sea of silvered faces, feeling himself gliding in to meet their expectation. "Still, it's hardly any time in the life of a species, of a world. Do you think three hundred sixty-three years has given you enough perspective?"

"Perspective on what?" Kona asked, impatience in his voice, but anticipation too, as if he was getting exactly what he wanted out of Lot.

"Well, on the future, real one. Do you have enough experience now that you can see into the future?"

Kona rolled his eyes. "Each day has always been a surprise to me."

"Sure. The future is inherently unknowable. No one can predict even the next moment. So what difference does it make if we are twenty years old or seventy-five or a thousand? None of us is really fit to gauge our next best move. Maybe, instead of lowering the voting age, we should raise it."

That drew an approving chuckle from the attentive ados. Lot watched them closely, willing them to belief. "Experience is an illusion. We're faced with the unknown, and our judgment is equal."

Kona laughed . . . rousing Lot's ire. But Lot knew he was able to do that only because he was a projected image, his human self locked safely away from the dangers of contact.

"It's not as simple as that," Kona said. "Experience doesn't mean only knowing what to do, but what not to do. Especially in the young, enthusiasm has been known to overcome good sense—"

"Good sense?" Lot could hardly believe Kona would choose such vulnerable ground. "Has the council shown good sense? By hiding this city's resource problems? By adopting the tactics of the Chenzeme and attacking a living world? A world fully capable of defending itself?"

Kona didn't try to answer. He held his silence, as if waiting. . . .

Lot let instinct guide him. He stood slowly. Cameras tracked him. Millions of eyes were watching him tonight. Never before so many. A fine silver current seemed to flow through him and out, into the heat of the mob, before returning to him in a circular path. "What good sense did the council show when they condemned my father's people to die in the packed corridor of the industrial core? Where in that action can goodness be found? Or sense? For all their experience of centuries, the council acted out of reflexive fear, and thousands of people died." He turned back to Kona's image, and asked, in a soft voice picked up by the camera bees and flung around the city: "If not goodness and sense, what is it that makes you qualified to determine our collective future?"

Kona nodded, a look of grim satisfaction on his face. "That will be for the voters to decide."

"Are you crazy?" Urban screamed at him. "Why did you bring Jupiter into it? Is that supposed to convince the real people to trust you?"

Kona's image had winked out. Now ados swarmed over the gazebo's railings and roof. Lot slouched in his chair, feeling slightly embarrassed by Urban's bout of hysteria.

"They needed to hear it. They wanted to hear it. No one's ever called them to account for what happened that day. It's been festering."

"And you just had to slit open the gutter doggie to-night."

Lot shrugged. "A lot of real people believed Jupiter. They trusted him. They'll trust me too. I have that power. *I* want the initiatives to pass. So they will pass. Trust me, Urban. Believe in me."

"You and the angels and the fairies?"

"It'll be okay."

Urban shook his head. "Look at yourself, fury. Crazy cult leader. You finally get to play the role. But for how long? If you don't pull yourself together, you'll be back in the monkey house tomorrow."

Lot smiled at him. Even Urban could not shake his confidence tonight. "Wait a bit. You'll see that things have changed."

"Yeah. I'm sure it's nice to think so."

Lot still presided from his chair within the gazebo when the vote was taken. It would have been possible to display the tally on the soccer fields' scoreboards, as city authority compiled the results, but real people liked to keep certain privileges for themselves. So the results were tabulated privately, and broadcast first through the atrial net.

Little groups of real people were scattered among the ados on the fields. Lot watched them closely as the results arrived. He saw them murmur in surprise, saw the sudden blossoming of relief on their faces. Some of them started to laugh. Not in any mean way, but as if a child had done something cute though unadvisable and now it was over and they were delighted with the harmless performance. They looked at Lot and they looked at Urban and that kind of laugh was on their faces.

"It's over," Urban said.

Lot felt his guts twist. The flowing silver current that had carried him all night finally began to break up, patches of turbulence rocking his surety. Perspiration broke out across his cheeks as he tried to convince himself he misunderstood. He wiped his face on his sleeve. His hands were wet, his skin a slick, brassy color. He stood slowly, and walked to the edge of the gazebo's deck. Seconds later the tally appeared on the scoreboards, while a booming male voice read off the results. First the new council, nine seats. Two point nine million ballots had been cast, producing eight clear winners and lastly the chair and that was Kona Lukamosch again, no surprise.

"The initiatives," Urban growled. Lot felt suddenly dizzy. Ord shifted nervously under his hair as the results of the first initiative appeared:

On lowering the voting age from one hundred years to twenty years: 219 for, 2,924,339 against. The measure fails.

For a moment the park was utterly silent. Lot could hear his breath whistling in and out of his lungs. Two hundred nineteen. He looked at Urban. Two hundred nineteen had to be statistically less than they could have expected from the inadvertent votes of drunkards. A low babble of disbelief erupted from the ado mob.

The results concluded: *On adjusting the citizenship requirement of Level 1 psychological profile to Level 2.5: 187 for, 2,924,371 against. The measure fails.*

Lot swayed on his feet.

Statistically less than voter error.

The clustered knots of real people on the lawn smiled encouragement at him. Such a bright child. Wait until he grows up.

Around him, ados whispered his name. They climbed the gazebo railings, crowded the stairs, bumped against him. Foul language and loyal sentiments. A display of bigotry to cement their devotion to him. He felt Urban's grip on his arm, on his shoulder, "Come on, Lot. Let's get out of here."

"No."

He felt the city around him, like an entity. Felt the brush of its cells against his skin as a hundred fingers touched him. Felt the wash of its breath across his face. He'd tried to knit this city to his will, just as Sypaon, in her endless silver circuits, had sought to bind the ring. Like Sypaon, he'd failed. He couldn't touch every cell at once.

Time for another rule change?

War is change. Sypaon had said that.

"Come *on*," Urban commanded, but Lot planted his feet solidly against his paternal tug.

Ados whispered his name. He could feel the sweep of their presence like an extension of his body, silver tendrils winding around the hard, dead knots of the real. "We are *nothing*!" he shouted to them.

The whispers subsided to silence. In the sudden stillness the night air seemed to shiver with infinitesimal specks of silver, a glittering, self-replicating storm that roiled across the upturned faces, dividing and rebounding against lips and eyes and the moist cavities of open mouths that were desirous of this contact. Lot beheld the phenomenon in a state of awe. *Chemical sight:* reason told him he must be watching the crowd-fed spread of an aggressive charismata.

He leaned forward. His voice carried in hard tones across the entranced ado faces. "In the eyes of the real people, we are nothing. How many times have you heard it? Ados don't think. We are despised." For a moment his perspective shifted, and he saw himself through eyes that weren't his. Was he inside them? Nurturing their frustrations.

The volume of his voice rose: "We live at the discretion of a people ruled by fear. Time to change that. Sooth. The time is here." Their readiness touched him, moist against his sensory tears, and he loosed himself into that receptive space and roared: "The real people will never give us what we want! If we are to be real too, we must *take* what is ours. Against objections. Against resistance. We will have our rights."

The words were an artificial structure, a gross formality strung together for the benefit of the real people. The ados didn't need words; the ados were already far beyond words, requiring only his presence to see inside themselves and know their own wills.

From the edge of the crowd came a shattering crash like a great weight of stone thrown down and rebounding in a thousand broken pieces. A terrorized scream followed. On the distant courtyard fronting Old Guard Heights a sluggish spire of flame erupted, rising slowly against the face of the Heights, its light reflected a thousand times in the banks of rectangular windows. Lot reached a hand toward it, the lurid orange glow playing off his fingertips. People shoved past him, streaming down the steps of the gazebo to join a sudden torrent of human motion across the lawn. A hysteria of voices arose on all sides. He felt he could take the column of fire in his hand, that he could hold it, close his fist around it and absorb it into his body, let it fill him, tip all systems far past maximum until he could—

Something struck him across the face. Pain flared in his mind, and then he was down on the gazebo's deck, on hands and knees, perspiration dripping off his nose, or maybe it was blood, his hair lank, stuck against his cheeks. Urban crouched beside him screaming, completely hysterical, bruised fist pressed against his chin. *"Do you know what you're doing, fury? Do you know what you've done?"*

Lot wasn't sure, but he could count more fires on the perimeter of the park and that was crazy, because the buildings wouldn't burn . . . though maybe the sump pipes would? The city's resources becoming volatiles and ash.

Already the air was thick with a vile smoke. Security officers had appeared on the seething, screaming promenade. Stun wands for the running ados. Loudspeakers advising everyone to be calm, to go home. Inciting to riot was a serious violation of city law.

"Come on," Urban growled, and he pulled on Lot's arm until Lot was faced with the choice of losing it, or of standing up.

He stood, and let Urban drag him down the stairs and across the soccer fields, unsure if this was the proper next step in the drama, or if something more was expected of him tonight. The silver tide had shattered into fragments, and for the moment anyway he couldn't perceive its will.

He was still puzzling over this when a security officer spotted them. She yelled at them to *stop right now,* then brought up her trank gun without waiting for them to comply. Urban froze before she could fire. Lot stopped too. Cool, minute explosions touched his cheeks, like droplets of mist that evaporate in the instant of contact. He lowered his chin. "Be very sure," he warned her.

A look of confusion passed over her face. Her gun hand lowered a bit. Lot felt her determination collapse. He turned his back on her, walking away across the fields while Urban hurried to catch up, leaping after him in quick, deerlike bounds. "Shit, fury, what are we doing?"

How could Lot answer that? He wasn't sure himself.

They skirted the rising face of Old Guard Heights until they reached the line of trees that marked the boundary with the neighborhood of Spoken Verities. They could hear shouts and concussions in the distance, up on the Heights. But here not even a night breeze disturbed the quiet.

Passing under the trees, they stepped out on the luminescent street. Gent was waiting for them. His face looked eerie in the upwelling light. "You've crossed over," he said softly. "They won't forgive you now."

"Shit!" Urban hissed. He was shaking. "Dammit,

Lot, you know he's right. It's over. It's the monkey house now . . . or cold storage. For all of us. After tonight, they won't let us out in the life of this city."

Which might not be too long, Lot reflected. He looked at Gent, and saw in his eyes a quiet expectation. They had only one option left. "We're leaving the city tonight."

Urban blinked. "Fury?"

Triumph gleamed in Gent's eyes. Lot nodded, feeling detached, as if instinct alone was moving him through the patterns of a dance that had been written for him long ago. "We're going down the Well."

Chapter
20

Though the Silkens tried to plan for disaster, twice now they'd failed to predict the form of its appearance. Ten years ago Captain Aceret's assault on lift control had taken them by surprise, immediately overwhelming their slim security forces. Tonight's riot had done the same thing—every trained officer must have been called out to restore order in Splendid Peace. Lot suspected that even if authority was aware of their flight, no officers would be diverted to pursue them. After all, Silk was a closed city. There was no place to run, and miscreants could be gathered up at authority's convenience.

Gent opened a doggie-door on a side street in Vibrant Harmony. The old tunnel had a sour, rotting smell. Gent crawled inside. Lot shooed Ord off his back, then squatted down to look. The tunnel walls glistened with reflected light from the street. He wrinkled his nose in distaste, but he got down on his hands and knees and followed Gent, his shoulders scraping the tunnel walls while his hair rubbed at dew beaded on the ceiling. Behind him, Urban swore softly at the reek.

They found the doggie at home, spread in a thin membrane across the side walls and ceiling as its carry pouches emptied into nanodrizzles that skittered away deeper into the unlit tunnel. The doggie watched them with dull, dark eyes. Its body felt squishy and wet as Lot scraped by beneath it. The odor of rot grew briefly stronger. For one giddy moment he felt sure the doggie would drop on him, wrap him up in a putrid cocoon and hold him until his body had been converted to nanodrizzle.

"God," Urban said, as he pressed up close to Lot. "Was that its tongue?"

Then Lot was past and Urban behind him. At the end of the doggie's crawlway he followed Gent through a thick gel membrane, into a maintenance tunnel on the other side.

The gray-walled corridor was ablaze with lights for sixty feet in both directions. Pipes ribbed the ceiling. Shimmering nanodrizzles scurried along the walls. Ord crawled out of the doggie's tunnel and climbed up a wall, causing turbulence among the nanodrizzles as the tracks shifted to get around him.

Lot got to his feet. He sniffed at the air, finding it cold, and suspiciously thin. Urban burst through the membrane behind him. "This is crazy!" he shouted. His fist pounded the wall in frustration. "You know we're not going anywhere. The elevator system doesn't work."

Lot's gaze cut to Gent. "Not taking the elevator, huh?"

"Course not." Gent seemed anxious now. "Come on. We've got to be long gone before they have time to look."

He set the pace: a fast run that left no breath for questions. Lights flashed on as they advanced; flashed off behind them. Gent led them a long way down the maintenance tunnel, past numerous cross corridors, each one sealed with an opaque white gel membrane, numbers etched into the walls beside them. The maintenance tunnel was built on a slow curve, limiting their view. So Lot sensed her before she came into sight. *Alta.* He quickened his pace and pushed past Gent.

She waited at one of the sealed cross corridors, dressed in an odd, skintight coverall that gleamed dull gray in the tunnel lights. A pile of equipment lay at her feet. Her dark eyes watched him uncertainly. Caution and anxiety braided her mood. Lot took that as a challenge.

Jumping over the piled equipment, he caught her up in his arms, using his momentum to swing her around, his mouth on her neck, just over the hard, rasping collar of her coverall. She tried to push him away but to his satisfaction she started laughing too, pounding at his shoulder with half-force and ragging him: "You idiot! Put me down. *Now.*"

He obeyed, and she backpedaled, suddenly nervous, her burst of humor gone. Wariness lay in her eyes now. He could feel her thoughts clicking over, could almost hear the voicing of her doubts. Doubt like rot, black rust in his silver armor. Anger stirred in him. But he held on to his humor, a mask to hide the deeper processes. He dropped his chin low, a tight smile on his face as he began to stalk her. She stepped back in sudden alarm. "Lot, stop it!"

Gent clapped a rough hand on his shoulder. He yanked him off balance, then sent him stumbling hard against a wall. Lot was so surprised that for a moment he couldn't react. "Gent?"

"You want to be that kind?" Gent shouted at him. "You like scaring people? You like twisting them?"

Lot's gaze cut to Alta. He didn't try to hide his resentment. She glowered at him in return, her dark eyes furious. His sensory tears caught the taste of her mood. He cooked it for a second, then threw it back at her. "You want me to be like the old man! So I am."

Gent crossed his arms over his broad chest, his gaze fixed on the ceiling. Lot could feel him gathering himself. Urban stood a few paces back, hangdog, embarrassed and scared. Alta had adopted a defensive posture, her shoulder turned to Lot. "You're not like him," she said. "Jupiter invited love. He didn't coerce it."

"I don't remember it that way."

Her brows rose. "How then?"

Lot shook his head. He didn't want to say it. But Alta pressed him, stalking *him* now. "How'd you feel back then? Tell me, Lot. I want to know."

His gaze cut away. "Scared all the time."

She frowned. "Scared of what? He loved us."

"Sure. Long as we believed."

"You never stopped believing."

"I don't know. He thought so."

"Uh-uh. He loved you."

Lot shrugged. Maybe he had. But it had never felt like any kind of permanent state. *Scared all the time.* He'd been a kid, but he'd understood the situation. He'd *felt* it. Jupiter could shuck the bonds of love as easily as a doggie could empty its pockets. Let it all run away in darting nanodrizzles. Every day, Lot had dreaded that possibility. If Jupiter got angry, or unhappy, or just found something that interested him more, he would turn away. Lot had felt it. He would be gone.

And isn't that what finally happened? Jupiter had disappeared that day, leaving his army twitching behind him like the severed tail of a lizard pretending it was whole.

Lot shoved off from the wall, annoyed with himself, because he'd let Alta get inside him. He scowled at Gent. "We going?"

"Yes." Gent was cool now. He bent over the pile of stuff and selected a cylindrical gray pouch, about the length of his forearm. He reached in, pulled it inside out, and shook it until it unfurled into a coverall like Alta's. He tossed it to Lot. "Strip and put that on. If you've got to piss, save it until you're in the suit. It can recycle the waste, and we'll be glad to have it before we reach the bottom." He repeated the procedure with another pouch, and tossed the resulting coverall to Urban. "You can still back out."

"Hell."

Urban dropped the coverall on the floor and started to strip, his anger like a slow, persistent pressure wave pounding against Lot's senses. Lot dragged off his own clothes and stepped into the suit, feeling it pull snug around him. The feet and calves had an odd, spongy feel to them. The knees were heavily padded. A hood dangled at the neck.

Gent handed him a soft-sided backpack. It was heavy, and Lot hefted it uncertainly. He could feel himself coming down fast from the high he'd been riding all day. *Nutritional deprivation leads to imbalanced body chemistry.* "Gent, I'm hungry." Seriously hungry. He could feel a hollowness inside him, an unhealthy languor spreading like dark syrup through his veins.

Urban squinted at him. "Crash time."

Gent growled something unintelligible. He took Lot's pack again, and fished out of it a cylindrical bottle. A flexible tube extended from the bottle's base. Gent snapped that off, then popped off the bottle's top. "Drink this. But come on. We've got to move."

Lot tossed it down: a mildly sweet, unremarkable brew. Alta was winding her hair up into a bun at the back of her neck. She caught him watching, and smiled. He could get no trace of anger from her. But then, why should she be angry? She'd beaten him this time, and that victory had allowed her volatile mood to shift back to a charitable affection. A needling voice whispered that she would not be playing these games with Jupiter.

She might have read his mind. Her smile widened. "Don't look so somber, Lot," she teased. "We're finally going home."

He felt the raw edge of her enthusiasm as it played against his returning doubts. "Do you really think we'll find him?"

A radiant smile graced her face: that was all the answer she would give to such a factitious question. She pulled her hood up over her head. "Seal up," she advised him. "The core isn't pressurized anymore."

Lot nodded, feeling his own eagerness rekindle. He imitated her, winding his hair up into a loop at the back of his neck before pulling on his hood. He press-sealed a seam at the neck. The hood fitted itself to his face, molding into an arched, translucent bar over his eyes. At first he couldn't get a breath. "Activating respiratory function," the suit informed him in a patient, feminine voice. The language was Silken, but the accent . . . it reminded him of Jupiter.

The respirator kicked on, and air started to flow from a muzzle fixed over his nose and mouth. Gent's voice spoke to him through the suit's audio pickup: "Put on your backpack." He did it. "Now plug in."

Twisting around, Lot spotted another flexible tube dangling from the bottom of the pack. He caught it in his hand. It wriggled across his palm, seeking a socket in the suit just over his hip. As it burrowed into the orifice, golden liquid appeared in the tube. Gent checked the connection, pronounced it satisfactory, then turned to do the same for Urban.

Alta already had her backpack on. Her eyes crinkled over the muzzle of her suit in what must have been a smile. Then she slipped through the gel membrane. As Lot started to follow, Ord dropped down from the ceiling, landing on his shoulder. Its face was tweaked in a plaintive expression and its little mouth moved. Lot could just hear its soft voice through the muffling barrier of the hood, though he couldn't make out the words. He shrugged, then pushed through the membrane.

No lights came on as he emerged on the other side. A soft illumination filtered through the membrane, but that would be lost in a few steps. Alta waited for him, her suit glowing a dim gray in the shadows.

"Fifteen millibars positive pressure," the suit commented casually. Lot hissed. Fifteen millibars was a ghostly thin atmosphere; hardly better than vacuum. A sense of anxiety moved in on him. He tried to turn it away, knowing that inside the suit he could get no input from anyone else; it would be so easy to sink into his own emotional pit.

One of Ord's tentacles snapped past his face in weird, jerky motion. Lot reared back, expecting to see the haze of a trank expelled against his helmet . . . but Ord only spun its tentacle into a whip-thin cord that wrapped around Lot's back, snaking beneath his pack. Its gold body lay stretched on his shoulder.

"What's it doing?" Alta asked, more curious than wary.

Lot tried to turn his head far enough to see. "Securing itself for a ride, I guess."

"It's not moving."

Lot nudged the still form, but got no response. Ord's face lay pressed against his neck so he couldn't see if it was speaking or not. "Guess it's not going to make trouble."

Alta just shrugged. Then she turned and started trotting down the tunnel, her backpack bobbing up and down. Within a few steps she'd become almost invisible in the darkness.

"Hey, wait!" Lot called.

She slowed briefly. Her taunting voice reached him over the suit radio. "Hey no, *fury*. You catch me." Then she took off, darting around a junction in the corridor and out of sight.

His brows rose in surprise. What could he do but take the challenge? He sprang after her, running hard, his own pack strapped tight against his back. Around the junction, he plunged into almost total darkness. Instinctively, he blinked his vision down to IR, but the walls were cold and barely visible. Alta was a gray flame, far ahead of him. He sprinted after her.

At the same time he felt himself running away from his own foul feelings. Layers of emotional sediment that had accumulated on his brain over the years began to dissolve under the rush of his blood. His sweat pushed a ruined straitjacket of dirty feelings out through his pores. His lungs grabbed at recycled air, scrubbing it clean of antique emotion. And gradually, he felt himself shed the weight of fear that had held him down since he was a kid. *Free.* Exhilaration rang through him. He'd waited so long for this. Belief and doubt didn't matter anymore. All good lay in the *doing,* and he pushed that as hard as he could.

Ahead, Alta darted from one corridor to another. Lot tracked her, plunging through the dividing gel membranes, drawing always closer to the core until finally he sprang after her into the spiral corridor that wound around the stacked loading bays. Here the angle of descent was as familiar as the feel of his own body. His boots skimmed the rough gray floor. He plunged headlong, tracking the remembered curve and slowly gaining on Alta until they broke together into the lower chamber. He pulled up then, though his momentum still carried him halfway across the broad, empty floor.

Empty. He looked around with detached curiosity. All the bodies were long gone and the foul air too, with its ugly stench of fear. Still, the past pressed hard against the present. He saw them again in shadowy proximity: an ocean of dead, dried up, gone away. The floor beneath his feet was a playa smoothed by their blood and the spillage therein of frantic, disintegrating Makers striving to heal wounds that were no longer within the reach of microscopic hands.

He stepped up to the transparent wall that sealed the pit and looked down the shaft, but it was night outside, and he could see nothing.

"I never got this far," Alta said, her voice soft, seeming to speak from just behind his head. He smiled, and nudged the transparent wall with the toe of his boot. One last barrier. He felt Alta's hands tugging at his waist. "Come away. We're going to blow it open."

"*Huh?*" His head swiveled in surprise. "No Makers?"

"Can't trust them to work," Gent growled.

He'd come silently from behind, and was squatting at the base of the transparent wall, carefully spraying a chemical across its face in a three-by-seven-foot rectangle that glowed incandescent in the infrared. "Go find something to hold on to. The pressure here is still higher than outside."

They retreated a few feet, and took a grip on the railing that ran around the pit wall. Urban stepped up close to Lot and seized hold of the railing too. He wouldn't meet Lot's eye. Gent joined them, trailing a wire linked to the painted rectangle. A moment later the explosive coating burst in a blinding infrared flash. The rail shuddered, and incandescent dust was sucked into the pit, where it swirled in thin, glittering vortices that curled off the pit walls. Across the bay, the pressure doors sealed with a palpable thud. Lot clung to the rail while the mild pressure blew itself out.

Gent moved first. "Come on," he said. "Not much time now."

He dropped his pack. From a sack inside he pulled out a thing similar to the slug in Lot's apartment—a transparent, gelatinous blob—though this one was larger, almost the size of a soccer ball, and it had numerous fan-folds of a thin gold cord embedded within its body, all radiating from a central point. Lot touched it. The slug had a hard surface. He felt as if he were stroking a hide of scaly armor. Dangling beneath it on a line of the same gold cord was a cassette, its spool visible through the transparent casing.

"This hooks to your suit," Gent said. He held the cassette against Lot's abdomen and numerous filaments extruded from the suit's fabric shell, hooking through six eyelet holes in the cassette's rim.

"Auxiliary organ plausibly compatible," the suit informed him. "Stand by for attempted integration." Then a moment later, "Integration complete."

A new voice came online. "Cooperating intelligences ninety-four-percent compatible."

The suit responded: "Affirmed. Six-percent negative compatibility isolate from integrated processes."

"Isolation confirmed."

Lot listened in fascination to the voice of the slug's DI. It too was feminine, though distinctly different from the suit's voice—softer, more demure—a subordinate persona. But it too spoke with an accent like that of Jupiter . . . and Nesseleth as well, now he thought about it. Curious, he asked Gent, "Where did you get these suits?"

Gent gave him an impatient look. "City library."

"We mined the design," Alta added eagerly. "Deep run. Nobody had accessed the file in maybe twelve hundred years."

"Bit garbage, then," Urban said. "They're probably seeded through with decay errors."

"The design's clean," Gent said sternly. He pulled

several meters of gold line from the cassette, letting it drizzle onto the floor. "All degeneracies removed."

"All identified degeneracies."

"Is it from the Vasties?" Lot asked, thinking of what Yulyssa had said about Jupiter's age and wondering if these suits had been designed by a culture known to him, their DIs endowed with the accent of that time. The Vasties were more than one place, and far more than one culture. Could an accent be a clue to Jupiter's origin?

But Gent dismissed the question. "It doesn't matter."

He stepped up to the opening he'd made in the transparent wall. Holding the last couple of yards of gold cord in his hands, he started to swing the slug from the end of it. He took a moment to build up momentum; then he let the slug fly across the pit. It hit the far wall and splashed into a broad film, then held tight. Its edges were ragged: a smear on the wall glowing bright in the infrared.

Gent turned to Lot. Over the muzzle of his hood, his gaze was hard. He tugged at the tube that connected Lot's suit to his pack. "Think of this suit as a living creature," he said. "It eats just like you do; the same liquid nutrients that'll be sustaining you over the next several hours are also powering critical portions of your suit. The gloves, the boots, the leggings"—he slapped each part—"are hot zones. They'll form temporary bonds with the elevator's molecular structure. Enough to support you—"

"Fly walking?"

Gent scowled. "The process is overseen by the suit's DI. It operates with discretion, but you can override with a repeated request."

"Okay."

"The second DI controls tension and flexibility in the cord and the anchor."

"It lowers me down?"

"No."

Alta giggled. Gent gave her a scathing look. "It only slows you down. Are you ready?"

"I don't know. How—?"

"The suit will take care of you," Gent interrupted. He stepped away from the neatly blasted opening, hooking a thumb at it as he did. "Coriolis forces will carry you slightly away from the column. You just have to jump."

Lot's heart lurched. *Jump?* He peered at Gent, and

saw that he was serious. A nervous laugh bubbled up in his throat. Bit garbage? It was too late to go over the suit design now. He stepped cautiously up to the opening, sweat prickling under his arms. *Jump.* Gent would have done a thorough search for degeneracies. He knew that. If this was what the suit had been designed for, then there was nothing to fear.

Clutching the sides of the opening, he gazed down into the dark void while his lips moved in silent recitation *Jupiter, Jupiter, Jupiter.*

"Fury," Urban said, his voice breaking between the syllables. "This is crazy. These suits are antiques. Dammit, we—"

Lot jumped. He yelled as he did it, a long defiant roar that blasted the fear out of his throat as he plunged downward. Dark walls flashed past while the cord fed out behind him. He shot below the floor of the city. The milky glow of the nebula suddenly surrounded him, its few permitted stars peppering his retina. The seconds stretched, until, with a bone-jarring shock, he hit the end of the cord.

The pressure snapped him faceup, but it didn't stop his plunge. He continued falling, but slower now, as the Dull Intelligence wound throughout the cord smoothly adjusted the tension to absorb his velocity, gradually arresting his momentum until he came to a full stop, without recoil.

He found himself facing up, the faintly glowing bulk of the city looming like a planetary mass. Then, in his peripheral vision, the infinite face of the elevator column came rushing in to meet him.

He twisted on the end of the cord, trying to get his feet around to cushion the impact. The wall slammed against his shoulder. He twisted further. The pads on his hands and his leggings skragged across the surface. He felt the rake of tiny claws creating friction to slow his skid, and finally he felt the suit's hot zones fusing with the vast, vertical surface.

He couldn't move. He didn't want to anyway. His heart was running so fast he could hardly breathe, while in his mind a dread awareness of the abyss below had brought on a kind of fibrillant shock. Empty space seemed to pull at him. Two hundred miles of nothing lay between him and the planet's surface.

Only gradually did he become aware of a buzz of anxious voices, barely audible over his own frantic heartbeat. "Gent?" he asked, in a hoarse croak. "Alta?"

"Lot! Are you secured?"

"Yeah, I'm okay. Shit, what a ride."

"Hold on. We're behind you."

Hold on? Lot didn't know how to let go. His hands and legs were locked on tight. He prayed they'd stay that way. Sweat dripped in his eyes. He shook his head and looked up, to see two more objects falling after him, then a third. Spidery, faintly incandescent figures against the dull cloudy roof of the city. *Oh, Jupiter.*

He pressed his sealed face against the column's smooth surface, not sure if he felt more terror or joy that he'd finally made it out of the city, and was on his way at last.

Part
III

Chapter 21

Lot watched the three descending figures, and soon realized only the last two were human. The first was far smaller and hotter: a plunging globule arcing gradually out from the column. Its identity puzzled him, until with a start he remembered the slug that had anchored his fall. He telescoped his vision, but couldn't make out any detail. If it was the anchor, who controlled it? Who had signaled its release? Not him. Gent then? It was possible. But more likely, control lay with the suit's DI. *Bit garbage.* He ruefully reconsidered Urban's objections: any mutations in the suit's neural architecture could easily prove fatal.

Higher than the plunging anchor, though dropping at precisely the same speed, he could make out a human figure, arms and legs askew. He told himself there was no way their cords could cross. But he glanced at his own line anyway. The gold thread of it was visible for only a few feet before it disappeared against the dim glow of the night sky. But the section that he could see was pointing down, not up. A U-shaped loop must have formed as the full length of the cord plunged through vacuum at the same rate as the falling anchor. Against his belly, the cassette fought the slack, sucking in line in an intense, vibrationless spin.

The anchor swept past him—well out from the column—at what seemed like meteoric speed. Lot half-expected the momentum of its plunge to yank him off the column. But instead the cord stretched, absorbing the kinetic energy so that he felt only a hint of recoil before the cassette busied itself hauling the anchor back up.

"Get out of the way, fury, I'm coming in!"

Lot started at the shouted warning, then ducked hard as Urban swung in nearly on top of him, boots striking the wall just inches above Lot's head. "Alta's right behind me," Urban panted. His gloves locked onto the column. Lot watched him struggle to pull them off again. "Shit, how are we supposed to move?"

"Dunno."

"Urban!" Gent barked over the suit audio. "You secure?"

"Stuck fast."

"Heads up, then."

Alta swung in hard, but she moved with more grace than Lot or Urban, running sideways along the wall for a few steps before her boots locked on. Obviously, *she* knew how to handle the equipment. "Secure," she called, with a glance back up toward the city. Lot looked up too and saw Gent begin to descend. "You guys want to get out of his way?" Alta asked.

Lot felt a flush work its way up his cheeks. The anchor dangled at his waist, once again a sluglike knot of protoplasm encasing a thready flower of gold cord. "Maybe I should have taken a tutorial," he said, not quite able to meet her gaze. Gent was approaching swiftly.

"Cue your suit," Alta said, as if the procedure should have been obvious. " 'Hark: climbing, climbing.' You'll get one limb free at a time."

Lot tried it. He managed to scramble a few feet toward Alta before Gent hit.

"Now spread your anchor against the wall," she went on.

Lot frowned at the globular slug, then tried pushing it flat. Alta laughed at his effort. "Come on, Lot, we have to move fast. Just slam it. Punch it down."

His cheeks grew hotter still. But he shoved the slug hard against the gray, stained surface. When it stuck, he punched it square in the center. Ripples ran out from the point of impact as the anchor spread in a large patch across the wall. "Okay?" Lot asked.

"Clear to jump," his suit answered.

He gritted his teeth. His muscles still hummed from his first jump. "Why can't we just use the mats to slide down the column?"

"Generates too much heat," Gent said. "Besides, this way's faster. You're clear, Lot."

"I know." He closed his eyes. Then, with a spasm of leg muscles, he launched himself away from the elevator column. This time he managed not to scream. He remembered to start counting, and reached a slow eight before the cord played out. Despite the cushioning effect of the stretching cord, the abrupt deceleration hit with jarring force. His head rang; his vision swam. Then he had the wall under his hands; locked on.

Again Urban came down almost on top of him. "Some fun, huh fury?" he panted, landing a little more gracefully than Lot this time.

"Sooth." The suit offered him a straw, and he took a long sip. Only two jumps, and already his body felt like it was about to give out. The suit gave him clearance. He jumped again.

After they'd traversed five miles, Gent let them rest for a few minutes. The city no longer loomed like a roof over their world. It had shrunk against the vast spread of the milky sky. Far below, tiny sparks of lightning flickered among the cloud tops.

Lot huddled against the column, too tired to feel either fear or wonder. He hadn't slept for almost two days. Slowly, his eyes closed. He only opened them again when he felt a nudge against his arm. He turned his head, expecting Alta. But it was Urban.

"What's with the little monster?"

Lot followed Urban's gaze. With a start of surprise, he realized Ord still clung to his shoulder, its tentacles looped under his arms. "Hark, climbing, climbing," Lot muttered at his suit. He got a hand free, and used it to nudge Ord, but the robot didn't respond. It felt stiff; its tentacles almost brittle.

Urban stared at it malevolently. "It's gone dormant?"

"Guess so. It must need O_2 to function."

"Then dump it, fury. Just drop it."

Lot's eyes widened in shock. "Why?"

"Come on. It's your best chance to get rid of the thing. You like it tagging after you?"

Lot frowned. Ord *was* annoying. Certainly it had messed him up in front of Kona. But Ord hadn't reported him to authority when they'd been down in cold storage. And Ord hadn't tried to stop him running away through the tunnels. . . .

"You know," Lot said, feeling himself on the defensive. "Ord has a lot more data storage and analytical facilities than we do."

Urban rolled his eyes in disgust. "Come on, Lot!"

"It might be useful on the planet," Lot added quickly. "You never know."

"Or it could trank you when you're not looking."

True. Still, Lot couldn't bring himself to just drop the DI. "You like it," Urban accused.

Lot shrugged. "Hark, release both hands."

In a voice that sounded distinctly disapproving, the suit asked, "Are you sure?"

"Yeah. Let's try it." Lot strove to keep his weight over his calves as he slid first one arm, then the other, out of Ord's frozen embrace. After that he carefully pressed against the tentacles, and with some effort was able to squeeze them down against Ord's body, winding them into tight coils.

"Now drop it," Urban said again.

But Lot just swung his pack down on one shoulder and stuffed the robot inside. "Could be useful," he said again.

Urban swore softly. He slammed his anchor against the wall and punched it flat, then kicked off the column, dropping away while Lot was still trying to get his pack strapped down.

Authority found them just before dawn. They'd dropped almost a hundred miles beneath the city. Lot's body felt numb. Whether that was because his onboard Makers had flooded him with painkillers, or because he was just too tired to feel anything, he couldn't say. Gent moved with him on every jump now, reminding him to grab the wall, to lay out the anchor, encouraging him to drink from the suit's feeder tube. Lot tried to talk to him, but his words slurred. He would find himself gazing down at an infrared glow that spanned the thickening atmosphere below them, wondering what produced it, and what it might be like to be down there in that light. The glow had beckoned to them for hours, so he guessed it was a chemical or electromagnetic effect rather than a harbinger of dawn. He was locked in one such circular contemplation, waiting for Urban to complete a jump, when a new voice broke into his sensorium.

"Urban!"

Lot started. He swiveled his head wildly, looking for the speaker.

"Urban, I have to hope you can hear me."

"Daddy?" Urban croaked, as he swung into the column.

"It's your old man," Lot blurted the obvious.

"Urban, I don't know what you're doing. I don't know why. But if you descend any farther, we can't let you back in the city."

Urban froze up, dangling on the end of his line, only one hand secured against the column. "Hark: climbing, climbing," Lot growled at his suit. He shrugged off Gent's cautioning hand, then traversed the wall until he could reach Urban's arm. He yanked hard, pulling Urban against the security of the column's face.

"Urban, listen to me. You might not be able to ascend, but don't go any farther down. We'll send someone for you. . . ."

Lot put his arm around Urban's shoulders.

"I'm okay, fury." His voice overrode Kona's continued pleas as the suit sought a clear channel. He glanced up, as if he might see Kona looking down on him, like some dark god at home in the sky, the deity that had ruled his life . . . or that had sought to. Urban's apostasy had begun years ago. "Think he can hear us?"

"It's not likely," Gent said. His voice was soft, as if that would make any difference. "The suit transmissions are fairly weak."

"—a lot of anger. Too many people are in custody. Urban, we need you to speak to the ados—"

Alta completed her jump, her boots touching lightly over the column's face as she slowed. "Urban as authority's mouthpiece. Now that's an enthralling concept." She swung in close, peering into Urban's eyes past the distortion of his visor. Lot could see the humor in her own eyes gradually drain away. "Hey. You're thinking about it, aren't you?"

"No." Urban ducked his chin and started pounding his anchor against the wall.

Lot backed off, but Alta did not yield Urban any space. "You're thinking your old man might still forgive you."

"I'm not asking for it."

Alta said, "I hope you're not looking for it, either. You know Kona wouldn't be so nice if he had the deck guns at hand. It's lucky for us they were moved out to the burster's orbit."

Lot shivered. The city's bulk shadowed them from the defensive lasers on the upper column, but they would have been wide open to the deck guns that were normally mounted below the city . . . if those had still been in place.

Urban's hand stiffened against the anchor; he seemed ready to denounce what Alta had said. But then the rigid set of his fingers relaxed. He stroked the anchor's smooth surface. "You might be right."

Lot felt his own heart hammer, wondering how long it would take to retrieve the deck guns from their high orbit and bring them into firing position. "We should hurry."

". . . won't be any prolonged internment. We've contacted Null Boundary and he's agreed to come in-system. Lot, return to the city. You'll be given passage on the ship. Freedom. We won't—"

Urban hissed. He twisted around to look at Lot and excitement enlivened his eyes. Freedom. It was a rousing promise: Get out of Silk free. Go away. Find new worlds, new systems. Never have to face the Well, not ever. Lot felt the temptation himself—and immediately reviled himself for it. He slammed his anchor against the wall, and started pounding it flat, unnecessarily chasing the moving ripples outward from the mat's center. It was empty temptation anyway. "You think Kona would let you go?" He glared at Urban, the charismata of his anger impacting against his own cheeks. "Kona didn't say he was getting on the ship. He'll exile me, but he won't risk you on it. You said it yourself: Null Boundary's same as the old murderers in their eyes."

"You don't know."

"So climb back up and ask him!"

"What's rotting you? You know I'm never going to

be authority's puppet. But if there is a real chance of getting out—"

"I don't want out! I'm going down. That's why I'm here. That's what we came here for." Lot adjusted his cassette, ready to kick off. But then he hesitated. He looked at Urban, while something seemed to open up inside him, a blade of loneliness cutting a red swath through his chest. The tension gathered, while Kona's pleading, reasoning, rational voice worked on.

Finally, Gent broke the spell. "What are you going to do, Urban? Going up? We'll need the supplies you're carrying."

Urban laughed softly. "Shit. Say it. You'll need *me*."

"Maybe."

Urban nodded slowly. "Lot's probably right anyway. The old man wouldn't let me near that ship."

"Does seem likely," Gent agreed.

Lot wanted to say something, but his own pride was so thick in his throat he couldn't force words past it.

"Let's get going then," Urban said. His voice sounded strained, but there was a note of victory in it too. "Before they bring the lasers around." He looked up at the city one more time, while Kona talked ineffectually on. "Hark," he said to his suit DI. "Edit that. I don't want to hear anything else from the city." Then he kicked off the wall.

Lot watched him fall, and when Urban completed his jump, Lot followed. But it was three more jumps before the tension had bled away enough that he could talk to Urban, and that Urban could talk to him.

Dawn came quickly in a glare of white light that swept across the massive cloud structures below them. Their suits glittered silver, reflecting away the radiation. The sight triggered memories, and for a moment Lot felt as if his will had slipped away. He felt hollow inside, waiting . . . for something, he wasn't sure what.

Gent nudged his elbow. "You okay?"

Lot shook his head to clear it. "Yeah. Just tired."

Fatigue had become a real hazard, and they moved more slowly now. Spots drifted in Lot's vision, disorienting him, so that more than once he thought he saw the lasers drifting into position in the dark void overhead.

Daylight also revealed a knob on the column below them. Urban mentioned it first. "Yeah," Gent said. "I think it's an elevator car."

Lot leaned away from the wall, looking down past his shoulder. Half in light, half in shadow, a tiny bump was visible on the column. He couldn't tell how far away it was, or how large. He tried blinking his eyes up to telescopic, but he couldn't get his vision to work right.

He didn't think about the car again for a couple of hours. By then the anomaly had grown large in his vision, and he could clearly make out the truncated crescent of the roof. Even through his fatigue, a chill knotted his gut. Jupiter had left the city. But even authority didn't know if he'd ever reached the planet.

They climbed out on the car's roof around midmorning. They'd come down 140 miles, but a 60-mile climb still lay between them and the planet. They'd gotten no glimpse of the land yet. A storm system hung over the ragged edge of the continent, and all that lay below them was a white glare of cloud tops.

The elevator car hung like a small building against the column, slightly curved to match the slow curvature of the wall. Alta jumped down on the roof first, her bundled anchor swinging at her waist. Lot followed her to the roof's outer edge. They looked over the side, peering down the building's face. He could see the glitter of windows, and seams that marked three sets of doors at the car's lowest level. "We could climb down there." He looked at Alta, and she nodded.

Gent had already gone down the car's side. Now he climbed back up, examining the seam between the car and the elevator column. "It's fused. All around, as far as I can tell. It must have bonded when the tracks were slagged."

Lot looked up. The column above the elevator was scarred, as if it had been partly melted and the slag dragged downward. "You think it's still pressurized?"

Gent shrugged.

"We need to look."

"Sooth." Gent dropped his anchor at his feet, then stepped on it a bit to smooth it out. Lot copied him. He ordered his cassette to feed slowly, then dropped over the side, letting his boots stick and rip across the face of the wall.

He looked in a couple of windows, but they were opaque against the sunlight. Next, he dropped down to the bottom of the car and examined the middle set of doors. But he couldn't find any way of opening them. Gent swung over to join him. "Have you got any more of that explosive spray?" Lot asked. "We could try it on a window."

Gent nodded. His eyes looked grim.

Lot hung on his cord while Gent painted one of the midlevel windows; then they both retreated several yards.

The window blew out in an explosion of debris: blankets like slow birds, dropping in long arcs, keeping pace with squat pillows and pieces of electronic junk glinting in the sunlight.

When the debris had cleared they returned to the window. Looking inside, Lot saw a small cabin. Double bunkbeds hung on two walls, stripped of their bedding. The door was open only a few inches; it looked to have been wrenched off its runners. Debris clogged the gap: blankets, packs, shed exoshell armor. Lot swallowed hard, then climbed through. He pulled some of the debris clear of the doorway, then leaned on the door, forcing it to open wider. "Careful," Gent said.

Lot glanced back, to see Urban and Alta climbing in through the window. He nodded at Gent, then squeezed through the gap and into the hallway.

Doors on both sides stood partly open. Gent joined him, and together they moved cautiously down the hall, glancing into each cabin, stepping carefully over debris that had been scattered across the floor by the sudden depressurization. Lot saw a thigh guard and helmet. A pack of the design issued to Jupiter's army. A woman's white crystal hairbrush.

At the end of the corridor an escalator descended to the next level. They walked down its frozen treads, counting three more levels of deserted cabins. Dust clung in static attraction to the walls, growing thicker as they descended.

They found the bodies on the lowest floor.

Lot performed a rough count, and decided there had been perhaps 180 people aboard. They'd gathered in concentric prayer circles in the open space of the lobby. A few had been reduced to white bones bedded in dust. Others were mummified, their skin like rough wood, stretched taut over protrudent bones. But most had avoided decay.

Lot walked between the kneeling figures, gazing into faces that seemed almost alive beneath an encasement of wrinkled, glassy skin. They were terribly thin. Their fat and muscle had burned away as their Makers had used the only available energy source to secure the sanctity of tissue pattern. But their structure remained. They could be brought back. Maybe. If their Makers had successfully preserved the patterns of their brains.

Lot walked carefully between the circles, crouching to examine each preserved face, trying to see in the withered features people he'd once known. He accessed fixed memories he hadn't explored for years, and gradually attached identifications. Gent helped, and Alta too.

Urban kept his distance. He sat on the escalator watching them, his dark eyes unreadable. Lot tried to copy his expression, scared again of falling down a pit of black emotion. Trapped in his suit, with no outside input . . .

The harsh croak of Urban's voice interrupted his thoughts: "There must be a radio system in this car."

Lot looked at him, not understanding. "You want to call your old man?"

Urban shook his head slowly. "These people. They must have screamed for help for days . . . over the radio. The real people must have listened to them begging for help . . . *for days.*"

Lot frowned. It could be. The direct-line transmission would be easy. "They would have switched off their atriums, I think."

Urban stared at him, and Lot figured he'd said something dumb, but he was too tired to think about it.

They were nearly through the prayer circles when Urban asked in an artificially casual voice, "Jupiter with them?"

"He's not here!" Lot snapped, not knowing until he said it how much that question had been weighing on him.

"Be sure of it, fury," Urban said. "I don't want to drop into the Well if there's not even a ghost to chase."

They made sure of it. Alta and Urban searched the upper floors, while Lot and Gent recorded the identities of everyone in the lobby. They didn't find him. "There could be more cars," Urban said.

Gent nodded. "We'll check them too."

After nearly an hour they gave in and retreated to the upper floor. Gent told everybody to rest, then went outside to survey the elevator column and the void overhead for any sign of pursuit or attack from the city.

Lot kicked a clear space on the floor and settled into it. His suit offered him a straw, but he ignored it. Through a dull buzz in his ears he only half-heard the start of a conversation between Urban and Alta on the dwindling state of their nutrient supply. Alta asked him a question, but he didn't remember answering. The next thing he knew Gent was shaking him awake. It was past noon, and they had to get moving if there was any hope of getting down before dark.

Chapter
22

A grim mood settled on Lot as he worked his way across the face of the car and back to the elevator column. His body hurt, and hunger cramped his belly. The suit didn't offer to feed him anymore. It was the same for all of them. Nutrient reserves had been consumed far faster than expected, and the suit DIs had changed strategy, conserving what was left for their own use.

"It's bit garbage," Urban told Gent. "The way these suits are sucking energy, they have to be flawed. There's an error in the reconstructed design, and you didn't catch it."

Gent answered stonily, "There's no flaw in the design."

Lot nodded, fairly sure the real source of the drain lay elsewhere. "It's us. We run hot." And the ripping damage of jump after jump had placed a high demand on all their self-repair systems.

"Sooth." Gent sounded worried. "Our metabolic rates are likely higher than the norm when these suits were written. I didn't take that into account."

"Then," Urban said, "we better start breathing slow."

Alta answered him, her voice softly confident. "This is not a bad thing. If we run hot, at least we fix fast. An antique metabolism might have failed the cumulative repair."

Lot liked the neat circle of her reasoning. "So we're paying for an advantage?"

"Sure."

"That's very nice," Urban said, "if we've got the currency."

Gent slapped his anchor against the wall. "I should have foreseen this. Dammit. Lot, ready? Then jump."

Lot stayed close to Gent. They checked each other's jump procedures, on guard against the stupid mistakes that always followed in the wake of an exhausted mind.

For Lot, the next couple of hours passed in a blur. They made good progress, dropping forty miles down the column. His mood picked up a little. The sunlight dazzled him. He felt as if he were soaring above the landscape. Though he was still cognizant of the curve of the Well, it was an arc broader than anything he'd ever experienced. Less a curve now than a cloud-covered plain, flat enough to fire the ancient synapses in his mind that had been first arrayed on primeval savannahs. But this was more. He *floated* over the surface, like a spirit in a vision quest, looking down on an ocean of brilliant white clouds piled upon each other in a creamy spiral, completely obscuring the grasping fingers of land that he knew lay beneath. He could see the bulk of the clouds below him, building up like a circular mountain range. He would lose himself sometimes, gazing at the structure of it, taken by the hypnotic beauty of the flowing white vistas. For a while, the clouds became his destination, with the land below of no more interest to him than the bones beneath Alta's smooth white skin.

Later, Lot began to experience a curious pressure at his back, as if some rogue force pushed at him. When he jumped, he sailed a little farther from the column's surface than he had before. It gave him a creepy sensation, and he thought about the phantoms below and Urban's remark about chasing Jupiter's ghost. Then Gent said, "We're deep enough in the atmosphere now, we can feel the wind."

They fell more slowly, held back by atmospheric resistance. Within half an hour they'd entered a dense cloud deck. Visibility dropped abruptly. Water clung to Lot's suit and the wind blew in fierce whispers past his hood. Gent shortened the length of their jumps, and their progress slowed again. But caution paid off. Through the ripping fog Lot saw below them the looming shape of another elevator car. Legs would have been broken if they'd hit the roof in a state of free fall.

They explored the car, but it was empty, and from the track damage they guessed that it had been ascending when its progress had been stopped. Inside, they found the discarded power pack from a bead rifle and graffiti on the wall that declared in a long flowing script: *on this day we have entered a higher existence.*

"So they got all the way down," Urban said.

Lot ran his fingers across the graceful alphabet, then turned to look at Gent. Gent's eyes crinkled in what was probably a smile, lost behind the muzzle of his respirator. "Soon," he said, and Lot nodded.

They set out again, descending through the troposphere in storm conditions. Gent wouldn't let them drop more than seventy-five feet at a time—about the limit of vision in the day's fading light. Progress was reduced to a slow creep. The pace was frustrating, but Lot could only feel grateful for the respite from the horrible jarring of the long jumps. He was beyond tired. The false clarity of exhaustion ruled him. He babbled philosophy over the suit comm, running on about the encroachment of entropy upon the Universe until Urban kindly told him to shut up. A few minutes later he noticed that his gloves had begun to slip.

He blinked hard, not sure he was getting the facts right. But there. When he laid his right hand against the column, he could drag it. Beneath his palm he could feel the rasp of the hot zone against the column, but it refused to take solid hold. His left hand had a better grip, though it slipped a little too. So far his leggings seemed to be holding up. Next, he slapped the anchor out flat and examined it. With a sinking feeling, he watched the edges curl. And still seven miles to go. Softly: "Gent?"

"Yeah?"

"My equipment's failing."

"*Shit.*"

Lot showed him the condition of the gloves; the peeling edges of the anchor. Gent checked his pack. "Your nutrient reserve's been sucked dry."

"The suit didn't warn me."

"The suit's as dizzy as you are."

Or maybe there really had been a flaw in the design . . . though Lot didn't suggest that out loud.

Gent called Urban and Alta in, then carefully checked the state of their equipment. It seemed to be fully functional. He inventoried their remaining reserves, then divided it, linking a couple of full packets into Lot's system. Lot's gloves still slipped, but the anchor held tight. "Your suit's putting energy where it's needed most," Gent said.

Lot nodded.

Urban smoothed his anchor against the column. "We're going to have to start risking longer jumps. We can't keep moving at this pace, or the suits will fail before we reach the ground."

Gent was a silhouette in the gathering dark. He nodded. "I'll go first." That assertion was greeted by a three-way chorus of dissent, but Gent silenced it with an angry chop of his hand. "This is my expedition," he said.

"But—"

"No. Don't follow until you get my all-clear. I want Lot coming down second. Then Urban, then Alta. Understood?"

"But Gent—"

"*Understood?*" Something in his tone left no room for argument. They nodded. Gent checked his anchor, then kicked off, disappearing swiftly into the running clouds.

Near full dark the clouds around them began to flicker dully with distant lightning. Thunder rumbled in ominous warning, and Gent began taking longer and longer jumps. Over the next twenty minutes the thunderheads moved closer. The surrounding clouds began to light up like lanterns, and a few minutes later they could see lightning bolts forking across the cloud faces. The thunder was so loud now it could be felt as much as heard. The column itself seemed to hum with an inner vibration that intensified with every deafening clap.

They were quiet, their pensive gazes fixed on the storm around them while they waited for their turn to jump. Like small animals, sensing the approach of a predator.

Gent kicked off. Lot checked his anchor, waiting for permission to follow. Nearly forty seconds passed. He started to get scared, but finally Gent called up. "Okay, Lot. Set your cassette for maximum range. Check him, Alta."

"Checking."

Lot dropped. Lightning flickered twice during his fall, and somewhere near thirty-five in his count it began to rain. He hit the end of the cord, every muscle in his body braced against the impact. Then he swung into the wall. Rivulets of water ran sideways around the column, blown by the wind. More water skittered across his visor, blurring his vision. He secured a grip with his leggings, using his hands in a near-useless attempt to screen his visor from the rain. "Gent?" He could just make him out, about twenty feet below. The DI called his anchor down.

"Stay there," Gent said. "I'll climb up to you."

The cassette spun. Gent had covered maybe half the distance when the next bolt struck. It hit Lot's dangling anchor, then forked, one branch leaping onto the column, another blasting up the anchor cord and through the fabric of Lot's suit. Lot felt a sense of compression. Something wrenched at him. Then abruptly, he was falling.

He didn't have time to scream. He brushed past Gent, feeling the harsh jab of grabbing fingers. The suit DI was running a technical chant in some foreign tongue. Then Lot remembered the anchor at his waist. He clutched at it, expecting to find a ruined mass. But it felt spongy, and whole. He pitched it back toward the elevator column. An edge caught. He remembered to brake the cord. A bone-jarring jolt, and his descent stopped. "All systems nominal," the suit announced, in its accented Silken voice. "Please secure position immediately."

Lot swung frantically toward the wall, his gloved hand out. But before he could touch it, the anchor slipped. He bounced down several inches.

Another bolt of lightning ripped close by. In its glare he saw the anchor . . . hanging by its edge. As the bolt flickered, another couple of inches peeled off. He dropped again. With a desperate effort he lunged for the wall. But the wind was against him, blowing him out over the abyss. He screamed, bracing himself for the moment when the anchor would rip free.

Gent dropped out of the clouds. Lot saw him in IR. Gent used his boots to brake his descent. As soon as his leggings locked on, his anchor came plummeting after him. He didn't have time to secure it. He lunged for Lot's anchor, grabbing it with both hands just as it peeled off the wall. Lot felt the sickening plunge, and squeezed his eyes shut. But he was brought up again with a sharp jerk. He flailed for the wall. Maybe the wind had eased, because this time he got a finger on the column, though he still couldn't get close enough for the glove to knit. He could see Gent overhead, secured by only his leggings as he bent nearly double in a struggle to hold on to Lot's failing anchor.

Lot swung closer to the wall. His ankle brushed the column, though the legging didn't seize. Another bolt of lightning cracked overhead. He slipped down with a sudden jerk, then slammed hard into the wall. This time his leggings knit, and one of his gloves too. He felt a snap-pressure at his waist, and looked down to see his bundled anchor hanging at the end of his cord. Then he looked up. Even through the rain-blur, he could see immediately that the wall of the elevator column above him was empty.

"*Gent!*" His hoarse scream cut through the cacophony of voices on the radio. He started crabbing down the column, as fast as he could move while the suit muttered soft warnings in his ears. "*Gent!*" he screamed. "*Gent!*" Until finally Gent's voice reached him through the lightning crackle.

"Secure your anchor, Lot!" He was breathing heavily, his voice pitched metal-tight. "*Now!* Get it secured."

"Gent, where are you?"

For long, dark seconds the suit radio was silent. Then Gent's voice came to him, as close and familiar as his own skin. "Convince them that it's right," he said.

"*Gent!*"

But Gent didn't speak again.

Lot hugged the wall, his hooded cheek pressed against its slick surface, while Alta and Urban's panicky voices played in his ears. "I'm here," he croaked. "I'm okay. But Gent's gone."

He thought of Nesseleth and her own dreadful plunge into the Well. He pressed himself harder against the wall, his hood's optical band filling up with liquid that he only gradually realized was tears. He closed his eyes tight and the suit quickly absorbed the excess.

By the time Alta and Urban found him he was calm again. They huddled together, sharing the pressure of bodies, if not heat, and waited for the storm to pass.

* * *

Around midnight the sky started to clear. A few bold stars appeared, and then the dim wash of the nebula, though the wind didn't ease. Lot's anchor had begun to curl at the edges again, but there was nothing they could do about it. They started descending, calling constantly for Gent, in case a swirl in the wind had swept him back against the elevator column.

Near four in the morning they began to see vegetation on the column: at first only clusters of lichen growing in tiny, scalloped depressions in the column wall. But soon they saw small shrubs too, rooted in pockets of windblown soil that had collected behind the lichen patches. At about the same time, Ord woke up. It slid silently out of Lot's pack, sending one tentacle probing across his face. He jumped so hard he almost lost his failing grip. Ord mouthed something, but Lot couldn't make out the words past the muffling layer of the hood and the sough of the wind.

Dawn had begun to lighten the sky when they finally reached the last elevator car. Lot remembered the day he'd seen it through the warden's eyes. Now he dropped down numbly on its roof, his boots sinking deep into a soggy moss that supported a thick assortment of sword-leafed plants and several small trees.

"We should be careful," Urban said. "Could be animals here."

"This high up?" Lot asked. They were still some twelve hundred feet above the terminal building.

"Some things fly."

That brought a dark shadow to his mind. *Some things don't.*

Alta crossed the hummocky roof, to peer down the car's front.

"We can't break in," Urban said. "No explosive spray."

That had gone with Gent.

Alta turned back to look at him. "The doors are open."

Lot frowned. He and Urban went to have a look, and saw that she was right. All three pairs of doors stood open.

"It could be drier in there," Alta said.

Lot shook his head. "We can't stop. We're not down yet."

Urban laid a reassuring hand on his arm. "Easy, fury.

Nothing's going to stop us now. But we should rest, for a few hours anyway."

Lot felt uneasy, but he didn't argue. Maybe Urban was right.

They dropped down the front of the car. Lot dangled outside the central entrance, carefully scanning the interior. Vegetation choked the lobby. Using IR, he sighted several small warm-fuzzies within the foliage. Urban confirmed that interpretation. "Things in there," he said warily.

"They're small," Alta countered.

"Could be toxic. You don't know."

"We'll move through quietly. Find a back room."

Urban went in first. As he clambered across the vegetation, one of the warm-fuzzies in Lot's field of view began to stir. "Watch out," Lot warned. "There's something—" A horrible screech ripped through the air, almost enough to separate skin from muscle, even within the muffling barrier of the suit. Urban dropped flat on his face just as a swarm of warm-fuzzies popped out of the vegetation, shrieking and darting for the doorways, their ribbed wings scratching at Lot as they passed.

"Well, I guess it's ours now," Alta said, when the commotion finally died down. Lot could only see a few small IR points still lingering in the lobby of the car.

Urban got up, cursing softly. "Nice world you inherited here, fury."

Lot smiled. As soon as he got inside the car, Ord slid off his shoulder and across the floor. Urban jumped as it swept past him. It slipped up the escalator and disappeared. "Where's it going?"

"Check things out, I guess."

Lot stood quietly in the doorway, while Alta pulled in her anchor. Outside, he could see tree branches swaying grandly up and down in what was still a powerful wind. He could hear the wind's own raspy voice as it growled past the corners of the suspended car. *Deception Well, real time.* "We're not dead yet," he observed.

"Haven't breathed the air," Urban pointed out helpfully.

Lot nodded. That was true. The governors hadn't passed judgment yet.

He stepped closer to the door, feeling as if he were a

rogue spirit floating high above the forest. *We came here for a reason.* He reached up to squeeze the seam of his hood.

"Do you wish to unseal the hood?" the suit asked him.

"Yes."

"Are you sure?"

"Yes."

The suit's queries must have been audible over the general comm, because Urban was staring at him. Alta too.

He turned away from them. Looking out over the wind-tossed forest, he touched the seam again. It split under the pressure, and a finger of warm, humid air touched his throat. He pulled the hood back, off his face, and drew in a cautious breath.

With his nose he could smell a sweet, heavy scent. With his sensory tears he caught stray wisps of human emotion: curiosity, anger, pent-up sexuality, as if someone were snapping open select pheromonal capsules several hundred yards away. He rubbed at his sensory tears, but the sign persisted, diverse as a night in Silk. . . .

"I can sense them," he whispered. The suit mike was still against his throat, picking up his voice. He leaned out the doorway, searching the forest and the terminal building below. But even in IR he could detect no large life-forms.

Urban had come up behind him. Now his hand closed firmly on Lot's elbow. He tugged him back from the edge. "Come on." His voice sounded tinny and distant, coming from the crumpled hood. "Let's sleep. A few hours, that's all. Then we'll look."

Ord found them a room on the third floor. The carpet and walls were black and moldy, and the air in the room had a sour smell, but at least there weren't any animals. Lot and Urban dragged the door mostly closed; then they settled down with Alta, leaving Ord to watch.

Lot lay on his back, staring at the ceiling. An odor of hot spice and rot rose up from the carpet, pressed out by his weight against the fibers. He snuggled close to Alta, but she held herself stiff, and did not respond. After a minute, she asked, "Urban?"

"Yeah?" Their voices rising faint from somewhere behind his neck.

"These suits won't last much longer without a resupply." Urban lay on her other side, and she turned now to face him. "The nutrient reserves are so low . . . if the rebreather function fails, we could suffocate in our sleep."

"Yeah." Urban was silent a moment, then he sat up, and started rummaging in his pack. "There's some reserve left in here. I'm going to transfer it to your pack—"

"No." She put her hand on his.

Lot stiffened, but he didn't move, or say anything. Several seconds of silence passed. Finally, "You're right," Urban conceded, his voice curiously full. "We should save it for the climb down tomorrow."

They initiated the query sequence, then opened their suits—at precisely the same time. Abruptly, Lot could sense their fear . . . and other things he didn't want to examine too closely. Still, he couldn't completely stifle the sense of dread that bloomed in his belly. He lay quietly, listening to their whispered conversation about the quality of the air, the slimy dark walls, about Lot.

"Is he asleep?"

"I think so."

But he remained awake long after they'd slipped out of the room. When the wind blew hard, he imagined he could feel the elevator swaying slightly on the column. Ord came over and laid its tentacles on his forehead and tut-tutted . . . and Lot drifted into a—dream? Strange. He'd lived most of his life without being aware of any dreams. Now he climbed through an endless, dark descent with Gent falling, always falling, and no matter how many times the dream looped back Lot could not reach out a hand in time to catch him.

He cried out and woke himself. Muted sunlight streamed in through the filthy window. The room was stiflingly hot, and he could feel the slick, sticky burden of perspiration on his cheeks. Alta and Urban had come back. They slept quietly at his side. But there was something more here. His hackles rose as he sensed a foreign presence in the room. He held himself still, trying to determine what and where it was. Until, near the door, the pattern of mildew seemed to blur and shift, briefly outlining a tiny human form.

Chapter
23

It stood no more than three feet high. Lot watched its vague shape blur and shift as it moved cautiously along the wall, drawing slowly nearer to where Urban slept. He didn't dare to even tense his muscles, lest it suspect he was awake.

He waited, while it crept to within three feet of Urban's sleeping form. Then he launched himself on it, diving over Alta and Urban to hit it with the full weight of his torso. It disintegrated beneath him. A gelatinous mass splashed across his chest, then wrapped around his right shoulder in a smooth, hot flow that reached as far as his exposed neck. He hit the floor with only a thin membrane beneath him, and that was flowing away fast.

But the impact had weakened its camouflage function. He could see it clearly now: a pool of green liquid interlaced with gold wire, petite human arms and legs rapidly reforming as the liquid congealed. The warden lifted a head to bear on him. *"Lot, look out!"* Alta shouted; Urban's roar of outrage filled the room.

Lot kept his gaze fixed on the warden's thickening tissues, searching the semitransparent ooze for an object of greater density: the green aerosol capsule that carried the assault Maker Placid Antigua had used. He hadn't noticed the weapon when he'd run the wardens. He hadn't thought to look.

A tiny green hand lifted toward him, still partly viscous liquid, the fingers not quite formed yet, but suddenly Lot knew the capsule would be there, embedded in the palm or the forearm. He struck the limb with his fist, over and over again, using his enhanced reflexes to smash the tissue against the floor. On the third stroke he felt the poison sack. It slipped like soft rubber beneath his coiled hand.

He changed tactics. Digging his fingers into the gelatinous mix, he groped for the poison capsule, determined to tear it out. Urban appeared at his side. Lot shouted at him to search the warden's other arm.

He got his fingers around the capsule. The warden's flesh tightened as it strove to use pressure to immobilize his grip. But Lot hooked the capsule anyway and wrenched it out. Urban was shouting, cursing, as he dug into the other arm. Alta screamed at them to *"Get out! Get out!"* Urban yanked the second capsule free and dove for the door.

The warden's face was nearly complete now. Lot found himself eye to eye with soft green features vaguely sketched in beaded lines. It seemed familiar, and yet, not quite *believable.* Too abstract; too stylized. A generic representation of a human face.

Lot raised his fist. The warden's self-repair function probably demanded a heavy load of metabolic energy. It had already drawn deeply on that. If he could damage it again, it might take longer to re-form. He drove his fist against its face, smashing down through the small nose, driving all the way to the floor below. The green tissue sloshed in grotesque, blunted fountains.

Then Lot was on his feet and squeezing through the doorway's narrow opening, into the shadowy corridor. Urban and Alta were ready. They leaned hard on the smooth door. It popped forward on its track, sliding shut with a harsh *snick!*

Lot stood in the shadows, breathing heavily. A soft pounding played out against the closed door. He didn't think the warden would have the strength to open it, but Alta wasn't taking any chances. She leaned hard against the door, her eyes red-rimmed, silent rage on her face. She'd managed to toss their packs into the corridor. He started to reach for his, then remembered the capsule in his hand.

He looked down at it. It was about two inches long, teal green in color with a spray head at one end. An innocuous sheath for a deadly poison . . . could they use it?

Urban was already shouldering his pack. "Come on, fury. Let's jump before the commandant brings up another warden. Now they know we're here, we've got to get as far into the forest as we can before—"

"Where's Ord?" Lot interrupted, looking up and down the corridor in sudden concern. He scooped up his pack with one hand while his gaze searched the shadowy junctures of ceiling and wall. "It was supposed to be watching." He frowned, retrieving a detailed picture of the room from fixed memory. He searched it, but Ord's spidery body was not part of that scene. "Where did it go?"

Alta could not bring herself to say it out loud, but the look in her eyes clearly communicated her opinion: he was a fool to waste concern over the device.

"It's a tool," Lot growled at her. "It's got a design similar to the wardens. Maybe we could arm it with these capsules." He held the poison sack out for her to see, but she wouldn't look at it. The charismata of his displeasure had fallen across her, and she'd turned her head away. Once again her vulnerability was exposed. *And she resented it.* In a moment of sudden clarity, he understood that. For Jupiter she would have done anything. But he was not Jupiter, and she resented the power he held over her.

As if to confirm that conclusion, her small hand closed into a defiant fist. "You never get it straight," she accused. "Authority would have used Ord against you. They made it. They controlled it."

Lot felt his heart lurch. "What did you do with it?"

Alta just glared at him. Urban stepped close to Lot, dropping the second capsule into his hand. "We dismembered it," he said. "Then we tossed the pieces into the wind. It had to be done, fury, or this expedition wouldn't have lasted another day."

Lot looked at the twin capsules in his hand. He tried to tell himself Urban was right, that it had to be done. But the viciousness stung, a brute execution no different from what the warden had attempted to deliver. (Or had the warden intended to hurt them? It hadn't actually attacked.)

A sick feeling settled into Lot's belly. His hand closed over the capsules, ready to fling them to the end of the corridor. But at the last moment he reconsidered, and instead put them in a small pocket at his waist.

Alta and Urban had already started trudging down

the escalator. "Come on, fury," Urban called. "If your old man's here, it's going to take some work to find him."

Beneath the elevator car, the column's surface appeared heavily damaged. Last night they'd seen shallow scallops in the wall where plants had taken root. That deterioration increased dramatically in the last thousand feet of their descent. Here the scallops were up to ten inches across, and some of them overlapped. Lot pulled out the vegetation, to find hollows as deep as his fist.

"It looks like an infection," Alta said, stroking the curve of a smooth depression. "It looks like it's eating right through the column."

"It's not," Lot told her. "It's quiescent now. Kona said it happened around that day."

Lot went first in the rotation, leading the descent in a series of short drops, no more than fifty yards at a time. The flat black roof of the terminal building spread out beneath them, filling the valley floor. It looked slagged; half-melted by some great heat. Thick patches of gray lichen filled the folds and furrows. Alta hissed as she studied the damage. "Did authority turn the deck guns against him?"

No one answsered. Kona had sworn to them he knew nothing of what happened here that day. That day, the wardens had been lost, and the column had been damaged by some unknown mechanism. Lot almost wished it *had* been the deck guns. "Let's just get down."

The elevator column was anchored within the heel of a U-shaped bay cut into the side of the building. The open arms of the U embraced the beginning of the weathered road that ran out of the valley. The day was cloudless, and in Kheth's noon glare the roof radiated a baking heat. As they drew closer, Lot pulled his hood half over his head to shield himself.

He remembered the time he'd seen this valley through a warden's eyes. Fog had draped the land, and possibility had seemed to lurk just beyond the obscuring mists. Today Kheth shone with the force of rational inspection. In its glare the forest appeared dully normal.

Lot looked closer. He studied the shapes of individual trees and the way they interlocked in clusters of shape and texture to make the weave of the forest. Here and there, distant trees flowered in mushrooming canopies of red and yellow. Leaf color varied too. Though green dominated, there was green seamed with yellow, or rimmed with red, green in a hundred variants of shade and shininess. Some trees sparkled as their waxy leaves moved in the slow breeze.

Lot squinted, trying to push his vision into telescopic. But the system kept falling back to standard. He sighed. It was just another symptom of his deteriorating condition, as his body reserved his declining physiological energy for more essential tasks.

"Look there," Alta said. "There. Just a few feet out." He followed the white glare of her pointing arm until he sighted a transparent . . . *insect*? hovering on buzzing horizontal wings in the updraft that rose from the terminal roof. Its body was shaped like a rounded fin, deep in the belly, but extremely thin, perhaps three inches long. He could see the shadowing of its internal organs through its transparent flesh. Another glass fin glinted just beyond the first. Then abruptly, he was aware of the creatures all around him, hundreds of them, hovering innocuously in the rising heat. They showed no awareness of the intruding humans.

A pack of black-winged flyers appeared suddenly from one end of the valley. They remained distant, staying close to the valley wall as they skirted the forest canopy.

"Looks like no bogeymen today," Urban said. His tone was cocky, but his nervousness worked on Lot like a high-pitched whine.

Urban stopped the descent when they were level with the roof. A horizontal gulf of some sixty feet separated them from the slagged rooftop. "We don't have any way to get over there," Urban said. The heat had raised a ruddy sheen in his dark cheeks.

Lot nodded. He looked down, examining the base of the column. Where the elevators had once come to rest in the heel of the open bay, there was now a broad, sunlit apron of ferns interspersed with spindly trees. The vegetation spilled out through the bay, only gradually giving way to the valley road. *Jupiter would have gone that way.* But nobody knew how far Jupiter had gotten. Alta dangled overhead, silent, her mood sharp and critical. "We'll go all the way down," Lot said.

The heat eased as soon as they dropped below the level of the roof. Once they'd descended several feet, they stopped again. The terminal building stood only four stories high. Each floor opened onto the elevator terminus. Daylight fell dimly on the smooth expanses, finally giving way to full darkness in the building's cavernous interior.

Wherever Kheth's light touched, there was vegetation. Trunkless plants like ribbed fins were most abundant, clinging to the floors and the soaring pillars, their emerald green faces spread in overlapping clumps. There were a few small trees too, and a trailing, fernlike growth in the distant zones that enjoyed at best a half-light. Small bright shapes whirled in the air just on the border of light and shadow, turning erratically like falling leaves, but never quite descending. The same sixty-foot gap separated them from the empty floors. Apart from the epiphytic vegetation, it all had a very utilitarian look, reminding Lot of Silk's industrial core, rather than the graceful city itself.

He wondered what great project this building had been made to serve. Looking at its empty decks, he suspected it had never seen real use. The Old Silkens had been taken away so soon.

They started down again, examining each level as they dropped past it. On the ground, they paused to gather up their climbing gear, stashing it in their packs. Ferns crunched under their boots, the broken fronds releasing a tight, dusty odor. Lot listened carefully, but heard only the skittering of tiny, hidden creatures.

Since awakening this morning, he'd caught no sign of human presence. The jumbled auras of last night had taken on a dreamlike quality in his memory. He shouldered his pack, gazing out of the bay, to the road . . . and the forest. Something was out there. He couldn't sense it. Not yet. But anticipation pulled threads of tension through his body.

He felt Urban looking at him, so he turned his head, to encounter that familiar, cocky grin. "So where to, fury? You do have a plan?"

Lot smiled, as the tenuousness of their situation rolled in on him. Leaving the city had been something of a spur-of-the-moment decision. Now they were isolated on a potentially lethal and little understood world, without food or communications or transport or data analysis. His smile faded. With Gent gone, they didn't even have good advice. He winced under a sudden surge of harsh emotion. Gent had died to save his life, to get him down here. *Why?* What was he supposed to prove? That he could die here too? Or that he could live here?

No. Something more.

A tiny flitting creature landed on his gloved hand. He looked down to discover a fly, a perfectly ordinary little fly, exactly like the ones so irresistibly drawn to his sundews. Its triangular wings lay like glass panes across its back. He squinted at it. Had its kind been here since the days of the Old Silkens?

Part of the system.

He could not say yet just what that meant. So. Perhaps he was here to find out.

He looked tentatively at Urban. "We should probably get out of this valley. Away from the elevator column. There's bound to be more wardens around. We might as well make ourselves a little harder to find."

They debated whether they should use the road. Alta wanted to seek the depths of the forest, hide themselves as quickly as possible. Urban wanted to keep to the open, arguing that their presence here was no secret, and that it would be easier for them to spot a warden on the road than under the speckled shadows of the trees. Lot stepped away from the circle of their tension.

Beyond the sheltering walls of the terminal building, the old road struggled to hold back the advance of the forest. It was not in good condition. The pearly gray surface looked as if it had been preserved at the peak of a fine-grained boil, each tiny, rising bubble flash-frozen at the moment of bursting. Where overhanging trees provided some shade, rainwater glistened in the hollows. Lot stepped out onto the surface. With a disheartening *crunch* the fragile bubble walls collapsed into dust.

Yet despite the damage, the road retained much of its former glory. No weeds had taken root on it. In fact, only a handful of leaves and a few scattered blossoms cluttered its tortured surface, hinting at the survival of at least one class of maintenance nanomech. And it cut an impressive swath through the forest: 150 feet from edge to edge. Trees crowded up against it, though, in dense, leafy walls that sight could not penetrate. A slow thermal current rose from the artificial surface, setting some of the leaves asway. Anything could be hiding in there.

Lot squinted along the roadbed, trying to remember exactly where he'd seen the phantoms the day he'd run the warden. Suddenly, he blinked hard, trying to get his eyes to focus on a spot about a quarter-mile away. "Hey!" he called to Alta and Urban. "Check that." He glanced back at them. "There. Where the road begins to curve."

Urban trotted to his side, his gaze fixed on the point Lot had indicated. He wasn't squinting. Maybe his eyes were working okay. "Banana trees, fury!"

"They're fruiting, no?"

"Ripe and ready!" He looked at Lot. "But where'd they come from?"

"The Old Silkens. Must be. Nothing's lost in the Well."

" 'Cept people."

"Maybe."

The presence of food decided them. They stuck to the road. To Lot's surprise, the condition of the road improved steadily as they left the terminal building behind. By the time they reached the banana grove, they were walking on a smooth, flawless surface.

The bananas seemed as normal as any in the gardens of Silk, unaffected by the manipulations of the elusive governors. After that they found other fruit trees growing along the road: mango and rambutan, lychee and ahuacatl. They stood in dense groves, the vigorous descendants of what must have been an allee of young fruit trees in the days of Old Silk.

Lot climbed one of the ahuacatl trees. It was hung with spiderwebs. He brushed them aside and climbed higher, up to the pendulous bearing branches. Reaching out, he plucked one of the heavy green fruits, then dropped it for Urban to catch. Soon they had enough to fill one pack, and he jumped down. Alta had gathered some of the spiny rambutan.

They ate quickly, squatting in the shade of the trees. "We need to refuel the suits," Urban said, looking thoughtfully at the green rind in his hands. "I wonder if they can use this stuff?" He started playing with the tubes that fed out of his pack, while carrying on a soft conversation with his DI. Lot listened for a while, but the food in his belly had made him sleepy and soon his attention drifted to the darting pattern of a swarm of tiny flies as they buzzed over a rotting ahuacatl that had smashed against the leaf mold. Another spoiled fruit looked half-eaten. He could see the scrape marks of small, sharp teeth in the exposed green flesh. Some of the flies were buzzing very close to him now, their black bodies like darting specks in his vision. He jumped at a sudden, sharp sting on his cheek.

Alta looked at him, eyes wide. "There's blood there."

He swiped at the spot. A minute smear of blood reddened his finger. *Biting flies?*

Urban crouched at his side, taking a closer look. "You think it's poisonous?"

Lot shrugged, wondering the same thing himself, but not wanting to admit it. "Our Makers can handle it."

Alta's fear touched him then, like a dark mist under the trees. The city suddenly seemed very far away. What was going on there, in the aftermath of the riot?

"Let's get out of here," Alta said.

They slipped back up to the road. Lot emerged last. As he stepped out onto the gray surface, he thought he heard a rustling noise behind him. Turning quickly, he saw a blurred smear of motion deep in the shadowed brown world under the low-hanging branches. The disturbance took only a second to slide out of sight and into the deeper forest.

"Fury?"

Urban had already gone with Alta several steps up the road. Now he looked quizzically back at Lot.

"A warden's trailing us."

Urban's face darkened. "You still have those capsules we took from the other one?"

"Yeah."

"Get 'em out. We might have to use them."

Lot retrieved them from his pocket, giving one to Urban. They experimented a minute, until Urban managed to eject a stream of the poison—so fine it couldn't be seen—but they all knew it was working because at the point of impact the road began to melt and boil in a self-sustaining reaction that swept outward in an ever-widening circle, chewing up the pavement, forcing them to scramble out of the way. "Oh, shit," Urban whispered, when the infection approached the edge of the pavement without showing any sign of slowing down.

"No," Alta said, still backing away. "It can't keep going. It has to have some limiting mechanism—"

The boil reached the edge of the road. Lot held his breath. But Alta was right; the reaction failed to spread into the forest. And when he looked again, he saw that the damage to the road had slowed, and soon it stopped entirely. The pavement had not quite been melted fully across.

"Thank you," Alta whispered, though it wasn't clear to whom her gratitude was directed.

"Yeah, fun stuff," Urban said. He fingered the capsule cautiously, before slipping it into his suit pocket.

Lot put the other one away. The melted section of the road glittered, its surface rough and uneven . . . though it was still discernibly a road—unlike Captain Antigua, who had not much resembled a human by the time the warden's disassembly Maker finished with her.

Lot tried to push the thought away.

He turned to Urban. "Did you find a way to refuel the suits?"

Urban shook his head. "Bit garbage. The suit design is so primitive, it doesn't have the nanomech to handle anything but dilute liquid recycling."

Lot puzzled over that. "You mean pee?"

"Hope you've got a high sugar content in your urine."

Lot groaned. "Sounds like an awfully slow way to refuel."

Alta seemed confused. "Refueling never seemed important. We wanted to bring enough juice to get here. Nothing else mattered."

Lot stared at her in consternation. He wanted to yell at her, *What were you thinking when you brought us here?*

But they'd been in it together, he knew that. And the reason they'd done it involved nothing of thought, or planning. It was all about the way Jupiter had left them. Lot knew he would have come here if it meant dropping naked and alone into the forest. *Why* he felt that way he still couldn't say.

With the caloric energy of the ahuacatl flush in their veins, they moved quickly, keeping strictly to the center of the roadway. At first they went in dead silence, listening for any telltale rustle. But by the time the road began its climb out of the valley they'd relaxed a little. Lot had been trailing behind, his gaze roving constantly over the vegetation and the shimmering heat waves rising on the roadbed. Now he hurried a bit, catching up with Alta. She glanced at him warily. He stepped a pace farther away, trying not to let it touch him. "Did Gent talk to you about this?" he asked her. "Did he say what he expected to do when . . . ?"

She actually relaxed a little. "He said we'd find Jupiter. That's all." She held out her hand to Urban as he dropped back to join them. Lot tried not to see it. He took another gander back over his shoulder, his gaze sweeping the heat shimmers, trying hard to focus on what counted. *Gent expected to find Jupiter . . . alive?*

"Do you know if he . . . had any contact with Jupiter, since that day?"

She looked at him curiously. "He's in all of us, Lot. I can feel his presence now, like a guiding light."

Sound seemed muted. Lot could hear the dull wash of his own breath, the tramp of their feet. "What are you talking about?"

She looked startled. "You don't know?"

"Alta . . ."

She stopped abruptly, her gaze troubled. "You have to know."

"Know what?" Urban asked softly.

She looked at him, as if for reassurance. "He's here." She tapped her breast. "I can feel him inside me, like . . . like a plexus. Tendrils of warmth. Emotional warmth, like comfort, like love. That's the seed, Gent said. And it'll grow when we're with him. It'll fill up our bodies, and we'll forget all the bad things we've ever done, all the conflicts and the jealousies. We'll be perfect then. All of us together. Part of the soul of this world."

She looked again to Lot, this time with a pitying gaze. "You can't feel it?"

He shook his head, resentment rising in his throat. She couldn't sense Jupiter. If she felt anything, it was an infatuation, a delusion, a mental illness that the monkey house had not detected. He didn't need her sympathy.

But in her dismay, she missed the shift of his mood. "I don't understand. It was the same for Gent. It was the same for everyone else in the quarter. But not for you?"

He didn't answer.

"Lot, you should know him best."

His temper snapped. "I don't know him at all!"

She stiffened, but she held her ground. "Then I'm sorry for you. But if Jupiter's left you a harder path to walk, it's for a reason. You have to believe that."

"I don't believe anything." He turned away from her and strode fast up the road, feeling like an idiot and on fire and not understanding why. After a few minutes he remembered to be alert for the wardens' telltale blur. Alta and Urban trailed behind him. He could hear them talking sometimes, though he didn't try to understand the words. Slowly, his attention shifted back to the forest.

As Kheth swung round to late afternoon, animal life began to stir. Lot could hear a distant chorus of hooting, and closer, a bell-like clanging call, rising over a piping bird song.

The road climbed the valley wall, its broad expanse supported on pillars that held it like a shelf above the forest canopy. As Lot neared the peak of the ridge, an eerie ululation rose from somewhere just below. He paused, gazing over the ornamental rail. Through a break in the trees he saw something moving. At first he thought it was a warden's blur, so closely did its mottled brown and black hide match the leaf litter through which it crawled. But after a second, his mind distinguished its shape: it was a serpent. Or at least, that part of the thing that he could see was serpentlike. Tentacular. It slid from his view without giving him a look at its head, leaving him uncertain of its real appearance. But he had the distinct impression that it had been huge. The sliding section he'd seen had been twelve feet or more. At least it had been moving away from the road.

A few minutes later he reached the ridgetop—and the end of the road. He stared in surprise at the abrupt termination. The edge of the pearly gray paving looked as if it had been torn, twisted, ripped off from a ribbon of similar tissue. The ragged edge had been stretched thin as human skin in some places. Beyond was only undisturbed forest.

He glanced back over his shoulder. Behind him all was normal. He could look back into the valley and see the black terminal building, the elevator column rising from it like an overlay dividing the sky. Alta and Urban were small figures, trudging steadily up the slope.

He frowned again at the unfinished road, wondering

which way they should go now. On the far side of the ridge, the land fell away in an exaggerated panorama that echoed on a grand scale the slopes of Silk. Narrow valleys cut the slope like giant claw marks. Steep ridges rose between them, thrusting knife-edged profiles into the hazy late-afternoon sky. In a few places the brown, upside-down teardrops of recent landslides scarred the nearly vertical valley walls, but for the most part the land wore a uniform skin of hearty green.

Far below, a thread of gold held the horizon. Lot frowned, then realized it was the ocean, reflecting Kheth's burnished light.

A cool breeze moved up the slope, bearing with it a sense of human presence. Lot stiffened. Then he held his breath, focusing all his concentration on impressions drawn in by his sensory tears. *Jupiter.* The aura was weak, barely perceptible on the failing breeze, but he had no doubt of its identity. *Jupiter.*

Somewhere below them, and whole.

Chapter
24

He turned at the sound of a step, startled, because he'd thought Alta and Urban were still a hundred yards or more behind. He froze as he recognized a warden. With its camouflage mode switched off, its skin was a dull jade green. It stood facing away from him, staring into the forest along the descending spine of the ridge. He couldn't see its face. Who possessed it?

He edged away, back over the ridgetop, back where Urban and Alta were still climbing up. His fingers slipped into his pocket, to curl around the capsule. The warden on the road turned to look at him. Its mouth opened, but no sound came forth. Its face scrunched up in a parody of severe mental effort.

"This has nothing to do with you!" Lot shouted at it. "Leave us—"

The face changed, startling Lot so badly his shouted defiance broke off. Its features blanked, then quickly re-formed in minute detail. Its mouth was beaded with hundreds of tiny mouths; its eyes the same. Every shadow of Sypaon's features was drawn with a sequence of speaking lips. But Lot heard no sound; sensed no emotion from her.

She seemed to realize the pointlessness of her efforts, for the face blanked again. Then she turned and plunged into the brush.

Almost immediately, a loud sound of thrashing vegetation erupted from the forest, punctuated by a steamy hiss. An acrid, acid stink exploded from the site. Lot scrambled back, as a plume of white smoke filtered out of the leaves.

Urban and Alta had heard the commotion. They called to him. Lot started to look back, to turn in their direction, when the vegetation under the smoke plume exploded upward. From amid the chaos of spinning leaves and swirling steam he watched the serpent rise.

It was like no snake he'd ever seen in the VR. Its head was a flattened disk ringed by a fringe of arm-long tentacles patterned in black and brown, smaller versions of the exaggerated tentacle that had evolved into its massive body. As it reared high among the trees, it lifted its head, exposing the underside of the disk, where it held the warden's jade body clenched in a black, star-shaped . . . Lot could not quite bring himself to think *mouth*. It was a pit, a black hole, and the inset points of the dark star worked on the warden like teeth.

The warden had frozen. The green gel did not flow. It had become inanimate bait, basted in an acidic drool that made Lot's eyes burn even at a distance of almost fifty yards.

The obvious truth of it hit him. Sypaon had tried to warn him. And when that failed, she'd lured the thing out of hiding.

The spell that held him shattered. He jumped back six feet as the serpent tossed its head in a grotesque spasm of chomping, swallowing, primitive effort to work the warden into its belly. The jade green body disappeared just as Lot turned to run. Acid spattered around him. He glanced back, to see the serpent head rise high among the trees, the black star pulsing open and closed, surrounded by a necklace of glistening blue beads that could only be eyes. The creature seemed to gather itself; then suddenly it sprang forward, falling across the road with a resounding thud. Lot jumped hard and reached the far embankment as a stream of acid sprayed past his legs.

Down the road he could see Alta and Urban. They'd stopped yelling. Alta's eyes showed white all around as she darted with Urban up the embankment and into the shelter of the bordering forest. Lot caught all that in a glimpse as he balanced on a cushion of soft soil. Then he sprang up the embankment himself, to the top of the road cut, crashing through the shrubbery, sending clouds of glassy-winged insects into the air. Behind him a sizzling crackle and hiss arose, and he felt the heat of acid burning through the foliage.

He was over the ridge. The descending slope was steep, barely thirty degrees from vertical. He found himself in a half-controlled bounding slide, zigzagging down between the tree trunks. The soft ground gave way under his feet at every step, tumbling behind him in tiny avalanches of humus and soil. Overhead, the canopy blocked out most of the daylight, allowing only a thin understory of ferns and head-sized green globes accented by the occasional spindly sapling. He could hear no sound of pursuit.

He fetched up against a tree. His gloved hands tried to grip the marble-smooth trunk, but the effort did little more than slow him. Still, he managed a half-turn as he slid past; his gaze swept the slope behind him.

The serpent had crested. It slipped now in silence over the humus, its mottled brown and black body flowing downward like liquid.

Lot's grip on the tree failed. He stumbled, and dropped to one knee, sliding down the steepening slope. To his left he caught a flash of silvered motion: Urban or Alta. "Watch out, fury!" Urban's shout rang through the forest. "The land drops out beneath you—"

Lot saw it before the final word was out. A natural drainage cut at a shallow angle across the slope. It was twelve feet down to a bottom of black rock. No way Lot could stop in time. So he jumped, shooting for the far side of the narrow gorge. Two-thirds across, and he knew he would never make it.

He hit about halfway down the rocky wall. The impact knocked his breath away. But the gloves seized on—for a second anyway. Then their grip failed, and he half-fell, half-scrambled to the bottom, landing with a splash in a knee-deep pool of slowly flowing green water. He glanced over his shoulder. The serpent was already descending the other side of the gorge, running down the wall like a liquid flow of humus. Without slowing, it raised its head and spit a stream of acid at him. He twisted, dodging the strike.

Pushing hard, he plunged out of the pool and onto a water-smoothed rim of black rock. He teetered there a moment, then got a direction on his momentum and took off down the gorge, holding hard onto his balance on the slippery rock, going down once, then again, on patches of green algae, the second time drawing an explosive pain in his knee that was quickly damped by his medical Makers at the same time his leg went numb from the knee down. He half-stood, hobbling, almost knuckle-walking around the shimmering pools of slow water. The serpent drew near, skimming in silent sine waves over the reflective surface of the ponds. It raised its head again and in his eyes Lot could feel the smarting of its acidic breath.

He remembered the capsule. He groped for it, sliding down a shallow step between two ponds. He could hear the rush of wind in the treetops, though around him the air was perfectly still, only the dribble of water, the buzz of insects, and his own frantic breathing audible. He got the capsule out and had it pointed behind him as the serpent's head poked out over the rock rim, its rows of sapphire eyes glinting just over his head. He squeezed the capsule, firing a brief, invisible stream that sliced across the spangled eyes, igniting a line of steam, a boiling, stinking, fast-forward putrefaction as the cellular material began to dissolve into baser structures.

The serpent reared back, its acid factories temporarily on hold. Lot tucked the capsule away, then threw himself forward, rolling, half in, half out of the water, his leg dragging behind him, useless dead weight. He glanced over his shoulder, hoping for a reprieve, hoping that by now the serpent's face would be entirely consumed in a black boil. Instead he saw only a livid pink scar slashing across the closed mouth. A wad of corrupt tissue oozed from the end of it, but the reaction had ceased.

Urban's voice rang out overhead. "Come on, fury! Go! You've got to jump!"

Lot glimpsed him, capering on the rim of the gorge, now almost sixty feet overhead, his fist bunched and his face a featureless black against the bright green of the foliage.

"Jump, fury!"

Perhaps Urban's voice distracted the serpent, or maybe it had learned caution, for Lot was able to scramble a few more feet, a crawl that brought him to an abrupt edge, and suddenly he understood Urban's exhortations. The wind he'd heard was no wind at all, but instead an airy waterfall, a long, long, plunging veil, greenish white ghost hair streaming against a cliff face into an emerald pool perhaps two hundred feet below him, first in a series of pools that stepped down the center of a narrow valley. Lot clung now to the valley's sheer headwalls.

"Jump!" Urban screamed. "Lot, *now*!"

Lot didn't look back. Once again he could feel the serpent's acid breath. He got his good leg under him, balanced a moment, then leaped off the cliff face.

The waterfall blurred in his vision, spraying him with a fine mist that clung despite the rush of air past his face. He struggled to keep his feet beneath him. He thought he heard Alta's voice echoing off the cliff walls, and then he hit the water's surface—*hard*.

His breath slammed out of his lungs as he plunged deep into the fall's splash pool, and he felt like he'd taken a kick to his genitals. He opened his eyes, to find himself submerged in water like green tea, black darting shapes streaking away from the rising net of silver bubbles that surrounded him. He followed the bubbles up, kicking hard for the gleaming white surface.

His pack held him down.

He knew he should abandon it, but he'd been too hungry too long—he didn't want to lose the food he carried. So he kept trying and finally his head slipped past the surface. He gasped, drawing in a lungful of cool, wet air. Water splashed in his mouth, washing out the taste of acid. Mist rained down on his face, and the waterfall purred as it trickled and spun down the long scooped face of the cliff.

He worked his way to the edge of the pool and hauled out onto the sun-warmed rock. He rolled onto his side, surveying the cliff face. There was no sign of the serpent, but Alta and Urban were clearly visible, gray figures dropping down the precipice in slow increments. He couldn't see the gold cord at this distance, but he thought he could pick out their anchors, secured to a face of clean rock.

"Lot!" Alta's tinny voice came to him from the suit's hood. *"Are you okay?"*

Not really. He ached all over, and his leg was still numb. But he didn't want to admit that to her. So he pulled his hood partially up, activating his radio, and in a show of bravado he called out, "Next time, remind me to fix my anchor before I jump."

"Lot!" she shouted. "Can you hear me?"

He sighed. Perhaps they couldn't hear his transmission with their hoods down and the noise of the waterfall so close. Or maybe his radio wasn't sending anymore. He waved to them, to signal that he'd heard.

As they continued their descent, he spent a minute listening to the forest. All he could hear over the mutter of the waterfall was an insect chittering. If insect was the right word. He slipped out of his pack and scooted back down into the water.

Slow green ripples marched across its surface, and it was icy cold. He hadn't noticed that before. Still, he slid all the way in, until the water was over his head. He could both feel and hear the boiling pulse of the waterfall. He let the current work past his face, ease through his hair, sweep away the bitter acid and his own last lingering expectations.

The Well had tried to kill him—and not with anything as sophisticated as a governor. Macro-scale life could be fatal too. He would be dead now, if Sypaon had not given him a moment to leap away.

The Well was deadly. Kona had said so a hundred times.

Where was the harmony Jupiter had promised? Where was the Communion? Surely not in the belly of a radial snake.

He popped back up to the surface, then stroked awkwardly toward the shallows. His lower leg remained immobile, but he could feel a heat working inside it now as his medical Makers rushed to repair the damage.

When he could balance against the bottom, he cupped his hands and scooped at the water, watching the afternoon light play upon the liquid. It didn't look like regular water. It was tinted a soft green and seemed too viscous, almost gooey as it settled in the reservoir of his palms. He held it to his lips and drank a tentative sip. Cold and slick, with a slight, sweet taste. He drank more, then crawled out on the rock and sat in the liquid afternoon light, contemplating the strangest fact of the day:

The serpent had reacted to the assault Maker in much the same way as his own body, sloughing off the infected tissue to limit the reaction. Was it the bloody Chenzeme influence again? In the Well; in him; in Jupiter. *Why?*

Urban and Alta were finishing their descent, coming down on the farside of the pond. While they worked their way through the vegetation to the water's edge, Lot squeezed the seam of his suit, opening it in a line from his throat to his belly. He shrugged out of the sleeves. Kheth's warm rays played against the bronzy skin of his back and chest.

He thought about going in the water again, then decided to scrounge in his pack instead, pulling out a smashed ahuacatl. He scooped at the browning pulp with two fingers. On the other side of the pond, Urban squatted at the water's edge, and grinned. "I never knew nirvana could be so exciting."

Alta stood behind him, her face pale, her eyes still wide with lingering fear. "Are you okay?" she asked again.

Lot shrugged. He ate another bite of ahuacatl, then said, "Leg's kind of numb. I think it'll fix."

She couldn't let it go. "It almost killed you!"

"Guess it was hungry."

She didn't appreciate the humor, and suddenly he was glad they had a body of water between them. "Dammit Lot! What's the matter with you?"

He scooped at the ahuacatl's mushy green flesh, his hunger a never-declining demand. "You know," he mused, "we could have just missed the door to nirvana. What if it was through the belly of that snake?"

She didn't bother to answer that, just dropped her pack in the bushes before stomping to the end of the pond, where she sat down with her back turned toward him. Her anger boiled like mist off the waterfall.

Urban frowned after her, seeming perplexed. But he let it go and turned to Lot. "So where to, fury? Got any ideas? I don't think we're going to find our way back to that road."

"Doesn't matter," Lot said. "The road ended at the top of the ridge."

Urban laughed shortly, then turned to fish an ahuacatl out of his backpack. Lot tossed him a smashed one instead. "My load didn't come through too well. Better eat it first."

Urban made a face at the damaged fruit, but he took a tentative bite. Lot didn't try too hard to dodge the sudden rise of bitter feelings. "Oh yeah, and here's one for your girlfriend," he said, lobbing another ahuacatl across the water.

Urban scrambled to catch it with his free hand. He gave Lot a long, cool look, then called to Alta, tossing the fruit in her direction. "It happens sometimes, fury. It's nobody's fault."

Down the valley, the edge of Kheth's disk had been

cut off by the peak of a jagged ridge. Lot reached into his pack and pulled out a lychee, feeling his bitterness coil upward like cool steam into the dying afternoon. "Jupiter's out there. I caught his trace up on the ridge, just before the serpent hit. Only . . ."

He frowned at Urban. How to explain? "It wasn't really him, I . . . don't think." Alta had turned around. She stared at him, raw anticipation shoving her anger aside. "It felt too . . . too distinct, maybe. Almost artificial. Like a lure?"

"He could have changed," Urban said. "That's what he came here for."

"I guess." Lot didn't feel sure of anything anymore. "Anyway, it's something to follow."

Chapter
25

Daylight was fading by the time they reached the valley's end. They stood at the head of a six-foot waterfall, looking out over an eroded volcanic crater, its gray walls forming a shallow ring around a plain of low-growing tussocks and sedges and the odd green globular plants. Shadows ran long across the level ground. But where Kheth's light still reached, tiny white diamonds glinted within the green and bronze turf. "Weird," Urban said. "Looks like a park, doesn't it?"

"Yeah."

The stream dropped into a small splash pool that had no obvious outlet. Lot leaned forward, gauging the distance to the opposite shore. He could jump that far.

He was eager now to get out of the highlands. All during the hard scrabble down the valley, as he'd limped over the slow repair of his knee, Jupiter's presence had continued to brush him, sweeping past in irregular wisps, mingled with a sensory packet that brought him a tangy salt scent. In his ears he could half-hear the purring sound of waves on rocks, just as he'd heard it at times in the VR. He was being called to the ocean. There was something here that was aware of him, that expected him. A straw to grasp. He wanted to find it.

So he jumped first, going long over the tiny splash pool and into the tussocks beyond, landing so most of his weight was taken by his good leg. Green water splashed up around him, splattering the leggings of his suit, and he sank calf-deep into a soft, boggy turf. He looked down in surprise, to discover green water gradually pooling around his legs. "This place is like a sponge!"

"Can you get out?" Urban asked. He crouched anxiously at the top of the falls. "We could throw you a cord."

"No, I think it's okay."

Carefully, he pulled out first one foot, then the other, stepping lightly onto the center of a large tussock. He sank only a few inches this time, the water lapping over the toes of his boots. "The splash pool must have saturated the ground all around here." He bounced up and down on the springy surface. "This is really weird."

"I'm coming down." Urban and Alta climbed down the rockface, then waded through the shallow pool.

Lot had already started hobbling across the crater, making a line for the far wall. A flock of four-legged, scarlet avians startled at his approach, blasting into the air with a noise like farts, leaving an equally foul odor behind them. Other flocks winged past overhead.

The light faded abruptly as Kheth dropped below the crater rim. Long shadows weighted the tussocks, and the brassy afternoon sky swiftly gave way to mild pink and then deep, deep blue. The elevator column still had the light, and as the illumination on the ground faded, it gleamed like an optical fiber, with a pearly luminescence. Though they'd been walking away from it for hours, it still seemed to be almost directly overhead. Now that the day's glare had faded, Lot could see the swollen joint of the city, with a few stars emerging from the nebula's veil.

"Lot."

Alta stood close at his side, her breath laced through with nervous tension. She touched his elbow. "Did you see that over there? What is that?"

She pointed tentatively, as Urban puffed up on her other side. Lot looked, but saw only a mound of upthrust soil. He'd seen many like it as they'd followed the stream. He hadn't thought much about it. He'd seen the same thing that day he'd run the warden, and no one had suggested then the structure held any interest.

"Use IR," Alta said.

The shadows were deepening, the land rapidly yielding its heat to the atmosphere. Lot blinked until his visual receptivity expanded far down the spectrum. The bog glowed softly warm, but brighter still was the mound. Its heat signature outshone even Alta's mammalian intensity. "That's not just soil," Lot muttered. It wasn't a plant either.

He started toward it. Alta hesitated only a moment, then followed. Urban swung wide, to come at it from the side.

It proved to be thigh-high, almost circular, and nearly five feet across. Like all the other mounds Lot had seen that day, it neither moved nor gave any other hint that it was aware of their approach.

The day's light had faded further. Now Lot could make out a temperature gradient in the mass, zones that varied in warmth by two or three degrees. He crouched beside it. Water puddled in his footprint, and where the edge of the puddle touched the mound's base, the water began to steam.

In the cooling air, Lot could feel the heat radiant against his face, probably fifteen degrees above human body normal. He reached out a gloved hand and tentatively touched the mound. Alta gave a small gasp, but the mound made no response.

Lot pressed against it. It felt spongy beneath his fingers. He pressed harder, driving his fingers into its tissue. He heard a faint hiss. A noxious odor exploded under his nose. He whirled away, an incoherent bellow ripping out of his throat. He was vaguely aware of Urban and Alta running, a fact registered and swiftly forgotten as a fiery pain swept across his eyes and his sensory tears. He tripped and went down, water splashing up on his face. It cooled the heat.

He pressed his face against the turf, scooped water from the hollows of his footprints and rubbed that against his cheeks while an uncontrollable stream of childish imprecations ran past his lips, *"I hate this place, I hate this fucking, dirty place . . ."*

Urban squatted next to him, chuckling softly. "Well gee, fury, you didn't like that smell?"

"Fuck off." He was still dabbing water at his cheeks, but the burn had mostly faded.

"Let me see."

"It's almost fixed." But he tilted his face up anyway, so Urban could check it out.

"Wow, your Makers are blazing." Urban watched for several seconds. "You're right, though. It's fading." He cocked an eyebrow at Lot. "You want to curb your curiosity a little?"

Lot looked back over his shoulder. The mound still glowed, an organic factory of unknown purpose. Alta had approached it again. She stood a few feet off, staring at it, an air of expectation rising from her. Maybe she sensed his gaze, because she looked at him then. "How did it know what chemicals to hit us with? That was the worst stink I ever smelled, but it didn't stir up my defensive Makers at all."

"It's got a good defense," Urban said. But Lot sensed uncertainty behind his words.

"Or maybe it's adapted to people?" she asked softly.

"Yeah. Anyway, we're not supposed to touch it."

Lot stared at it too, feeling curiosity stir again. *Not supposed to* was sometimes pretty hard to distinguish from *Gotta try it.*

He started to pull his hood on. He could protect his eyes and his face while he took the thing apart—

"Uh-uh, fury." Urban caught his wrist. "Just let it go. You've got Jupiter in your sights. Let the exploring come later."

"But it'll be at our backs," Lot argued. "We don't know—"

"Yeah, that's right. We don't know anything. So walk softly. Speak softly. Don't pick any fights. Okay?"

Lot twisted his arm out of Urban's grip. He wanted to attack the mound again, just to see if he could, just to try to wrest one small victory out of this miserable day. But he knew Urban was right. "Okay. Let's get going, then."

Alta was making her way back toward them. "It's night. Maybe we should sleep."

"Here?"

"Yes. It's a good place. It's open. We could hear things, see things coming."

Lot looked again at the mound.

"And we can keep an eye on it," Alta admitted.

Lot climbed to his feet, suddenly aware of his fatigue. And hungry again. The fruit wasn't a very concentrated source of calories. "Maybe we should move a little farther away."

They found an elevated site, where several tussocks had grown together to form a platform slightly higher than the water level. Lot blinked his vision back to native range, finding comfort in the darkness. They ate more rambutan and ahuacatl, and watched the gathering of stars overhead, and later, the swan burster rising over the crater rim. It looked like a thin gold rod when it first appeared. The color startled him, and he wondered if something critical had changed. But as it climbed out from behind low layers of obscuring atmosphere, it regained its perfect white surface.

Sypaon had saved his life on the road today. Why? Why had she even noticed his absence from the city? He looked at Urban. "You know that warden we smashed on the elevator car? I bet that was Sypaon too."

"You think she's keeping authority off our backs?" Urban asked. He lay with his head pillowed on a tussock, one arm around Alta as she snuggled against his shoulder.

"Seems like it. If she commandeered all the wardens in this area . . ."

"How many do you think there are?" Alta asked.

"Dunno." He looked at Urban. "Not too many, I guess."

"Don't know how they make more, though."

"Yeah." When it came right down to it, they didn't know anything about anything. "I really miss Gent."

"Sooth."

Alta shifted, her eyes glinting in the ring light. "Have you sensed him at all, Lot?"

"No."

Her disappointment gusted softly over him. "The fall would have shattered him."

"Sure."

"But there could have been something left."

"Tissue remnants," Urban mused. "But there would have been a lot of heat on impact. Information content scrambled. Some of his Makers might have survived, but they wouldn't have enough information to rebuild."

Lot again went over the sequence of events in his mind: the shock-blast of lightning that had driven him off the wall. Gent's scramble to catch him. Gent gone.

Alta's voice whispered softly in the night: "I know he couldn't have survived it. But do you think there was enough left that . . . do you think he was brought into the Communion? Or some part of him. It was all he wanted, Lot. The harmony. The union Jupiter had found. . . ."

To become part of something bigger than one's self.

It was a desire that had burned across the Hallowed Vasties, fusing cultures into the singular organism of a precisely integrated cordon, only the oddballs left on the fringes, but they held the desire too. Or maybe the desire had flared again, under the tutelage of fear inspired by the Chenzeme. The Well was not a human thing, but that only made it grander. Shared biological histories defined the clade of species whose ancestors evolved on Earth, or the clade of species descended from the Chenzeme. But such distinctions became irrelevant in the Well, where peace was literally mixed between warring clades.

Lot said, "I think Gent's been known to the Communion since he descended the elevator that day. I think we all have."

The ring was beginning its turn from zero to one. Lot looked away from it, seeking Alta's face in the darkness. She still cuddled close to Urban. But standing behind them was the dim suggestion of another figure. Lot started badly. He was on his knees before a rational thought could slide past his instinctive panic. Through the figure's torso he could see stars, and the hard line of the distant crater wall. But slowly, slowly, the apparition gained definition. It began to glow with a faint blue luminescence. The strong legs, the muscular shoulders and powerful arms and the face: Gent's own smooth features.

He heard a tiny cry from Alta.

It seemed perfectly formed. Each finger of each hand carefully distinguished. The nipples on his chest, the pattern of his abdominal muscles, the vertical line of hair beneath his belly button spreading in a patch across his groin and the complexities of his genitalia. His hair was not arranged in the ringlets Gent had worn. It was a short, unkempt mane. But the eyes were Gent's: a perplexed concern glinting in the night. *It looked so real.*

But Lot knew it was not. He could get only mechanical snatches of human emotion from it, a subtler replay of the previous night. "It's an illusion," he whispered. "A phantom."

"*No!*" That was Alta. She dove at the apparition. But as her outstretched hand swept its belly, it shattered, collapsing in a shower of unlinked, half-liquid molecules like a breached soap bubble. Alta's raw scream echoed across the crater, "*No!*"

Urban was on his feet, shouting his own indignation.

"What was that supposed to be?" He turned his frustration on Lot. "Who's playing tricks on us?"

Lot settled back against the spongy ground, his heart still running double-time. "Maybe we bring it on ourselves."

"You think this place can get inside our minds?"

"It's already there." He stretched out on the ground, using the butt end of his pack for a pillow. The Well was in them. He had no doubt about that. In them, and waiting to act. He fretted now over the question of whether they would ever be able to get it out.

Exhaustion feathered his body, but his mind was jumpy, and he didn't feel a closure with sleep. So he told Urban he would stay awake and watch for a few hours. The swan burster tumbled in a leisurely path across the sky. For a few minutes it was bisected by the elevator column, which had finally passed into the planet's shadow. Silk glowed faintly against the velvet night.

Around him, the crater buzzed with a chittering, croaking, whooping concert of night sounds, some familiar, most not, alien reverberations that set his nerves on edge.

The ring had begun to drop behind the far rim when he saw the phantoms. He stiffened, but he did not wake the others. The silent figures glowed cool blue, just as Gent had. When Lot first saw them, they were near the splash pool: two men and a woman, nude, their hair clotted in feral manes. They crossed the floor of the crater, drawing closer, though they didn't move directly toward him. He could hear no sound at all of footfalls, though he thought he heard voices: faint, almost imperceptible even with his enhanced hearing. He wondered if the erratic whispering might be only in his imagination . . . and if so, was it a product of his own mind? Or put there by something else?

The phantoms drew nearer. He could not tell if they were aware of him. The woman's mouth moved as if in speech, but all Lot heard was a soft buzz. She swung slowly away from her companions and nearer to Lot. He watched her feet step gracefully across the tussocks. The grass didn't bend at all beneath her step. Yet she had a presence. He caught it on his sensory tears. Anxiety. Anger. Anxiety. Guessing wildly, he whispered, "Sypaon?"

She did not answer. She squatted close to his side,

staring at Alta's sleeping figure. The two men had continued in their stroll across the crater floor.

The woman's lips parted. *"Another,"* she said, her voice barely audible. She lifted her head to peer after the men. They were halfway to the far wall now. Their blue glow had faded, so that Lot could hardly see them. *"Another comes,"* the woman said, her accent thick, sounding like the recorded images that had testified about the plague that ruined Old Silk. *"Within us."* She looked to the sky, but not in the direction of the setting ring or the elevator cable.

"Tell me what you are," Lot whispered.

She stood, with no creaking of joints. Her gaze remained fixed on the spot where Lot had last seen the men, though they had vanished now from his sight. "Don't go," he urged her.

She stepped away, her path taking her over Urban. She seemed to float over him, walking on a thin cushion of air. Lot hesitated, debating over the sleeping figures. Then he made up his mind and followed her. She did not object, or even seem to notice.

He trailed behind her across the crater floor. The men did not reappear, but her own image held strong as she drifted over the tussocks. He looked ahead, wondering where they were going, or if they even had a destination. She seemed very real, but not at all human. He had a thought that maybe, the passage into Communion was gradual—a gestation—and learning the new consciousness was a long process, these Old Silkens now only mature enough to emerge from whatever slow womb had contained them over five hundred years.

He saw the mound ahead of them. It was not the same one he'd tried to breach before. This one seemed twice as large, its heat signature like banked coals on a barbecue, steaming beneath a cool, crusty surface.

The woman approached it, and without slowing or changing her stride, she waded into it. Lot watched in astonishment as her feet, her calves, her knees disappeared into the mound's rising structure. A wave of denser blue color ran across her, from her legs upward, flooding her whole body. And when the wave crested her forehead, she burst into a blue-tinted mist that showered outward in all directions. Lot cried out in shock and surprise—he had seen it clearly this time, *she'd been hollow.* Nothing more than an inflated vessel. Nothing more? Without internal structural support she'd still seemed to move exactly as a human woman. She'd spoken to him. All this passed in the brief moment before her misty remains rained down upon him, wetting his sensory tears and he could feel himself backing away.

He tripped and went down and though his body got up immediately, scrambling like a clumsy drunk across the uneven ground, he saw himself as if he looked upon another, and even that slim awareness of his own discrete existence began to fade, overwhelmed by a volant expansion of perception as he felt himself shunted through a gateway into a foreign sensorium, his own locus shrinking rapidly to inconsequence within the awareness that contained him.

Him?

There was no such distinction. He had unfurled, run liquid across a thin fabric of intentionality, at once touching upon the anxious dead of Old Silk, the serpent, the breath that flowed through Alta's body, the struggling fly against the sticky cushion of the sundew's paddle, a raging echo of the ado riot, and other, nameless things, little more than shadows, their substance hidden in a dark, ponderous ocean, its depths running far, far beneath his own shallow reach. Higher: flowing across the hide of descending Nesseleth, sliding the circle of the swan burster, murmuring voices in the accent of Old Silk and a sense of discrete nodes of human thought locking in around him, bound in place by the intoxicating molecular code of want, and of desire. All this at once and yet not at the same time.

Past time: cold, airless, void, the magnetic fields of a great ship that is not Nesseleth singing through his awareness as he follows the field lines, inward toward the hull.

Another comes. Skimming on the surface of the dark ocean of being.

He enwraps this other, and it feels wrong.

Present time: the nebula glitters overhead, faint wash of light and Urban screaming his name.

His name?

Past time: the ring swollen into a searing disk of brilliant light pure energy bearing down—*it is wrongness*—frantic thrashing reaction communicate panic panic panic across the void—skip time ski—disassemble, dissolve, destroy destroy destroyed—

"Lot! Come out of it, come back, come back."

He winced as Urban's hysterical voice roared in his

ears. Icy water flowed across his face, got in his nose and he coughed hard, rolling onto his side, Alta's hand against his back and Urban trying to hold his face above the shimmering film of water that pooled over the mosses.

In the distance, he could make out the chittering night song of the forest. But close by, all had fallen into stunned silence.

He shuddered, lying exhausted against the turf, water seeping into his ear, saturating his hair.

"Lot?" Alta whispered, her hands stroking his cheeks, his shoulders, as she instinctively used touch to focus his consciousness, fix him here in his own body.

But he had never left it. . . .

"What happened?" he whispered.

"We woke up," Urban said. "You were gone. We ran to look for you, and Alta saw the other mound." He stared past Lot's shoulder. Lot sat up, twisting around to look at the structure: a black silhouette a stone's throw away. He blinked into IR and the heat strata appeared. "You were on the ground," Urban said. "Your whole body was trembling. Your eyes were moving beneath the lids. I thought it was eating your nervous system—"

"What was?"

He shrugged. "I don't know! This place, the Communion. . . ."

"The Communion," Lot echoed, putting a name to it. "It's what we came for."

"No! We came to find Jupiter."

". . . and the mitochondrial analog." Did the analogy hold? The Communion he'd sensed had been no more than a thin fabric, the surface tension of a vast ocean of being. A dark ocean, the pull of it strong beneath him.

"You saw it, didn't you?" Alta asked.

He nodded. Only a thin awareness, yet it had been so vast—

"Thought you were dying, fury!"

"Maybe." He felt confused. "I don't know. . . ."

"Is that what you wanted?" Urban demanded.

Want, desire. Lot trembled, remembering. "Once you're in it, it's all you want."

"Are you in it now?"

"No. It's over. It's gone."

But for how long? He'd sensed a compelling structure falling into place around him, as if an old, half-eroded intellectual pattern had begun to reassert itself in his presence, fitting him with enzymatic perfection . . .

"We've got to get out of here," Urban said. "The old man was right. The Well is going to eat us alive."

. . . locking them all into a foreign structure.

Fear crept over him, the same deep panic he'd felt that day when the troopers had begun to stampede. His sense of self wouldn't last here—he knew it—and was that really any different from dying?

He glanced uncertainly at the night sky. Fear existed within the Communion too. "There's something wrong out there." *Another comes.* Null Boundary? The Silkens had long suspected that ship. Could their misgivings have been communicated to the Communion? Despite its vastness, the awareness he'd sensed was only an overlay on deeper processes. "We still have to find Jupiter."

"Jupiter's dead," Urban said.

"He's not." Lot could sense traces of him even now, a dilute mist on the still night air. "Down by the ocean. We could get there tomorrow."

"Fury, it's over and you know it. We barely made it this far."

Across the crater, some small creature called in a soft, three-note song. Lot listened, trying to devise inside himself an analog of calm. "So what do you want to do? Wait for your old man to find us?"

Alta responded first, as he'd known she would. "Kona would have killed us, if Sypaon hadn't held the wardens."

Anger flared in Urban's aura. But then his gaze cut away. Lot could see his braids swaying slowly against a milky background of thinly scattered stars. "Sooth. You're right."

Lot nodded. "So we've got to go on. Find Jupiter. He knows more about this world than anyone."

"There's no way out, is there?" Alta asked him, her voice soft, resolute on the cool air.

"He planned it that way, when he sent Nesseleth down." But Jupiter had made mistakes. "We have to find him, then maybe, we'll find a way."

Chapter
26

Lot opened his eyes to a dawn sky, broad wash of deep velvet blue with the white points of the Committee still peeking through. Translucent wings soared overhead, and he felt rested, for the first time in days. He sat up and tested the air. Jupiter's presence was strong, mixed with an image of the ocean, tang of salt spray over the mellow rotting scents of the bog. Alta was awake. She looked at him, her expression questioning. Urban lay between them, still sleeping. "Did you see anything?" he asked her.

She shrugged. "Some ghosts. They didn't come near."

Lot smiled at the casual way they'd already come to treat the phantoms. Alta misread his mood. She turned away, struggling with something. Lot was pretty sure he wouldn't want to talk about it. "Let it go," he told her.

"I have to tell you why—"

"No. It doesn't matter."

Lot got up, the sun flashing glitter across his eyelashes. He squinted at her. "You still feeling Jupiter in you?" he asked tentatively. "Same as always?"

She nodded. "It's not changed. Not at all." Her hand touched her chest. "He's here."

No change. Faith as a chemical concept Jupiter had

implanted in those around him. Not even a DI to adjust its measure.

He was not Jupiter, and she knew that. She'd tried to pretend otherwise, but it hadn't worked.

"We should go soon," she said.

He nodded. Here on the ground it was still fairly dark. He could hear the hiss and gurgle of the splash pool at the upper crater wall, though he couldn't quite make it out. "Why don't you wake up Urban? I'll be back in a few minutes."

He headed across the crater, enjoying the freshness of the dawn. He thought he could sense others besides Jupiter, but the traces were faint, not like the night he'd first opened his hood. That had been the night Gent died, his tissue smeared across the land. Had the Communion been reacting to that?

Nothing is lost in the Well.

But the Well and the Communion were different things. He'd learned that, anyway. The Communion was a veneer, like the conscious mind of a man vibrant over the older, deeper, unconscious mental patterns.

Jupiter had found the Communion here. Lot chewed over that odd fact as he made his way across the crater.

In the predawn darkness he felt almost alone. The air tasted cleaner and freer than any he had ever breathed. He reached the edge of the pool. In the dim light, the thick green water looked almost black as it moved in slow waves away from the trickling splash of the little waterfall. Lot split the front seam of his suit and peeled it off, throwing it into the water, then wading in after it, the cold liquid closing hard around him, squeezing his lungs so he could hardly pull in a breath. He forced himself under the water anyway, shaking out his hair, letting the water work against his skin. His Makers would always keep him clean, but there was something satisfying, sustaining, about the touch of water, even fake, thick green gooey water. It still felt clean. And it tasted good. He drank some, then popped back up to the surface, his skin puckering and his balls trying to climb up into his body. He grabbed his suit and swished it around, letting the water fill up the sleeves and the pant legs.

"Lot!" Urban's voice rang out across the crater. Dawn light had begun to pick out the gray shapes of tussocks, and the sky over the crater rim glowed.

"Yeah, I'm coming!" Lot yelled, his voice echoing in the quiet air. Still in the water, he pulled the suit back on. He was wading out onto the spongy turf when a familiar voice broke into his reverie: "Messages, Lot. Busy morning."

He jumped three feet in the air, landing with a splash back at the water's edge. *"Ord?"*

The robot crouched on a tussock, its long tentacles folded accordion style across the front of its tiny body.

Lot squinted at it, sputtering his surprise. "But Urban said he—"

The DI stood on its squat legs and looked quickly around. "Master Urban's aggression is treatable."

"I doubt it." Lot grinned. "You okay?"

"Messages," Ord repeated.

Lot squinted at it. It seemed whole, though now that he looked, its tentacles were distinctly shorter. "You put yourself back together?" But that was not a question Ord could really answer. Self did not exist for it, and the pronoun "you" Lot so casually used had no referent in its system of thought. It considered his query, then declined a response.

"Urgent messages," it said this time.

Lot found himself reluctant to receive any "messages," suspecting that any such must be either threat or entreaty. He especially dreaded encountering Kona's so-reasonable and knowing manner as he voiced the same doubts and implausibilities that already plagued Lot's own mind. But he knew Ord would not shut up about it until he'd done the task.

So Lot held a hand down to it and Ord caught hold and swung up, then shinnied to his shoulders. "Go ahead then," he said, without enthusiasm. He started back across the crater floor, just as Urban bellowed for him again.

Suddenly, Ord was speaking in Yulyssa's voice. "Lot! Stay out of sight. Stay under cover. Oh, I don't even know if your attendant is still with you, or even if . . . if you're still alive. Kona thinks you are. Oh Lot if you can hear me, hide yourself. The deck guns have been recalled. Shao is certain of it. He believes they were remounted tonight. Things are falling apart up here. City security has collapsed. Half the officers were ados, and they're in open rebellion. People are going crazy, and authority's blaming *you.* They're hunting you. They'll use the guns against you, if they get a visual sighting—"

Lot didn't wait to hear more. *"Urban!"* he screamed. "Alta!" He bounded across the crater floor. The dawn was cloudless, and in the open bog there was no shelter at all from the sky. They were camped at the center of a bull's-eye, and full light was only minutes away. Maybe authority didn't need visible light to resolve them. Maybe IR was enough. But they were still alive. . . .

Urban and Alta were on their feet, silhouettes in the dimness. "Get the packs!" Lot roared at them. "Grab them and get over the crater wall. Get under the trees!"

A flock of tiny brown fliers sprang up in front of him, their chittering as alarmed and incomprehensible as Yulyssa's voice in his ear. A glance at the sky showed him brightening blue, only two or three of the Committee still present, almost invisible beside the blazing, bisecting line of the elevator cable that had long since caught the full light of day.

Urban grabbed his pack. Alta already had hers on. Lot bounded between them, scooped up his own pack, shrugged it on—*"Come on!"*—and together they ran toward the edge of the crater, while Lot's shouted explanation tore out of his throat in coarse lumps: *"Deckgunsback— aimedatus—gottagetouttasight—'foresunup."*

Light drenched the land. It would be only a moment before the search programs in Silk spotted them. The rim wall loomed ahead, only about twelve feet high, but nearly sheer. How could they get over it?

"There!" Alta said, pointing at a small rockslide. She scrambled up the unstable slope, Urban and Lot on her heels, then caught herself just before she spilled over the other side. *"Oh Jupiter,"* she whispered.

The outer wall of the crater fell away beneath them in mossy ribs of exposed rock that dropped in a sliding descent of some twelve hundred feet, ending in a wide green river that tracked the bottom of a gorge. Vegetation kicked in maybe six hundred feet below.

"We have to do it," Lot said.

An electric potential hummed around them. Then, within milliseconds, a tremendous concussion slammed through the air, louder than the thunder they'd heard that first night, and the crater behind them exploded in a searing, billowing column of steam.

Alta jumped first. She hit the mossy rock and started to slide, her gloved hands grasping at knobs, at bumps, to slow her descent. Lot glimpsed the grim determination on her face, then jumped after her, already half a step behind Urban. Their suits flashed brilliant silver, reflecting away the heat that blasted out of the crater.

Lot landed hard on a shelf between parallel ribs of rock. Urban hit higher on the angled surface. His feet slipped from under him. He went down on his ass, then slid, shooting down the natural drainage. Lot started after him.

Overhead, the crater wall exploded.

The concussion knocked Lot off his feet. Pain knifed through his injured knee. Then his head slammed against a wall of rock, and that was worse. Maybe he blacked out for a second. He had to open his eyes. Urban was hauling on his arm, while a rush of debris swept around them, a river of gravel and stone. Urban dragged him up on top of it while they continued their downward slide, the land moving beneath them.

The toe of the debris hit the vegetation. Lot tumbled into the whipping stems of a dense shrub. Urban's clawing fingers wrenched free of his arm. The landslide swept around him. Hanging suspended in the fragile branches, head downslope, face up to the sky, he caught a glimpse of the crater rim. It was far above him now and it was . . . melting? Boiling? *Disintegrating.* Like a high-speed video of organic decay, it was breaking down into a shimmering particle soup. Billows of steam roared upward, obscuring most of the rim, developing into a gigantic thermal plume.

The branches broke. Lot held on long enough to get his feet under him; then he was stumble-running down a scree-covered slope, past half-buried bushes and, finally, under the shelter of trees. He saw Urban ahead of him, and through the obscuring leaves, the green glint of water. Alta was already down there. She jittered on the shore of the river, screaming at them to hurry up, hurry up.

Urban was limping badly, so Lot caught him in a few steps. He got his arm around his shoulder and took some of his weight, so they slid down the balance of the slope together. The roaring steam bore down on them, searing the back of his neck where his hood dangled uselessly, while Alta pointed behind them, her mouth open as if she were screaming, though her voice was inaudible now against the pounding gush of the steam.

"Into the water!" Lot shouted. He could hardly hear

himself. He was half-carrying, half-dragging Urban, riding their momentum down the slope. Urban sensed their imminent collision with Alta and tried to pull up, but Lot wouldn't let him. They slammed into her, knocking her into the water. The impact ripped away his grip on Urban, but did nothing to slow his forward progress. He plunged into the river, green water closing over his head and he hoped that Urban and Alta would stay down, stay under as long as they could.

The river was deep and fast here as it chugged through the gorge. Lot bumped along the scoured bottom staring up at an expanse of green-tinted light, streaks of foam like green clouds far overhead, the roar of the river in his ears and the high-pitched crunch of his pack against the river bottom. It held him down. He twisted free of it and rose, floating, soaring in the current, a fabric of green waving around him, carrying him in a vast, intricate flow, eddies and tiny whirlpools tracking along his sides, spinning, aligning the viscous water and giving it form, green among green, Gent beside him now, eyes like faded emeralds, blank as emeralds.

Lot wrenched away. He sought the surface, but the direction eluded him. Green everywhere. The pressure of the Communion tugged at him. It *knew* him. He felt its want as it pulled him under, fitting him into a shattered intellectual pattern that quickly coalesced in powerful order all around him, an amalgam of diffuse minds taking solid form, growing outward like frost across a dark oceanic surface, self fading. Information flow: link to link, he fed on data rising from the Well's oceanic depths, mostly cold chem-flow, but hot currents too: UV/light/radio burst of sensory input from a planktonic cloud of tiny sentries scattered across the nebula. Pirating their data, his reach leaped wide. He could feel Null Boundary moving through dimly scattered edges, a sharp, fluted, diamond body, blazing fusion jets dumping velocity in profligate abandon, a solemn human voice in the radio spectrum *a debt owed, a debt owed*. A façade. The mindless sentries of the Well hardly cared, but *he* could feel its wrongness. Tremulous suspicions and the land torn beneath him, the sky torn overhead, alien panic obeying ancient, opaque commands, destroy information content destroy—

His shoulder struck something hard, and the pain slammed him back into his own limited awareness. His head burst above the foam. He gasped in a great gush of air; his lungs forswore collapse for a little longer.

The river swept free of the gorge, and immediately slowed, its velocity spread out now across a wider track though it still moved with good speed. Trees stood on banks of mud, bending over the water, forming a lacy canopy that did not quite meet in the middle, and it was through that gap that Lot could see the great column of steam still rising, well back up the ridge.

No laser gun had caused that. The first explosion, yes, accompanied by a great crack of thunder, that could have been from the city. But something had happened after that. The Well had objected. It had writhed in a suicidal foam of self-destruction. General destruction. *Destroy information content destroy*. Insubstantial words inadequate to frame the vision he'd brushed in the Communion. There, the meaning had been far more deeply felt. He'd caught memories of other woundings. Terrible woundings, the Well responding with indiscriminate dissolution *destroy information content* willing to rend itself to dissolve the aggressor. Willing to rend anything that was not a recognized part of the Well, anywhere within the system.

The current swept Lot into the bank, where he caught the loop of an exposed tree root with fingers numbed by the cold water. He scaled the knobby wood, climbing to the top of the fragile, overhanging bank. There he collapsed between the buttressing walls of the tree's surface roots. The river grumbled on below him, while overhead, animals chittered in the canopy.

The world he could see was only a skin over layers of finer processes: first the conscious veneer of the Communion, and beneath that the unconscious deeps of the Well itself. Lying on the riverbank, he tried to discern some hint of it, but he could not.

Ord shifted on his shoulder, making him jump. "You're still here?" he blurted in surprise.

A tentacle unfurled to pat his cheek. "Lot needs to eat. Lot needs to sleep."

"Lot needs to find Urban and Alta," he muttered. And across that concern there gathered another layer of anxiety as he recalled what Yulyssa had blurted during her frantic message: half of city security in open rebellion. It didn't seem possible. He'd assumed that the election-night riot had ended within minutes after mass arrests. But if security had fallen apart . . .

Lot thought about asking Ord to contact Yulyssa. But wouldn't authority use the signal to target him?

He needed to talk things over with Urban and Alta. Together they could figure out what to do.

He stood up, feeling a weakness in his limbs: the debt for days of deprivation. What little food he'd had was at the bottom of the river now. He pulled his hood partially up, activating the radio. "Alta," he called. "Urban." He waited a moment for an answer, then tried again. When he got no response, he queried the suit. "Is the radio working?"

"Equipment diagnostics green light."

"Why can't they hear me?"

The suit didn't answer.

Lot crouched on the riverbank, carefully examining both shores. "Alta!" he yelled. His voice reverberated through the forest. "Urban!" He waited several seconds, listening for a response, then yelled again. He heard no answering cry. Neither could he get any trace of them through his sensory tears. But if they'd stayed in the water (he flashed on the cool green deeps, the helpless way hair and limbs would sway in an insensate current) their passage would have left no trace that he could read. He tried the radio again, then called a few more times. But he got no response beyond the mindless echo of his own voice.

His isolation weighed on him, made worse because he knew, close by, was the Communion, and maybe he could slide beneath the visible skin of this world and reach it, pirate the Well's oceanic currents of data and find them. If he knew how. If he dared. His heart boomed. He could drown within the Communion, as easily as he could drown in the river, his self dissolving across the links of its sensorium.

He took refuge in ignorance. He didn't know how to peer under the skin, short of half-drowning himself. "Urban!" he yelled again. The silence hung on. So finally, he started down the river, knowing that if they were ahead of him he would pick up their trail, and if they were behind, then they were likely already dead.

Chapter
27

The vegetation grew in lush, almost impenetrable thickets on the riverbank, forcing Lot away from the shore and into the forest. Under the trees the air was still and close. Scent would not disperse far. Still, Lot hunted for some sign of Alta or Urban. He used the radio. And whenever he could, he pressed a path back to the water to search and call.

Along the way he passed numerous mounds. Some were almost four feet tall and six across, but most were small, little more than knee-high. Plants didn't grow on them, so they were easy to identify. He beat a wide berth around the first few, but as time passed, his caution faded and he drew closer, sometimes even laying his hands on their hot surfaces.

The sun was only an hour high when he stopped to rest. He chose a site by the river where a tree had recently fallen, tearing an open space in the bank. He walked out on the trunk—its diameter only slightly less than his own height—taking a seat on a thick cushion of moss. Already, the day was oppressively hot. He lay down on his belly, folded hands pillowing his head while he stared at the steadily flowing current. Green water dripped down the rounded sides of the log, pressed out of the mosses by his weight. Something screamed a loud, ugly note high in the canopy on the other side of the river. In the center of the stream, something else swam just beneath the surface, leaving a trail of v's in its wake. He tried not to think about Urban and Alta. But not thinking left his mind curling around a central void that expanded with the passing seconds, a weighty darkness poised to fully infiltrate him.

Ord touched his cheek. "Lot needs to eat."

The gentle voice ran in ripples through his mounting depression, a kinetic input to disturb the deadening latticework of his mood. He smiled faintly. "Hey Ord, you got anything to eat?"

"Yes, yes! Good Lot."

He raised his head in surprise, but Ord had already dropped over the side of the log, into the calm water trapped between the fallen tree and the riverbank. Lot sat up, watching Ord's wavering image move slowly along the bottom, apparently exploring the underside of the fallen log. Soon a tentacle snaked up the mossy surface, and Ord pulled itself up again. Its other tentacle coiled around a collection of snails. They had tawny gold shells, and looked just like the snails in the koi ponds at Vibrant Harmony.

"Safe," Ord said, using its dexterous tentacles to pull one of the creatures out of its shell. The snail's soft body stretched for a moment, then snapped free. Its tentacles immediately contracted, and its flesh began to foam. Ord held the specimen out to Lot. "Eat it please good Lot."

His body greeted the proposition with a bout of nausea. "But it's alive."

"Smart Lot."

"It's an *animal*."

"Know its name?"

It was a game Ord had played with him when he'd been nine and still unfamiliar with the Silkens' language. He answered the query as accurately as he could. "Writhing, tormented mollusk."

"Smart Lot. Yes. Please eat."

His blood felt feathery, empty. Hesitantly, he took the bit of flesh out of Ord's tentacle. It felt squishy and dreadfully soft.

He'd seen carnivorous eating in the VR, but that had been drama. He'd never thought about doing it himself, in real life, real creatures dying inside his gut. He almost retched then, the taste of acid burning in the back of his throat. "It's an Earth species, isn't it? From our clade?"

"Yes, Lot."

He popped it quickly into his mouth. He couldn't bring himself to chew it, so he just swallowed hard. He waited a moment, half-expecting to feel it wriggle inside him. He got ready to puke. But instead a sensation of warmth spread out from his stomach, soothing, dizzying. He lay back against the soggy moss, while a slight buzz rang in his ears. Ord handed him another shelled snail and this time he ate it mechanically, not sitting up. Another and another until he'd had ten. "No more," he told Ord.

He gave his body a few minutes to settle the meal; then he got up and paced the log. Still no hint of Urban or Alta. So he moved on, telling himself that at the ocean shore, everything would be pushed out into the open.

He'd gone only a few hundred yards when Ord leaned down over his shoulder and announced, "A message for Lot."

"Yeah?" He turned his head eagerly. "Is it Yulyssa?"

"Lot?" Her voice emerged from Ord's mouth with an anxious edge. *"Lot, are you there?"*

He started. "You're in real time?"

"Yes, Lot. Thank goodness. You're okay?"

His hackles rose. Communication with the Well was strictly controlled. If authority wanted to target him, they'd just had their signal. Suspicion tightened across his mind. "Is Kona with you?"

Yulyssa hesitated. Weighing options? "He's not with me."

Something in her voice told him she was lying. Authority was always lying to him. His frustration broke through: "Kona! You hear me? Urban's gone. He's missing. You tried to kill us this morning. And maybe it worked. Alta's lost too—"

"Lot." Kona's cool reason sliced through Lot's dumb ado rant. "I need you to listen. The situation's slipping out of control."

"Never been under control," Lot growled. "Never. We hold on and we ride."

"Maybe. But it's gone too far. What happened this morning, it was a mistake."

"No shit! You boiled the back off that ridge."

"That wasn't us—"

"You fired on us!"

"—thority abandoned the guns! They stopped after the first barrage."

Frenzied breaking, splitting, boiling . . . Lot saw it all again. The crater rim hadn't vaporized. It had simply *dissociated*. Lost structure. A chill touched him. "Yeah," he conceded. "That was the Well. Defending itself." Tiny governors everywhere, poised to react, even at a distance, even in the city. The Silkens were only probationary members of this system.

"Authority won't risk firing again," Kona said. "They're convinced of that, finally."

Something in his voice worked at Lot. "You didn't approve it?"

There was a knife edge of anger in Kona's voice. "You understood it. The governors are everywhere. Even in Silk. We were wrong about the city gnomes. They're not in decline. Their protective envelopes had changed to make them harder to detect. You were right, Lot. What happened to the Old Silkens could happen to us."

"Yeah."

"And the guns, they just weren't *necessary*."

Rarely were Kona's emotions so exposed. Even with voice-only, Lot could pick up the flow. "I don't know what happened to Urban," he offered. "We went into the river. He was okay then. But if he got hung up in the gorge—" He caught himself, though the image played on in his mind: frantic fingers stripped of skin, bone dissolving. . . .

Ord's mouth moved, emitting a simulation of muffled whispering. Then it spoke again in Yulyssa's voice. "Lot, the city's breaking down. Since you left, mobs of ados and refugees—they're acting crazy. We've had vandalism and sabotage. We tried to calm them with a psychoactive virus in the air supply, but something's breaking it down. Lot, we've had open battles in the street, and it's all in your name. Silk is fragile. City security's doing their best, but half the officers have deserted and . . . we think we know why." He could hear in her voice a quaver of fear. "You wanted to know why the Old Silkens died."

"Yeah."

"We have a theory. It's tentative—"

"Tell me."

"They had trouble. Or possible trouble. They'd discovered a parasitic neuronal infection. One hundred percent of the population had it. It was a stealth structure—very difficult to detect, especially because it had no apparent effects beyond a tiny production of heat as it metabolized normal cellular energy sources. But as its structure was mapped, it was found that it shrouded the hypothalamus, the part of the brain that controls emotions—though it had tendrils elsewhere, with especially strong links to the olfactory bulbs. Not knowing its function, the Old Silkens decided to get rid of it. In their place, we might have made the same decision." She sighed. "They designed and released a Maker for that purpose. Within thirty-six hours, they were all dead."

Lot tried to make sense of it. "You're saying the Maker killed them."

"No. I don't think so. They believed the Well killed them." *A vast, opaque ocean, supporting the Communion, but not part of it . . .* "It's only a guess," Yulyssa continued, "but what if the Well's defensive system detected the Maker, and coded it as a threat? The Old Silkens might have been inadvertently destroyed when the Maker was wiped out. . . ."

Destroy information content: accidental death, on a massive scale. Chance hovering over every moment of every life. Lot shuddered, remembering the tunnels.

"Tell him the rest," Kona growled. "You agreed we should."

There was silence; then she said, "The parasitic structure appears to be a simpler form of the chemically receptive atrium you carry, Lot. And it still exists. We've found it. In me. In Kona. In sixty percent of the people we've tested so far. But in the rebellious ados it's denser and far more active."

Kona finished for her: "While in the few loyal ados there's no sign of it at all."

Lot's gloved hands kneaded in slow fists. He didn't feel much surprise. Alta had as much as told him she carried her faith in physical form. Captain Antigua had said much the same thing, describing Jupiter's abiding presence forever dwelling inside her. Now he thought of it, David had confessed similar feelings, though he'd caught the faith from Lot, that day in the tunnels. The most dangerous viruses were those with a long latent period. "You think I did this."

"*No.*" That was Yulyssa's voice, edged with anger. "We think—we *know*—it started long before you. The Old Silkens were gone before Jupiter ever reached this system."

Tiny flies buzzed in a shaft of light that had found its way through the thick canopy. Lot's gaze fixed on them. "Jupiter found the Communion here. It infected him here. So it didn't start with the Hallowed Vasties."

"It started with the Chenzeme," Kona said. Then, to Lot's surprise, his voice softened. "And that's in you."

Sure. The "chemical atrium" Dr. Alloin had found constituted a different perceptual system. He could see what others could not. Silvery faith, and the interlocking pattern of the Communion.

Kona again: "The rioters are acting in your name, Lot. They know you're down there and it's made them crazy. They want to follow you the way they followed Jupiter. They want the Communion—"

"Oh." He felt a resonant sense, as if a maelstrom of unrelated facts was about to collapse into coherent order.

"You . . . haven't found it?" Kona asked.

"The Communion? I have."

Stunned silence followed on his pronouncement. Finally, Yulyssa asked, "Then is it real? Do you . . . understand it?"

Lot frowned. "I don't know. It has to do with the phantoms, I think." The blue woman had pulled him under the first time; and Gent's image had accompanied him in the river. "It's a human thing anyway, and not really part of the Well. That's . . . something else. Older. Alien. A mechanism . . . to preserve data? Biological data. From the Communion I can . . . look into it?" He shook his head, frustrated by the inadequacy of words. "The Communion's a place for thinking, though it's only a veneer on top of the Well system, tapping the Well's data sea. Still, it's *big*. It reaches around the planet, and across the nebula too. The nebula's populated by more than butterfly gnomes. Did you know that? It's replete with governors too. Microscopic sentries. They pass their data inward, across the nebula. I saw Null Boundary through them. He's coming in-system."

The nebula's debris field had forced the great ship to slow to a tiny fraction of its interstellar speed. Maybe that was part of the reason for the nebula's existence. *The Well protects itself.*

"Something's wrong with that ship, Yulyssa. Watch him closely."

"Lot? I don't understand. Is the Communion a sculpted entity? Like a great ship?"

"No. Not like that at all." If he could explain it to her, maybe she could make sense of it. "The Communion's made of . . . well, it feels like lots of small, hungry points of awareness, diffuse minds. Maybe that's what's left of the Old Silkens. I don't know. When I first . . . well, when I first encountered them, they were scattered and weak. Then they began to link together, focusing around—"

He broke off abruptly, startled at his own blindness. *Focusing around me.* Gent had said something like that once: *You're the gateway to the Communion. The focusing lens.* Twice now he'd felt a powerful order congealing around him. Suppose the Communion he sensed was only a half-made thing, weak and unfocused and in need of a seed crystal around which to congeal? In need of *him.* Great cult leader—or reservoir of rare biochemical structure? He supposed it was much the same thing.

Given all that, what might the Communion grow into?

The vast and intricate information currents of the Well loomed in his consciousness. The Communion had only a loose attachment to it now. But might a deeper synthesis be possible?

"That's what Jupiter was after," he muttered, his thoughts bouncing hard now. "The mitochondrial analog. Remember, Yulyssa? He always used that—"

"Yes, but—"

"The mitochondria retains its own primal identity. Its own DNA, though it can't survive outside of the cell . . . and the cell can't survive without it."

"Basic doctrine," Kona interrupted.

"But how long for that synthesis to evolve?" Lot asked.

He could almost see Kona's famous scowl. "It had to work right away, or the cell would have metabolized—"

"No. Bacteria have their own strategies."

"Oh, Lot," Yulyssa sighed, despairing at the unkind analogy.

He shook his head and pressed on. "It might have been only a clumsy association, at first. Things would need to change—a lot—before the invading bacteria became fully integrated. How long would that take?"

"How should we know?" Kona growled.

"Jupiter knew. It could take a long time. Hundreds of years. Thousands. Maybe more. It didn't matter to him. That's how we survive, no? We turn our backs on the Hallowed Vasties and let the past slip away and tell ourselves it doesn't matter, a year, two years, a thousand, what does it matter? Once we cut ourselves off from our past. . . . Because most of us don't understand time. That a thousand years is nothing. Ten thousand years is nothing. We're awed by life spans that touch a millennium, but in the life of a planet, it's nothing. On that scale even the Chenzeme are young."

Kona was not taken in. "We don't exist on that scale!"

"Jupiter thought we could."

"*Lot.*" Yulyssa's voice broke into his thoughts. "We need you in the city. The rioters will listen to you."

There. She'd said it. The reason behind this call . . . not that he wanted to face it. "Maybe you should listen to them. If people are rebelling, it's because they're scared. The food supplies are running out, and unless you want to chance the Well—"

"There are other options!" Kona insisted. "Null Boundary's coming."

"Don't count on him." Lot puzzled over the sense of threat he had felt when he'd slipped under the skin. "He's wrong, somehow. . . ."

Kona couldn't accept it. His voice was thick; every word must have cost him. "Understand it, Lot. We need you. The ados listen to you. The refugees listen to you. You could buy us the time we'll need to find a real solution."

Lot stared at the flowing green water, glimpsing in its eddies a shadow beneath the skin. "You're wrong. They don't want me. They want Jupiter. They want you to let them down the Well."

"I can't do that. It's the same as murder."

"I'm still alive."

"Jupiter's not."

Lot held his silence. Kona desperately wanted to believe Jupiter was dead. It was probably best to let him. He might blanch at murder now, but he'd let half the army die in the tunnels that day. To stop Jupiter?

Yulyssa was speaking, pleading with him to come

back. "I can't," Lot said. "Not yet." And then he added, "Beware of Null Boundary." Before they could say anything else, he looked at Ord and made a slashing gesture across his throat.

"Rest now?" Ord asked brightly.

He couldn't imagine it. "I've got to find them." Urban and Alta . . . and Jupiter. He envisioned them all, gathered together at the ocean shore, waves rolling in, spilling on white sand with a sluffing roar just like in the VR. They'd be waiting for him, all of them safe; merry teasing because he'd been the last one down. And walking there on the edge of the land he would discover what to do, what he owed. He imagined it that way, knowing it was the coarsest bullshit.

He reached the coast in late afternoon. The river ended in a wide, brackish marsh between the arms of two steep ridges. Lot slogged through, emerging on a beach of bright sand, eroded calcite mixed with specks of black lava. A light breeze flowed off the emerald ocean, tempering the lumbering afternoon heat.

He stood at the crest of the beach, feeling the sand sliding away beneath his feet. It was a dizzying sensation, as if the ground had been gutted of its solid structure, leaving behind an amorphous debris field, stone ashes that presaged the collapse of his own inner world as he looked up and down the beach and saw that it was empty, a wild shore, with no sign of human presence. "*Urban!*" he called. "*Alta!*" But the chuffing, growling ocean overwhelmed his voice!

Swells rolled in from the uninterrupted horizon. He watched them slow and steepen as they approached the shadowy outlines of submerged reefs. Their smooth faces glinted green, a moment before they collapsed into white breakers. The air was full of a salt tang, and Jupiter's presence was very strong. Yet there was no visible sign of him. No settlement. No evidence that anyone had ever been here.

He turned, gazing back up the broad valley, wondering if there was any point in searching the riverbanks again, when Ord spoke softly in his ear.

"In the water," it said. "Things swimming."

Lot turned swiftly. He scanned the shorebreak, and then farther out, to the dark green water that ran in a narrow channel through the reef. . . .

A swell rose over the submerged rocks and he saw it then: a silvery torpedo-shape darting across the wave's exposed face, a skirt of long tentacles trailing behind it. Size was hard to gauge against the waves, but he guessed that from tip to tail it was nearly twice as long as his own body.

He stared at the spot where it had appeared, hoping for another sighting, at the same time wondering what it ate and if it could come ashore.

CHAPTER

28

Chapter
28

The descending sun, low in the sky but still potent, poured its light upon the beach, drenching the viscous green swells with shining gold. Lot sat in the sand, watching the chaotic crash and backsplash of the surf, his thoughts equally choppy, insight as elusive as the occasional dark shape that sliced just beneath the surface. Time squeezed hard and he knew that an answer had to be found before Silk collapsed into chaos.

"Ord?" He twisted around, searching the vegetation line at the top of the beach for a glimpse of the robot. He saw it only when it moved, slipping down from a perch among the gnarled branches of a thick-leaved shrub.

"Yes Lot?" It picked a fastidious path across the sand, as if the loose grains irritated its gelatinous body.

"I need help," Lot conceded.

It squatted beside him, its tentacles folded neatly against its torso. "Yes, Lot, yes. Get food?"

"Maybe later. For now I need to know what's going on . . . or if I'm going crazy—"

"Lot's okay."

He smiled. "Thanks. Do you sense any other people around here?"

Ord snapped upright and spread its tentacles on the wind. Several seconds passed. "No." It folded in upon itself.

No people. No Jupiter. He couldn't dodge a sense of crushing disappointment, though he'd suspected it himself. The trace was so pure, so strong, so unvarying. How could it be anything but artificial?

But where did it come from?

"Do you sense anything similar to human?" he asked. "Something that imitates human?"

"Yes, similar," Ord agreed.

"Can you locate it?"

"From the ocean."

Lot stared at the jumbled, glistening water. "Do you think it's from those creatures we saw?"

Ord shrugged.

Frustrated, Lot got up and walked inland. The water in the marsh sat in gooey green ponds. Insects buzzed at the surface. He waded through the shallows, looking among the reeds until he found a mound, half-submerged in the water. The mounds in the crater had exhibited thermal layers. He pressed the flat of his hand against the surface of this one and felt the heat. What process produced it? He could detect no methane, or other gases of decomposition. No debris gathered over the surface. If it was alive, what did it feed on? What did it produce? He remembered the phantom, the way she'd waded into a mound and disintegrated. Was it coincidence? Or had the mound destroyed her? Why?

Maybe it had created her too. *An engine of the Communion?* He felt a brush of memory, but he could not hold on to it.

He glanced over his shoulder, to see Ord slinking through the vegetation. "Come here," he said, crooking a finger at the robot. "Can you analyze this? Figure what it's made of?"

"Sure, Lot." Ord scuttled over, then climbed up on the mound. It spread its tentacles out across the surface, its face wrinkled in a synthetic frown of concentration. Then it pulled its tentacles back to its body. The tip of one of them flattened into a hard, pointed spear. Lot quickly backstepped several feet. Ord pierced the mound. A hiss erupted from the punctured surface and Lot backed off even farther as a peppery sting reached his sensory tears. The robot withdrew its probe, seemingly unaffected. It hopped down off the mound and scurried over to Lot. "Many components present. City library suggests—"

"You're connected to the library?" Suddenly nervous, he glanced up at the line of the elevator.

"Yes, Lot. City library suggests a typical mix of common Chenzeme plague vectors, information storage links, Earth-clade genetic data—"

"Does city library suggest what the mounds are *for*?"

Ord frowned, its head cocked exactly like a real person under atrial link. "Guesses only. Information storage. Plague incubators. But a quandary exists. The mounds may be an historically recent phenomenon. The library's original records contain no mention of these structures. Apparently they were unknown to the Old Silkens. This is considered remarkable given the thorough observations these people made of other aspects of the planet's biology, leading some researchers to surmise the mounds did not exist in this period."

"But the mounds existed when the new Silkens arrived?"

"Yes. A preliminary report on the structures appears within the initial planetary survey."

The blue woman had spoken in the accent of Old Silk. Her people—or some part of them—still existed within the Communion, interlocking sparks of awareness awkwardly attempting half-forgotten ways of communication. . . .

Another comes within us.

Chenzeme plague vectors thrived within the mounds. Chenzeme neural patterns existed in his head and presumably in Jupiter's head too, generating chemical sight. Jupiter had lived in the Well. He would have been aware on some level of these soluble ghosts and their latent connective patterns. Lot fit that pattern with enzymatic perfection.

Why?

Jupiter could not have created the Communion, yet he'd been part of it. Chenzeme plague vectors; Chenzeme neural patterns. Could other communions exist in other places?

Jupiter had come out of the Hallowed Vasties.

A teasing trace of memory touched him, but he could not pin it down. Worry clutched at him. He looked at Ord. "What's happening in the city?"

"News brief?"

"Yes."

Yulyssa's voice startled him as it spoke from Ord's mouth in a swift mediot summary. "The election-day riot has continued to expand in scope, threatening the safety of all citizens. Protesting factions—composed primarily of refugees and adolescent Silkens—are demanding free access to the Well. Very little information can be confirmed, but indications are that most city functions are now under the control of dissidents. Certainly the decentralized recycling and security systems have been appropriated. City authority denies there's any immediate danger, but counsels everyone to check the pressure seals on their dwellings and to stay indoors until the emergency has passed. Scattered reports of warden activity in the city core and on the elevator column hint that this function too has been taken over by—"

"Stop it!" Lot barked. Yulyssa's recorded voice cut off. Lot stood in the muck, his hands trembling. *Crazy.*

They were all crazy, a veneer of madness sweated out of the real core of human civilization. All sane stock had made stable communities in the integrated cordons of the Hallowed Vasties. Only the misfits and the madmen had wandered on, sociopaths gathering on the frontier in unstable patterns, spilling over the edge of chaos.

He sat down abruptly.

Chaos.

Muck seeped up around him. Instability had hit the Hallowed Vasties too, if the disappearing Dyson swarms meant anything. Captive stars blazing bright once again; consciousness burning off in the stellar winds.

Had Jupiter brought the seed of destruction out of that core? Had he known it?

He looked at Ord. "You have to find somebody in the city I can talk to. Somebody in control. One of my—" He could hardly force himself to say it. "—one of my *followers.*"

"Sure, Lot."

Jupiter had reviled the Hallowed Vasties. He'd watched them fail. And he'd fled to the Well.

Nothing is lost in the Well. On a molecular scale alien biochemical structures could be identified within Well life-forms, from Chenzeme plague vectors to human genetic systems. But they were changed from their source. Evolved. Augmented. Hybridized. Winnowed? Perhaps. Complex systems could evolve through selective processes, reaching high states of organization without the guidance—or interference—of a conscious mind. Beneath the veneer of the Communion, the Well did not seem to be self-aware, not in the way of having an ego. Yet it had survived, while the Chenzeme were long gone.

Could human consciousness find a place within such a system? Jupiter must have thought so. Could human consciousness become its ego? Providing it with goals?

Natural evolution had no goal. That which survived, survived, and survivors tend to reproduce, willing their survivor traits. But egos function otherwise. Egos establish goals (illusions), they prattle on about destiny, they go crazy, they self-destruct, they burn out their existence in allegro tempo, building on themselves until the illusions are finally ripped aside or the whole system collapses of its own unsupported weight, but in either case it finishes. It finished the Chenzeme and maybe it was finishing the Hallowed Vasties even now, pulling them under a closed horizon of inward-turning minds, sucked down in an irreversible closure.

But the Well felt different. This was a greater thing. Ancient, wily, and powerful. Yet without ego, it remained curiously blank. Jupiter must have seen himself and his followers filling up that blankness, their Communion becoming the ego of a system that could pull every living thing of every clade into itself.

"Lot?" A suspicious-sounding masculine voice spoke from Ord's mouth, interrupting his thoughts.

Lot groped to identify it while flies buzzed over the mud. "David? Is that you?"

"Lot, we've won!" David crowed. "We've got wardens on the column, repairing the elevator system. We'll be down in a matter of hours."

The Well had subdued the Chenzeme. It would always defend itself. "No assault Makers, okay, David?"

"Sure, Lot." But doubt had crept into David's voice. "You okay?"

Unity. Harmony.

The promise of the Hallowed Vasties, but writ against the Well. The Well had healed Jupiter of plague. Had he believed it might also heal that greater flaw that was causing the Vasties to fail? Lot's gut clenched as he glimpsed the gamble Jupiter had taken. Unconscious processes could operate on only a pragmatic value system: *survivors survive*. Foresight, mercy, sympathy, forgiveness, love—all these were inventions of conscious minds. The Well could not love them.

Its governors could not forgive their mistakes. It could only react, according to its own, unknown protocols.

"Lot?" David asked in soft concern.

"Go slow," Lot warned him. "It's not a simple choice. There's more."

"It's endless, isn't it?" David asked, with a mix of eagerness and awe in his voice that sent a shiver down Lot's spine.

Believe in me.

Lot shook his head. He could not find his own faith, no matter how he groped. "It's alien," he whispered. The flies continued to buzz over the mud, tiny, oblivious immigrants from Silk.

At dusk Lot walked along the beach, Ord clinging just under his hair. David had called a couple of times to report that the work on the elevator was going slower than expected. Packs of repair Makers had failed, and needed to be replaced. More time had been lost when city authority launched an electronic counterassault aimed at disrupting remote communications. "But we'll get there," David insisted.

Lot urged him to be cautious.

The ocean had lost its greenish cast in the failing light. Still, the waves rolled forward with unnatural lassitude, ponderous swells that only reluctantly crested and broke in a brilliant white froth. "Ord, why's the water green?"

"The color and texture of the liquid is attributed to an elusive colloid that may serve an information-storage function."

The Well's library? Information moving through every facet of the Well's biosphere, hitchhiking on the water cycle. He imagined he felt the probing touch of molecular hands, assaying his cells and the odd, hybrid structure of his mind. To what end? He shivered, wondering what would happen if he ordered David to stay in the city.

Chapter
29

"Lot. Wake up. Something is happening."

He came awake instantly, his body stiff, fear threading his heart. Jupiter's presence hung thick in the still night air. There were no stars. A low cloud deck had formed while he slept on the beach. He could see the cloud bottoms, dimly illuminated by a reflected green light. He shoved himself up on his elbow and gazed out to sea.

Beneath the breaking waves, the reef was aglow with a blaze of emerald green.

Slowly, he got to his feet. He could make out the shape of the reef despite the refracting water: a long, broad spindle lying parallel to the shore. The waves dimmed when they passed beyond it into the near-shore shallows. And the expanse of the ocean beyond was dark.

A large mound? He wondered. The mounds he'd seen glowed only in the infrared.

Abruptly, the light began to pulse. It moved in swift ripples in a direction opposite the waves. Ord stirred, a tentacle tapping in soft concern against Lot's leg. "City library identifies this pattern, Lot. It is the bar code of a machine alphabet."

Lot breathed slowly, carefully, trying to restrain an anxious expectation. "A message?" he asked softly. "Can you read it?"

"City library translates it as *Help, Lot. I am your friend. I, Nesseleth. Do not forget me.*"

Nesseleth? He frowned, trying to discern some relationship between the narrow spindle of the reef and the vast structure of the lost great ship. "I don't understand," he whispered to Ord. "Nesseleth went down. She burned in the atmosphere." A shudder passed through him. There was no way she could have survived it. Her hull would have been burned away, her insulation, her engines, her decks, all the way down to—

"Her core!" Lot shouted. He leaped high into the air. The core shelter, where the ship's mind was housed. It was the sternest part of her construction, the last refuge for ship and crew alike. He ran down to the water's edge. "Nesseleth!" he shouted, on the chance that she could hear him. The pulsing lights ran on, and he felt as if he could almost read them now: *I am your friend. I am your friend.*

Ord was speaking, demanding his attention. "Good Lot, the city calls you. Speak to your friend David in the city. Lot?"

"Later," Lot said. *Nesseleth had survived.* Ignoring the objections of his suit's DI, he pulled on his hood, sealing it over his face. The respirator kicked on. Ord's tentacle wrapped around his gloved hand. Lot gently removed it. He waded into the surf until the water ran past him knee-deep. Then he dove under the froth of a wave and stroked hard.

Nesseleth's core was covered with weeds like fine, emerald streamers. The light pulsed beneath them, a softer green. Dark shapes circled over the electric ground. They moved in neat groups of two or three, like guardians on patrol. They were twice Lot's size and fishy-sinuous, propelling themselves with strong strokes of their long, trailing tentacles. Undulating fins on both sides of their smooth torsos seemed to provide balance and steering. A pair of the guardians jetted toward him. Lot decided to make for the bottom. He kicked hard, fighting his own buoyancy to get down among the weeds. The pair spun off into darker waters.

He grabbed the soft sea plants with both hands to keep himself low. The pulsing light of Nesseleth's core blazed up from beneath their holdfasts, pressing against his retinas, feeding the anxious pace of his nervous system.

Then the light went out.

He felt blind in the utter darkness, until a small green glow caught his eye. It grew swiftly brighter. He kicked hard for it.

A trio of guardians passed in front of him. He could see their eyes, bedded in sockets on their bullet-shaped heads. Gill slits flared like skirts just above the tentacles. They rounded the light, then swept back, circling several feet above him. He pulled himself through the weeds, toward the light. One of the creatures dove to intercept him. In the faint glow he could see its eye rolling back, tracking him as it passed only a few inches away. Then another one charged. As it came at him the lower half of its snout peeled back to expose a wide star-shaped gullet filled with tiny, needle-sharp teeth. He twisted aside, but it rolled with him, catching his arm in the crushing rim of its maw. He yelped in pain and surprise. Then his suit froze at that point, preventing further damage without discouraging the guardian at all. It remained locked on to his arm; already he could feel his hand going numb.

So with his free hand he jabbed at its eye. But it blinked, raising an armored lid to protect the orb. He glimpsed another guardian darting toward him. He didn't think they could breach the suit, but they might be able to keep him under until his sparse energy reserves ran out.

Angry now, he used the leverage from his pinned arm to throw himself against the guardian's side. He reached far down its torso, plunging his gloved fingers into its gill slits, the suit translating for him the rough, bony texture. It reacted violently, thrashing in the water so that he was snapped back and forth by its convulsions. Then its grip slipped. He tumbled a few feet. Another guardian swept past, brushing against him, knocking him toward the bottom. He spun, searching for Nesseleth's light. There. Only a few feet away now. He pulled for it, reaching the glowing membrane just as another guardian lunged at his lower leg. He kicked hard, hitting its snout and at the same time knocking himself into the grip of the gel lock. The membrane seized him with a gentle pressure. It ferried him through its glowing expanse, then spilled him unceremoniously onto a curving white floor.

White: the soft glow of it surrounded him, emanating from the walls of a small vaulted chamber without furnishings, equipment, or inhabitants. The chamber's orientation was wrong. It lay at a right angle to the pull of gravity, so that he sat on the curved wall, white light welling up around him. After the long trek through the forest, after the emerald green glow of the water, white seemed almost a magical color, a symbol of artificial forms, the chamber itself a bubble of pure order.

"I thought you were dead," he said softly, speaking into the suit's mike.

Perhaps Nesseleth no longer had radio capabilities; she didn't answer.

He sat up amid a puddle of green seawater, eyeing the membrane with some suspicion. But no guardians burst through. He queried the suit about the quality of the atmosphere, and it expressed no concern. So he pressed the seam of his hood and pulled it back over his face and head. His hair spilled free. He sniffed at the air, and suddenly he was shaking.

Nothing had changed.

The atmosphere aboard Nesseleth was a thick, complex, nurturing stew of warmth and humidity—nothing like the cool clarity of Silk. He'd tried to duplicate this air in his breather and he'd failed at it, he knew that now. Childhood memories came flooding back, the cradling air, dense with floral scents from the gardens and—

Emptiness.

Empty.

There was no hint of human presence. The complex weave of the ship's company was absent. And worse, there was no trace of Jupiter at all.

He bowed his head, understanding coming as a crushing loss. Nesseleth had manufactured Jupiter's sense to call him down to the shore. *So?* Hadn't he known all the time it was an artificial lure? And still he'd let himself hope.

He rose to his feet, sliding a little on the curving surface while his fists clenched inside their gloves. "Nesseleth!"

His own sense had begun to permeate the air in the little chamber: an unsettling combination of joy and sadness; loss, fury. He ignored it, trying to reckon where he was. A diagram of the ship came to him from fixed memory. He studied the layered sections, frowning.

Nesseleth had been a long ellipsoid, her warrens

turning in countermotion beneath the tanks of water that had been her shielding. Her core had been stationary. It had housed the ducts that funneled the dust gathered by her ramscoops. And beneath more insulation, it had housed the core shelter—an armored spindle that contained the ship's mind and her records, as well as the cold-storage units that could preserve her crew should all other systems fail.

Lot stepped carefully up and out of the chamber, balancing with some difficulty on the curved, seamless wall. The chamber opened onto a crawlway, with grab slots all over the wall for fast travel in free fall, and a flat path for use under acceleration. But the path was turned on its side, and Lot had to scramble on the curving wall, bent at the waist as he tried to match the topography of the core with his mental map. He'd come in through a receiving chamber. There were twelve of those, scattered around the spindle's hull. Soon now—

Yes. A few more steps and he reached a tunnel that led to the cold-storage facilities. He scrambled down its short length. A gel membrane sealed the end. He slid through it—

—and almost plummeted over a sheer edge. He jerked back, lost his balance, and went down on one knee. He knelt there at the aperture, the membrane still clutching at his shoulder and looked—up and down—at a vast wall of cold-storage cells on the other side of a narrow chasm. Three and a half feet of open space separated him from the stacked ends of the square-footed boxes. They were packed together like cells with no space between them, climbing in a slow curve from far below him, rising over his head at a similar slow turn, a long curving bank facing its mirror image across the open chasm.

Looking down the chasm, he could see openings like the one in which he knelt, scattered at wide intervals on both the inner and outer walls. Those openings would have been easy to access in zero gravity. Now . . .

He shook his head. The cold-storage cells did not appear to be active. They measured about three feet square, a blank indicator panel on each hatch. He could not remember hearing of any of the chambers ever being in use.

"Nesseleth?" he called softly. Her mind had existed on a substrate at the center of the core, protected by the double banks of storage cells. But her senses had extended throughout the ship. She had been ever-present. "Nesseleth?"

No answer. This armored spindle had been only a

small part of the ship; now it was all. He wondered how much of her mind could have survived such extreme truncation.

He activated the climbing pads on his suit and edged cautiously over the precipice, fly-walking across the outer wall of storage cells until he arrived opposite an aperture on the inside wall. He reached across the chasm with first one hand, then a foot; then he swung over and eased through the gel membrane.

The passage on the other side was nearly ten feet long and very narrow. He crawled through, the soft white glow of the walls so consistent it dazzled his eyes and seemed to vibrate at the edge of his vision. He could still smell the garden scents, though he felt sure that was synthetic; there'd never been gardens in the core shelter. Maybe the scent had always been synthetic, a selected environmental parameter in the ship's systems.

He went on, pushing through the final gel lock into the central chamber. As he emerged, he slipped down a curving slope; it was only a few feet to the bottom. The chamber was oblong, shaped like a bullet lying on its side, and about four feet high: no point in trying to stand, so he remained sprawled on the floor. The walls projected an image of the surrounding water. Nesseleth must have switched on her hull lights again, because he could look out through the clustered holdfasts of glimmering green weeds to see the tentacled guardians cruising past in small groups of two, and three. At the chamber's curved end drifted the human image that served as Nesseleth's personal interface with Lot, its angle of vertical orientation slightly skewed from his own.

Chapter
30

Her interface appeared just as he remembered. A young girl, eight years old, her skin as brown as her eyes, her hair long, golden. He felt a smile on his lips. He'd never noticed before how much she looked like him. She might have been his sister. "Nesseleth."

The child's mouth opened in a soft, round circle of pained surprise. "*Oh!* You've grown up. I forgot . . . to do that."

"It's okay. I like it this way."

Her eyes chided him. "You always wanted to be older than me."

He laughed softly, while a sudden, fluttering sensation slid through his arteries. Nesseleth had used other interfaces with other people, but to the boy he had been those were only masks. This was her real face, and she'd revealed it only to him. A devoted, secret playmate. Not even Jupiter had stood between them. He closed his eyes, feeling almost at home. "I missed you."

"Did not!" she accused. He looked, to see her pretty lips turned into a pout. "Did not, or you would have come for me sooner. I've been so lonely here."

That stung. "I thought you were dead. They said you'd burned in the atmosphere."

A sudden pallor affected her face. "Jupiter wouldn't let that happen to me. I'm still here. I'm just the same. I am the same."

"Sure," he said quickly, hoping she wouldn't observe his doubt. "I can see that." But she retained only a fragment of her former self: this core shelter was all that was left of her.

Perhaps she guessed his thoughts. Her hand rose to her mouth in an anxious gesture. "I was scared that day," she admitted. "It hurt a lot to come down through the air like that. I said bad things. But I didn't mean them! *I didn't mean them.* Why didn't he come for me, Lot? I did everything he said, but he never came."

There was bewilderment in her voice and on her face, but he could get no *sense* of it. He frowned, realizing he'd never interacted with her that way. As a kid it hadn't bothered him; maybe he'd just been used to it. Not anymore. Without supporting traces playing against his sensory tears, her grief seemed false, an act designed to touch his own emotional core and extract the truth of his flawed convictions. . . .

He pulled back: a gesture at once both physical and emotional. He wasn't going to let himself be put on trial. "Maybe it just wasn't your time."

She shook her head, her small white teeth clamped down on a trembling lip. "No. It's just that I got scared and did it wrong. I went too deep, and he couldn't find me. I couldn't call him. I couldn't see anything, or hear or talk or move. The water tried to smash me open!"

Lot glared at her. Without an accompanying chemical sense her grief seemed mechanical. He tried to conjure some sympathy for her by imagining what it might have been like alone on the ocean floor, her sensory gear seared away, the world outside this core shelter an impenetrable blank. But the hovering sense of his own impatience spoiled the exercise. "You survived it," he pointed out coldly. "You rebuilt your senses."

"Too late! He was gone."

"Yeah, well I'm not."

Her image froze at that suggestion. Then it seemed to run backward for a few seconds, her gestures oddly stripped of meaning as her hand dropped stiffly into her lap. A little smile flitted across her lips. "I've been thinking about that since I sensed you in the world. Do you think he knew . . . ?"

"I think we got lucky." Overhead, a trio of shadowy gray guardians darted through the curtain of green light cast by Nesseleth's hull. He followed their motion until they disappeared back into the surrounding darkness. "What are they?"

"Just animals. But they were drawn to his sense, just like you."

He felt his skin crawl. *Animals.* Unconscious and reactive, yet he'd responded exactly like them, chasing mindlessly after Jupiter's trace, even when he'd *known* it was artificial. What did that make him?

He touched his sensory tears. "He was sent out from the Hallowed Vasties, wasn't he? And you with him."

She smiled and nodded. Her face seemed radiant with the memory, and he realized abruptly that she wasn't a child any longer. She'd grown up without his noticing. He stared at her, while his throat tightened in awful recognition. *"Mother?"* he croaked.

Her eyes widened in surprise. The image twitched, then re-formed instantly into the golden-haired child. Too late.

He was on his knees, his heart racing. Why? He'd always known the image he called Nesseleth was only an interface. Now he knew how Jupiter had seen her. *So what?*

He tried not to care, but twisted jealousy wormed through the air. Why? Because, dammit, he'd thought he'd had something unique. What a joke. Nesseleth had served the old man for centuries. She'd probably been made for him. . . .

"Who was Helena?" he blurted out.

The child looked at him calmly. "Your mother."

"You?"

"Silly Lot. We're best friends."

"Sooth." Easy to see why. A derivative interface for a derivative madman. *I'm not him.*

He gazed at her, feeling something break inside him. "I don't think this interface is going to work for me anymore."

She looked pained, but she returned to Helena's image.

No, he reminded himself. *This is Nesseleth.*

Lot straightened his shoulders, trying not to let the

reverberant memory touch him. "Tell me what he was," he commanded stiffly.

She sighed. *(—Mother?—)* "You already know that. He's the seed, the center of the Communion."

"But the Communion was already here. Jupiter found it here . . . didn't he?"

"What he found here was unique."

Lot swallowed hard against the desire to touch this maternal ghost *(only an image)*. ". . . and elsewhere?"

She watched him closely. "Do you remember?"

He realized that he did. Faint memories licked at him; vague images—not of things he had done or seen himself, but there in his fixed memory, just the same. "There were other Communions, weren't there? In the Hallowed Vasties?"

Did she nod in confirmation? Her gaze was so stern. "You should know these things, Lot. You're unschooled. You've been negligent with your heritage."

Sooth. A sorry runaway. No keeper like Nesseleth to guide him in the proper path. Instead he'd had Ord. *Good Lot, smart Lot.* "Tell me now."

Her critical gaze softened as she explained it to him. "Each Communion starts with one man. The faithful know him. They're drawn to his hand. His will becomes their will."

And sometimes their will becomes his, Lot thought. His gaze cut away as he remembered the silver interlock of emotions he'd discovered in the city.

"The Communion takes form around him. It grows outward, and as it does it changes form. Gone are the antique loci of man and man and woman and woman. Minds that were once sequestered now conjoin in bundled nerve systems that twine about each other, extending in electronic link over cities, then over entire planetary surfaces."

Lot could almost see it. "They make the Dyson swarms?"

"Linked by light, yes. They are the blessed. The nature of their existence is not comprehensible to us."

He breathed deeply, slowly, counting the guardian shadows. "Why did he leave it all behind, then?"

"That was his purpose. They made him for that."

"To make more of their own kind."

"It's your gift too."

Lot nodded his bitter understanding. "It's like an infection."

"It's the Communion."

And I'm its agent.

He shook his head, striving to see the whole. "But in the Hallowed Vasties it's a human thing, isn't it?"

"Yes, Lot."

"Then why did he come to the Well?"

Her face seemed troubled. He imagined hot points of visible light searing through the perforated cordons. "He suspected that the Vasties were not . . . stable."

Lot snorted. Good guess.

But then he reminded himself: Jupiter had known. He'd seen the problem. He'd been thinking about it. He'd been trying to find a way out instead of stumbling and bumbling around like an animal surrendering its fate to luck and natural selection. . . .

"I brought him out of the Hallowed Vasties," Nesseleth continued. "We roamed the star cluster called the Committee, but it was an unfriendly place. So many of the people there were strangely blind to his gift. He could have made a Communion despite them, but he hesitated. He was troubled. He didn't want to repeat the mistakes of the past. He would have a clean pattern, without flaws or resistance. So he accepted only those who came to him freely. Then we left to find our own world."

She hesitated. Her face emptied of expression. "The hopes of our first Communion died in the plague that I could not shed. But the Well saved him. He found a half-formed Communion already here. How it came to be he didn't know. It was strange and unfinished, yet full of promise. He knew it was holy, and that we'd been guided here by the hand of the Unknown God, that we could heal the flaw of the Hallowed Vasties.

"You see it? Don't you, Lot? In natural systems, stability is found in diversity—"

Lot nodded. "And the Well is diverse, and very, very stable."

"Our enemies discovered peace here."

He frowned, wondering at the meaning of that word. "The Well has its own mechanism. Jupiter wanted to integrate his Communion with that." The mitochondrial analog. Two distinct systems merged into one. A union of long-term potential.

But it had failed.

"What happened to him? Do you know?"

"He gave himself to the Communion. He waits at its center."

But there had been no center. "You're just guessing. You were in the deep ocean. You didn't witness it."

She shrugged. "They needed him. He would have gone to them."

They? Lot felt his skin crawl. He'd felt their need too.

Nesseleth smiled in a superior fashion that said she'd worked this all out long ago. "They couldn't be complete without him. So he went ahead."

"I think you're wrong. I think this place killed him."

Her face spasmed. Doubt was there, but only for a moment. Contempt quickly won out. "You've forgotten him," she accused.

But Lot had not. He clearly remembered Jupiter's ruthless determination. Jupiter had sent Nesseleth down. He'd been ready to use assault Makers against the Silkens. It wasn't hard to imagine him standing at the bottom of the elevator column, waiting for cars that would not come, knowing his grand scheme had failed, that his people were dying uselessly overhead and that he wouldn't have enough human tools to shift the balance of this world to his control, his conscious control. Foresight, mercy, sympathy, forgiveness: all were products of the conscious mind. But so was revenge. "He released an indiscriminate strain of assault Maker, didn't he? A virulent strain." That was why the elevator column had been scarred near the surface. Pitted and scoured so that dust could collect and plants take hold. "You've examined the traces, haven't you?"

Nesseleth didn't blink. "Whatever he did, he did it with cause. He had to force them down when they refused to come to his call. The Silkens are dangerous. They're old and scarred and they never sensed him clearly."

The sociopaths of the frontier. Restive descendants of the mavericks who'd deliberately fled the Hallowed Vasties, reveling in their isolation, while the sane and stable remained behind. Such selective pressures might mold a resistant strain. On the frontier a prophet might have to struggle to raise a following, forever coping with malcontents like Captain Antigua, who would slip away from his union.

"He meant to attack the Silkens. He meant to sever the elevator cable if they didn't give in. But his assault Makers damaged the Well, and the Well defended itself. It killed him."

"No! He entered into the Communion. He's here now. He *is* here." And if she said it often enough, would that prove its truth?

Lot remembered the boiling, seething slopes of the crater: a chaotic storm, its only purpose to destroy information content. *Nothing is lost in the Well.* Jupiter had made that claim, but Jupiter had been wrong. The Well was not analogous to the Hallowed Vasties. The Vasties were a celebration of consciousness. The Well had none. The Vasties burned themselves out in a few hundred to a few thousand years. The Well had existed for eons.

Survivors survived.

Millions of years before the first human had even come into existence, the Well had hunkered down against the assaults of the old murderers, shedding consciousness . . . to survive?

Lot looked at Nesseleth *(Mother)*, wondering how much she really knew. "The Vasties evolved only after our ancestors left Earth." Less than three thousand years ago. "How did they start?"

Her expression was wary. "We received a gift from the void."

An infection. A plague of the Chenzeme? Buried under the skin of a man like Jupiter, *of a man like me*, perhaps existing in a latent state for years or even centuries, passed benignly through planetary populations, before finally being triggered to virulence. Viruses with long incubation periods had ever been difficult to detect, and to resist.

"Softly, Lot," Nesseleth/Helena urged, detecting his rising tension. "It's your purpose. You'll make us whole."

But he couldn't calm himself. What if the Chenzeme had fought this virus too? *And what if it had destroyed them?* Leaving behind only their unconscious machines, their unconscious systems, guided by an artificial instinct to destroy anything that hinted at technology . . . ever a strong indicator of conscious processes, where remnants of the virus might still thrive.

The gray guardians slid past. There seemed to be

more all the time. Drawn to the sense of Jupiter, and maybe to Lot too. Cult leader. Cult virus. He watched them, the tips of his fingers pressed against the smooth wall. Were these the remnants then, of the designers of the Well system? Still vulnerable to the pull of the cross-clade infection, even through the limited self-awareness they'd left themselves.

And the ados in the city . . .

They want to follow you. Knowing you're down there—it's made them crazy.

And Alta: *I can feel him inside me.*

His gloved fingers slid into a fist. "Why don't *I* feel it?" he whispered. He could believe it only during the crowd furor; never in the clean bitter moments of isolation.

Nesseleth's lost warrens had been cramped and close and he'd never been truly alone for the first eight years of his life. Jupiter must have known how tenuous faith could be.

Softly, Nesseleth/Helena reminded him: "All doubt will vanish when we cross over."

Resentment made him strike out. "You want too much. The Communion's not what you imagine."

Her cheeks darkened. "Don't say that."

"It's not what he said it would be!"

Her smooth face went abruptly blank. Her image began to fade, and he could almost hear the awesome flux of her mind. Then her projection strengthened. She drifted on air, closing the gap between them until her hand *(his mother's hand)* rested without weight on his thigh. He wanted to touch her; wanted it with an ache that pulled all his muscles into taut, painful cords. But she wasn't *real.* He couldn't sense her, and the disjunction set him on edge. She said, "You were a child then. You didn't understand what he promised."

"Maybe he didn't want us to understand. He *needed* us, or he couldn't grow. He would have promised us anything."

Now it was her turn to be angry. "It's not for us to question him. Not even you, Lot. You were born in the void. But Jupiter is from the Communion. He came out of the Hallowed Vasties and he carried the memories of those places inside him. He sees farther than any of us ever could—"

Lot interrupted her with a soft protest as implanted memories began to unfold inside him. "I can see some of that past too, and I think it's all illusion."

She pretended not to hear him. "Jupiter has gone

ahead of us." Her unexpected smile wooed him with sweet insistence. "You're our guide now."

"*No.*" He felt hemmed in, trapped. The smell of the tunnel came back to him, the obsession that would not be put off even by the close threat of death. *Crazy.*

"It's an illusion," he insisted, forcing the unwilling words past his throat. "I think we've been poisoned. We're not supposed to be like this."

"Oh but we are. We've always been this way. Lot, always. From Old Earth, from our earliest histories, from times that are not even remembered we were sensing the Communion. Desiring it. Making up stories about it, myths, legends. Trying always to achieve it. Now it's here. The true Communion. So close. And *you* are the gateway. Only through you can we reach our end, our reason for being. All of human history has been a process that is finally nearing its completion."

And the lights burned through.

He closed his eyes, trying to calm himself, trying to synthesize something of her mood.

"Lot?"

He looked at her, struggling to hide his growing terror. For ten years she'd endured an excruciating isolation. How might she react if he denied her now? He groped for a new subject, hoping to distract her. "Null Boundary's approaching. Do you know anything about him?"

"I know of him. He came out of the center long, long ago."

"You mean before the Hallowed Vasties?"

"So it's said."

Lot stared at the guardians coasting silently past Nesseleth's hard shell, struggling to keep his breathing shallow. *"That's so old."* Could Null Boundary have witnessed the change?

"You're impressed with his longevity? But time isn't always correlated with illumination."

"Sure, I know it." He rubbed his hands in nervous motion, striving to become someone else for a few minutes, someone Nesseleth would trust—in deceit, truth worked better than lies. "You know, it's almost time. City authority's been displaced. The elevator's being repaired. People will be coming down."

He caught from her the false sound of an indrawn breath. "Sweet Lot. You won't forget me?"

"No." He almost choked on the word. "Never." He rubbed at his sensory tears, blunting the taste of his own treachery. *(Mother!)* "I have to meet them."

"But you'll come back?"

Another guardian glided past, its eye fixed on some invisible point, an indeterminate distance away. "I won't forget you," Lot told her. "I swear."

Chapter
31

Nesseleth had modified her structure over the years, building slow mobility in the form of a swarm of tube feet on the ventral side of her hull. She'd gained some buoyancy in the deep oceans with electrolytic reactions to produce gas floats. But she would not go ashore. "I'd be helpless," she explained. "I need the water to support my hull; I need the nutrients it carries to survive."

But she didn't want to risk Lot against the guardians again, so she eased in as close to the shore as she could. Lot left her through an access port on her dorsal surface. The water was only knee-deep here. He clung to the green-glowing weeds to keep his balance as frothing waves swept past. He waited for the largest swell in the set, then dove with it toward the shore, letting its power carry him across the shallows. He thought he felt a tentacle brush his leg, but if there was a guardian in the dark water, it did not attack.

He waded ashore. The surf was still running past his knees when he caught the trace. He shook his head, for a moment not daring to believe it was real. Then he blinked his vision down to IR, and scanned first the beach and then the vegetation line. *There!* Just where the plants began to grow he caught a patch of heat. "Urban!" he screamed. "Alta!" The wave pulled back, leaving only sizzling wet sand under his feet. "Urban!"

The warm patch rose. It floated ghostly for a moment then responded with an answering whoop—"Yeah, Lot!"—and Urban came lunging down the beach.

Lot met him halfway in a furious embrace: "God, I thought you were lost! Dead."

And Urban talking at the same time: "You crazy, fury? Swimming at night? No old piece of a broken ship is worth that risk! I almost stripped Ord apart again for letting you go."

Then Alta was there, her arms around him, her lips against his cheek, her presence rolling silvery and bright across his sensory tears, an intoxicating, commanding tide. His eyes widened in surprise. He pulled away from her, suddenly terrified that he might slip under. She let him go with a gasp of her own. Maybe she felt it too.

He backed off a few steps, letting the clean night air run between them. Urban grinned, a hand on Lot's shoulder. "Hey fury, did you ever think we'd last this long?"

Urban had held on to his pack after the tumble into the river. They huddled together at the top of the beach, sharing out the last of the fruit while Urban recounted their adventures. Somehow, he and Alta had managed to stay together in the water. They'd washed up on a shelf inside the gorge, and had taken shelter there under a rock overhang. "We didn't dare move," he explained. "We didn't want to call the city's guns down on us."

The river had carried a lot of debris, among it a mound, torn free of its substrate and floating upside down in the swift current. It swept close to the shelf, and Alta had grabbed it.

Now she grinned at Lot, her cheeks warm with a faint flush of pride. "It was hot, even after soaking in the river. I guess it was still functioning, but it didn't shoot any stink at us . . . maybe because it was upside down. There probably is no defensive mechanism on the bottom."

They'd discovered they could peel away thin layers from the mound's underside, gooey, discrete levels connected by tough, vertical white fibers. "Like nerves," Urban said. "Anyway, it had been floating so high that Alta had this idea we could use it for a boat. So we hollowed it out, and what was left was still buoyant. We waited till dark, then got inside.

The current brought us all the way down to the edge of the marsh."

"Was the mound still hot?"

"Yeah. Real cozy."

Lot frowned, unhappy with the image that suggested. But Urban didn't seem to notice. "So what did you find out from the ship's core?" he asked.

Lot shifted, suddenly apprehensive. "A lot of history, mostly. She doesn't know what happened to Jupiter."

He lay back on the sand, not quite ready to talk about his suspicions, afraid of how Urban might react. Instead, he entertained them with the story of Ord's snails. They laughed like drunks over the incident, pulling jokes out of it long after the humor should have been spent—not touching on anything more serious until finally Ord interrupted: "A call for you, Lot."

Urban scowled at the robot. "What's it talking about?"

"It's got a link to the city."

Urban's eyes went wide. "Shit, fury! They'll target us again." He was already halfway to his feet. Alta had made a quick grab for the pack.

Lot held out a restraining hand. "It's okay, really. They're not going to use the guns anymore. I talked to your old man. He wasn't in on that. He tried to stop them."

Urban considered a moment. He didn't seem fully convinced, but he did settle slowly back onto the sand. "Maybe you better catch us up."

So Lot told them what he knew: that the riot had not been quelled, that the rebellious ados were all infected with a neural parasite, and that authority had lost control. "David said they were repairing the column; that they'd be down in a few hours." He could feel Urban's tension doubling, then doubling again, filling the space between them.

"This neural parasite, fury—it's why the ados follow you?"

Lot answered cautiously: "Sooth. That's why." But still Urban's tension rose another notch. Lot studied him closely, trying to discern the reason. With a start of surprise he realized how haggard Urban looked. His eyes were hollow, his cheekbones prominent. His mood tasted sharply bitter. Lot caught on. "It's not in you, of course," he said firmly.

"You know that?"

"I know it sure."

Urban thought it over; then his teeth flashed in a quick grin. "Sooth. I never followed you. It was always the other way around."

"That's right. You got it."

"A call for you, Lot," Ord said again. So Lot reluctantly told it to go ahead.

It spoke in David's voice. "Hey, Lot. Things are going a little slower than expected. We found only three cars on the lower tracks."

Lot felt a chill across his back.

"We brought the cars up," David went on. "City authority can't stop us. They've retreated to a remote complex in the industrial core. We want to start loading. But Lot, one of the cars—"

"I know, David. We saw it on the way down."

David didn't speak for a moment. Then: "There's at least a hundred and eighty bodies."

"*I know.*"

"Do you . . . want me to send them down? Maybe they've got enough physical structure left that you could . . . reach them? Somehow?"

Lot caught a foreign thread of human emotion on the air. He turned slowly, to see the softly glowing blue figures of two phantoms on the beach. Urban swore in ugly whispers. Lot felt his hackles rise. "Yeah, David," he said, his voice suddenly hoarse. "Go ahead. Send them down." The Old Silkens had been resurrected here . . . sort of. And a cargo of dead would at least keep the living at bay for a while longer. "Send them down first."

He signaled Ord to cut the connection.

Urban had moved protectively between Alta and the dim blue apparitions. The phantoms were perhaps fifty yards away, two masculine figures standing just above the splash zone, both of them nude, their long, unkept hair framing stern faces. "They've followed us down the river," Urban said.

"The same figures?" Lot asked.

"Sometimes a woman's with them."

Lot knew her.

Urban added: "They're drawn to Alta."

Lot looked at her. He remembered the blue woman crouching, staring hungrily at Alta as she slept. But there was no concern on Alta's face. She wore a faint smile. In her eyes was a faraway look, like a real one who senses something pleasant over an atrial channel. She seemed limned in silver.

Alta had the neural parasite. She was part of the cult and the phantoms sensed it. Lot edged away from her, shaking his head to dispel the pressure of her presence against his sensory tears. "Listen, I'd really like to get a look at what's left of that mound."

"Yeah," Urban said. "Let's get out of here." He touched Alta's elbow. "Come on. You don't want to go that way." He pushed her gently; got her to turn around. But her eyes remained dreamy. Lot stayed well away as they waded back through the marsh: night creatures seeing heat in the darkness. He continued to sense the vague presence of strangers, somewhere in the still night air.

On a muddy bank, where the river surged whenever there was rain in the highlands, Urban showed him the overturned mound. "See, it's made of layers," he said, peeling back a section of the gooey material a couple of inches thick. Long white filaments poked out of it. Urban pulled the layer off them as if he were pulling a bead free of multiple strings.

Alta helped him. She seemed to have forgotten about the phantoms, though she stood closer to Lot now than she had before. The clouds had begun to break, and some ring light shone through the wrack. Silver glinted everywhere on the edge of his vision.

"Look here," Alta said, pointing to a tangled web of the filaments. The mass layered the hollowed-out interior of the mound and nested in the bottom. "It has to be some kind of nervous system."

Neuronal architecture.

Urban handed him the stripped layer. It was heavier than Lot expected; dryer too. He squeezed it, and it yielded, soft/firm like a sleeping pad. Cautiously, he held it near his face, but it had no sense that he could perceive. He wondered again if it had anything to do with the phantoms.

He was getting ready to throw the stripped layer back into the hollowed-out mound when a hint of motion among the reeds drew his eye. He half-turned, expecting to see Ord, for Alta had sent it off to hunt snails. Instead, he recognized the diminutive figure of a warden hardly an arm's reach away. Its body glowed faint red, like a fading emergency light.

Urban saw it at the same time. His hand dropped to his waist. From his suit pocket he retrieved one of the capsules they'd captured from the warden that first day.

This new warden raised its hands. They dissolved, flowing down over its forearms like candles melting, while wisps of steam rose into the night air. "No armaments here," it said, speaking in a multiplex voice that issued from hundreds of tiny mouths strung together in lines to suggest a human face.

Lot laid a hand on Urban's arm. "It's Sypaon." He stepped toward her cautiously. She'd lowered her hands. Now the steaming limbs were re-forming. "We want to thank you," Lot said. "You saved us there, on the ridge."

The substrate that held her face seemed to liquefy. The tiny mouths slid into meaningless patterns—for a moment only—before order returned and her face reemerged. "This language: it is difficult to re-master," she said. "I've strung neural patterns together—"

Lot interrupted her. "How many wardens do you control?"

She seemed puzzled. "This one is all that's necessary."

But that snake thing had surely not disgorged her whole. She must have had another warden under her command. "You can access others?"

"As needed."

"Can you stop the wardens that are repairing the elevator column?"

She frowned. "Translate for me. Why have you driven our people from the Well?"

Lot held himself very still, sensing that his position had grown suddenly more precarious. "I have not done that, Sypaon."

"They've retreated," she insisted. "They say you carry plague. They fight among themselves."

He backed up half a step. His throat had gone dry. "It wasn't me. Your people vanished from the Well long ago. I'm trying to understand it."

"Is that why you were made?"

"It doesn't matter why!"

This outburst startled her. She went still for several seconds. Perhaps she'd withdrawn from the warden, to run her own assessments in the vast body of the ring. But soon her face coalesced again in sharp detail. "The Well holds me hostage. I cannot penetrate this system."

So. Was this the root of her interest in him? He knelt cautiously in front of her. "I can. Sometimes. Perhaps we can help each other."

She seemed to consider this. "A tool may be useful for things other than its intended purpose—"

"Shit, Lot," Urban interrupted softly. "They're back."

Lot turned. Some twenty yards away, three blue figures, two men and one woman, walked toward them across the surface of the water. He could see their reflections in the smooth mere as they strode silently forward. They made no disturbance in the surface tension.

Alta seemed mesmerized by them. She stared across the water, her expression vibrant with expectation. Silver glimmered in her eyes and across her face. Lot stepped close to her. "Do they talk to you?"

She glanced at him, a childlike smile of wonder on her face. "Not in words. But I've begun to feel them, like I feel Jupiter."

He looked out across the water. The trio had stopped perhaps ten yards away. He could see their features clearly. Worse, he could feel their desire and it pulled at him. They knew him. He had no doubt of it now. Expectation seeped from their strengthening auras.

"Translate for me," Sypaon said. "What system is this?"

Overhead, a cloud shifted and ring light turned the water silver. Or was it something else? Lot felt a gathering pressure on the air, as if an unseen crowd had suddenly risen from the ground around him, their bodies flush against him. He shook his head, backing away from the water, rubbing at his sensory tears as if he could rub their influence out of him.

Alta smiled. "They're from the Communion, aren't they?"

"The Communion?" Sypaon muttered. "Archival reference—"

"Sooth, it's so."

Urban's hand fell roughly on his shoulder, spinning him halfway around, leaving him staggering on the slippery ground. "That's bullshit, Lot! You know it. That's not transcendence. It's stinking marsh gas."

Lot caught the sense of his anger and felt it resound inside him, amplifying in a knee-jerk reaction as if he were some kind of dumb machine. Alta caught his mood shift and melted back into the silvered reeds. But Urban was blind to it. Dark. Forever separate, a flaw in the silver net. Lot grabbed at the open neck of his suit, his fist closing around the supple fabric. "They would have killed you in the Hallowed Vasties," he growled. "They destroyed everyone like you who couldn't feel it, who couldn't believe."

The dark souls had been quickly isolated wherever the Communion grew. The tendrils of light that flowed through the growing network had closed like a garrote around the throats of those who could not conform to the pattern of the Vasties.

Crowds seemed to whisper around him, tugging at him with a silver tide. He felt himself slipping.

I'm not ready for this. He grabbed for Urban with both hands now, trying to reach into that dark space, clinging to it like a drowning man clinging to a rock against the rising waters.

Silver flow of thought running in tides around a star.

"I can remember it," Lot said. Urban's eyes went wide. His hands closed defensively on Lot's arms. His skin stank of fear. "It starts small, with a man like Jupiter. They made him for the purpose. He carries their seed in him. Call it the cult virus, though it's more than that—and it's older than the Hallowed Vasties. Some people sense it right away. Like Alta, they're vulnerable; they're drawn to him. Others get it when they've been with him awhile. He changes people, Urban. He parasitizes them. He makes a place for himself down inside them. His desires become their desires. They accrete around him. It begins."

"He's *dead*, fury."

Lot nodded. Out on the water, the phantoms stared at the shore debate in cool blue constancy. "Sooth."

"*No.*" Lot was suddenly aware of Alta, circling slowly round them, a shining, shimmering entity. She pointed toward the phantoms. "He has to be with them."

Lot shook his head. "I remember what it was like in the Vasties." His voice was hoarse, his grip on Urban never lessening. The tide ran past him, like a physical force. "Not like this."

"They're Old Silken, aren't they?" Urban asked.

"I think so."

Alta tentatively touched his shoulder. He flinched. He could feel the buzz of her, a high, tight silver vibration. "But they've made a Communion," she insisted.

"Sooth. It's so. The cult virus must have been latent here."

"It killed them?" Urban asked.

Lot shook his head. "I think it was the Well that killed them. The virus took over what was left—when they had no way to resist it—tried to knit it together maybe, but there was no focus, no center."

"No Jupiter, you mean."

"Or a man like him." *We are always men.* He could sense the predecessors vaguely, like shadows in his memory. Imprints of each other, stamping out their silvered shapes against a dark background of collapsing worlds.

"But Jupiter's here now," Alta insisted.

She glistened silver. He felt the gleam of it flood his own skin. Felt his heart racing. Deliberately, he kept his senses fixed on Urban, lightless well in a glistening net. "Jupiter used assault Makers on the column. The planet reacted. It destroyed him."

"You can't know that!" Alta cried.

But he could. The Communion made here was flawed and corrupt. It had no center, no focus, and so it could not grow by conquest but only by slow accretion, a confused, disjointed intellect operating forever out of sync.

"You're a liar," Alta said. "You're jealous of him and you never really *believed* anyway. But I know. He brought us here. He has to be here. He brought Gent back from death. He bound him inside his own soul, and he'll come for me too."

Lot felt himself falling into her tide. She was so close, her body hot, liquid, a mercuric fluid that melted through his skin, all the way down to his bones until he felt more her than himself, and she—

He looked in her eyes and saw only himself, eyes wide in awe, and then her again, inconstant perception like the fluttering of a falling leaf, self/other descending to a silver core. *"You don't need him."* Lot knew the words were his, though they were said in Alta's voice. And in his own speech: *"I am him."*

From somewhere close by he could hear Sypaon's

cool warning. "A feedback reaction has begun. A biochemical dialogue in the Chenzeme way. The suspended data patterns seek consensus."

But it was only background chatter, a temporary flux in the silvered tide. The tide ran through him strongly. Entities whispered around him. Not wholly human. Partly made into something else that was at once new to him and deeply remembered. They brought him the history of Silk, swift joyous years in the city and then dissolution, their biosystems crumbling. They are captured. Suspended in a slow disjointed union they had never sought. Now with him, sinking into him.

A spike plunges into his awareness, a black needle in the silver flow. He is cognizant of his body once again, and a fiery eruption that runs along his skin beneath his suit. He claws at the seam, scratches it open, a mechanical voice pleading with him *are you sure? are you sure?* Shrug out of the shoulders. A half-seen crowd presses close around him. He peels the leggings off, mud between his toes, ring light casting his skin unnaturally white, small animals leaping away from his running feet, Alta just ahead of him, her body already a dissolute blur as she throws herself upon the tide he jumps—

—and does not come down. He floats in suspension, the tide winding around him. He is the core cell in a plane of awareness that locks in place as his perceptions expand, until he can see the full surface of the world and the broad sweep of the void that holds it.

The geometry is not flat. Yet it seems flattened somehow—or else he's been raised beyond it, because he can see it all in a glance linked through an hours-long interval of time.

They cling to him. Bright points of awareness. He is many at once, the same in all places, tendrils of man reaching outward to gather the selves to him, he can see with their eyes, feel with their hearts and they with his, one feeding the other—

He leads them.

They lead him.

Synchrony building between them and the sense of self fading

Becoming another

Awestruck

Jupiter knew.

Never has anyone seen so far. He is whole. All.

What had confused him
Now clear.

He understands why the Well abandoned all conscious mind:

Because that's what I attack and subsume, now, and in my ancient past.

What beings would deliberately choose mindlessness over this glory-state he'd just begun to taste?

The alien is a strong chord within him, blended with the newer harmonics of human desire, a natural desire for union, for something greater. Human culture had welcomed him. Human culture had sought this state for millennia.

He recalled the wonder of the Hallowed Vasties, long flowing skeins of thought encircling a captive star while subminds chattered endlessly on—

—until the light burned through.

Nothingness.

He cannot remember anything for a troubling long time. Then light again, thousands of lives his now—*Jupiter was right to flee*—here in the Well he will become something new. Already he's begun to mix with the alien traces gathered here. He sends exploring fingers into the mindless ocean of biodata, becoming an entity greater than the Vasties ever knew—

A black spike smashes into his world.

He can see for millions of miles and feel the tides of the Well run fast around him but he can't see his own core. Heat cuts him. The links unravel around him, tearing great sections of his mind away. A distant wind gushes howling in an animal voice and he is going blind. He would clutch at the core of his being but has no hands no mouth no eyes no senses at all only raw exposed nerves laid out over vasties and being trod upon pain driving him out into hopeless separation all sense of Communion fading fading and gone—

—and Lot can hear his own voice screaming, startled that the sound of it is coming from his throat until a moment later he feels the pain and understands it, curling flesh, snapping threads, his skin peeling away, the nerves exposed to hands *touching* him, clots of darkness, every contact an agony, lifting him, dragging him, the mud like a bank of knives under his legs he had almost melted away. *"Oh God Urban stop it!"*

"Lot?"

It's Urban's voice. It hurts his ears. He can hear the unsynchronized panic of two hearts and that hurts too. Urban's breath on his cheek: hurts. He blinks hard and the starlight sears, though it's muted behind a watery film.

"Lot?" Urban says again, his voice high and frantic.

Lot thinks his skull might split. "God, don't speak," he begs.

"You're *back*."

Urban's holding him in a half-sitting position. They are sprawled in the mud. Sypaon scuttles in staccato time all around a large mound, snatching up from the ground writhing, wormy things and tucking them into the gelatinous tissue of her arms. Her warden body casts a dancing red glow on the mound, revealing the recessed imprint of a spread-eagled man.

"*Alta*," Lot whispers. That imprint is his own shape. He knows it. The impression left by his body. There are fine wormy filaments trailing out of it. Other filaments emerge from the ground near him. They seek him like slim, hungry, blind worms. They move. Peristaltic motion pushing them gradually closer. The most vigorous of them tracks a scar his heel made in the mud when Urban dragged him.

Urban watches this one too. Lot feels him stiffen; a swift intake of breath. *Clot of darkness.* Lot twists around to look at him. "I know your kind."

Dark and empty men. Flaws in the Communion. In the Hallowed Vasties they'd been driven out or destroyed.

Urban lifts his hand. Glinting in it is the warden's capsule.

Lot is aware again of his sloughing, burning skin, his exposed nerve ends and he understands now that he's been wounded by the assault Maker, that Urban has used it against him. He cringes. But Urban reaches past him, squeezing a fine jet of the stuff at the closest tendril. It recoils, bubbling, the wounded section suddenly amputated.

"Come on, fury," Urban says. "They're hunting you now. You have to get away. Get clear."

"Yes," Sypaon says, pulling up a long filament, tucking it into her arm. "You must flee." Her many eyes glow like tiny embers.

Lot shakes his head, unable to deal with things. "Alta," he whispers again.

"Shut up!" Urban screams, an hysterical edge on his voice. "Just shut up and do what I tell you!"

Lot is on his feet now. His body's numb, so he knows the painkillers have kicked in. He tries to do as he's told. He walks. Urban keeps him balanced, steers him. Sypaon must be with them too, because over her red light shows the glinting marsh water, the reeds, the mud under his feet disturbed by the wriggles of emergent tendrils, a communal network like a vast fungus underground. Finally, he's stumbling on beach sand. It's dry under his feet and apparently uninhabited. The swan burster glides out from behind the clouds, a bright round oh of surprise tut-tutting over his pitiful condition and some long time later Urban finally lets him fall to the sand, the grains against his lips and in his mouth, tasting sand, scattered grains unrelated to one another except by proximity, shed from the greater mass of some volcano or continental shelf. Individuals, on the beach.

Chapter
32

Over the years, Lot had watched hundreds of tiny flies alight on the glistening paddles of the sundews that he grew in his breather. Never in all that time had he been moved to pull one of the mindless creatures from the sweet, entrapping secretions. What would be the point? The body could not come away intact.

He awoke to daylight. Kheth was already high, its fierce light burning against his exposed skin. He sat up slowly, his muscles feeling peculiarly distant and heavy. Sand had stuck to tiny sores all over his body. He had no way to check how much interior damage had been done, but judging from the numb state of his peripheral senses he guessed that it had been significant.

He looked around. The ocean was calm, small waves breaking in whispers against the shore. He could see Nesseleth's long silhouette under the green water. Far down the beach, Urban pitched rocks across the reef. Sypaon stood with him, a vague figure, the color of sand.

Urban's pack was close at hand. Ord scuttled out from under a small-leaved shrub and pulled a bottle of water from it. Lot drank half, watching Urban's distant figure as he bent to pick up a pebble, turned to pitch it into the water, bent to pick up another. . . .

Lot sensed a sullen fury in his tight, choppy movements. Dread nestled in his chest. He looked at Ord. "Where's Alta?" he asked, his voice hardly more than a dry croak.

"Mistress Alta's presence is not detected."

Gone over.

He nodded, unsurprised. He'd known it already in some part of his mind. He could remember some of it. He knew he'd tried to go with her. He *should* have gone with her. That was why Jupiter had brought him here. It was why he'd been made.

They were waiting for him.

Alta and Gent and all the Old Silkens, caught in an unfocused, rolling consciousness, thoughts sustained for mere minutes at a time.

He put the water bottle down and crawled across the sand to his suit. It was crumpled and covered with mud. Vaguely, he wondered if it had been Urban or Ord who'd retrieved it. He wormed his way into it without getting up. Winces of pain broke through the deadened sense of his muscles as he twisted and squirmed, sand scraping against his skin. He'd just sealed the front seam when motion caught his eye.

He turned, to see Alta only an arm's reach away. She crouched beside him, her body a faint blue nimbus, hardly visible in the strong daylight. Only it wasn't her, not really. The eyes were hers, and the breasts, but the nose was only a suggestion. And she had male genitalia, though incomplete.

He shrank away from her, sliding over the warm sand. Her expression made his skin crawl: she seemed to stare past him, as if she saw something coming that remained invisible to him. "*Apart,*" she said softly, in the Old Silk accent he'd heard before.

He trembled, trying to hold himself aloof. The blue suspension that formed her was tenuous at best. It could burst at any moment, spraying him with a toxin that would force him under the skin. Why did he resist that? It was what he'd been made for.

But made by whom?

A gift from the void. His kind had come out of the void. Maybe they were only another weapon of the ancient war—or maybe they were the enemy. Death masquerading as salvation. The infection might take millennia to run its course. But what did that matter? The cult virus had abided eons since the demise of the old murderers. A few thousand years must count as nothing. Yet the Hallowed Vasties would burn themselves out in that span, briefly glorious, but in the end gone, gone, gone.

He glanced at the phantom beside him. Ecstatic death was still death—and an ending—in a universe that might be infinite. How could he support that?

There is no place of permanence in the Universe, no golden existence, no finish line. We live on the edge of chaos, with all the turbulence that implies. . . .

"Hark," he said softly, rousing the suit's DI. "Seal the hood?"

"Energy reserves do not support the action," the suit informed him.

Lot kept his voice carefully unconcerned, not knowing how much intent the phantom might perceive. "Emergency override, then. Do it now."

Ord watched him, a peculiar expression on its face.

"Are you sure?" the suit queried.

"Now."

"Now," the phantom echoed as the hood lapped swiftly up around Lot's tangled hair. Some of the matted skeins fell outside its reach. It couldn't seal. The phantom looked directly at him, its color deepening, just as it had that night in the crater.

Lot turned away, groping in his suit pocket, hunting for his copy of the warden's capsule. He found it, just as a sharp *pop!* behind him announced the phantom's dissolution. *"No!"* he roared, and scrambled away, squeezing the capsule so that its mist sprayed indiscriminately behind him.

For a moment the world was depicted in silver: the ocean waves, the darting shapes of the guardians in the water, the miniature dunes that raced up and slammed against his face, and Ord, always before golden, melting now in a pool of pure silver radiance, flowing down over his face in a solid mask that blocked the air but kept out the poisons too.

Lot got his feet under him and ran. He couldn't see or hear or smell anything, but he could feel the sand sliding under his feet, and then he was splashing in the water. He pulled up sharply. Ord slid off his face, re-forming neatly against his chest while he gasped, drawing in great lungfuls of clean sea air.

Urban was racing toward him down the beach. Sypaon's shadow flitted across the sand as if she were dissolving then reappearing in frantic repetition. Lot looked back at a line of blackened, steaming vegetation, but no sign of the phantom remained. *Apart.*

If it had to be that way.

"Lot!" Urban skidded to a stop in the shallow wave wash. His shoulders heaved as he looked from Lot to Ord, now clinging contentedly at Lot's shoulder.

Lot knocked his hood back. "We have to get out of the Well," he said, as he gathered up his hair and tucked it neatly behind his neck.

"You're a little late, fury. David's coming down."

Lot's hands froze in the act of pulling up the hood. "He's got the tracks rebuilt?"

"He said so. They're organizing supplies at the top."

"When did you talk to him?"

"Maybe half an hour ago. He's got it bad, Lot. Worse than Alta."

Sure. Jupiter hadn't left his trace to interfere with the loyalties of the Silken ados. "We have to stop him."

"Yeah, fury? You know how?"

Lot hesitated, at a loss.

Urban said, "I told him what happened to Alta. He didn't care. He wouldn't let me talk to Kona, and Ord can't reach the old man. Sypaon can't either. If you don't control these crazies, Lot, we're all going to die."

Control them? How? He couldn't even control himself when he was around them. He looked to Sypaon, hoping for some bit of wisdom.

Her pointillistic expression was stern. He remembered her last night, collecting fragments of the communal fibers. "Sometimes we forget to ask who the Chenzeme were fighting," she said.

Lot took a step back, acutely conscious of the warden's capsule still in his hand. Had she guessed? "Jupiter said they fought themselves."

"Perhaps. Or perhaps it was something of their own creation?"

The cult virus. A gift from the void, a parasite that had lain in wait, patiently seeking a new host, since the Chenzeme vanished millions of years ago. Fear sweat jammed like wires through his pores. Sypaon had once declared herself at war.

She watched his growing panic, her mouths moving

in slow asynchrony—until abruptly, her expression gentled. "We should know these things, if we hope to understand them."

Lot felt as if he understood too much already. "I need to get off this world. It's the only way to stop it."

Urban touched his elbow. "Null Boundary's coming in."

Sooth. Lot lifted his chin, remembering his vision of the great ship sliding in through the veils of the nebula. Null Boundary had felt wrong, but maybe that only marked him as an enemy of the Communion. Scarred and ancient and older than the Hallowed Vasties . . . his crew mysteriously gone. Did he know of the cult? Had he survived it?

"Ord!" Lot snapped, suddenly desperate to make good his escape. "Tell David to bring a car down now. We need a way back to the city."

"There's no need for that," Sypaon said. "They're already here."

Sypaon seemed willing to do whatever she could to help them. She'd already assumed control of a second warden, walking it into the terminal building. Now it stood looking up at an elevator car stalled some eight hundred feet above the valley floor, where the tracks had been wrecked by deep scarring on the column. Back on the beach, she described the scene to Lot and Urban. "They have the doors open, though no one has descended yet. A device is being deployed. An aircraft. This first car carries almost three hundred individuals. You must stay away from them. They shed dangerous stimulants—"

"Message, Lot," Ord interrupted. "From David. Real time."

Lot nodded reluctantly. "Let's hear it."

"Lot!" David's voice danced with enthusiasm. "Lot, we're down! Almost down. There's more track damage than we anticipated, but that'll be fixed in a few minutes. Half the city's poised to come down behind us. Lot, we've won."

Lot drew in a shaky breath. Urban gave him a warning look. He nodded, closing his eyes. "It's up to us, David. Jupiter's gone."

"Into the Communion?"

Lot breathed slowly, deeply. He had to make it sound right . . . and nothing convinced like the truth. "No,

David. I've been under, and Jupiter's not there. He's dead. He failed. He let anger get him. There's no place for anger within the Communion."

Ecstatic death.

David didn't answer for a moment. Maybe it hadn't occurred to him yet that the Communion could be anything but automatic nirvana. When he did respond, doubt had crept into his voice. "But you can show us the path?"

"I need to be with you." The words came out in a rush.

"No—" Sypaon started to object. He raised a hand to hush her. He *did not* want to be with David, or with anybody else who was susceptible to the cult virus that he carried, manufactured nirvana, short-term plan . . . and that meant almost everybody except the few, dark souls like Urban.

But David misread his mood. "We want to come get you, Lot. We manufactured a plane from out of the archives."

"Good, David. Good. You've planned well. Send it down to us, then."

"Right, right. Uh, is Urban still with you?"

Lot tensed, wondering exactly what Urban had said to David earlier that morning. "We've had a rough time," Lot said.

David's voice was suddenly wary. "He's not one of us."

Lot met Urban's tense gaze. "You're wrong, David. Urban's fallout from the Hallowed Vasties, just like me." An unconvinced silence followed, and Lot knew he'd stumbled badly. So he fell back on arrogance. "Send the plane, David."

"Sure, Lot. Right away." But his voice was flat, a poor mask for his suspicions.

Lot jerked an angry hand across his throat, signaling Ord to cut the transmission. *"Shit."*

"That plane won't get here empty," Urban predicted.

Sypaon said, "They're launching it now. You must avoid direct contact with them."

"Can you communicate with the DI that's piloting it?" Lot asked her.

"No. It's not listed in the city registry."

"David'll have exclusive codes," Urban growled. "Anyway, it doesn't matter. So long as it gets us to the elevator column, we've got a chance."

"They won't let you on the plane."

"They'll do what you tell them."

Lot shook his head. "More than the cult virus has come down to me. I've been remembering things out of the Hallowed Vasties. David's right. You're not one of us. And when they feel that, you won't last."

Urban stomped off a few steps, muttering obscenities, more angry than scared. Lot followed after him. "It's not their fault," he said. "They can't help the way they feel. I've put that on them."

Urban turned around, his temper exploding. "So they can't help it? They'll kill me and sacrifice you and we just go along with it?"

Already, Lot thought he could hear the buzz of the plane's engines. "I think we can fool them for a while. We're the same size, aren't we? Almost the same build. Put your hood on, darken the lenses. Let them guess who's who."

Sypaon nodded in approval. "This could protect you for a necessary interval."

"You think they'll be that patient?"

"I won't leave them any choice," Lot said. "I'll just tell them the truth: that I'm on the edge." He couldn't see it now. He couldn't feel it. Still he knew the Communion was near, growing stronger and more coherent every time he entered it. Next time it might not let him go.

Great cult leader. He shook his head, knowing he was as vulnerable as any ado. He caught them with his charismata. They caught him with their silvery faith. It was a feedback reaction, notably devoid of choice. "If they don't want an early meltdown, they're going to have to put up with my eccentricities."

Urban frowned. His gaze cut away. "So then. Tell Ord to get clear, or it'll give you away."

The droning of the plane was suddenly loud. Lot reached for his hood. He pulled it up over his head and down across his face.

The suit spoke in a disapproving voice. "Without further supplies, the rebreather function has an estimated life of forty-two minutes."

Urban had fifty-three. "That doesn't leave us much time to convince them to let us on the cars," Lot said. He could see the glitter of the plane in the bright light of late morning.

"Verbal persuasion may not be adequate," Sypaon said.

Urban glared at the plane. "She's right. Give me your capsule."

Lot looked down at the little capsule he still clutched in his hand. Urban snatched it before he could think how to respond. "Hey! Wait a minute—"

But Urban ignored him. He fished the second capsule out of his own suit pocket.

"Urban, you can't—"

"This is about survival, Lot! For me, for Silk."

Sooth. "Then maybe you should just use that stuff against me. Get rid of the source of your problem."

"Placid Antigua already tried that. It didn't work, remember? You've got Chenzeme protection."

"Urban, you can't just kill them!"

"Why not? They want to die, don't they? Alta wanted to die. And she got her wish. You gave that to her, didn't you, fury?"

"Yeah." Lot sat down hard on the wet sand. "I did." First Captain Antigua, then Gent and now Alta. Jupiter Junior, for sure.

A shadow flitted across the beach. He looked up, to see the plane sweep out over the sand, then stall, to begin its vertical descent, the hum of its engines muted by his hood. "David could probably get treatment once I'm gone."

"We're not scrambled," Urban observed. "Your radio signal has gotten really weak, but it's not inaudible."

Lot felt a sudden flush in his cheeks. The plane was close enough that its communications system could be picking up their conversation. He plunged his fingers into the sand, trying to decide what to do. He could warn David. He had that option. But then Urban would be left exposed.

Sand billowed as the plane set down. Urban strode toward it and Lot rose to follow.

The door opened. David was first out. He skipped the descending step and jumped down to the beach, the tattoo on his arm squirming in the sunlight. Two more ados followed him. They both held bead rifles. Lot hurried forward. The plane didn't look big enough to hold any more occupants and still have room for passengers.

He saw Sypaon's warden-shadow slip under it. She melted up the stairs.

David looked from Urban to Lot with a quizzical expression. "You're suited? How come? Something wrong with the air down here?" His voice arrived muffled through the suit, barely audible past the grumbling of the waves.

Lot didn't bother to answer. Without a communications link, David couldn't hear him anyway. Maybe David realized that. He glanced uneasily toward the plane's open door, just as Sypaon reported in over the suit's comm link. "Nobody inside."

"Just these three, then," Urban said, breaking his silence now that he knew no one else was listening. He held his arms loosely at his sides; his fingers curled naturally over the capsules. "You ready, fury?"

Lot could see his left fist begin to close. "Don't do it." He touched Urban's arm—gently—not wanting to cause an accidental release. "It's not necessary."

But now David had seen the capsule in Urban's hand. His eyes got big. He backed off a few steps. His buddies with the bead rifles raised their weapons, settling their aim on Urban's chest. Lot stared at the tiny pore that tipped the nearest muzzle. It might take a bead several seconds to chew through Urban's suit, but once breached, the assault Makers in the bead would ensure he'd soon be dead.

"Lot," David warned, "you better tell me what's going on."

Maybe that would be best. "Hark," Lot said, alerting the suit. "Unseal."

"No!" Urban countered.

Too late. Lot's suit split on the seam. He reached up slowly and pulled the hood back. Like the rest of his body, his face was covered with sores. From the shocked expressions on the ados' faces, he knew he must be a ghastly sight. David's mouth opened, then closed, then opened again before he could get any words out: "*What happened to you?*"

Lot felt the brush of Communion like a soft, silver rain. Maybe the ados felt it too. The two holding the bead rifles shifted uneasily. Doubt flowed from them. Lot caught it, amplified it, mixed it with fear. *Jupiter Junior.* Grimly, he let himself slide into the role. Pointing at his wounded face, he announced: "The planetary wardens did this. They tried to kill me."

David frowned, perplexed. "But we couldn't locate any wardens here."

Lot blinked in surprise. His gaze cut briefly toward the plane's open door, where Sypaon had disappeared. But of course they wouldn't know about her. His mouth felt dry as he turned back to David. Still, he knew what to do. He knew what Jupiter would have done. "Liar. *You* sent the wardens after me."

David's eyes widened in shock. "No!"

Lot gestured at the rifles. "You came here to kill me."

"No. We only wanted to protect you—"

"You wanted to steal the loyalties of my people! Set yourself in my place."

"*It isn't true,*" David panted. "Lot, I only—"

"I'll find out what's true!" he barked, startling himself: it might have been Jupiter speaking through his mouth. He caught his breath. He could feel David's dread, as if it were his own. His hand trembled as he signaled to the two with the bead rifles. "Watch him closely. You'll be safe here, until I can send the plane back."

He looked at Urban. But he could see him only as a lightless rent in a world that he suddenly realized had gone all silver. "*Get on the plane.*" He had to force the words out. He wasn't even sure if he'd said them aloud. He wasn't made for this. Jupiter had never shown him how to successfully betray his own being. The beach and the air around him swirled in silver. He could make out vague shapes in the matrix, Alta and Gent and a hundred others, waiting for him.

Slowly, he turned back to David. He didn't *need* to cut David off. He could draw him in, make him part of a greater whole, they could all be as one—

Urban yanked his arm hard. "Get on the plane, fury." He half-pushed him, half-carried him up the stairs, then shoved him stumbling through the door. Lot went down on his knees in the tiny aisle, suddenly nauseated, his pulse pounding in his skull. Ord slipped past him. "*Believe in him!*" Urban shouted at the astonished trio on the beach. Then the door closed. Sypaon must have convinced the plane's DI to cooperate, because the engines started with a roar. Urban stomped past him, dropping into the forward seat. "Slick performance," he growled. "Now, why didn't I think of that?"

Chapter
33

Sypaon got them aboard the elevator car. The warden at the terminal building was still armed, and she used it to burn a perimeter around the loading bay. The plane set down on the charred ground between the wings of the building. A crowd of ados had fled to the road beyond. There were maybe six hundred altogether.

Lot watched them through the plane's window, picking out faces, setting names to them. They were angry. He could see it in their posture and in the way some of the ado boys paced the edge of the burned zone, back and forth, in ancient threat. The warden figure stood in the savaged ground, affecting a charred color and nearly invisible, though obviously the ados saw it, because it drew dark looks from knotted groups of them. They surged forward when the plane landed.

The warden reacted calmly, flitting toward the ados almost faster than the eye could follow, laying down a precise line of spray that caused the ground to bubble and steam. The surging ados fell back.

"That's dangerous," Urban said. "It could set off a defensive reaction in the governors."

"Unlikely," Sypaon responded. "The warden defensive mechanism is strictly limited by time and initial substrate.

Specific damage in the Well is necessary and must be allowed."

Lot pulled on his hood before the door opened. He had to do it manually, because the suit refused to do it for him. Energy reserves absolutely did not support the action. To his concern, the hood felt thin and insubstantial. He pressed the seam shut, hoping it would seal. Then he descended the stairs. The plane lay between him and the ado crowds. He kept his back to it, and did not look around.

Two elevator cars rested on the pad. Lot walked toward the nearest, concentrating on each step like a drunk pretending he was not.

He could hear a staccato noise behind him: sharp, commanding sounds muffled only a little by the decrepit hood. He hummed loudly so he would not have to hear much of it and ask himself if it was only creaking tree branches or his name barked out over and over again.

The elevator doors stood open. He walked past them. A warden slipped in beside him.

On the wall he recognized the graffiti he had seen once before: *On this day we have entered a higher existence.*

But they had not survived that long.

Regret rolled over him as he considered again the glory of the Communion. There had been beauty there, and a vast reach that already he could only dimly recall.

"Shut the doors," Urban said. "Let's get the hell out of here."

"They will wait for us in the city," Sypaon pointed out.

Lot felt the floor lurch. He staggered, lost his balance, and went down on his ass. He decided to stay there for a while. Exhaustion had made the blank white wall below the graffiti an interesting focus of observation. With some prompting from Urban, he remembered to unseal his hood.

He blinked. Urban had shoved something into his hands. "Eat fast, fury. We make the city in a few minutes."

Lot looked down, to see a rolled crepe filled with mint green cream, just like the ones Urban had served him that day. He chuckled softly.

Urban gave him an odd look. He had more of the

crepes piled on a plate. "Hey," he said with a shrug. "At least they stocked the kitchens."

"How are we going to get past them?"

"Ord got through to Clementine. She's coming for us."

"She still has a hand in it?"

"Says so."

The change of velocity was only half-sensed. Lot wasn't sure the elevator had come to a stop until the doors whisked open. He scooped the last crepe from the plate, then stood, gazing warily out into a cramped darkness.

The floor of the elevator had not aligned with the floor of this receiving chamber. A three-foot difference remained, with the elevator on the low side. An apron of light spilling outward from the open door showed a rough, unfinished gray floor—and only four feet higher, a ceiling of the same material. Lot could hear a ringing, pounding, erratic vibration, though he couldn't guess its source. The chamber beyond looked empty, though it was not.

The food had brought back some measure of alertness. Lot moved his head slowly back and forth, sampling the cold, thin air to confirm the trace. "Security's outside the door. They're hunting us."

"Clementine!" Urban shouted into the silence. "We want to help. We don't want to fight."

His announcement received an immediate response. Armored security personnel clutching bead rifles scuttled around both edges of the door. Ducking their heads, they dropped into the elevator car then drove forward into Lot, slamming him against the wall. The muzzles of two bead rifles thrust into his throat, aimed upward, at his brain.

From somewhere to his right Clementine whispered, "I told you I wanted *silence*."

Lot turned his head a quarter inch. They had Urban against the wall too. Clementine held a rifle at his chin. "We've got almost a thousand crazies on the floor directly overhead. They don't know we're here. We'd like to keep it that way."

The low *whump*! of a small explosion resounded on one of the car's upper stories. Clementine glanced up, her face flushed with anger. "Sounds like some children are coming to visit. But you two boys have been naughty. I'm afraid you can't play. So *let's go*."

The bead rifles pulled back. Lot could hear footsteps on the floor overhead. He scrambled for the door, using one hand to boost himself up to the chamber floor. Then he ran hunched, following Clemantine's security detail. He thought he saw Sypaon flit past before the elevator doors closed behind him, cutting off the light. He blinked down to IR. The sharp nudge of a rifle urged him toward an opening on the right. They were hardly through when the door slammed shut behind them. "Vent the chamber," Clemantine said. Beyond the thick, insulated walls came the scream of escaping air.

Lot still held the last crepe. He took a bite. Clemantine noticed. Cool amusement crackled in her eyes. She edged up close to him and laid a controlling arm across his shoulders. "How ya doing, Lot?"

He kenned her mood: raw contempt, edging onto hatred. He didn't want any part of it, so he breathed slowly, softly, seeking the cold, machinelike state that would let him pass through the minutes untouched.

Perhaps she saw this nonreaction as a challenge, for she leaned a little harder. "You know Lot, you really stink. Did your skin suit die?"

The idea startled him. Clemantine laughed in satisfaction at his obvious disconcertion. Then she slapped him on the shoulder—"Don't worry about it!"—and turned to the security detail. "Let's go," she barked, starting them all trotting up the narrow passage.

"No," Kona said, when Urban made their plea for sanctuary aboard the approaching Null Boundary. "The situation's changed. The crisis is past. The ados have been running on little more than a riot mentality, and without Lot, that'll quickly wind down. They still control the elevators and the main tunnels. But it'll take days to move even half of them to the planet surface. In the meantime, we have a lock on organic resources. When they get hungry they'll start to think—and after that it won't take long for most of them to go crawling back to Mommy and Daddy." He said this with confidence, though behind his words Lot sensed a disingenuous strain.

Such subtleties were beyond Urban. His anger flared across the narrow, echoing chamber to which Clemantine had brought them: a command center that had been set up somewhere in the vast, uninhabited city core. Tactical holos lined one long wall. Along the other a window looked into a factory room, where great stirring blades turned slowly in glassine vats. They'd passed sixteen pressure doors to get here. Clemantine had vented each corridor behind them.

"Don't you understand what I'm telling you, Daddy? Lot's a catalyst. The Communion will happen if we don't get him away."

Lot huddled cross-legged on the floor. The air was fiercely cold, and his suit wasn't keeping him warm at all. A foul odor rose from it, wreathing him in decay. Clemantine had ordered him to sit down and shut up. One of her assistants still held a bead rifle against his throat with a pressure that could not be described as friendly, so for the most part he'd obeyed, leaving Urban to argue his fate.

Now he felt Kona's gaze, framed on a ribbon of subterfuge. "Urban, we understand your concerns. Believe me, we share them. But it's important that we keep Lot here."

"You only say that because he's infected you too!"

"Don't you think I know that?" Kona's anger was a hot spike. But after a moment, he seemed to recover his composure. "This is Sypaon's wish. She wants him kept safe—and close."

Sypaon? Lot jerked in surprise. But the rifle's muzzle bit deeper into his neck, squeezing off his questions.

Kona turned again to Urban, his calm voice at odds with a tension he could not contain. "She feels sure that if she can compare the two Chenzeme dialects, she can learn enough details of the language to truly control the swan burster, and that would be a priceless breakthrough." He raised a hand to quiet Urban's protest. "She would not use it against the Well. But she could protect us in the void . . . if we cut the elevator. We could reshape the column into a great ship, Urban. We'd have to retreat to cold storage, but Sypaon would keep us safe."

Despite the threat of the rifle, Lot could not keep still for this. "She's lying to you!" he croaked. The rifle's muzzle suddenly withdrew, whirling away in his sight while the butt swung round—

He threw himself back as it whistled past his cheek.

"Stop it!" Kona barked. "Let him talk." Anxiety hung around Kona like a dark fog. He didn't trust Sypaon. Lot felt sure of it.

"It's not a language barrier that stops her," Lot said.

"It's the Well. It doesn't matter what language she uses to persuade the ring cells. The Well has arranged every decision to end in an inactive state."

"That can be changed," Sypaon said.

Urban hissed. Lot jumped at the sound of her voice. For the first time, he noticed her warden shape, darkened with shadows, pressed against the wall. The lines of her tiny eyes slid and folded, creating warped expressions as she groped for the proper words. "The Well sees me as the enemy. But it has not recognized you, child, though you carry the Chenzeme virus."

So. He'd wondered why Sypaon had chosen to protect him in the Well. Now he knew. She saw him as a key that might unlock her obsession with the ring. But she was mistaken. "It won't work," he said softly, aiming his words at Kona, not at the warden-fragment of Sypaon. "The Well made its defense against the virus millions of years ago. I can skim its surface, maybe delve a little into its depths, but that's all. The Well will never be dominated by conscious processes—" . . . *any more than we are.*

He broke off, startled by this unexpected analogy. But wasn't it so? So much of human thought was shaped by the unfathomable currents that ran in the dark mental oceans beneath the conscious mind. The intellectual processes that could be perceived were only a small part of a greater mechanism. . . .

Except, perhaps, in the Hallowed Vasties. Within the cradle of the Communion it might be that too much was perceived at once. Against that, the Well offered no shelter at all.

So Jupiter had been wrong. He looked at Kona, feeling stunned by this heretical certainty, rising whole like some mythical beast from the dark well of his own mind, sweeping into view like a Chenzeme weapon set to destabilize all that he thought he knew. Was it true? He whispered it aloud, to see how it felt: *"Jupiter was wrong."* Then again, in a stronger voice: "Jupiter was wrong."

Kona appeared unimpressed, but in his aura Lot caught a sense of wry amusement, marbling low-key pride. He grunted in an offhand way. "Huh. Maybe you're not hardwired after all."

But Sypaon objected. Her warden shape sparkled like

the tactical holos as she slipped away from the wall. "He's afraid," she accused. "He would say anything."

Kona shrugged artfully. "Maybe. We've time to give it some thought." His words were laced with clouds of subterfuge, but in her warden-fragment, Sypaon couldn't recognize it.

Neither could Urban. His temper exploded again. "There *is* no time, Daddy! We have to get Lot out now, or the Communion will happen. This is about obsession. That's what the neural parasite is for."

Scowling, Kona beckoned to two security officers. "Get him out of here."

They moved toward Urban. Lot closed his eyes, determined to keep his suspicions firmly locked inside him.

"Don't give up, fury!" Urban shouted. "There's no other way for us."

Sooth. But Kona already knew that.

They kept him sitting on the floor for nearly three hours. In the prolonged cold an implanted survival routine kicked in, causing his metabolism to slow and his body temperature to drop. His mind drifted on languid waves. The face of his guard changed, then changed again. This concerned him, until finally he observed the substitution of personnel and understood that they were minimizing individual exposure to the hazard of his presence. Sypaon's warden-fragment had been sent out into the tunnels on some errand.

An eerie silence dominated the command chamber. Despite the shifting complement of security personnel and council members, not one word was uttered aloud. Communication had been relegated to atrial links, and Lot could only guess at what was going on in the city by reading the tides of anxiety that puffed around him. As time passed, the density of concern mounted. He guessed the ados knew his situation and were protesting it. Once, Kona looked up from his deliberations to meet Lot's gaze. Regret plied his aura. Lot stiffened, suddenly sure Kona would buy peace by turning him over to the ado mobs.

No.

He set the thought adrift on the air like dust, charismata of negative intent. Kona's gaze faltered. He shook his head, as if dizzy, or perplexed. Then he left the room for a while, and when he came back, Clemantine was with him. "Take him to the shuttle," Kona said, nodding at Lot. The sound of his voice was startling after the long period of silence. "Make ready to leave before Sypaon is aware of you. This is not something we can learn to live with."

It took Lot long seconds to reawaken his muscles, a delay that drew angry accusations from Clemantine. But gradually a numb warmth flushed through him as his body woke. He stood on stiff limbs. Ord shifted under his hair. Silently, Lot willed the little robot to be still. So far, city authority had overlooked its presence, or perhaps hadn't attached any importance to it. Lot wanted to keep it that way. Clemantine frowned at him with a hint of suspicion. Then she nodded toward the door. "Out."

His suit had really begun to reek. As he passed Clemantine, she rolled her eyes at the stench. "That thing is definitely dead."

In the narrow passage outside she told him to strip it off; she wasn't going to spend three days in a closed ship with him smelling like that. She gave him some clothes and he changed. By the time he was done, her mood had lost some of its edge. "You're being awfully quiet," she observed.

He blinked, thinking the ceiling lights must have shifted color somehow. Her skin seemed highlighted in tiny points of silver.

"You were always a quiet child. You might have turned out okay if Urban had just left you alone."

Not likely.

She put her arm around his shoulders again. It seemed she liked to touch him. "You're a nice boy, Lot. I want you to know that no one here has anything personal against you. It's what you are that makes you dangerous. It's that we have to deal with."

The air shimmered silver. He felt the tug of it and the warning tap of Ord's soft tentacle against his throat. He closed his fist. *Clemantine.* She was as old and as tough as Kona. Her vulnerability now felt like a betrayal. Deliberately, he sought the vindictive state he'd used on David. One quick lesson would keep them both safe. . . .

The charismata of his anger flushed across the space between them. She breathed in the artificial construction—

and recoiled. He felt the sharp spike of her fear. But it fell back, giving way immediately to the fury he knew must come. Her face twisted. Then to his surprise her fist darted out, catching him hard in the throat. He choked and went down on his knees while she swore at him, "You dirty little son of a bitch! I don't know why Kona's giving you even this chance."

He coughed on the floor, struggling not to puke, chastising himself for not having the foresight to stand farther away. She jammed the muzzle of her rifle up against his head. "Thank you," she told him, in a soft voice that slid through the air like a razor. "Thank you for the warning. Really, you have my deep appreciation. And if it ever needs to be repeated, I'll kill you. Understand?"

He nodded against the pressure of the rifle, seeing specks of silver on her still. He could take her. He was pretty sure of it and the knowledge left him shaking. It was all he could do to stand, to walk docilely on, to pretend he did not want this at all.

They were far closer to the city wall than Lot would have guessed. Only three pressure doors separated them from a narrow receiving bay. Past glass windows he could see the shuttle craft Captain Aceret had flown into the city fully ten years ago: one of Nesseleth's shuttles. Silk had no other transport.

A cadre of security officers eyed him warily as he entered just ahead of Clemantine. To his surprise, Yulyssa was with them. She approached him tentatively, caution laid out cool around her. "I came to say goodbye."

He nodded shortly, not trusting himself with anything more.

She walked in parallel with him, her aura steeped in a welling sense of loss. Lot knew its cause, and that—as Clemantine had said—it was nothing personal. He tried to comfort her with that: "The parasite's been identified. It can be gotten rid of."

She shook her head, sending flecks of sharper emotions impacting against him. "The Old Silkens tried that."

"They tried to eliminate it from the Well. You can be more selective."

"And even if we succeed, you'll be gone."

He shrugged. "It won't matter then."

Her desire lapped at him. "It'll matter to me."

"That's just the charismata."

"It's more, Lot. I know it."

"That'll change."

They'd come to the ribbed tubeway that led to the shuttle's door. Now she hung back. Dark emotions seeped from her: regret and pain and purpose and other things he could not readily identify. "You're very young, or you would know this," she said, her voice hoarse and whispery. "But there is no end *unless we choose it*."

Her desire sparkled in the air, and suddenly it seemed absurd, unfair, disrespectful of the proud and independent being she'd been . . . and he had done it. The realization left him feeling as foul as the pockets of a gutter doggie.

Clemantine nudged him in the shoulder. He felt her impatience with a sense of relief. With a last glance at Yulyssa, he walked down the tubeway and boarded the little ship.

Chapter
34

The stations of his life seemed open for review. Over the previous days he'd stumbled in a chaotic procession from one monument of his past to another: the tunnels, the loading bay, the gathered dead in the elevator car, and Nesseleth herself. Now—as he stepped aboard the shuttle craft that had brought him into this city—he felt a circle of ten years begin to close. He'd reached the final station of his pilgrimage, though he did not know yet if a new cycle would open.

The interior of the shuttle didn't fit his memories. The partitioned cockpit with its complex control boards was gone. Instead, the forward cabin had been pushed all the way into the bow. Four acceleration couches sprouted from the deck, their long seats folded upward in graceful Us like unopened flowers. "Sit down," Clemantine said. "It doesn't matter where."

She was probably right.

He chose a rear seat, by the closed cargo doors. Touching a likely-looking green pad, he got the chair to open for him. Ord slid off his shoulder, disappearing under the seat.

Kona came in a few minutes later. He wore beige armor, just like Clemantine, though he looked so natural in plated skin that Lot felt shaken by a resonant sense, as if he'd glimpsed Kona's past and seen only a landscape of scars. Who had he been, the day the swan burster took Heyertori?

Kona conversed with Clemantine a moment; then he took a seat beside Lot. "My better sense tells me we should simply destroy you, by the quickest, most thorough method, and let the political repercussions fall as they will." His hand closed over the armrest of the chair. "Maybe it's the influence of the parasite, but I can't do it."

"Sypaon will be angry."

"Sypaon can be soothed." Then, after a minute: "You know Null Boundary has no crew. You'll be alone."

"That's the point, isn't it?"

Kona studied him closely, while moving his head slowly back and forth, as if he could sift the dust of moods from the cabin air and read in them Lot's intentions. "Null Boundary's a strange ship. The entity inhabiting it is not the ship's original persona. I'm not sure he even came to the position voluntarily. He's very old. Yet he has never fully integrated with the body of the ship. He sustains a separate identity. Indeed, he prefers it. Null Boundary is his metal jacket. Inside, he's still the man he used to be." Kona frowned and shook his head. "I wish I could tell you more about him, but we despised him in those years we were aboard. We blamed him for Heyertori . . . and still I don't know if he was part of it or not."

Lot shivered as he remembered the sense of wrongness he'd experienced. No one knew where Null Boundary had been in the millennia since his manufacture. No one knew what he had done.

"Strap in," Kona advised him. "We'll be leaving soon."

Kona moved to a forward seat beside Clemantine, but the door didn't close. Lot realized they were waiting for someone. A minute later, Urban hurried in.

Lot stared at him, astounded. Joy kicked through his system—but only briefly. Urban had discarded his skin suit for a security officer's plated armor. He had a bead rifle in his hands and a peculiar look on his face.

Stiffly, he took the empty seat beside Lot. At a reminder from Kona, he strapped himself in. The lock sealed. The forward screens winked on. Lot could feel the vibration of the engines as some silent command urged them to life.

Urban felt armored in aloofness. "Did they draft you?" Lot asked him.

"I volunteered."

"For . . . ?"

Abashment broke through his brittle shell.

"Say it," Clemantine urged. But Urban would not, so she explained it herself. "Urban has volunteered to be our Executioner."

Urban's aura hardened, as if Lot had physically assaulted him. "It's gotten too easy for you, fury. When you played that game with Clemantine—"

"I was warning her off!"

"And next time?"

"I don't want it."

"It's not always a rational choice," Kona said. "If things get out of control, we're vulnerable. Urban's not."

Lot looked away, feeling the severance of time flowing between them like an ever-widening river. He told himself they were not at cross-purposes. Not yet.

The shuttle edged out of the city on rollers, then plunged in a heart-stopping maneuver, before the engines finally fired. Thought seemed a luxury in the fierce acceleration.

"Message, Lot."

They'd been aboard less than an hour when Ord slid up onto the armrest. The hard acceleration had crushed it to little more than a gelatinous blob, though it could still form words.

"From who?" Lot asked.

"The sculpted entity Sypaon."

His heart seemed to swell in his chest. "Cut the connection."

"No," Kona said quickly. "Let her speak. Lot, I promise you, we won't turn back."

Urban's knuckles paled as he gripped the bead rifle.

"Okay," Lot said grudgingly. "Let her speak."

Ord's voice changed. "Child, you must reconsider." It was the voice Sypaon had used with her warden-fragment. The change struck Lot as mere ornamentation, for Sypaon had no real voice of her own. "Null Boundary is a corrupted entity. You know this, child. You've felt it yourself. He is older than the Hallowed Vasties, and quite insane. You risk your life with him. Return to Silk. Nothing will be done that you do not approve of."

"Shut it off," Lot pleaded, feeling the fragility of his position. Just a little more pressure, and Kona might change his mind.

But again, Kona countered his command. This time he spoke to her directly. "Sypaon, what do you really know of Null Boundary? You have not communicated with him."

"He will not answer my queries. But we all know he is the ship that betrayed Heyertori. He will betray you too."

Lot felt his position crumble. "Shut it off!" he shouted, knowing it was too late.

This time, Ord obeyed. But to Lot's surprise, the shuttle continued on its planned course to rendezvous.

They'd been aboard six hours, long enough for Lot to figure out it was Clemantine commanding the navigation DI through her atrial link. They were still pulling over two gees, so moving around was no pleasure. He remained in his chair, watching the image on the screen through half-closed eyes. There was little else to do.

The nebula hazed the darkness with a milky luminescence that suppressed all but the brightest stars. It appeared to be a stationary cloud, shot through with denser whorls and lanes of dust, ever-poised at an unchanging distance in front of them. Yet it rattled them, hurling bits of dust-shrouded stony matter against the hull.

Dust. It clung to the nebula's pebbles through static attraction, forming clumps that were too large to be carried off by Kheth's mild stellar wind. At relativistic speeds, every pebble was a potential bomb. Yet no clump could accrete to more than a few ounces in size, before attracting the attention of the butterfly gnomes that lived within the cloud. They would descend upon the aggregate, lashing it apart with an electric charge.

Dust clung to hulls too, and to the hides of any object that ventured within the system.

It seemed likely the nebula was an artificial construction. Yet Sypaon had overlooked it. She'd come here only for the swan burster, its weaponry and its promised secrets dazzling her into a debilitating tunnel vision. There was so much more here than Chenzeme fossils. Information streamed in slow chemical currents through the dust, flashing occasionally into the electromagnetic spectrum astride erratic signals barely distinguishable from the static. Halfway down the sheltered Well, human lives burned in the warm infrared, oblivious of the whispered exchange. Dust sifted past them, falling through the atmosphere, into oceans, taken into the colloidal flow, perhaps rising again with storms, escaping the atmosphere aboard some unknown ferry. Information was traded and adjustments were made in feedback reactions working on alien protocols encoded in the dust, long ago, while the Communion waited: alert, patient. . . .

The dust was alive. Lot wondered why he hadn't understood that before.

Halfway through the second day, Clemantine announced: "That bitch Sypaon may have been right." Fear popped in sensual bursts around the dead calm tone of her voice. "Null Boundary has begun to accelerate."

"Within the nebula?" Urban asked. "It'll tear itself apart."

"Not this far in," Clemantine said. "Inside the Well's orbit the nebula is thin."

Kona had his eyes closed, an intense expression on his face. "Modify our course to match—"

"That would be suicide. We're operating on no fuel margin."

Kona radioed the great ship and received reassurances that seemed nonsensical, given the circumstances. He contacted Silk, and was informed that Null Boundary's new course would bring it deep within the orbit of the elevator column.

At that point, Null Boundary ceased to respond.

Clemantine cut the engines to conserve fuel. Their rendezvous was blown and it was a fair question now if they'd have enough reserves to carry them back to Silk. A sheen of sweat began to accumulate on her face, as—with eyes closed—she frantically ran calculations, seeking a workable course.

Kona threw off his straps and turned to Lot. "You warned us about this ship before. What do you know of it?"

Lot shook his head helplessly. "Not much. It seemed

wrong. Different. Not like the city. Or even the ring. I thought . . . maybe it was an enemy of the cult."

"And now?"

He shrugged. "It still could be. I don't know."

Urban had been uncharacteristically silent for most of the trip, but he stirred now. "It's hard to tell sometimes what things really are on the inside. When you want to hide, you try to look like your enemy. Sypaon lives inside the burster. The cult virus lives inside Lot." He stared at the seat back in front of him. "It's easy to get close to your enemies if you look and feel and smell exactly like them."

Kona's teeth clicked together. "Damn the Chenzeme! Damn even their memories—"

"Then you think the ship's been infested?" Clementine demanded.

Kona glared at Lot. "It fits, doesn't it? A Chenzeme neural system inside it, *mimicking* something human."

"Then the Well will neutralize it," Clementine declared with rather artificial optimism. "It neutralized the swan burster."

They both looked at Lot, as if he had some magic atrial access to that era of prehistory and could confirm her speculations.

He shook his head. All he had was doubt. "It's different from the ring."

"You don't think the Well will interfere with it?" Kona asked.

He rubbed absently at his sensory tears. "It hasn't interfered with human ships before." Sypaon, Null Boundary, Nesseleth: all had glided unhindered through the guarded nebula. "I think the Well only attacks if it's been attacked."

"But if it *is* infested with Chenzeme protocols, it's not human."

Lot shrugged. "Maybe the Well doesn't know that yet." Foresight and deductive talents were facets of consciousness and didn't exist in the Well. The Well learned only by the harsh, irrefutable pain of experience.

"It'll hit the city first," Clementine predicted. "Even without weapons, it has enough momentum to shear the elevator column. The Well might pith it then, but for us it'll be too late."

*   *   *

Null Boundary continued to accelerate. Its changing course promised to bring it deeper into the Well, in a path that would burn through the sparse wisps of the upper atmosphere. Clemantine muttered and cursed over the poor course options available to them. At best, they could get back to Silk in some twelve days . . . not that they were supplied for it.

Lot decided to offer a suggestion. Swallowing his misgivings, he spoke in what he hoped was a reasonable voice. "If Null Boundary's infested, it won't do us any good to return to the city. He'll get there before us, and there won't be a city left."

"It's not *your* home!" Urban exploded.

"Sooth." Lot leaned back, watching the great ship's brooding image slowly grow on the screen. "But if we burn all our fuel to match course with the great ship, we might still be able to get inside—"

"Save your own skin?"

"Yeah. Even if Null Boundary's been made into a Chenzeme weapon, it's still got the structure of a human ship. And that means it's hollow. Made for us. Not like the ring. There's no place there to even *be*, unless you rewrite yourself into an alien mind. Null Boundary has an inside. We might be able to approach its neural centers; maybe even . . . communicate with it."

Kona had twisted around in his seat. "Could you do that?"

"I don't know. Sypaon—"

He turned to Clemantine. "Could we get a download of Sypaon?"

Her chin snapped back and she let out a sharp, popping breath as she broke her atrial links. "A download into what? Besides, if Null Boundary really is a Chenzeme weapon, then it's a plague ship. We'd die within minutes of boarding."

Kona watched her closely. "Minutes might be enough."

"It took Sypaon four centuries to understand the swan burster."

"She had to learn the system. Lot inherited it."

"I don't think the interior will be defended," Lot said. "No one's ever boarded a Chenzeme device before. How could they, when there's never been an inside? If these weapons are unconscious systems, that—like the Well—learn only through experience, then we might be able to take advantage of a naive interlude. . . ."

"And do what?"

"What the Well does: restructure its protocols."

There had been dust in the air ducts. Statically attracted wads of molecular machines, forever trading information. He remembered choking on them until his lungs bled.

Dreaming dust. A system replete with information, but operating without foresight, without consciousness. Selective processes rewarding survival.

The key to neutralizing Chenzeme weaponry was written in the dust. If Lot could only read it, he might activate it himself. Frustration surged through him. All the information in the world might be contained on the shelves of a library, but if one isn't able to read, the information may as well crumble to dust. . . .

Lot could read the dust . . . but only when he was spread thin, his vision linked to the communal web. He could write with dust too, through the linkage of his sensory tears.

Alta's face loomed blue and eerie in his memory, its tenuous membrane on the verge of an explosion of toxic fog. The phantom could carry him under. "Ord?" he asked softly.

The DI slid out from under his chair, gliding up its tentacles and onto the armrest. "Yes Lot?"

He glanced anxiously around the cabin. Clementine and Kona were glassy-eyed, involved in some internal debate. Urban's chin was drooping against his chest while the insane aura of dreams drifted from him.

Lot swallowed his misgivings, telling himself it would be all right, the Communion couldn't reach this far. Softly: "Did you get a record of the phantom's physical structure?"

"The record was forwarded to city library."

"Can you access it?"

"Yes, Lot."

The Communion can't reach this far. "Can you synthesize it?"

"Yes, Lot."

"Do it for me, Ord."

Its face twisted up in an expression of pained confusion. "Bad job, Lot. No good."

"I know it. But I need to."

"Not safe."

"I'll take the chance," he whispered fiercely. He hated being put in the position of arguing for something he didn't really want to do. Couldn't somebody just stand behind him for a change? But Ord wasn't really somebody. "You want to keep me safe. Well, we're all going to die if you don't help me. Now, Ord."

It seemed to struggle with the decision. He thought he caught a glint of silver in it. His eyes widened. Did the robot have a flicker of consciousness too? The cult virus was an opportunist, feeding even in the spare nooks and crannies of an aging dull intelligence.

Apparently, Ord reached a decision. "Good Lot. Smart Lot. Now?"

Fear burst through Lot in a sordid flush. Then it was away, leaving cold sweat as a tidal mark. "Yes Ord. Now."

He closed his eyes and leaned back, so he did not see the rain though he felt its misty touch against his sensory tears, anxiety tripping through brief moments. Then those perceptions vanished. He sank into a sea of dust. He almost choked, feeling blind and crippled. The liquid flow of data he'd experienced in the Well was nonexistent here in the dry nebular roof. Insight flashed across his awareness in spurts. Dust bearing history. History borne on dust. Slowly, he lowered himself to the pace. Different modes for different environments, all interconnected, shaking hands one to one to one, only rarely winking in lightspeed data transmissions throw and catch, dreaming dust circling Kheth, selective processes defending a system where the destabilizing influence of consciousness need not exist. In the tumultuous, evolutionary exchange of data within the living microbial dust, myriad ways had been found to strip the instinct from a Chenzeme machine, to feed new protocols to the alien cells, to corrupt their purpose. Lot felt his arteries running tens of thousands of miles long. Clever structures flowed through them, spilling into his fixed memory . . . while on the periphery of his awareness he felt the winking presence of the human ghosts as they railed in their unmet need. It was an old message, hours, perhaps even weeks in transit. He would be long gone before they could react, a minor god winking briefly into existence, determined to remain forever unmoved by supplications that would destroy him.

* * *

Lot roused slowly, forced back into the world by the pressure of hard acceleration. Urban was looking at him, his face drawn, the muscles in his neck standing out like cords. "You were dreaming again."

Lot grunted, still absorbed in the graceful geography of the charismata that sculpted Chenzeme moods. "Where are we going?"

"To catch Null Boundary."

And no going back. They could get aboard the ship, but even if they lived, the shuttle would have no fuel reserves to bring them home.

It's not your home.

The pursuit burned up another day. Time enough for a thin layer of dust to collect on the seat backs after seeping through the shuttle's supposedly impermeable walls. Lot brushed at the stuff and breathed it in. Breathed it out again, setting the glinting specks swirling in the air, tiny judges, forever untouched by mercy or forgiveness.

Chapter
35

Boarding Null Boundary was not a challenge. It had ceased to accelerate, and its hull was stationary. At the bottom of a deep pore penetrating the ship's insulation, a set of bay doors stood open. Clemantine edged the shuttle through the tunnel, then settled it against the mechanical locks. The ring of metal on metal resounded through the cabin.

As soon as the decision had been made to pursue the ship, Kona had set the shuttle's small factory to making skin suits for all of them. The design he ordered was thicker and heavier than the version Gent had used. Lot slipped it on, clothing himself in an intelligent skin. The sculpted entity occupying Null Boundary had clothed himself in the hull of the ship. But he had not become the ship. Instead, he'd stubbornly maintained his own identity. In the face of the Chenzeme threat, stubbornness had become an essential survival trait.

Lot pulled up his hood and sealed it. No one could predict what traits would be essential the next day, the next year, the next millennium. The future remained opaque at all wavelengths; chance and selection still ruled. Whether he chose to deny that fact or face it, its essential nature could never change.

*   *   *

Clemantine went first. She strung a line from the shuttle to a wide cargo lock, whose outer door stood open in apparent invitation. Lot hooked a short tether to the line, then glided across, carrying Ord's quiescent form on his shoulders. Kona and Urban followed. The lock was bigger than Lot's breather. When they were all inside, Clemantine closed the outer doors. Air flooded the chamber. The skin suits sniffed at it, chattered between themselves for several seconds in rapid machine twitters, then announced that the air was breathable. In fact, the ship's atmosphere registered quite high on the quality scale, receiving demerits only in the very low percentage of water vapor and in the ambient temperature, which hovered near freezing. Ord woke, though it seemed uncomfortable in the absence of gravity, and it continued to cling to Lot.

The inner door of the lock opened. In free fall there could be no true up or down. Yet Lot's first impression of the corridor that greeted them was that it was a shaft, plunging directly to the heart of the ship. Close by, the walls glowed soft white, but the illumination faded with distance.

"Awfully convenient," Clemantine said, her voice buzzing over the comm system in Lot's suit. "Do you get the impression we're expected?"

Kona edged into the shaft. "Maybe the bastard is prepared to talk. Come on. There's not much time."

"Wait," Lot said. He ordered his hood to open. Kona protested, but Lot cracked the seam anyway. Cold air stung his cheeks. His breath steamed. He moved his head slowly back and forth, then frowned in confusion. "Nothing."

Kona hesitated a moment longer, then opened his own hood. "You'd be able to scent a Chenzeme presence?"

"Maybe."

"Damn, but we could be wrong about everything."

They traversed the shaft rapidly, moving ever inward toward the ship's core. The walls lit up ahead of them, darkened behind. Lot felt his cheeks begin to chap in the cold. He'd just pushed off from a recessed handhold when he realized the shaft had come to an end. He tried to stop his flight, but his glide path had taken him temporarily out of reach of any grips. He shot past Clemantine, out the end of the tunnel and into the core chamber beyond, where he hit the far wall with a gentle thud. When he bounced back Clementine caught his hand, arresting his momentum.

He looked around cautiously. This chamber was much larger than the one aboard Nesseleth. Its walls were clean, opaque crystal surfaces, glowing softly like the tunnel walls, though the air here was warmer and more moist. For the first time, Lot caught a faint trace of foreign presence.

Kona edged past his shoulder, dropping in a slow whirl through the chamber's center. He looked around, his arms akimbo while his braids danced medusa-like around his head. "Still skulking, eh Nikko?" he said into the silence.

As if summoned by this taunt, a swarm of pixels suddenly appeared: thousands of tiny points of light that shifted and fluttered in a slow, dramatic assembly until finally a figure coalesced from the cloud.

Lot looked it over in close detail. It was huge, brooding, and not quite human. Where a man would have skin, this being was covered with minute blue scales. His long, long, fingers and toes twitched like a restless spider's legs. His head was smooth and hairless, the eyes obscured behind overlying crystal lenses, the nose quite small. His mouth was set in a hard, unforgiving line, while around his shoulders a small blue membranous cloak shivered and flexed.

"Cheap drama for the primitives," Kona said. "Nikko, you haven't changed."

"I have." Nikko's voice was deep, stern.

Lot started in surprise as he realized this was more than a visual representation. He could detect Nikko's presence in the Chenzeme way. Data packets peppered his sensory tears, just as they had that day Sypaon had come to him in the city library. Colors flashed in his optic nerve, without coalescing into discernable shape, but still carrying a cross-clade meaning: a livid rainbow spray of hatred. *"Kona,"* he whispered. "The Chenzeme influence is here."

The Nikko-creature's gaze fixed on him. Lot could read no expression on his face, but the air carried suspicion, and a flood of questions that seemed to form wordlessly in his mind so that he was shaking his head "no" before Nikko said anything aloud. That evoked silent packets of laughter. "You learned this in the Hallowed Vasties, didn't you?" Nikko asked. He chuckled. "I returned there once."

"Would that you had stayed there," Kona snapped.

"Daddy . . ." Urban clung to the tunnel mouth, his caution a weak accent to Nikko's bitter aura.

"You bastard," Kona growled. "We didn't die when you abandoned us here. Have you come back now to change that outcome?"

Lot sensed a momentary flicker of confusion. "I didn't want to leave you," Nikko said, his voice remote, as if he were reviewing historical records, and drawing his conclusions from them. "I'd hoped you'd be safe here . . . for a time."

"You left us with *nothing*!"

"I left you clean, *when I was not*."

Lot felt his skin prickling with unseen parasites burrowing into his blood, his bones. He cried out, slapping frantically at his arms before he realized the effect was an illusion, only a replay of something Nikko had endured.

The image glared at him. "What are you?"

"Leave him alone," Kona warned.

Nikko's short cape began to bunch and climb around his neck. "He's not just a refugee from the Hallowed Vasties."

Lot pressed instinctively against the wall. He imagined he could feel tiny hands reaching for him, poking at him, exploring his cellular structure. Ord tapped at his cheek in soft concern.

"He's not human," Nikko said. "Why have you brought him here?"

"Because we thought we might need him—to translate from the Chenzeme syntax that guides you, Nikko. Where is the infection that has turned you into a weapon against your own people?"

"I've destroyed it."

Kona might have been expecting any answer but that one. He was taken aback in surprise.

The image flexed its membranous cloak, letting it flutter in the laden air. "You were right, Kona. I was infested, even before Heyertori. I *did* bring the Chenzeme. Not knowingly. Not intentionally. But innocent motives cannot excuse the crime."

His image slowly shrank to more human proportions as he described how he'd discovered the infestation on the exodus from Heyertori. Tiny automata had been budding off his hull, dropping behind into the vacuum where they began to send out faint signals in the Chenzeme dialect. "I had to sterilize them, and to accomplish that, I first had to put you aside."

"So you chose Silk?" Clemantine scoffed. "It was a dead city."

"It wasn't dead. The city was alive and thriving. Only the people had been—"

"*We* are people!" Clemantine burst out. "We could have died, just like they did."

Lot felt as if a cord were pulling tighter and tighter around his throat. "You could have," Nikko answered. "It was a chance."

Suddenly, the pressure eased. Lot gasped. Kona shook his head. "That may be true, and it may be forgivable. By the Unknown God, we live in desperate times. But you did not even tell us. *Why?*"

The image looked away, its blue-tinged face absolutely still. Suddenly, Lot knew he would not answer, not in words. Still, Nikko's reasoning burst against his sensory tears: green flecks of guilt on muddy gray slopes of self-loathing, washed over by staunch, stubborn white sheets of pride. "He felt shame," Lot announced, in a low, defiant voice.

Nikko's queries snapped hard against his sensory tears. "What are you?"

Again, Kona turned the subject. "You're not driven by the Chenzeme influence now?"

Nikko chuckled faintly. "We are all under the Chenzeme influence, Kona. They've shaped our minds, and defined our values, and we'll never escape their meddling until we've destroyed them all. You think I've aimed this ship at your city, don't you?"

"You've served the Chenzeme before."

"I hunt them now. Don't worry. I'll slip safely past Silk. No harm will come to your people through me."

"Then what are you after?"

Vivid hatred, like fire in the air. It reverberated within Lot's own alien neural structure, and suddenly he could see their goal, a loathed beacon in the night sky. "It's the ring," Lot whispered. His gaze darted to Kona. "He's going to attack Sypaon."

Kona cocked his head in abject confusion. "That's impossible. Nikko, you don't have weapons for that."

"I have this ship."

"You're going to ram it?" Urban blurted. "Why?"

"You have to ask? It's no longer dead. I felt the flux in gamma radiation. It's been brought back on line."

"Sypaon has control of it now!" Kona said, his hand chopping angrily through the air. "She's not Chenzeme."

Lot shifted uneasily. Nikko caught his doubt. Dark amusement popped over an opaque wall of certainty. "You're not sure about that, are you?"

Lot swallowed hard and looked away, made guilty by his doubts.

"Tell me," Nikko urged. The others waited too.

Lot drew a deep breath, groping for words that would describe his vague suspicions. "It's the Well. It classifies Sypaon as the enemy, right? So it keeps her neutralized. But it hasn't done that to me, or to you, Nikko. She *says* she's human. But the Silkens couldn't even talk to her before I came."

"You translated from the Chenzeme?"

"Sooth," Kona said cautiously. "He was the link."

"Where did *you* learn it?" Lot asked.

Nikko lifted his chin, while the cloak on his shoulders went utterly still. "From the weapon that I mated with in the void."

Lot shuddered. He could remember asking Sypaon, *What have you learned*? And her laughing answer: *Evil*.

"You survived it," Kona said softly, wonderingly.

"It survived too." The way Nikko said it: as if that alone constituted another crime. "I can destroy this one, before its self-repair is finished."

Revenge. It was a human aspect, a facet of consciousness unknown to the Well or to the plundering servants of the Chenzeme. Jupiter had unleashed his assault Makers on the column, to no real purpose except revenge.

Lot shook his head. "Let it go," he urged Nikko softly. "Sypaon can't use the ring. It's harmless, and it's not worth dying for."

"I wasn't planning on dying."

Urban shifted slightly. "Then what are you going to do?"

Nikko activated the chamber walls, providing them a full view beyond the ship. Null Boundary skimmed past the Well, brushing the upper atmosphere. Nikko informed them that they'd safely passed the elevator column, though Lot never saw it. Sudden acceleration slammed him back against the soft gel image wall at the chamber's aft end. He hung there like a fly trapped on the paddle of a sundew, struggling to breathe.

Beyond Nikko's hovering figure, he watched an image of the tumbling swan burster. Sypaon must have finally guessed their purpose. On Lot's shoulder, Ord suddenly stirred. "Message, Lot."

"No."

Sypaon ignited the ring just as it began to fully open to a circle in their perspective. It glowed brilliant white as it entered the excited state that would feed its gamma-ray burst. Brighter and brighter it grew, its light spreading in a twisted sheet across the dark interior, until its luminescence surpassed the display's parameters and the optical system was forced to translate to safer artificial colors. Lot could see a spot of darkness at its center.

Nikko's worry moldered in the chamber. "It will fire on us."

"It can't fire," Lot whispered, past the constricting grip of acceleration.

"You deserve it, you bastard," Urban croaked.

Nikko did not deny it.

The ring loomed before them, growing larger until soon it overwhelmed the scale of the display. The spot of darkness at the ring's center also seemed to expand in size as they drew nearer. Null Boundary's prow was aimed at its center. Were they going to pass through? Lot had not known that was possible. The space inside a ring was warped by severe gravitational gradients. . . .

But the central eye? He knew starlight could pass through there unmolested. But could the same be said for Null Boundary?

"Message, Lot," Ord repeated.

Lot closed his eyes, trying to calm his pounding heart. "Okay then! Say it."

He flinched as Sypaon's voice hissed in his ear: *"My purpose is satisfied if you die with me. Come forward. The geometry will tear you apart."*

Lot looked at Nikko, but his image didn't waver.

"She's right," Clemantine warned. "You're going to kill us."

"I did try to avoid picking you up," Nikko reminded. "A small courtesy gone wrong."

"Not for the first time."

"We'll live if we keep dead center," Kona said.

The eye was a circle of flat geometry. Lot had seen stars shining there during evenings in the city that now seemed long ago. But the eye was also a rotating target. Nikko would have to thread the ship exactly through its middle.

The dark circle loomed before them, continuing to expand until it dominated the image wall. Faint stars became visible within that space. The ship's hull groaned in a dark metal voice as they entered into it. "By the Unknown God," Clemantine said. "I can feel it."

Lot could feel the presence of the ring too. It grabbed him, slamming him across the aft wall to the chamber's right side. Clemantine came down on top of him. He felt caught in the bite of an invisible vise clamped across the length of his body, all his muscles, his organs, and his nerves crushed and ready to snap as Null Boundary brushed the ring's plunging gradients.

A holographic image of the ship suddenly appeared in the center of the chamber. Nikko loomed over it, watching it closely, waiting. . . .

"*Now!*" Nikko shouted in a distorted voice that seemed to enter only into Lot's right ear.

Null Boundary shuddered. On the holographic image, Lot saw the flash of hundreds of small explosions all around the ship's hull. Null Boundary's hide and all his outer insulation shattered into thousands of tiny pieces that rocketed away from the ship in a storm of white-hot debris, leaving behind a glowing red, but intact, inner hull.

The crushing pressure climbed. Lot felt as if his lungs had flattened, as if his brain had flowed over to one side of his skull. The air that pooled around him moved liquid slow against his cheeks. His eyes had distorted too. The displays all blurred as the jettisoned debris rocketed outward, accelerating down the ring's twisting gravitational gradient. Lot watched the debris shift into red, then infrared as it sped toward impact with the burster's active surface. It hit, and beneath the crushing energy of impact the Chenzeme cells that coated the ring flared into plasma. Beyond the core chamber, alarms screamed overload as Null Boundary was swathed in an expanding bubble of radiation. The image walls flushed white. Lot told himself the ship's core would shelter them from the worst of it. Then the wavefront was past, and a starfield could be seen again across the prow, veiled by the milky light of Kheth's nebula.

As Null Boundary passed beyond the ring's grip, the crushing pressure vanished, leaving only the relatively mild push of the ship's continuing acceleration. "By the Unknown God," Clemantine whispered again, shifting far enough to the side that Lot could peel himself free of the wall.

"And damn all the Chenzeme," Kona added.

Lot rubbed at his arms. His muscles felt numb, indicating his medical Makers had gone to work on the radiation damage. He caught sight of the aft image wall.

Behind them, the swan burster still rotated from zero to one against the gleaming background of the blue-green Well. But its shimmering silver surface had been burned to volcanic red—a red-rimmed eye slowly closing over a plain of twisted darkness. Lot watched it, feeling himself set loose, adrift in the core as Null Boundary ceased to accelerate.

In nature, there were so many strategies for survival. The mitochondrial analog was only one, yet through the fusion of Chenzeme and human it had given rise to Lot, and Nikko, and even Sypaon, though for her it had failed. Though the ring still existed—its charred hoop still enclosing an inexplicable circle of twisted space-time—the Chenzeme cells that had been its mind and motivation were gone, and Sypaon was gone with them. The burster was a dead artifact, shining only dully with reflected light.

Why Sypaon had to die was still not clear to Lot. But perhaps there never were any real reasons. *Survivors survived.* And who could predict what combinations of traits would slide past the twin filters of rogue chance, and dire necessity?

Lot wasn't at all sure of his own success. He didn't even know how success should be measured amid the endless chain of disasters that marked the progress of life. Maybe success never could be measured except in the transcendent power of a moment, the grace of an hour, or a day, short spans of hallowed time like brief poems, sparkling gems set in the flowing matter of space-time. *There is no finish line. . . .* Only a collection of small victories, and the choice to go on. Choice was a privilege not shared by the Well or the Chenzeme marauders—

—and perhaps not even by the magnificently unbalanced human inhabitants of the frontier. Free will might be only an illusion generated by the unseen selective events within the human subconscious. But Lot chose to believe it was not. It seemed the ado thing to do.

Epilogue

adiation had damaged the farside of the Well. There'd been a limited defensive reaction there, but it hadn't spread to the city. The ados seemed chastened by the swan burster's demise. The exodus to the planet had stopped. Negotiations had started. Kona conceded that they might tap the planet's resources after all, if they went about it carefully. He said this as Null Boundary carried them ever farther from the city.

The ship's solenoids had been damaged during its sprint through the nebula. Nikko had chosen to conserve his limited fuel reserves. Null Boundary coasted now, on a trajectory that would eventually carry it out of the system, while packs of repair Makers set about the task of reconstruction.

Lot asked permission to stay. He didn't see that anyone had a choice about it, but it seemed polite to ask. Nikko shrugged. "If you want to take the chance." With the ship's insulation gone, the outer halls were exposed to a constant sleet of hard radiation. So Nikko promised to convert sections of the cold-storage facilities into housing.

Kona seemed satisfied with the arrangements. He extended a hand to Lot. "You're free now. For a while." Lot clasped his hand, though he couldn't make sense of Kona's bittersweet mood. "I wish you luck, son. And stealth. There are still Chenzeme weapons out there."

Lot's confusion must have shown on his face.

"We're going back," Kona explained gently. "Null Boundary has the facilities to generate the code."

"*Sooth.*" Lot nodded in understanding. Kona's atrium could assemble a copy of his persona and translate it to electromagnetic code. Lot knew it was possible for Kona to do the same thing with his physical structure. Kona, Clemantine, and Urban could return to Silk on a data stream that would be preserved in storage until new physical copies could be prepared. But only information would be transferred. The matter that had formed itself into the man before him would not go anywhere. "You'll have to stay here too," Lot pointed out.

Kona shook his head. "I've always had an aversion to a bifurcate existence. With only this one version of myself, I've already been at the root of too many disasters."

Lot nodded. Then he looked to Urban and Clemantine. "And you?"

Clemantine grinned. "Those charismata are wonderfully persuasive things." Lot didn't believe her for a moment. "I'm going back with Kona, son. But I'm also staying here—if Nikko will have me."

Nikko's image shrugged again, as if it meant nothing to him—though Lot could tell that wasn't true. Nikko had been alone for a long time.

Urban shifted uneasily. Lot could taste his anxiety, and guessed what was coming. But for once he guessed wrong. Urban stunned them all when he announced: "Daddy, I'm not going back at all."

Kona's shock was a palpable rain against Lot's skin.

"There's no place for me in the city," Urban said defensively. "You know it."

"We have the planet now."

"That's not enough."

The argument went on for over an hour, but in the end it made no difference. Their parting was bitter, and Lot held himself to blame, though Clemantine assured him he was not.

Several days after Kona had gone, Nikko startled them by appearing in physical form. He announced that most of the repair work on the coils had been done, and he invited them to walk the hull with him.

Lot was surprised to learn that Nikko required no

skin suit: his scaled hide kept him intact under vacuum. The short membranous cloak that grew on his shoulders displayed its purpose by rolling up over his nose and mouth, where it served as an organ of respiration.

They emerged through a small lock onto what was now the outer hull. This had been an inner wall before Nikko's assault on the swan burster. It had the look of a virgin surface, bearing none of Null Boundary's fabled scars.

Spurning a safety line, Nikko set out first, skating from handhold to handhold on his long prehensile toes. There was no rotation to contend with. Still, Lot preferred to be cautious. He anchored himself with a long tether secured to a handhold near the lock. Urban and Clemantine clipped to the same line; then they set out after Nikko.

Null Boundary still coasted within the nebula. It loomed behind them as a wispy, white presence. But they were nearing its edge. Ahead of them, beyond the sheltering span of the working ramscoop, the nebula was hardly visible. That was the direction called *swan*. There, a plethora of stars blazed against the dark molecular clouds that traced the inner edge of the galaxy's Orion Arm.

"Turn around," Nikko said. He spoke through his atrium, his voice arriving over the skin suit's comm system.

Lot had almost caught up with him by this time. He anchored himself with a second tether, then pushed gently at the hull, so that he rose in a slow ascent above the plane of the ship. Urban and Clemantine had fallen several yards behind him. He could see them, silhouetted against the nebula.

"Now," Nikko said. In magnificent silence, a blue fire stabbed from Null Boundary's distant stern, a fusion torch that sliced ruthlessly through the filmy nebula, burning dust, and the history bound up in it.

For a while they watched in silence. Their acceleration was almost too small to notice at first, but gradually it began to mount. Finally, Urban's voice came doubtfully over the comm. "I don't understand. The magnetic coils are sweeping a huge path through the nebula, and the jets are vaporizing even more material. Why do the governors tolerate that level of damage?"

Lot frowned. He'd never thought about it in quite this way before, but the nebula must be an almost irresistible target to a ramship. With an abundance of raw materials ready to harvest, and hydrogen for fuel, what ship could resist an investigation? He'd always seen the nebula as defensive, but it could also be interpreted as a lure.

"Probably, the Well recognizes scales of disaster," Clemantine mused. "The nebula's bigger and simpler than the planet, so it takes more damage to solicit a reaction."

Lot shook his head, unsatisfied with that suggestion. "The best way to defend the Well would be to simply disassemble any approaching ship. Break it down to dust."

"You couldn't do that soon enough with anything moving at relativistic velocities," Urban said.

Nikko chuckled darkly. "Anything moving at relativistic velocities would burn itself up in micro-collisions on the system's edge."

Lot squinted at the milky haze behind the ship. "So maybe this is a sundew."

"What?" Urban asked.

Lot's hand swept in an expansive gesture. "Like a sundew attracts flies by offering nectar, the nebula attracts ships."

"A sundew eats flies. The nebula doesn't eat ships."

"But it captured the ring."

"One ship in thirty million years."

Clemantine added her agreement. "Most Chenzeme weapons attack on a hyperbolic orbit. Sypaon's ring was probably the exception, culled because it assumed a circular orbit before attacking— Anyway, Nesseleth and Null Boundary were both able to leave the system."

"And they both returned."

"For their own reasons."

Lot nodded in grudging agreement. "Sooth."

Still, there was something tantalizing in this image. . . .

His eyes widened, as insight flooded him. "It's infesting them!" He turned around to look at Nikko. "The Well is infesting the Chenzeme weaponry—and not just those weapons that come through the nebula." He recalled his experience with Sypaon, when she showed him the workings of the ring, and let him feel the ecstatic mingling of alien cells in a multiplex information dump as the robotic weapons met one another in the void. "The dust could attack any information system. Infest it with Well protocols. When the weapon meets its own kind in the void, the information is spread—and spread again at the next meeting, and the next."

Urban sounded unconvinced. "But the Chenzeme must have developed defenses against viral pirates."

"I know I have," Nikko said in a cynical voice.

Lot countered that: "You're not Chenzeme."

For some reason, Nikko found that funny. He laughed, while a blush warmed Lot's cheeks. Lot turned back toward the nebula. Still, he was determined to make his point. "Think about it," he urged. "Evolution runs at a fast pace in the Well. Variation is forced; clades are blended. Keys capable of corrupting the Chenzeme system have already evolved, and they continue to evolve."

"But the Chenzeme are still out there," Nikko pointed out coolly.

"Or their weapons anyway." It was an important distinction.

"Right," Urban agreed. "They're here . . . in the Chenzeme intersection."

"Meaning, not in the Hallowed Vasties?" Clementine asked.

Lot could see bright blue reflections from the fusion torch as Urban turned around. "Yeah. So maybe we live on a border, where the Well is taming the Chenzeme threat."

Cautiously, Lot nodded. "That's what Jupiter believed." He hesitated, remembering. Jupiter had said the Well belonged to the peacemakers. "Maybe he was right." It pleased him to think Jupiter had seen that truth, even if others eluded him. He'd wanted to find shelter, a sanctuary from the failures of the Hallowed Vasties and the lingering evil of the Chenzeme. He'd been *trying*. And maybe that wasn't enough excuse for what had happened, but it was better than nothing.

Clementine had resumed her crawl across the hull. "New populations of weaponry must still be coming into this area, from some other direction," she said.

"It could be," Urban said. There was a rising excitement in his voice. "Do you think they're still out there? Nikko?"

"I don't know."

"Jupiter said the war was over," Lot added.

"But somebody modified the cult virus to work on us."

"Maybe."

"Maybe!" Urban snorted. "You believe it."

"Sooth," Lot admitted. *A gift from the void.* "But we don't know the direction, or how far."

"Far," Nikko whispered.

Lot turned again to peer at him, feeling a chill of anticipation on his spine. Nikko hovered above the plane of the ship, a black, almost human shape marked by random blue highlights. "You've been to look?" Lot asked.

"I set out once." By the way he said it, Lot knew he had not gotten far.

"We're a frontier people," Urban said. "It doesn't matter how far we go, because we don't ever come back. Once we cross the void, we're gone."

"That's true," Clemantine said softly. She settled on the hull near Lot. "Nikko? What do you say? You're not looking to return again to the Hallowed Vasties?"

Nikko laughed softly. "I think not. Not this time."

Lot gazed once again at the clouds of dust and the luminous stars that lay ahead of them. A thousand years down the Orion Arm, the Hallowed Vasties would fade to less than a legend. "Do you suppose anybody's still ahead of us?" he asked.

"I hope not," Urban said, with a feral note to his voice that set Lot's heart beating faster. "More than anything, fury, I hope we're the first ones standing on this shore."

ABOUT THE AUTHOR

LINDA NAGATA's short fiction has appeared in *The Magazine of Fantasy and Science Fiction* and *Analog*. *Deception Well* is her third novel, following the release of her Locus Award-winning debut novel *The Bohr Maker* and its highly acclaimed follow-up, *Tech-Heaven*. She lives on Maui, Hawaii, where she shares with her husband the joys of raising two active children.

She can be found on the World Wide Web at: http://www.maui.net/~nagata/

Get a preview of the future with

"One of the best thinkers in science fiction today." —*Newsweek*

BRUCE STERLING

"As with some of Heinlein's work, one becomes convinced that the world *must* and *will* develop into what Sterling has predicted." —*Science Fiction Age*

Holy Fire
____09958-2 $22.95/$31.95 in Canada

A chilling tale of an elderly woman who undergoes a medical procedure to restore her youth, only to jeopardize her newfound life.

Heavy Weather
____57292-X $5.99/$7.99

The Storm Troupe tracks monster storms across the Badlands. But they can't possibly prepare for the destruction of the mythical F-6 tornado that they seek.

Globalhead
____56281-9 $6.50/$8.99

Brilliant, satirical, and visionary. A stunning collection of thirteen cutting-edge stories set in strange futures and alternate nows.

The Hacker Crackdown
____56370-X $5.99/$6.99

An inside look at a new breed of cyber-criminals—their lives, crimes and adversaries.

and with William Gibson
The Difference Engine
____29461-X $6.50/$8.99

A detective story with an eye for period detail. A mysterious box of punched Engine cards is discovered, and someone is willing to kill to retrieve it.

Ask for these books at your local bookstore or use this page to order.

Please send me the books I have checked above. I am enclosing $ ____(add $2.50 to cover postage and handling). Send check or money order, no cash or C.O.D.'s, please.

Name _____

Address _____

City/State/Zip _____

Send order to: Bantam Books, Dept. SF 58, 2451 S. Wolf Rd., Des Plaines, IL 60018
Allow four to six weeks for delivery.
Prices and availability subject to change without notice.   SF 58 2/97